Methuselah's Pillar has it ⟨ ⟩ biblical mysteries, and even ⟨ ⟩ ⟨ ⟩ ⟨story⟩. And what makes *Methuselah's Pillar* so outstanding is that Griffiths works his literary magic and pulls the whole story together without stretching the boundaries of believability too far. The way he does it is the old-fashioned way – through character development, short chapters that end with cliff-hanging scenes, and ramped-up, non-stop action that leaves the reader gasping for breath.

Don't blink because you might miss something.

Quite frankly, the reviewer – yours truly – ranks W.G. Griffiths with Dan Brown, Vince Flynn and James Patterson. This guy can tell a story! Why no one has heard of him is anyone's guess. And why one of the big publishing houses hasn't signed him to a multi-book multi-year deal is beyond comprehension.

In any event, don't let anyone persuade you not to read *Methuselah's Pillar*. It's the sleeper of the year. Definitely one of the best thrillers to come along since *The Da Vinci Code*. If you miss it, you'll be sorry.

—BC, Blog Critics

"EDGE-OF-YOUR-SEAT SUSPENSE WITH EXPLOSIVE TALENT, and UNSTOPPABLE ACTION!"

W.G. Griffiths takes the reader on a fascinating journey that will send chills up your spine as you sit on the edge of your seat from beginning to end in a guessing game that makes you keep asking page-after-page, what horrific bit of evidence will pop up next? What kind of powers will the pillar infect the world with, and who will grab it? As the reader is introduced to ancient wells, enemies in Afghanistan and the translation of early writings, the characters come to life in a deadly game that becomes an obsession as the world begins to shatter like broken glass. Samantha finds herself playing monkey in the middle as danger becomes more intense, while the heart-pounding race between the CIA and the terrorist insurgents continue through unstoppable action that explodes like fireworks on each and every page of a thrill ride that will cause an adrenaline rush. What happens to John Decker, after he is taken hostage? Who will unlock the mystical, magical secrets on the pillar first, and will evil spread through the midst of a battle where the clock is ticking fast? I highly recommend this captivating, high-adrenaline, spectacular thriller to all suspense lovers. The author is a mystical mastermind who did everything in his power to create an incredible thrill ride with relentless action through an unforgettable plot made for the movie screen. The reader will witness descriptive ancient artifacts, biblical legends, international espionage and horrifying intentions from a terrorist group as deadly plagues and immortality reaches its highest peak in a gripping story through a compelling journey of the past and present. "METHUSELAH'S PILLAR" contains as much danger as TOP GUN, is as riveting as ARMAGEDDON and as thrilling as THE ROCK, with Hollywood superstar Sean Connery.

—Ahern Reviews

"As well crafted as a Pharoh's tomb, *Methuslah's Pillar* grabs you from the start and doesn't let go. WG Griffiths at his spellbinding best."

—Rick Robinson, Award Winning
Independent Author of the Year, *Writ of Mandamus*

"Move over, Indiana Jones; there's a new anthropologist/hero in town."

—Ron Kaplan, Clarion Review

METHUSELAH'S PILLAR

W. G. Griffiths

6/6/12

Publisher Page

an imprint of Headline Books, Inc

Terra Alra, WV

Methuselah's Pillar

By W. G. Griffiths

Publisher Page
P.O. Box 52, Terra Alta, WV 26764
www.PublisherPage.com
www.WGGriffiths.com

Tel/Fax: 800-570-5951
Email: mybook@headlinebooks.com
www.HeadlineBooks.com

Publisher Page is an imprint of Headline Books, Inc.

Cover Concept by Luke Griffiths and Stephen Griffiths
Cover Images by Maksym Yemelyanov and Karel Miragaya
Author Photo by Luke Griffiths

ISBN 978-0-938467-41-0 Hard Cover
ISBN 978-0-938467-46-5 Paperback

Library of Congress Control Number: 2012936898

Griffiths, W.G., 1955 -
   Methuselah's Pillar / by W. G. Griffiths
      p. cm.
   ISBN 978-0-938467-41-0
   ISBN 978-0-938467-46-5
            1. Archeology—Fiction 2. Afganistan—Fiction 3. Mystery—Fiction
4. Biblical History—Fiction

PRINTED IN THE UNITED STATES OF AMERICA

To David, Jessica and Michael

And the Lord God commanded the man, saying, "From any tree of the garden you may eat freely; but from the tree of the knowledge of good and evil you shall not eat, for in the day that you eat from it you shall surely die."

Genesis 2:16-17

And the Lord God commanded the man, saying, "From any tree of the garden you may eat freely; but from the tree of the knowledge of good and evil you shall not eat, for in the day that you eat from it you shall surely die."

Genesis 2:16-17

1

Samantha Conway spit into her diving mask, smeared the saliva around with her fingers and then rinsed it out in an old wooden bucket full of cool well water so the glass wouldn't fog. On-looking reporters made notes of every move she made, especially after she suited up. Photographers snapped away. They had positioned themselves to use the pyramids as background. *Some secret mission*, she thought sarcastically. She'd been recognized the moment she'd stepped off the plane in Cairo and, each day, her archaeological exploration had gathered more and more talking heads. She had to admit though; scuba diving down ancient wells near Egypt's famous Valley of the Kings wasn't the best way to avoid attention.

"My mouth is so dry, Paki, I can hardly spit," Sam said to her Egyptian assistant.

Paki furrowed his thick connected eyebrow. "Don't they make a spray for that?" Paki was a young man with big dark eyes, long eyelashes and a short but full jet-black beard. A sweetheart. He had headphones and a microphone growing out from a turban that seemed to be either screwed or glued on. Neither high winds nor gravity had any effect on it.

"Yes, but nothing except raw potatoes works as well as spit. Did you have any raw potatoes, Paki?"

"Potatoes?" Paki said. "No, Doctor Conway. I remember for next time." Sam smiled and more cameras went off. The media loved her smile. "Yes, write that one down. Next time you're assisting someone scuba diving in the Sahara Desert, make sure you bring raw potatoes in case their mouth is too dry."

Paki nodded and began feeling for a pen.

"No, Paki, I was only kidding," she said and rolled her eyes playfully. Sam was an ancient writing expert and well-respected among her peers. Her ability to translate the most difficult hieroglyphics, often reading through the characters and between the lines, had resulted in priceless finds for her employer, The New York Metropolitan Museum. With her inspiring archaeological insights, adventurous spirit and natural photogenic good looks, the media had painted Sam out to be a female combination of Indiana Jones and Sherlock Holmes. In fact, the History Channel had offered her a series, with a contract far in excess of what the museum was able to compete with. She'd slept on it and turned them down the next day. "Thanks, but I'm not ready to live in a fish bowl just yet," she had told them. "Maybe some other time." Fame and fortune weren't enticing enough to buy the freedom she enjoyed following up her own research and intuition.

The Valley of the Kings, or the official name used by the ancient Egyptians, "The great and majestic necropolis of Pharaoh's millions of years of Life Strength Health in the West of Thebes," enclosed sixty-two known tombs numbered chronologically in the order they were discovered. Ancient Egyptians were unreservedly obsessed with death, to put it mildly. Pharaohs would spend their entire lifetimes building their tombs. Nothing was more important. Whether you were an architect, priest, baker or a slave, your time and energy revolved around a tomb. Possibly one you'd been working on since childhood. And how you tended to this task had a lot to do with your life on the other side of eternity. Why? Because sooner or later you would be there with your Pharaoh who was now your god. In fact, the belief system and pressure were so great that some were actually known to commit suicide right after their Pharaoh died so as to be positioned favorably in the next world. Others, unwilling to make that ultimate sacrifice, would have to wait stressfully to see what would be waiting for them after death. Hopefully their king would be very understanding.

Consequently, most worked diligently to please their Pharaoh. Tombs were decorated with beautiful hieroglyphics recounting events during the king's life. From these artful writings, modern man has learned more about the Egyptians than any other civilization of the time. How they cut and drilled stone. How they conquered their enemies. Who their gods were. How they baked bread. And, sometimes, if one were brilliant enough to read between the lines, where treasures were hidden.

Sam dreaded to think what the papers would say if she didn't find what she was looking for, this being the ninth well in three days with the last eight being dead ends. But this one offered hope the others hadn't. According to her research, which fortunately was kept much more private than her physical whereabouts, Senenmut, a master Egyptian architect during the eighteenth dynasty, about fourteen fifty BC, stashed away treasures for his queen and rumored intimate companion, Hatshepsut.

Traditionally, entrances to most Egyptian tombs were displayed openly, to be easily guarded. Senenmut, correctly, didn't trust that method, especially since the tomb would have to be shielded from his lover's jealous stepson who would eventually replace her as Egypt's ruler. In a recent find that Sam also spearheaded, she found an obscure clue that led her to explore nearby wells for a secret entrance to Senenmut's hidden stash, intended for him and his queen in the next life.

The Aqua Video she used to scout the ancient wells had revealed a small opening in this particular well's wall sixty-four feet down. Now her heart was racing; she was anxious to get down there in person to test her theory.

Sam made a few last minute checks. Spare flashlight worked, tank was full, wristwatch told her it was 12:02 and her knife was strapped securely to her leg. She tied back her thick, curly blond hair into a ponytail, and pulled the mask over her entire face and breathed the cool compressed air. She had never used a full face mask regulator before, but being able to keep radio contact with Paki was something the museum insisted on when she proposed her unprecedented exploration.

"Testing, testing," Sam said, her own voice sounding strange through her earphone. She also had to remember to speak exactly what she meant if she cared to be interpreted correctly. Paki's English was decent but, apparently, he had not yet learned American euphemisms, taking everything she said literally.

Paki adjusted the microphone closer to his mouth. "I hear you loud and clear, Doctor Conway. Be safe," Paki said, his statement sounded more like a prayer than a request.

"Always. And call me Sam, Paki," she said, for the tenth time. It was a joke by now. She took a final look below. The well opening was a mere six feet in diameter and ten feet down to the water's shadowed surface. She moved and tiny pebbles plopped into the still water. She held the mask to her face with one hand and pushed off the stone edge to the clatter of cameras and braced for sharp. Nothing. The Aqua Video had already revealed adequate depth and no protruding objects but, there was always that unshakable thought of... *something,* beneath the water's dark surface. Relieved, she came back to the surface and looked up to

Paki, who was leaning over the well's opening, his turban, of course, stuck to his head.

"All good. Send it down," she said.

Paki nodded and lowered the underwater camera assembly with a rope and pulley. She took hold of the yellow housing, a little larger than a loaf of bread, and turned it on, along with its "Super Nova" lighting system. She unclipped the museum's precious camera and pointed the brilliant light downward. Blackened stone walls that had been in dark shadows for thousands of years were suddenly exposed.

Sam held the Aqua Video in both hands and swam down into the tight, black abyss. She soon found the water to be surprisingly cold for a blistering hot African country a stone throw from the equator. Cold and dark. The walls were so black and non-reflective that the high-lumen power lamps could only penetrate an eerie fifteen feet ahead.

Sam tried to ignore the pressingly claustrophobic environment. A mischievous tomboy as a child, she'd explored local storm drains, using candles for light, with the manhole covers clanging overhead. In an oddly similar environment, she spotted a large hole in the wall about thirty feet lower and was anxious to look in.

So much time and energy and money had been invested, or rather, gambled, at her recommendation. She aimed the lamp into the opening and, for the first time in millenniums, the cavity was filled with light. She paused, while bubbles massaged her cheeks and ears.

In treasure hunting, things were not always as they appear. The entrance, if indeed it was an entrance, was about five feet in diameter and shallow. Dishearteningly shallow. Maybe seven or eight feet deep before it ended in a sheer wall. Possibly a door of some kind, she hoped.

She moved forward into the hole until the lamps almost touched the rear wall. The side walls were also discouraging. Broken natural stone without evidence of human sculpturing. In other words, simple erosion. Another dead end. But maybe not. She unsnapped the knife from her right leg and reached to scrape the rear wall. Her leverage wasn't good and multi-tasking with the camera and lamp soon became too difficult. She re-clipped her knife, turned around and put the Aqua Video near the entrance on the cavity floor, carefully aiming it at the rear wall. That was better. She quickly found her knife and went back to work on the wall. Sam poked and scraped off thousands of years of residue buildup in seconds. After a few minutes, she found nothing and was becoming impatient. She only had so much air before she would have to resurface, and she desperately wanted a reason to return. Something. Anything.

"How are you, Doctor Conway?"

"Wonderful."

"Have you found anything?"

"Just manatee's and leprechauns, Paki."

Paki didn't reply. Sam figured him to be paging through an English/ Egyptian dictionary.

Sam dug and gouged at the wall's edges looking for a seam. She cursed.

"Did you say something?" Paki said.

"Duck, Paki. The leprechaun has a duck."

More silence.

Sam backed away from the wall for a new point of view. The solid stone could be man hewn, but not necessarily. It could also be the side of a great flat boulder, like so many others in the famous valley. She reexamined the walls all around her and wondered how the cavity could exist if not by design. It occurred to her that the well's water level could have changed throughout time. Could the treasure have been discovered by others at a time when the diving depth was reachable without modern diving gear? Could grave robbers or....

Suddenly, the cavity went dark.

2

Sam turned her head fast enough to see her entire camera assembly slip over the edge. She must have inadvertently backed into it and knocked it off with her fin. She swam as fast as she could to the cavity's opening, but the Aqua Video had fallen out of reach.

Her heart sank as she watched a ring of light on the well's walls sink further and further, smaller and smaller. "Great," she said sarcastically. Not only did she *not* find the treasure, but she'd lost a fortune in camera equipment. In her mind's eye, she saw the deep frown on her boss's face. Michael Garmisa, director of the museum, threw nickels around like manhole covers and would call her in for a meeting for every expense and how it needed to be negotiated lower somehow. She sighed, but then her brow rose. The light was just a dot, but she could still see it.

"Doctor Conway?"

"Hold on, Paki," she said and looked up. She could see the light of day but having passed through a thermal barrier along the way, there was no clear definition. She imagined Paki was still looking down into the well, and had likely misinterpreted her last couple of comments. She shook her head. He was probably optimistic and holding tight to the edge of the well.

She looked back to the dot of light below. The camera had stopped maybe seventy or eighty feet lower, putting it at a hundred and forty, hundred fifty feet deep, more or less. A bit too deep for the simple compressed air in her tank. Without a helium/oxygen mixture, she would get nitrogen narcosis at that depth. The question was, how bad? She had never had the "rapture of the deep", that euphoric, drunken-like experience that happens under the higher pressures. After three atmospheres, (about sixty-six feet), nitrogen dissolves in the brain and nerve tissues at an abnormally high rate, acting like an anesthetic gas. The deeper the body goes, the higher the degree of absorption. Like alcohol consumption, everybody's tolerance is different. Her body might not feel any affect until eighty or ninety feet. After a hundred and twenty, things were bound to get weird and that could mean trouble in a world where lapses in judgment could have severe and immediate consequences. "You idiot!" she shouted and bubbles erupted outside her mask. How could she have been so clumsy?

"Doctor Conway?"

"Sorry, Paki. The camera and light fell to the bottom of the well, very deep."

"How deep?"

"I don't know. Around one hundred and fifty feet."

After a long moment Paki said, "You must come up."

Sam didn't reply. To return to the surface and face the paparazzi without evidence of the treasure wouldn't be fun, but she couldn't let them influence her decision. But losing thirty-five grand worth of underwater camera equipment with nothing to show for it would be a strike against her credibility. Exploration support and liberty had been earned with recent success. The museum was banking on her decisions and she wanted to keep it that way.

Think, think, think.

"You must come up, Doctor Conway. I have long rope and hook."

If only that made as much sense to her as it did to him. She would be dinking and dunking for hours and what were the chances it would even work? "No rope. Keep thinking."

"Come up and we will get you air."

A heliox gas mix? That was exactly what she needed, but they didn't have any. "That would take too long to get, Paki. Two steps backward," she said and then realized he would have a problem understanding her analogy. She looked down again at the dot of light. She could just *hear* it calling her. Too deep. Or was it? Maybe she had a high narcosis tolerance. She had never had it before. Maybe the depth could be considered borderline if she would only be down there long enough to grab and go. But if she went too fast she could get the bends. Another lovely thought.

She looked at her air gauge and thought about it some more. A bad sign. She knew herself well enough to know that once she began rationalizing in one direction or another, it was only a matter of time before she did what she wanted to do, and time was not on her side. *Okay, breathe regularly, go slow, get the freakin' camera and get back up, slowly.* A moment later she was on her way down, down, down, constantly squeezing her nose to equalize the pressure in her ears. Focused only on the pin beam of light, she extended her spare flashlight into the darkness so that she wouldn't hit the sidewalls. This was stupid, the kind of thing bad stories at diving classes were made of.

"Doctor Conway? Are you coming up?"

"Uh, not yet."

"Are you going down?"

Sam rolled her eyes. He was getting to know her. "Yes."

After another long moment, Paki said, "We need to keep talking."

"Agreed," Sam said. "You'll be my voice of reason."

"Then come up."

Sam smiled. "You might not always find me reasonable."

"I know this."

Sam passed a hundred feet and was feeling good. This was not necessarily a good sign. Narcosis was all *about* feeling good, too good.

"Doctor Conway?"

"Yes, Paki?"

"How deep are you?"

Sam looked at her gauge. "One hundred and twelve."

"How do you feel?"

"Fine."

"Do you mind if I ask you some questions?"

"Shoot."

"Shoot what?"

"I mean, ask me whatever you want."

"Okay, uh, what's your maiden name?"

"I'm not married, Paki. But if you find me the right guy, I would consider it."

"How would you know if the guy is right?" Paki said.

"That's easy. He would be my hero."

"Hero?"

"Yes. My whole life I have had to rescue myself. The right guy would be not just be my best friend, but also my hero. At least sometimes," she said.

"Is now a good time for a hero?"

"Let's hope not."

"Then you must still tell me your name."

"Paki, Paki. To make you happy, my name is and always has been Samantha Conway."

"Count backwards from ten."

"In what language?"

"Egyptian."

"Modern or ancient?" she said, and then laughed easily. Maybe too easily.

"Modern. I don't know ancient."

Sam counted backward from ten in ancient Egyptian.

"You only said nine numbers."

Sam ignored him and continued. The camera was just below and she was glad she had made the choice to go after the it. In a moment, she would slowly ascend with the museum's property.

"I'm almost there, Paki."

"When you come back remember to go slow and stop after every fifty feet."

"Yes, Darling."

"Doctor Conway?"

"Come on Paki, what happened to all that zeal, determination and fight you used to have when you beat out millions to reach the ultimate goal?"

"When was that, Doctor Conway?

"When you were a sperm."

"A sperm? Please get the camera quickly and return at once."

"Next time, I put the thing on a leash. Like a pet. A barking camera, sniffing to relieve itself, and pulling to find treasure." Did she really just think that? She laughed and bubbles gushed around her. Just above the camera, she stopped and checked her depth gauge. One hundred and fifty-three feet. Yikes! She pinched her nose and equalized one final time before ascending, but her fingers were having trouble closing. Finally she managed, but her ears didn't pop, or did they? She was going to try again, but gave up and took hold of the yellow camera case. Again her coordination was off, but she made do, one hand holding the light stem. The light worked and the yellow housing didn't appear damaged, but at the moment that didn't really seem to matter.

Sam turned and was about to push off the bottom when she saw something that made her gasp and startled backward. Her violent reflex caused ice water to enter her mask and she choked. She coughed repeatedly but, kept the camera's brilliant light trained on a human skeleton crumbled inside a cut stone tunnel entrance.

"Doctor Conway! Are you all right?"

3

Hakeem Salim heard thunder. He looked up and saw nothing, but then felt a mild rumble and some loose pebbles rolled lightly off a rock. After a long moment, his attention went back to the sheep.

Sheep die easily. Without fangs, claws, speed or intelligence, they need constant surveillance. Without a shepherd, their only defense is death. A predator can manage but one sheep at a time, giving the flock a chance to run.

Hakeem had spent more than half his twenty-two years shepherding the family flock. Ninety-seven sheep at present. His dog, Caleb, was a perfect complement. A team for years, each knew the other's thoughts. Caleb, a skinny mutt with black and white hair and a pointy nose, would tirelessly run random circles around the sheep while Hakeem kept a slow steady pace forward, throwing sticks and stones.

The sheep's search for another patch of grass was never ending. The stubby Afghani terrain offered little nourishment but plenty of rocks and sticks to throw ahead of wandering sheep. A rock or stick strategically placed would always send a sheep running back to the safety of the fold. Hakeem would do this as long as they were moving and often considered how Allah had done the same to him to keep him from dangers he could not foresee. Lots of time to consider such things. Like the time...

Hakeem paused. Listened. A gentle breeze feathered his cheeks and cooled his sweaty face. More thunder? He scanned the horizon and saw a clear desert sky, as it had been for weeks. Caleb stood still as stone, his ears forward and nose high. There, again, louder, closer. Pebbles danced as the ground trembled under his feet.

Hakeem hurried ahead of the flock to look over the hillcrest. His eyes bulged. Tiny flags on antennas, the sun's glare flashing off windshields. Grills and tires rose through thermal heat waves, all speeding in his direction. A plume of smoke rose directly in front of a small group of racing vehicles, more thunder followed. Another explosion and one of the racing tan vehicles flipped, losing debris and passengers as it tumbled.

The sheep froze in place, all staring straight ahead with Caleb. Fear quickly coursed through Hakeem's veins. Bombs and trucks would be on them in a moment with no regard for their safety. Run. His first impulse was to sprint in the opposite direction, back the way they had come, but no, they would be overtaken, shot down, run over. To the right, wide open plains with no place to hide, to the left a wide crevice with jagged stone walls emptying into a large valley. He whistled for Caleb and bolted into the ravine.

A loud explosion made the ground shake. Rockets were crashing ahead of their targets. His eyes darted about for cover. Nothing. He looked behind and saw Caleb running to him and the sheep bleating and stampeding through thick clouds of dust. Dirt and pebbles were falling from the sky.

The swoosh of a missile was followed instantly by a deafening blast high on the wall of the ravine. Hakeem fell to his knees. He covered his head and curled his body as rocks rained painfully on his back. Caleb yelped and snuggled tightly against him, trembling. The sheep huddled against the wall to his right, crying nervously to him for direction and protection. He cupped his arm around his dog and told him he was a good boy and everything would be all right, then scurried on his hands and knees to the flock. Several thunderous impacts on the other side of the wall shook the earth behind them. They couldn't stay here. The valley below was their only chance.

"Caleb *come*," he ordered and then took off down the ravine toward the valley. Hakeem heard another swoosh and explosion and, suddenly airborne, was unable to discern down from up. He hit sand on the opposite slope and couldn't move. He slowly lifted his head. Blood dripped from his brow and curled around his eye. Through a swirling cloud of dust he could see his sheep scattered about, many very still. Caleb crawled next to him, whimpering. Dazed and weak, he thought, *move or die*. Hot wind cleared away the cloud and some of his sheep gathered in the middle of the ravine, confused, bleating. Beyond the sheep, he could see where the missile had cracked open a crevasse into the base of the hill. A jagged crater surrounded by sharp boulders. Immediate shelter from the constant bombardment.

He blinked and tried to clean his eyes with a dirty hand. Now the hand had blood on it as well. He rolled down the sand and hobbled across the ravine. Caleb followed. More explosions above. He stumbled, caught his footing and hurried around a sharp boulder. Another swoosh and he quickly looked up. A missile zipped past. He didn't see the impact but the detonation almost took him off his feet. He dashed for the crevasse and was surprised to find how deep it was. In fact, the new crack in the hill had a hole in it, with broken brick around its edges. Did the missile find a tomb? Man had walked this country for thousands and thousands of years. Ancient tombs were common and it was impossible to know when you were walking over one. Natural as sand. Harmless. But to Hakeem, scary as the death it contained. Caleb poked him in the leg with his nose and Hakeem jumped.

"Don't do that!" he said and then exhaled and looked into the hole. He heard another whoosh and heard an impact on the wall about fifty feet away, but no blast. It just rested there, a thin white tube with fins. A dud or just a delay. More bombs and rockets hit lower in the ravine. No time to peek into holes. He kicked at the broken brick edge until the hole was big enough and then climbed into hollow darkness. Caleb quickly followed.

Hakeem tumbled into darkness onto a stone floor. The only light came from the hole behind him. His eyes adjusted slowly. A room of some kind, as big as his parents' mud home. The ceiling was too high to reach. The perimeter was dark, but he didn't see any skeletons or coffins. Just a room, but not entirely empty. He squinted. A couple of big rocks at the other end took shape as he moved toward them. One was rectangular, about the size and height of a small bed. The other stood tall behind it, and round, like a column.

The room shook. The bombing outside continued but the sound was muffled. Dirt and pieces of ceiling fell. *Caleb would be better off outside,* he thought. No question, they'd both be better off in the valley below the ravine. But he couldn't still his curiosity. He walked cautiously to the two stones, his eyes well adjusted now. He stood over the first stone and then smoothed his hand across the surface. Flat like a table. An altar? He looked at the tall column-like stone behind it. Different in color, darker than anything else around. He walked around the flat stone for a closer look. His eyes widened as he drew close to the surface of the stone. It was carved.

"Words," he whispered, as if someone else would hear. Etchings. Unbelievably fine and clear. His fingers moved slowly down ancient characters. These were not words he was familiar

with. Not Arabic. Not Islamic. What did it say? At the top of the
stone were characters with other characters connected under
them, like a hierarchy or chain of command or... ancestry? *Were
the characters people,* he wondered. And below the text was dense
but clear. Much too small and fine to see in the darkness. The
government would probably want to destroy such writings. They
were always destroying old writings in fear of new ideas that
would make one think. He puzzled over the color and texture of
the stone itself. Very different, he thought, being strangely drawn
to it. *What kind of stone was this?* Not usual for this area, that was
for certain. *And how old?* It occurred to him that he might be the
first person to see it in thousands of years. He frowned. Something
else occurred to him and he turned and looked back at the flat
surfaced rock. A chill ripped up his back. He looked around the
room. Plain. No writing on the walls. No seats. Nothing. Very
simple. Possibly simple by design. His hand reflexively came off
the stone. He had been touching someone's holiness. The slab
was an altar and the writing was the writing of someone's belief.
A different belief. He considered the beliefs he had heard about
ancient peoples and stepped back. He looked at the altar again.
For sacrifice, he thought. Sacrifice to some god?

Sheep? He remembered his flock.

Another missile hit and the room rocked. Hakeem struggled
for balance and fell. The stone wavered. Hakeem tried to find
his footing while reaching to stabilize the pillar. Too heavy. He
let go as it fell against the wall behind it, breaking the top into
several pieces.

"Idiots!" he shouted, glaring at the light coming in though
the wall. He bent down and picked up a small piece the size of
his palm. He put it in his pocket and then picked up another the
size of a large book, with both hands.

More thunder. A section of the ceiling caved in and the light from the hole dimmed as he again fell to the floor. Caleb ran to the hole and looked back. The dog knew it was time to leave or be buried alive. Hakeem sprang to his feet and ran for the hole as the ancient room of worship rumbled and collapsed around him. He looked back and saw the altar disappear. Gone. Buried. The floor heaved and, as he fell, the stone jumped from his grasp and slid across the floor. "Aghh," he cried and bolted to his feet in a sprint. He snatched the stone from the floor and held it tight as he dove through the hole into the light. Hakeem tried to stand and run as the hillside slid behind him and cleanly covered the opening like it had never been there. He tried to jump away but the landslide caught his legs from behind before his feet could leave the ground, as if hands had reached out of the earth and grabbed his ankles. He fell forward and whacked the ground with a loud grunt. The stone tablet had cracked and split in half, right down the middle. He struggled to get free, twisting, pulling, and felt a searing pain in his knee. The earth continued to mount up, higher, over his thighs and back until it reached his armpits. When it stopped, he was pinned and could hardly breathe.

Caleb came to his face and licked it and started to dig, but then stopped and turned his head. Hakeem strained his neck and eyes to see.

Trucks.

The vehicles that were being fired upon turned into the ravine for protection and were headed toward him. He could see the men inside, but they didn't look like soldiers. His cousin was in the military. He was familiar with the uniform. These men were dressed more like *he* was. Government trucks but not government soldiers. *Who were they? Asad al Adala?* Even he had heard of the Lions of Justice, but he had never personally seen them. Being a shepherd, he hadn't seen much and that was how he liked it. *Would they help him or harm him?* From what he had heard, they were capable of both and he wasn't in a hurry to find out firsthand.

The trucks hugged the opposite wall. Shells and rockets were flying over but unable to find their mark. The trucks slowed to a crawl and then stopped. Caleb growled.

"Shhhhh," he whispered. With no place for him to hide the best he could hope for was to be considered a waste of their time. "Caleb, go," he whispered, the dog was confused and stayed.

One man jumped out of a truck and grabbed a wandering lamb. Hakeem wanted to speak, but didn't.

"Look!" he heard someone say. He raised his eyes and saw a few looking at him. Maybe they would leave him alone because he was not in a protected area like they were. That hope was immediately dashed when two of them left the truck and hurried toward him with guns in hand, staying low. Hakeem was suddenly terrified. He let go of the ancient stone. Maybe they would not notice it.

"Get back here," someone yelled.

The two men continued. They stopped a few feet from him. Hakeem strained his neck to see above their boots.

"Shepherd. What happened to you?" one said with a voice that sounded concerned.

"Leave him," someone else at the truck yelled.

"He's alive."

"Then shoot him!" someone else yelled. "You'll get killed."

Caleb snarled viciously.

"*Caleb… no! Lay down!*" Hakeem ordered, fearing his friend would be shot.

Caleb obeyed but snarled quietly at his master's side.

"Can you please help me?" Hakeem said. "The bombs caused a landslide and I could not get away. I will be in your debt."

One of the men bent down. "Take my hand. We'll try to pull you out."

Hakeem reached out with both hands. The two men grabbed him tightly and pulled with grunts and groans. No good. The hillside held him fast.

"Get a shovel," one said to the other. Another explosion caused both to cover their heads and then one ran back to the truck. The other started digging by hand and then stopped. Hakeem saw the man's hand pick up the ancient stone pieces.

"What is this, shepherd?"

"I don't know."

"Where did you find it?" he said, his fingers smoothed lightly across the ancient characters.

"Here. I found it here."

"Here?" he said incredulously.

"Yes."

"You lie."

"No."

He frowned and examined the stones closely. "This may be very valuable. Do you know what it says, shepherd?"

"I... I don't know."

"You found it here?" he said and looked around. *"On the dirt?"*

Hakeem didn't want to answer. He was the only one who knew where the rest of the pillar was and he would keep it that way. "You can have it. Please help me get out," he said and immediately a bomb hit the ravine wall, causing more debris to fall. The man tucked the ancient stones in his loose jacket and left. He met the other man with the shovel halfway, turned him around and together they ran back to the truck. The vehicles started moving again. A gunshot was fired exploding the sand next to Hakeem's face.

"Aghhh," he screamed. *"Please no!"*

Another shot rang. His face suddenly felt very different. A strange sound entered his ears, like waves on the seashore. The sound of bombs slowly disappeared. His head became very heavy. He wanted to sleep. Quiet. Darkness.

4

Sam was no longer concerned about the extreme depth she had descended to. The skull in the stone tunnel smiled at her. Did it wink?

"Hi there!" she said, brightly, her words and vision slurred. "Can you please direct me to Senenmut's treasure?" Sam half expected the skull to answer or for a hand to rise from the bone heap and point.

"Doctor Conway?" Paki said. "I didn't understand your question."

"I wasn't talking to you," she said.

After a pause, Paki said, "Who were you talking to?"

"One of Senenmut's friends."

"One of Sen... are you ascending yet?"

"No. There's a tunnel here," she said, as she stared into a rectangular shaft, large enough for her to fit through. Beyond the skeleton, the tunnel appeared to go back thirty or forty feet and the walls were consistent in dimension, definitely man-made.

"Doctor Conway. Sam. You must come up now. It is not safe for you to be at your present depth. I must insist you come-up- now!" he pleaded. "You can return later with the proper air mixture."

Inside her head, somewhere, misfired sparks of thought told her Paki was right. His voice of reason reminded her of how she felt just before speeding through a red traffic light or before putting wasabi in her mouth or using the sound shooter, that marvelous toy her father had adapted for her when she was a kid.

The sound shooter. Floodgates of childhood memories opened wide. She could see her father in that comfy overstuffed chair looking over his reading glasses at her as she entered the family room. He would later fall asleep there before Mom called him to bed. After breakfast, he would kiss them all good-bye, Mom, Jesse and her, and go to work as the senior scientist at IST. She suddenly missed them all terribly. But those days were gone forever. Mom had died six years ago and dad was a year into quadruple bypass recovery after a heart attack he'd barely survived. And Jesse, her brother, suffered brain damage from a drunk driver that had crashed into his jeep almost a decade ago. She had been caring for their needs until the museum hired Miss Cox, a professional full time attendant, to free Sam up for her explorations. Guilt suddenly filled her chest. What the hell was she doing in an ancient Egyptian well when her family needed her? Her eyes began to well up as she saw Jesse as a healthy little boy on his dad's shoulders.

"Doctor Conway?"

Sam blinked.

"Doctor Conway! Where are you?"

"Who is this and how did you get my number?"

"It is Paki."

"Paki? How can I help you, Paki?"

"Please listen to me."

"No."

"No?"

"If you're selling something, I'm really too busy right now."

"But... I'm not selling anything."

"Then get rid of that accent."

Silence.

The skull still smiled. Entreating. "Okay, if you say so," she mumbled. The brain said "go," sort of, but her legs lagged, like they weren't really hers. Slowly, she moved passed the bone pile. When she got to the back wall, there was an opening above her. Maneuvering the camera housing up was difficult. Her hand and finger muscles couldn't move.

"Samantha Conway?" a voice said with a British accent.

"Who is this?"

"George Rivers, London Times. Your assistant is very concerned that you are in grave danger. Is this true? Do you need help?"

Danger? She didn't *feel* like she was in any danger. Speaking to the media. Now *that* was danger. "I'm fine, thank you, and very busy."

Finally, she managed to shine the Super Nova lamp into the upper opening. The tunnel went straight up with more dark walls, like a chimney. She had never seen an entrance like *this* before but anything up seemed like a good idea. Her muscles had all the spring of a sponge. They moved, but without power. She inched upward until she was vertical, then kicked weakly, ascending at half the speed of her bubbles.

"Samantha?"

She ignored the annoying voice. Near the top of the shaft, there was another ceiling and another horizontal tunnel. The entrance, if indeed it was an entrance, was not made for walking. Her fingers felt cold, but she seemed able to hold the camera easier. It also occurred to her that she would have to probably go back the way she came, which meant down. The narcosis was reversing and her thoughts were beginning to come together.

Unlike alcohol intoxication, nitrogen narcosis is completely depth related and leaves as quickly as it comes. Her head was clearing fast. She looked at her depth gauge. Eighty-one feet.

And her air was low, less than a quarter tank left. Jesus. She had barely enough air to return if she turned back now, but she would have to go back through the narcosis, where she might decide to do, well, *anything!* She pointed the lamps down the new tunnel. It seemed to end about fifty-feet in. Where was she going? How far to the end? With her muscles stronger, she swam through the tunnel to the back wall. Another pile of bones, only this time with two skulls. Again the ceiling opened as it had at the first level. She was in a series of shafts and tunnels, but going where? She looked back at the bones. Did they have the same questions? Senenmut's tomb had never been discovered. Were any of these skulls his? She turned the lamp upward. Another chimney, but no ceiling in sight.

This was crazy. If she didn't leave now *she* would be the *next* pile of bones. Sam turned around and swam back the way she came. If she was lucky, she had enough air to get halfway back and then would emergency ascend, exhaling all the way to the surface from the expanding air in her lungs. At the hole in the floor that led back to the bottom, she stopped.

"Doctor Conway?"

"I hear you, Paki. I'm at eighty feet," she said, and then suddenly remembered what she had said to him earlier. "My God, Paki, I'm sorry for the way I spoke to you before."

"It is all right, Doctor Conway. I understand."

"No, I don't think you do. I'll explain when I see you."

"I don't see your light yet."

"That's because I'm not in the well anymore."

"Then where are you? At eighty feet?"

"In a parallel shaft," she said, her predicament fully realized. She had other tanks, but there was no way for anyone to get them to her because she had the only regulator.

"Then you will have to go back down to get back up?"

It occurred to her that she had traveled almost a hundred feet horizontally and the well itself was near the ledge side of a steep hill in that same direction. "It seems that way, Paki. But I still don't know where this tunnel leads to."

"What do I do?"

"For the moment, nothing."

She turned and went back to the bones, no longer interested in asking skulls their opinions, she swam directly into the ceiling hole and up the shaft. Careful not to ascend too quickly, she considered that all her sideways swimming had helped lessen the chances of bends.

Well into her ascent, there was still no sign of a ceiling. But, there did appear to be a surface. Her light reflected off ripples made from the bubbles. Sam slowed and then, excited, she had to hold herself back from going too fast.

Sam broke the surface cautiously, lamp first, her gaze fixed on the camera screen. She didn't like what she saw and brought her head above water for a better look. The shaft continued, but she no longer had water to help her climb. She lifted her mask to her forehead and sniffed the air. Odorless, cold and dank. She pointed the light up and could see the shaft end about twenty feet higher and a natural stone ceiling about thirty feet above that. A cave? The dark walls of the tunnel lightened up dramatically above the water level with the exception of a soaked corner where a steady trickle overflowing from the top had eroded a dark groove. She figured the groove had been formed over hundreds, maybe thousands of years.

"Doctor Conway?"

She imagined Paki was nervously checking his watch and shooing away reporters. "Paki. Relax. I broke surface. I have air."

"You have air!" he said, surprised.

"Yes."

"Where are you?"

"I don't know. Stand by."

She held the camera between her knees and pulled her inflatable vest over her head. She secured the vest around the camera and pulled the inflation cord. The camera now floated on its own. Her hands were free to work. By extending her arms she figured the shaft to be about four feet by six feet. She stretched out, touching hands and feet to opposite walls, but the weight of her tank and belt made it impossible for her to get out of the water. She was not strong enough. Treading water, she assessed her situation. She had air and water and she was in communication with Paki. A rope would be great, but there was no rope.

Sam took off her harness, unlatched the tank and released it to sink. She then took off her weight belt, slipped off the lead weights and used the strap to tie the camera to the tank harness, light forward. Without the tank and weights, she was light enough to attempt the wall again. With feet and hands outstretched, she strenuously inched her way up but, after a few feet, the pain and fatigue were too much and she fell. After a brief rest, she tried again but with the same end result. She thought for a moment, then took the harness back off, slipped her legs through one of the shoulder straps, put her feet and backside against opposite ends of the shorter wall. Again she inched upward, but less strenuously than before. The camera dangled under her as she climbed, light pointing down.

The closer she got to the top, the more tempted she was to reach under for the camera and shine the light upward, but she didn't want to mess with her success. Finally at the top, she sat back on the ledge and, swung her legs around in the dark. The ledge was about two feet wide so it was sufficient to perch herself on it. She quickly took hold of the camera and aimed the lamp.

"Jesus, God!" she said, as she found herself sitting on an island surrounded by skeletons and… Senenmut's treasure. There was very little in the way of wall art, but this was a lover's stash, not a king's tomb. And the skeletons? Possibly workers buried alive for secrecy. Possibly fellow treasure hunters from a time without scuba gear and two-way radios.

"Doctor Conway?"

Sam took her mask off and spoke into it. "It's all good, Paki. We found what we were looking for."

Silence. "The treasure?"

"Yes."

Paki laughed joyfully. "Congratulations. This is very wonderful for you. What do you want me to do now?"

"Call Michael Garmisa at the museum. Tell him we need some divers with the appropriate air mix and extra tanks within the hour."

"Absolutely. Anything else?"

"Yeah, have him send the air tanks in with that hero we talked about before."

Paki chuckled lightly. "He would be a little late, I think. You saved yourself again."

"Better late than never, my friend. Oh but, you would be my hero if you get me a hot chocolate and a bacon cheeseburger, dripping with ketchup."

More laughter. "How am I supposed to get that to you?"

"Ask Garmisa. When they find out what we've got here, they'll find a way, pronto. Oh, and make sure to tell them to burn the fries. I like 'em hot and crispy. And tell him I also want the biggest Porterhouse steak he can find, smothered with mushrooms and smashed potatoes."

"I think your eyes, they are getting a little too big for your stomach."

Sam laughed. "The steak is for *your* stomach my friend. You earned it."

There was silence, but she knew Paki was smiling.

Sam examined a gold artifact as Paki relayed the news of the findings back to New York. The glittering art and writings matched Senenmut's time period and could give further clues to more discoveries. She felt euphoric in the accomplishment. The hard work had paid off.

"Doctor Conway?"

"Yes, Paki."

"How are you?"

"Wonderful, did you reach New York?"

"Yes," he said, but sounded less than thrilled.

"Is there something wrong?"

Silence.

"Paki? What's wrong?"

"Your father."

Sam's eyes widened as she stood up. "What about my father?"

Silence.

5

Ramses al Tarik sat calm, like the eye of a hurricane, behind a large stone table in his private chambers within his elaborate cave complex in the northern mountains of Afghanistan. Over the last few months the cave had become home. The room was decorated with art and small niches in the stone held oil lamps and random replicas of ancient Egyptian artifacts that included a tall wooden black statue of Anubis, the Egyptian god of death. The oldest and most feared of the gods, Anubis had the head of a jackal and the body of a warrior and carried a staff. According to Egyptian lore, Anubis held the keys to eternal death and could be entreated by worship and sacrifice. It had been fitted with real fangs and emerald eyes. One of two he had had expertly carved for himself by a highly talented sculptor who had since died of a sudden blood deficiency. Tarik didn't like the idea of any further replication of his prize possession.

Tarik wondered for a moment what time it was, if it was actually day or night. Hiding for weeks at a time inside the cave had confused his internal clock, though he would often stare at the hard stone walls without knowing the hour and feel the cold glimmer of a crescent moon or the warm crimson glow of a sunset. At the moment, however, he didn't need the sun to raise his temperature. Anger had him boiling hot. He had just finished reading another very disturbing message regarding the organization's financial status. Business was terrible. Tarik was the current leader of Asad al Adala, translated, Lions of Justice.

He was also the current leader on both the DIA and CIA's list of most wanted terrorists on the planet, thanks to the organization's enduring résumé of merciless death and destruction.

He closed his laptop hard and furrowed his brow as he looked across the table at the translator.

"Well?"

The old man's head jerked up from his focus, a bit startled. Zahi Hassani, a world class archeologist, was one of the best ancient writing translators in the Middle East. He had been brought to Tarik's main cave blindfolded and would leave the same way, if at all. "Excuse me?"

Tarik felt his blood pressure tick up another few digits but spoke calmly. "What does it say? What is it? You've been staring at it for over *an hour*," he said, pointing at the broken artifact. "Is it worth anything? And before you answer, you should know that I've killed messengers."

Tarik had succeeded founder and mentor Abdullah Fahri Mohammed after Egyptian authorities sentenced Mohammed to life imprisonment. The organization's original primary goal under Mohammed was to overthrow the Egyptian Government and replace it with their own religious state. But in recent years, the outside flow of financial support had slowed to a trickle due to economic distress and increased money tracing measures implemented in the global crackdown on terrorism. Consequently, Tarik, Egyptian from birth, believed the original founder's ideals needed to be reexamined and reshaped to allow a wider mouth for funds to enter the organization from the less willing contributors. He still believed in overthrowing the Egyptian government, but mostly because it would give him control and access to the country's many treasures and a platform to pilfer millions in the name of faith and country.

Tarik enjoyed his command. A student of military history, he learned that men preformed well if they loved you but that the best results came through fear. In Rome, Caesar was looked upon as a god because he conquered swiftly and mercilessly and marked his highways with crucifixions as a symbol of Roman greatness. Hirohito's Japanese Empire spread amazingly fast during World War II, easily defeating its giant neighbor, China. The Japanese armies had instructions to rape and pillage villages and establish terror as their most potent weapon. Fear meant power and power meant control.

"Where did you get this?" Hassani said, holding both pieces, unblinking.

"That is not important. Is it valuable?"

"Where it came from is very important. I must know."

"Can you read it?"

Hassani paused. "Some of it, possibly. This will take more time to work out."

Tarik closed his eyes and said, "Why more time? You are an expert. 'The best translator possible', they say."

Hassani frowned, deep gullies formed in his forehead. His fingers gently feathered over the artifact's surface. "This is not a language anyone is familiar with anymore. Translating will be difficult."

"Is it very old?"

"Very. But so precise. So detailed. Astonishing. Please tell me where you found this. It can only help."

Tarik paused. "About three hundred and twenty miles north."

"Of where? I do not know where I am."

"Somewhere near Ab Gach, by the Daryoi Pomir River."

Hassani paused. "There is nothing there but hills and mountains. There was never anything there. This came from somewhere else. A city."

"How do you know that?

"Because it is from an ancient pillar. Even if it is not the one I hope it is, it is still an ancient pillar. Most ancient cities displayed them prominently to give important information."

"What kind of information?"

"Where to water your camel or pay a tariff or worship a god, or declare ownership," Hassani said.

"Water your camel? Is that all this will say?"

Hassani was quick to shake his head. "No, this is different, but still from a pillar."

"Different how?"

"I would need to study it more, but it is very unique."

"Ah. What city could it be from?"

"I don't know. I need more time to study it."

"Then it is rare."

"Yes. It might be a pillar from an undiscovered city. Or...."

"What?"

"I'd rather not say just yet."

"Then it could be valuable?"

"Valuable?" Hassani said, and then laughed. "Yes, you could say that. But, it is incomplete. Where is the rest of it?"

"This is all I have."

"But there is more. We must find the rest," Hassani said louder.

Tarik was surprised by the sudden insistence. "Why?"

Hassani turned the stone so Tarik could see and pointed to the top. "Above the text, these two characters stem down to these three and this one branches down to this group and then here and here and..."

"Yes, yes," Tarik said. "But what does it mean?"

"It's a succession. There are several common types but this one is clearly lineage."

"Lineage?"

"Yes, a family tree."

Tarik narrowed his eyes and nodded. "Okay. So?"

"It's a very unusual one."

"How?"

"Well, to begin with, it is not Egyptian. The Egyptians were the first and, ultimately, the only civilization in their time to keep detailed ancestral records on stone. At least the only ones known. Later, others were recorded by mouth and by animal hides. But this is not Egyptian."

"Does that make it more or less valuable?" Tarik said.

Hassani ignored the question. "What is more unusual is that it is not a typical genealogy record. Normally ancient records of this type are formed backwards. They would start with a particular ruler and work back to a previous ruler, leaving out incidental descendents of little or no consequence. This does the opposite, as if it was recorded by the by the oldest."

Tarik frowned. "But that would be impossible."

"Yes, quite," Hassani said, turning his gaze back to the artifact. "The originator would have lived long enough to know his descendents. He would have to be hundreds of years old."

"Then what is your point? No one has ever lived that long."

"True, not as far as we know," Hassani said, his focus glued to the artifact. "But there are legends."

Tarik paused. "The writing tells a legend?"

Hassani shook his head and smiled, his crooked finger tapping the stone. "I'm saying that this artifact could *be* a legend."

Tarik stared blankly. "Explain," he said, with his full attention.

"Methuselah's Pillar."

Tarik paused and then shook his head. "I have never heard of this legend."

"It is not a common legend like Isis and Osiris or Noah's Ark or heaven or hell."

"You do not believe there is a heaven?"

"Belief has nothing to do with something being a legend. Without proof, even truths are legends."

"Yes, fine, tell me about Methuselah's Pillar."

"It is simple. It is said that Adam gave his great grandson of several generations a record of information. And some of the information helped Methuselah to become the oldest man ever to live."

"How old?"

"Nine hundred and sixty-nine years."

"Nine hundred. Obviously, this is not a true legend."

"No, you would not think so. But an interesting part of the legend is that Moses also read what was on the pillar. Maybe *this* pillar," Hassani said, turning his gaze back to the artifact. That would make this very valuable. Priceless in fact," he said with a thin smile.

Tarik started to smile but then another thought took it quickly away.

Hassani continued. "If you could find out where this was found and piece it together with the rest of the pillar and it actually wound up being a record from Adam, it would be the most valuable find in human history. You could name your price," Hassani said, but Tarik was no longer listening.

"Moses?" Tarik said.

"Uh, yes. Moses," Hassani said, matter-of-factly.

"The same Moses who inflicted Egypt with plagues?"

"Well, yes. There is only one."

"The same Moses that single-handedly defeated the most powerful army on earth."

"Uh, yes, with divine help, according to legend."

"Maybe that was part of his divine help," Tarik said, motioning at the etched stone.

"If. If this *even is* a piece of Methuselah's Pillar."

"You said it was."

"I said it could be. Possibly. Not definitely."

Tarik stood up and looked Hassani in the eye. "I want to know what this says. I want to know exactly what it says."

"To know for certain, we would need the rest of the pillar. This is incomplete."

Tarik marched to the door and called to his nearest assistant and ordered him to get the two soldiers who had found the artifact. A few moments later, the two soldiers were standing before him at attention.

"I want the rest of this," Tarik said, motioning to the artifact on the desktop.

The two soldiers shared a glance at each other.

"Is there a problem?" Tarik said unblinking.

One of the soldiers spoke up. "My Sheikh, we took this from a dying shepherd. And he told us we could have it but this was all he had."

Tarik exhaled. "What is your first name?" he said to one of the soldiers.

"Rashid."

"And yours?" he said to the other

"Saleem."

"Rashid and Saleem. I promise you a great reward that will make you and your families very wealthy. But you must find the rest of the artifact and bring it to me. Dig. Find his family and get it from them. Just get it," he said and waved for them to go. The soldiers quickly bowed and rushed away, colliding through the doorway.

6

Sam unbuckled her harness and opened the door before the helicopter came to a complete rest on the Saint Francis Hospital helipad. Ground attendants reached in to assist her off the aircraft but she blew past them before they could be of any help. She ran across the tarmac through the emergency room doors to the reception desk.

"I'm Samantha Conway. Where's the Coronary Intensive Care Unit?" she said before the receptionist could speak.

A man appeared next to her in green scrubs. "Come with me, Ms. Conway," he said. "We've been expecting you."

Sam followed him at a rapid pace, afraid to ask for any details. They hurried down the hall, into an elevator, up one floor, and down another corridor. Her usual good sense of direction was lost.

The flight back from Egypt to New York's JFK Airport had been the longest fifteen hours of her life. Forget sleep. She hadn't been able to even think of the found new treasures in the ancient well. And her gratitude for being whisked away by authorities to a waiting chopper was lost on the fact that it was done so as to race her to her father, who was calling her name while clinging to life.

Sam followed the man in green scrubs through the double doors of the CICU. They passed several private rooms until he opened a door and motioned her in. With the long anticipated moment of dread and truth upon her, she exhaled but entered without pause.

The room was alive with beeps, hisses and blinking lights. Her first sight was the silhouette of her brother, Jesse, in front of a large window that glowed with the afternoon sun. Her eyes quickly found her father in the lone bed in front of Jesse and she hurried to his side.

"Daddy," she said, her eyes instantly filled with tears as she touched his hand between wires and tubes. Next to her a beeping green monitor told her his pulse was one hundred and twelve. She tried not to shake.

Jack Conway's eyes opened slowly and then brightened dimly. "Sammy," he whispered. "You're back." His fingers worked around her hand and gently squeezed. She always loved his hands. The same hands that had picked her up and mounted her on strong shoulders countless times.

"Yes, Daddy. Back and here to stay."

Jack smiled thinly. "No one can put a leash on you, Sweetie. Not even you," he said, and paused to allow the oxygen tube in his nose to help him catch his breath.

"I love you so much, Daddy."

Jack closed his eyes and nodded slowly, tears squeezing out from under his eyelids. "I... I need your help," he whispered.

"Anything. What?"

"Jesse."

"Jesse?" Sam repeated. She looked up at her little brother. His bloodshot tear-soaked eyes matched his curly red hair. "Don't ever worry about Jesse, Dad. That base is permanently covered. You two own my heart and always will."

"You're a good girl, Sammy," Jack managed.

Sam tried to smile. "You've never accused me of *that* before."

49

"Our secret," Jack said. "Has your knight in shining armor showed up yet?"

"Yes, when I was born. You've always been my hero, Daddy," Sam said, her voice cracking.

Jack smiled. "I mean the other one. The one we've talked about."

Sam tried not to close her eyes as they flooded. She had always been able to reveal so much of her heart to him. "Not yet, Daddy."

"Don't worry, he will suddenly appear," Jack said weakly and the beeps from the monitor next to her became noticeably faster. Jack grimaced, pulled his hand from Sam's and grabbed at his chest. The door opened and several people in scrubs scrambled in.

"You'll have to leave now," said a nurse.

"Daddy!" Sam cried. Jesse came around to her side.

"Please, now, you're in the way. Out!" said a male in scrubs.

Sam stepped back and then, as if guided by her father's will, she put her arm around Jesse and led him out of the room.

7

Tarik sensed he was in the presence of greatness- his own. He stood behind the window of his new lab and watched Zahi Hassani, his world class translator, and Doctor Dulai, his newly acquired Indian scientist, as they worked shoulder to shoulder exploring the mysteries of what they believed could be Methuselah's Pillar.

Like Hassani, Dulai was ambitious and had an impressive résumé, his being in microbiology. Unlike Hassani, Dulai wasn't already famous and wealthy. Tarik promised him unlimited funds and his own prestigious lab to spearhead work on the greatest scientific discovery since gravity.

"They are here," said a voice from behind.

Tarik turned. "Who?" he said to the soldier.

"Rashid and Saleem," he said, but his expression was not excited.

Tarik said nothing else. He marched from the viewing window, his jaw muscles tightening. They had been gone over a month without communication. He had anxiously sent scouts out to find them two weeks ago. They had better had found something to show him. When they saw him coming, they both looked first to the ground.

"What did you find?"

They both lifted their shoulders and looked to the other.

"Look at me and report," he demanded through gritted teeth.

"We went back to where we found the shepherd," Saleem said.

"And?"

"And he was gone," Rashid said.

"Gone!"

"Yes," Saleem said. "As if he was never there."

"Did you try to find him?"

"Yes, my Sheik," Rashid said. "It was far from any towns but we went to all within fifty miles."

"Fifty?"

"Yes, maybe more."

"What leads did you find?"

After a pause, Rashid said, "No one seems to know about a missing or injured shepherd."

Tarik gazed back to the lab. Down the hall he could see Dulai and Hassani watching him. "You've been gone more than a month. You could have told me this weeks ago."

They both looked back to the ground. "We did not want to return back to you empty handed," Saleem said.

"But you have. After a month, you have brought me nothing."

Rashid and Saleem stood mute.

Tarik wanted to grab a gun and kill them both where they stood. He wanted more. Much more. He turned on his heel and stormed down the hallway. Disappointment hung on the face of both Dulai and Hassani. Their silence rang loud in his ears. His soldiers' failure to him was his failure to them. He had shown them weakness. *I must never appear weak to them*, he thought. He turned and pushed through the privacy curtains of his chamber where he could be alone and think. He sat down at his stone table. His laptop was open and scrolling financial information.

He closed it. Nothing compared to the pillar. He was destined to receive the power of its secrets.

Tarik's chamber walls flickered softly with the golden glow of oil lamps. He could hear hushed conversations beyond his curtains, probably about his disappointment and anger. They should be silent. *How dare they speak where I could hear*, he thought, and then saw the shadow move on the wall next to the curtain. Did it move, or was it the flickering light? He stared at it. It was always there when the lamps were on, but now it seemed to hold his attention. He turned around to see the source of the shadow. The tall wooden statue of Anubis, the Egyptian god of death. The tar black jackal head with canine fangs faced him. Flames from the oil lamps danced in the polished emerald eyes. His gaze locked, unblinking, paralyzed. His breathing slowed as he felt tension leave. He looked to the statue's feet and saw the sacrificial knife.

Tarik opened his curtain and summoned a guard.

"Saleem and Rashid. Bring them here to me. And bring the two doctors also. And bring two ropes."

The guard vanished but soon returned. "My Sheik?" called the guard from outside Tarik's chamber.

"You may enter," Tarik said.

The curtain parted and the guard entered and stood to the side as Saleem and Rashid and then the two doctors stepped in, followed by a second guard.

Tarik remained seated behind his stone table and first addressed the doctors. "You are here to observe only, like you did before. You may not interfere or leave until I tell you. Is that understood?"

The doctors nodded and shuffled into a corner. Tarik turned his attention to Rashid and Saleem. "Who killed the shepherd?" he said evenly.

Rashid and Saleem looked at each other and then Saleem said, "We all did."

"Everyone?" Tarik said incredulously. "That was not the report I heard."

"As a group we thought he should be shot."

"As a group," Tarik said.

Both soldiers nodded and said, "Yes."

"And everyone shot him?"

Both soldiers frowned nervously and then Saleem said, "No, my Sheik, but we all agreed."

"Why?"

"He saw our faces."

"I see. Why did you not take him prisoner?"

"He was half buried. Stuck in the ground," Rashid said.

"Then why didn't you dig him out?"

"We were being chased. Bombed," Rashid said.

Tarik turned and picked up the ancient sacrificial knife from the statue's base. He then laid it on the table in front of him. All the eyes in the room instantly widened. "Who pulled the trigger?" he said calmly.

After a moment of silence, he repeated the question.

Saleem exhaled and said, "Rashid."

Rashid looked at Saleem.

"Then Rashid shot the shepherd?"

The soldiers were silent.

"Rashid?" Tarik said, his finger slowly feathered the handle of the knife.

"Yes, my Sheik?"

"You shot the shepherd?"

Rashid swallowed and his words came softly. "Yes, my Sheik."

"And the knowledge of our treasure's location died with the shepherd."

"The shepherd was gone. He may have been taken by the army," Rashid offered.

"But you were gone for over a month and you have not found him?"

Rashid was silent.

Tarik nodded. "Then our treasure is lost."

"There was no other treasure," Rashid said.

Tarik glared at Rashid. "There is. I know there is. And I will have it."

Rashid nodded eagerly. "Then I will find it. I will not fail you."

"No you will not. You and Saleem will search much better this time and will find it."

Saleem also nodded eagerly.

Tarik stood up and took the knife in his hand. "Good, now lay down on this table," he said to Rashid.

"My Sheik?" Rashid said.

"There is a price to pay."

"A pri.... You just said I will help Saleem."

"As a powerful reminder. Lay down on this table," he repeated, and then looked at the guards by the exit. The guards were immediately at Rashid's side.

Rashid glanced up to the jackal head of Anubis and then to the table and took a step backward. The guards instantly grabbed his arms and held him fast. Tarik looked Rashid in the eye and then motioned to the table. The guards applied the needed pressure.

Rashid shook as he walked, his legs buckling. "Please forgive me."

"Take off his pants," Tarik said. "And then tie his feet and his neck."

The guard hesitated, but then ripped down Rashid's pants. The horrified soldier urinated uncontrollably as he was laid onto a stone table before Anubis. Rashid's neck and ankles were quickly roped and secured tightly under the table.

"My Sheik!" Rashid choked.

Tarik examined the knife before the soldier's widened gaze. He placed his middle finger inside the upper right leg, next to Rashid's genitals. He lightly slid his finger about three inches up the diagonal crease of the soldier's quivering leg and found what he was looking for. The femoral pulse.

"Stop shaking," Tarik said, quietly.

"I... I can't."

Tarik put the point of the sharp knife over the pulse and pushed it about three inches into the flesh. The soldier instantly tightened and screamed. Tarik gently tilted the handle, severing the femoral artery.

"Aghh," Rashid cried, struggling against the rope.

"Shhhh," Tarik said as he withdrew the knife and put the bloodied tool on the table. The guards stepped back as blood poured through the puncture and quickly drenched the table and floor.

Rashid breathed fast and heavily. When he finally caught his breath he said, "I'm cold," his teeth chattering, body shaking. "Very cold."

"And pale," Tarik said. "That's because your blood is almost gone. In about two minutes you won't feel cold anymore and you will become quiet and blue."

Rashid could not respond and soon his glassy eyes dulled translucent.

Tarik turned to Saleem, who was almost as pale as Rashid. "Now, are you going to find the missing pieces?"

"Yes, my Sheik."

"Good. Rashid's fate will accompany you in your mission. I will also send someone else with you to help you get back as soon as possible."

"Yes, my Sheik."

"You may leave."

Saleem bowed and stumbled through the curtain.

Tarik turned to the doctors. "Have you seen enough?"

They both nodded silently.

"Then I think it is time you get back to work."

The doctors hurried out and Tarik ordered to the guards to also leave. He then stood before Rashid's body. He picked up the bloodied knife and held it palm up to Anubis. "I gave you what you required. Now I ask for you to bring me what I need."

8

Sam pinched the dime-sized silver iron and counted out five spaces. "*Uh Oh*, luxury tax, pay seventy-five dollars. Can I buy it?"

"N-no," Jesse said. "Y-you ha-have to pay seventy-f-five dollars."

Sam counted out seventy-five monopoly dollars and handed them to the banker, Miss Cox. Miss Cox was middle aged plus and made no attempt to disguise the years. Curled gray hair, glasses and neatly dressed with a few extra pounds. She reminded Sam of her third grade reading teacher. Soft-spoken and functional, she breathed appropriateness. The museum had made a perfect choice as far as Sam was concerned to help her with Jesse. At least, that was how she felt before they started playing monopoly.

Jesse rolled the dice hard and one jumped off the table. "W-what number is it?"

Miss Cox leaned from her chair with a grunt and picked it off the floor. "Roll again," she said.

"W-why?"

Miss Cox smiled. "Because it went off the table."

"W-what was the n-number?" Jesse asked.

"It doesn't matter," Miss Cox said firmly. "You have to re-roll it."

Jesse looked at Sam for help. She shrugged. "You've got two choices. Flip a coin or just roll again."

Jesse frowned. "W-what if the c-coin goes on the f-floor?"

Sam laughed. "Just roll it again, Jess."

Jesse smiled and rolled. "Se-seven. R-reading Railroad. Yes! I'll b-buy it," Jesse said and gave the dice to Miss Cox.

Miss Cox did some calculating, counted out some money and put a house on both Broadway and Park Place. Now every side of the board had houses, all belonging to Miss Cox. She then shook the dice, blew into her hands and rolled. "Six, *yes!* Pennsylvania Railroad. I'll buy it," she said decisively.

"D-damn," Jesse said. "I w-wanted that."

Miss Cox smiled.

Sam rolled. "Uh, six," she said and moved. "Income tax, pay ten percent or two hundred dollars. Great. I guess I don't get my two hundred for passing 'go'".

"Nope," Miss Cox said and then pushed the dice to Jesse.

Sam's cell phone lit up and danced on the table. *Thank God,* she thought and looked to see who had just saved her. She would not have answered if it was a collection agency but the name said 'Michael Garmisa', director of the museum, her boss.

"Sorry, guys. Gotta take this," she said and got up. "Just go on without me."

"We can wait," Miss Cox said.

"Michael Garmisa," she said, and then answered. "Hello."

Miss Cox nodded. Jesse started to get up but a quick look from Miss Cox caused him to sit back down.

"Sam, hi, it's Michael," he said.

"Good timing, I owe you one."

"For what?"

"I'll tell you later. What's happening?"

"You are. CNN called. You're going on the Larry King show."

"Really?" Sam said. "Very cool."

"Yes. We're very excited about it. We'll push up your new Senenmut treasure presentation."

"When is it?"

"Two weeks."

"Two weeks? That's not enough time. The exhibit won't be ready."

"Then we'll show them what we can. It will be a exhibit in progress."

"I was also hoping to focus on some of the new writings we found in the well. There might be some more leads."

"I know, I know. We talked about that, but you can always do that after the show. We are only talking a couple of weeks. In fact, you can mention that and some other exploration plans on the show."

"What other exploration plans?"

"We'll make some."

"Like what?"

"I don't know. The Arc of the Covenant."

Sam rolled her eyes. "Well if it's attention you want."

"Exactly. If we can mix in a lead on a legend people are familiar with while we have Senenmut's treasure displayed, we'll double our membership."

Sam shook her head. "We don't have any leads on biblical legends."

"Then find a lead on a lead. We can start a rumor and then have 'no comment'. Who knows what could develop?"

"Sounds like we're becoming the Weather Channel."

"And Hurricane Sam just hit the Doppler radar," Garmisa said.

"Calm down, Michael. Hurricane Sam doesn't need any hype. Our discoveries can speak for themselves."

"They speak to you Sam. The rest of us need a hearing aid."

"That's why you pay me the big bucks. And speaking of bucks. I'm due for a raise."

"Yes you are. By the way, how is Miss Cox working out?"

"Don't change the subject."

"I'm not. Miss Cox is…"

"Don't even say it Michael," Sam interrupted sharply.

"Say what?"

"Miss Cox does not represent any part of my salary and she's not part of a raise. Are we in agreement or are we going to have to step outside."

"Okay, okay. I was just asking how you're getting along with Miss Cox and you want to beat me up. That's employer abuse."

"Fire me."

Garmisa laughed. "If I did that, you'd find my bones around the campfire of the Neanderthal exhibit across the park."

"I'd make sure to wave 'hi' as I pass you on the way to my new office. Natural History has already asked me to call them if I ever want another view."

"Ha, ha. Seriously, how is Miss Cox doing?"

Sam looked toward the kitchen. "She's… winning us over."

"Excellent. I knew she'd be perfect for you."

9

The Defense Intelligence Agency's fundamental mission is to provide timely, objective, and cogent military intelligence to warfighters, soldiers and sailors, airmen, marines—and to the defense planners, and defense and national security policy makers right up to the secretary of defense. The DIA achieves this with the integration of highly skilled intelligence professionals with leading edge technology to discover information and create knowledge that provide warning, identify opportunities, and deliver an overwhelming advantage to the mission.

D IA agent John Decker's orders left little leeway for interpretation but plenty for imagination. Find Tarik at any cost and kill him. Simply put, the United States had its best agent going after the world's most dangerous terrorist. Decker was a magician, but so was Tarik. Both were capable of the impossible.

Decker drew a mouthful from the Coke bottle and then stole another look at downtown Kabul through the ratty hotel's second floor window. Two men in faded Islamic garb shouldering machine guns walked casually through the shadows of the afternoon sun. They gave a nod while passing another man of similar attire who was leaning against the building across the street, enjoying a cigarette. A hundred feet up the dirt road, two children were playing with a soccer ball. Decker watched them for a while longer and then shook his head. In this country, machine guns and soccer balls could share space on the same postal stamp.

A dog trotted past the kids, up the street and under the window. Decker knew the dog, a mangy mutt. Probably hungry. Probably looking for him. He had fed it a couple of times. Actually more than a couple and more than he'd admit, but it didn't seem that anyone else fed it and, if he had to see it from time to time, he'd rather not see its bones.

The booming mechanical wail, or as they called it, 'prayer', through the city's loudspeakers wasn't noisy enough to quiet the rhythmic bumps and groans that vibrated through the hotel room's paper-thin walls. He wanted to sit. The stained bed mattress or the dusty floor. No chair. He stood. *How much longer*, he wondered and then drained the remaining Coke and set the empty bottle on the windowsill next to some dried flies.

He looked at his cheap watch; bought just two blocks away at the Kabul market, where he bought everything else he owned on this side of hell... the hot side. He exhaled and shook his head. They had been going at it strong for almost an hour. He tried not to think about it and took another glance out the window. The man across the street was still there, waiting for his friend, the brother of a known insurgent, presently getting in his weekly exercise in the next room.

His job for the last four years, which was the last time he'd touched a scissor or razor, was to become a fly on the wall in Afghanistan's most notorious city. Over the years, Decker had developed a skilled nose for trouble. A knack for recognizing enemy optimism in the midst of hardship. The fact that he was still alive was not the only measure of his success. His anonymity had paid big dividends in locating leadership movements and heading off strategic weaponry before installation.

Many of the insurgents had close local relatives who supported them with food and faith. The support often carried back a word or two of encouragement. These morsels were often all Decker had to work with, and he would make the most of it. Lately though, the information had been especially sparse and, in light of his new orders, it was time to push himself past the comfort zone.

Decker took another glance out the window. Nothing had changed. The man was enjoying another smoke and the kids were still kicking the ball around. In his peripheral, he saw movement. He looked left. A scorpion walking on the floor. He shuddered. Being from Chicago, he'd become used to the Kabul rat population fairly quickly, but the scorpions, no. Little amber land-lobsters with translucent legs and a poison stinger at the tail's end looking for something to stab. Well, it wasn't going to be him.

Decker reached through his goat's hair vest and found his knife. A heavy double-edged, soft-steel thrower he'd found at the market. A little smaller than his Bowie knife and sharp as a razor. He preferred a knife to his handgun, which he kept well hidden. The very last thing he wanted was a suspicious relative of an insurgent searching his room and finding a government issue pistol and silencer. Finding a knife would mean nothing in Kabul. Everyone had knives, although few had his… touch.

The scorpion was about sixteen feet away. In an instant, he calculated his turning cycle to be one and a half, bent his wrist precisely and then uncoiled his fluid, high velocity release. The knife flashed across the room and cut deeply into the wooden floor.

The groans grew louder and louder and then finally stopped. Decker clapped silently and walked across the room to the halved scorpion and retrieved his knife. By the time he walked back to the window, there was a soft knock on the door. He readied his knife for another throw and spoke in the native Farsi language without accent, "Come in, it's open."

The door opened and in stepped the young woman from the other room, though she had looked younger earlier in the day when he'd first propositioned her for information. In Kabul anything could be bought, but quality or its lack was too often discovered in hindsight. She paused when she saw the knife.

"Are you all right?" he said in Farsi. He took another glance out the window. Her last customer had just joined the man across the street for a cigarette. Decker put his knife away.

She shut the door and peeled back her head covering. Long black hair fell over her shoulders and, in spite of her harsh environment, she was quite pretty. "Same as this morning," she replied and walked toward him.

Decker looked at her from head to toe and then into her large brown eyes. Eyes that had seen too much. "Do you have something for me?"

She gave him a blank stare and then loosened and dropped her garment to her bare feet. "I have more than what you want."

The second place Decker's eyes went to was her scar-laced abdomen. Discipline, torture, she had no doubt experienced both. He hated the Taliban when he had first arrived, but now, after seeing what the religious fanatics had done to people like the woman before him, hate was too soft a word. "How old are you?" he asked sympathetically.

She smiled thinly and said, "I have forgotten my name and you ask my age? I don't know, perhaps twenty-one. Does it matter?"

Decker sighed and then lifted her clothing back over her copper shoulders. He didn't need to ask. Like thousands, she probably had a dead husband, again, compliments of the Taliban. Her shamed life was kept a deep secret from family and neighbors and, if she knew of another path that would feed her children, she would have taken it. The whole country was trying to regain a decade of lost sanity. "I only want the information," he said. "What did he tell you?"

"Nothing of any interest," she said, apparently surprised she was clothed so soon.

"I'll be the judge of that."

She rolled her eyes. "He only wanted to talk about my body and his wife."

"I'm paying you well now and you'll be the richest woman in Afghanistan if you can tell me where to find Tarik."

It was faint and fleeting, but Decker saw it. A question like that would work a glimmer of fear or greed on the coolest expression. He was hoping for greed... but she was scared to death. This was not necessarily all bad. She wouldn't be afraid if she didn't know something that could hurt her and help him.

"Did you ask him about his brother?" Decker said.

"I want more money. Such questions could get me killed."

Decker frowned and paused. After a fruitless moment of trying to read her further, he reached into his pocket and took out a thick wad of cash. She reached for it but Decker pulled it back. "Did he speak of his brother or not?"

"Aghh! He is a son of a dog! He didn't want to talk to me of his brother today. Why don't you ask him yourself?"

Decker quickly glanced out the window. The two men that were across the street hadn't left. In fact, they seemed to be arguing when, the man who had been waiting, pointed at the hotel and pushed the other man toward it. The man made a nasty hand motion, cocked his machine gun and started toward the door. He was coming back.

Decker looked back to the woman. "You told him?"

She shook her head rapidly. "No. I only did what you asked. I cannot *make* him speak."

Decker stared into her eyes for a moment, knew she had lied to him and then said in English, "Wonderful. Time to meet more interesting people, and kill them."

"He probably wants me for his friend." the woman said.

"Yeah," Decker sighed casually at her betrayal. "So ends another promising friendship. Looks like my lunch break is over." He took the cash, held the wad as if he were going to give it to her and then tossed it out the window behind him. "If you hurry down it might still be there."

"*What are you doing?*" she shrieked, reaching for his hand, but the money was gone. She looked at him in disbelief and then rushed past him to see where it landed.

Decker found his knife, a little scorpion juice still on the tip. The woman was leaning out the window. He set the knife handle between his fingers and watched the door bottom for a shadow. In English he spoke to her, knowing she didn't understand him. "I had a choice when I was eighteen. Student loan or the military. The Army said they would pay for my schooling. And the benefits were second to none. This hotel, however, didn't make their brochure and they didn't say anything about scorpions."

She frowned slightly, confused.

"I guess what I'm trying to tell you is to read the fine print before you sign up with Tarik," he said in Farsi.

Suddenly, the door smashed open and two men rushed in. Decker threw the knife, dove into a somersault, sprung to his feet and pulled his knife from the first man's neck and kicked the machine gun from the other man's grasp. As the injured man fell onto his face Decker grabbed and pulled down the second man's left sleeve, pushed the guy's right shoulder backward while placing his right leg behind the man. In an instant, the overmatched man was up off his feet and hard onto his back with Decker heavy on his chest, the point of his knife under his prey's chin.

Decker looked into the man's frightened wide eyes. "You can wind up like your friend over there, or we can talk about…" was all he said before hearing an explosion of pain shoot through the back of his head. He toppled sideways and saw the young girl with an empty Coke bottle in her hand, and then darkness.

10

Tarik traversed stealthily across rocks and boulders under the cover of a thickly clouded moonless night with his two man escort. His arrival at the cave was unscheduled. His time away at his primary headquarters on the oil rig was necessary but torturously long and financially frustrating. Nothing seemed to be going right. His thoughts and hopes were concentrated more and more on the work conducted in the cave. He constantly fantasized of launching the greatest terror offensive in modern history and was driven to micro manage the progress. He could taste his future dominance in the air. He would punish over three thousand years of injustice and shift the global balance of power forever. No longer would he have to worry about investments or burrow underground like a rodent.

"In the storm…" called a voice in the darkness.

Tarik and his armed men stopped. "…we have shelter," Tarik responded, giving the correct password. The guards scurried to announce his surprise arrival. A half mile later, Tarik disappeared into the mountain through a narrow crevice behind a huge boulder. The entrance was virtually invisible, even up-close in full daylight.

Watchmen bowed respectfully as the word of Tarik's presence spread quickly and deep throughout the massive cave complex. A shepherd hastened to separate a small flock of sheep as he passed through a cavernous foyer and continued down a central rock corridor. Sleepy-eyed soldiers scrambled from side rooms to greet their leader with reverence. He felt their warmth but also sensed their fear. Fear was good. Very good. A reputation for being spontaneous and impulsively violent had helped keep his people in line.

A man hurriedly adjusted his clothes, rushed to Tarik's side and said, "It is good to see you, my Sheik. I have been praying for your safe travels."

"Your prayers were heard, Asad," he said to his officer. "I will hear your reports in the morning."

The officer paused. "Of course, Tarik," Asad said with a bow.

"What is wrong?" Tarik said. "Is there something I should know sooner?"

"We have had additional concern because of the new prisoner."

"What new prisoner?"

"An American agent. He had been asking about you in Kabul."

"Everyone is asking about me," Tarik said.

"He wasn't taken easily. The American killed Amir's brother." Asad explained how the American had hired a prostitute to seduce information from a soldier's brother and, in the end, killed him expertly with a knife thrown in the neck.

"And Amir?"

"Grieving, my Sheik."

Tarik's chest filled with rage. He looked over his shoulder in the direction of the prison. He would deal with the American soon. Blood for blood. "Tell Amir I will avenge his brother's death personally."

The officer bowed. "You will lift his heart, my Sheik."

"Where is Doctor Dulai?" he asked sternly.

"In the lab with Hassani," he said.

"Good," Tarik said and immediately left. He passed several offshoot tunnels until he came to the lab in the far end of the cave. He looked into a viewing window and saw his two experts hard at work with their assistants. He tapped on the window and one of the assistants saw him and quickly to opened the secured airtight steel door, one of only two secured doors in the complex, the other being to the prison.

The door creaked open. "Sheik!" said a wide-eyed young bearded man in a white lab coat.

Tarik nodded, looked past the man to Doctor Dulai who had his hands busy in the glove box, a glass clean-room container the size of a coffin with arm-length rubber gloves allowing the doctor to work inside without letting anything outside get in, and more importantly, anything inside get out. Dulai turned and saw him and then continued working, rubber gloves up to his armpits. The lab was cold but humming with activity. Electronic boxes with fluctuating needles and gauges were stacked higher than his head. Tarik had no idea what any of it did. An IBM super computer with three white cabinets each the size of a refrigerator blinked little green lights. Several monitors lined up along a stainless steel counter were manned with more bearded lab techs in white coats. Cameras and scanners, mounted on a chrome tree, focused upon the ancient artifact inside another, smaller glass box. Hassani scrolled images on a large monitor and compared them to magnified images on the artifact.

Tarik walked to the glove box. Dulai appeared to be dissecting dried decomposed meat that might have once been a small monkey. In the far corner of the container sat another monkey, alive, alert and, by all outward appearances, perfectly healthy.

"How close are we?" Tarik said.

"To being raided by the Americans?" Dulai said, keeping his eyes on his hands. "They should be here any minute, looking for your latest prisoner. I understand he's CIA or something."

"Don't worry about the prisoner. He's my problem not yours."

"Let's hope you can keep it that way," Dulai said insolently. "This work requires all my concentration."

Tarik paused. If he didn't need the doctor, he would be immediately sacrificed to Anubis. Just the thought stirred him. Maybe the new prisoner could serve as a fresh reminder. He tried to refocus on what Dulai was doing. He seemed to be snipping a piece of rotten flesh with a round tip scissor in one hand and a pair of long tweezers in the other. "How close are we?" he asked again.

Dulai shook his head and then carefully placed the specimen in a test tube, laid his stainless tools on a tray and took his arms out of the gloves. He took his glasses off, cleaned them with a handkerchief and then wiped the sweat off his forehead. "How close are we? Very close. Very far. I do not know," he said and motioned to the glove-box. "Your ancient text contains monsters."

"Monsters?"

"Yes, you were correct. The information is very prescient, very innovative. Extremely precocious."

Tarik's expression went blank .

Dulai rolled his eyes. "As if brought from another world," he said. "Science usually advances by building on what it already has. This information hovers above anything I've ever seen. I don't understand how something so old can be so far beyond current knowledge."

Tarik fought to contain his smile. "I told you," he said proudly.

Dulai nodded. "You told me it was lethal."

"And?"

"And… it's quite lethal."

"Its effectiveness is well documented."

Dulai frowned. "Possibly, but I can not simply assume it has the history you claim it has without proof."

"Its history is everything," Tarik shot back angrily. "History justifies and demands revenge."

"Regardless of where it came from, you asked us to find your Angel of Death and we've found something."

"What have you found?" Tarik said, trying to contain his excitement."

"A germ."

"A weapon?" Tarik gushed.

"To call it a weapon presumes one side has control. I'm not sure this germ can be controlled."

"Explain."

"We were looking for a biological agent, but we were not prepared for *this*."

"Tell me."

"What we have here is a simple airborne virus that, once contracted, produces snake-like venom that is completely systemic."

"How does it work?"

"Deception. There is much I don't understand, but it appears the entity enters the body and immediately begins rapid reproduction. It doesn't seem to harm anything, but being foreign, it gets promptly attacked. The immune system engages the fragile invader and easily kills it. In fact, the antibodies literally tear it apart. But it's a setup. Inside the carcass is powerful venom that the immune system cracks open. The immune system bites into poison fruit and the circulatory system spreads it everywhere in the body. In other words, it's evil. Think mail bomb."

Tarik nodded slowly, his heart warmed with gratitude to Anubis. "And death follows?"

"Fast. The carnage left by the germ's slaughter is explosively lethal, more than anything I've ever seen. It dissolves living tissue like gasoline on Styrofoam. Simple exposure killed that monkey in minutes. It died and decomposed faster than you could... smoke a cigarette. But there is still much unknown here. For instance, I don't understand how following the instructions produced the entity in the first place, only that it did. And the bigger mystery is why the other monkey was completely unaffected."

"Did they both receive the same exposure?"

"Yes. In fact, the other monkey remains in constant exposure."

"Then dissect it."

"But it's perfectly healthy."

"Then kill it."

Dulai was about to respond again but paused, nodded, and barked some orders in the direction of his assistant, who immediately ceased what he was doing and attended to the glove box.

"You will probably find your answer in the text," Tarik said.

Dulai shrugged. "Perhaps. We've come a long way in being able to isolate many of the compounds and replicating the atmospheric conditions, but we are still uncertain of precise measurements and contaminant blocks because of translation and missing text that may or may not answer our questions. Which brings up another point," he said and then spoke closer and quieter. "Your translator Hassani seems..."

"Is the dead monkey a firstborn?" Tarik said.

Dulai paused and exhaled. "I don't know. We're still narrowing down the DNA marker that would distinguish that since your text seems to be missing that minor point. Either that *or* Hassani can't decipher it. Again, my reliance on his interpretations is something we need to talk about. I think we've reached his translating limits."

"Nonsense. He happens to be the best hieroglyphic translator in all of Egypt," Tarik said.

"Then perhaps you should look elsewhere. Obviously, the more precise the translation, the faster we can move forward."

Tarik glanced at Hassani. Elderly with a long white beard, craggy skin and thick glasses, he was glued to the largest monitor where the scanned text was magnified over a dozen times. "I will consider your request. In the meantime, push on. Explore whatever possibilities you can think of. That's why I hired you, and supplied you with everything you've asked for."

Dulai snorted. "Yes, but you failed to mention the lab would be hidden in a mountain in the middle of an American search and destroy campaign. I haven't seen sunlight once in the last month and wonder every day if I ever will. And while I appreciate you giving me the 'best space available' in the cave, I can hardly consider this to be the appropriate quality for microbiology. Pollution is a constant concern and the clean room I requested is a glove box with zero external decontamination."

"Moses had nothing," Tarik pointed out.

"We don't know what Moses had except that he had more text and less guesswork."

Tarik grew instantly impatient with Dulai's whining. "These experiments require the utmost secrecy and cannot be conducted in a university laboratory where our information can fall into the wrong hands."

Dulai gave him a look. "Yes. One could see how badly that could go."

Tarik glared at his scientist. "Doctor, perhaps your responsibility has become too much for you. You have been entrusted with knowledge hidden from man for millenniums and you complain. Maybe you would like me to find you a successor? I could arrange for your quick departure if that is what you really wish. We would part company with mutual respect and understanding for the other's future needs. I will consult Anubis."

Dulai became silent and looked around the lab and then at the lone steel door. "I'm sorry if I gave you that impression. The close quarters and long hours sometimes get to me and affect my... perception... of the goal. And honestly, the arrival of the new prisoner has been a distraction."

Tarik nodded. "I understand. I will tend to him now. In the meantime, dissect that monkey and make ready another for infection. This time, human."

Dulai paused, looking into Tarik's eyes without a blink. He then nodded and went back to work.

11

Decker slowly opened one eye, the one that wasn't in the dirt. A rat ate calmly from a wood bowl on the floor about five feet away. Decker lifted his head and felt the dirt stick to his face. He was nauseous and had a splitting headache, probably coming from the burning pain in his right eyebrow. Where was he? The last thing he remembered was being screamed at by his high school wrestling coach. Not good, considering he didn't have a long beard then and he had never worn... orange pajamas? Why was he wearing orange scrubs? What had happened to his clothes?

He pressed himself further up with his arms. He hurt everywhere. Knuckles raw and swollen. Probably someone else was hurting too, but he couldn't remember. Light came from a single light bulb dangling ten feet over his head and revealed a steel door about twenty feet away. He tried to get up and realized his right ankle was shackled. He was also barefoot. "Wonderful," he mumbled.

"Glad to see you're awake," a scratchy voice said in English. "I was getting worried."

Decker turned his body painfully to see another man. He had close cropped blond hair and was dressed in a dirtier version of the same orange jumpsuit. He sat against a stone wall. "Where am I?" Decker asked. "Who are you?"

"We're prisoners inside a cave somewhere, probably Afghanistan. I'm Private Glen Fields."

Decker hadn't heard about any soldiers being kidnapped. It was possible that an American soldier could have been taken prisoner without him receiving intel. It was also possible that the terror cell hadn't advertised that they had him yet and he was still just listed as MIA.

"Army?" he said, trying to appear nonplussed.

Fields nodded. "And you are?"

Decker was about to speak but paused. For all he knew his roommate, blond or not, was an enemy plant looking for information. "John. John Chase. Tea merchant."

Fields smiled. "You handle yourself pretty well for a tea merchant. It took six of them to shackle you and your hands were tied. By the time the entertainment was over you and *three of them* were unconscious. They seemed to think you were some sort of Special Forces agent."

Still cautious, Decker said, "It must have been the caffeine."

Fields lifted his hands in surrender. "Works for me, John Chase, special tea agent. By the way, you have a nasty cut over your right eyebrow. I think you caught a rock with it."

"That might explain the headache. Have any aspirin?"

Fields smiled. "Sorry. I'd ring for one but it would probably arrive in the form of another rock."

"Maybe later. What is that... smell?" Decker asked.

"The good vanilla-like smell is Angelica. The bad smell is everything else."

"Angelica?"

"Yeah, an herb they brought in a few weeks ago. Lots of it."

"For what?"

"I don't know. You're the tea merchant. Maybe they're trying to impress you with their secret formula."

"Their marketing plan needs work. How long have you been here?" Decker said.

Fields shrugged. "A month, maybe two. It's hard to tell without daylight. I wake up without any sense of how long I was asleep."

His beard length seemed to coincide with his timetable and the sun-deprived white skin and drawn cheeks also fit the bill, but Decker wasn't convinced. He wanted to ask about his company and commanding officer, but what tea merchant would know what to do with inside military information? "Where are you from, originally?"

"New England."

Decker nodded. "What state?"

"New Hampshire."

"Ah. Beautiful state. I dated a girl from Dartmouth once," he lied. "Whereabouts did you live?"

"Enfield."

"Patriots fan?"

Fields paused and then shrugged. "I guess."

"Helluva game they played in eighty-six."

Fields gave him a look. "Yeah, they got their butts kicked by the Bears. Okay. For the record, my folks have a beef farm on Jones Hill Road and, as far as I'm concerned, you can stick that Anubis and that Tarik moron where the sun don't shine, Sir."

Decker was about to smile but then said, "Tarik? Ramses al Tarik?"

Fields nodded. "Yes, Sir. We're in a viper's nest. From what I've gathered, this is a Tarik operation."

"Is that a fact?"

"I think so. Met him once about a week after I got here. Scary dude."

"How so?"

"He asked me intelligence questions. When he didn't get the answers he wanted, he told me I would be useful when they ran out of monkeys."

"Monkeys?"

"Yes, Sir. He bragged about some sort of Doom's Day weapon and, if I would pledge my heart to Anubis, I would go to paradise after dying in a scientific experiment for their cause. I think he was trying to scare me."

"Did he?"

"Uh, yes. I've heard the rumors. Being sacrificed to Anubis isn't in my preferred top ten thousand ways to die."

"What else did he say?"

"He gave me the seventy-two virgin speech. I told him he should try one before signing up for other seventy-one."

"No, I mean what did he say about the weapon?"

Suddenly, the steel door opened and two soldiers with automatic weapons entered and flanked the opening. Following directly behind them entered a man Decker had only seen in classified photos and video tape. With no more than a quick glance at Fields, Tarik glared at Decker.

Tarik stopped just out of Decker's reach and crouched to meet him eye to eye. "Looking for me?" he said with a mock smile.

Decker glanced at the gunmen. If he wasn't shackled Tarik would be dead before the soldiers could pull their triggers. "I wanted to join your cause."

"Lying will just make your death more painful."

True, Decker thought. Maybe if he could sufficiently anger the man, they would bring him somewhere for execution where other options would open up. He had always found action to be more reliable than words. "Seriously, I want to help you rid the world of peace and sanity, and if possible, get your autograph for my terrorist memorabilia collection."

Tarik didn't blink as the veins in his neck visibly grew and pulsed. "You killed the brother of one of my men."

"He didn't knock. I was with a lady, and he had already had his turn."

"You are CIA?"

"I sell tea."

"You expect me to believe that?"

"Bring me back to Kabul and I'll get you a real good deal on cardamom seeds. Fifty percent off."

Tarik's glare became more animal than human. He suddenly turned and marched for the exit, a trail of dirt kicking up from his boots. He ordered his gunmen to stay put. His soldiers looked at each other blankly. A moment later, Tarik returned and, in one hand, dragged a bleating sheep by a rope and in the other hand, gripped a long knife.

The animal offered no resistance as Tarik removed the rope from around its neck directly in front of Decker, who was measuring the distance to Tarik's knife. If the knife got within reach, Tarik would be dead, for sure.

"They tell me you are good with a knife," Tarik said.

"I don't need a knife to kill *you*," Decker said, trying to goad the terrorist to lunge. "All I need is a finger."

"A finger? Then maybe I should cut your fingers off."

"Start with this one," Decker said, holding his middle finger up in Tarik's face.

"You'll be taught respect," he said and then quickly slit the sheep's neck so deeply that the head hinged backward and blood shot into Decker's face, soaking his orange suit.

Decker turned away and spit, but then steeled back his glare in Tarik's direction. If he could just get him a little closer he could end his mission. "I think you missed a spot behind my ear."

Tarik dropped the limp carcass on the floor like a wet towel and then walked over to Fields. He grabbed the private's hair with his bloody left hand and pressed the dripping crimson blade to his throat. "Your insolence has earned your comrade his death. He will suffer the same fate as the sheep and then so will you."

Decker saw Fields' eyes fill with fear as lamb blood dripped down the private's forehead from Tarik's knuckles. The terrorist appeared insane, his gaze big and wild. But was he crazy enough to discard his priorities. Headquarters hadn't clarified why they had suddenly stepped up efforts to find Tarik, but chances were they had discovered something a bit more disquieting than kidnapping and murder. "But then you wouldn't have us for your little science project when the monkeys are gone, would you?"

Tarik froze. But then his knuckles tightened and squeezed lamb blood between his fingers. He pulled Field's back further and squared his stance and stared unblinking and defiantly into Decker's eyes.

Jesus! No! Decker thought but, remained silent.

"Tarik!" cried a frantic man in a lab coat. He stood in the doorway panting. "Come with me, quickly," he shouted in Farsi with an Indian accent.

Tarik looked at the man and then back at Decker and then back at the man. "What is it?" he snarled, and then turned so the man could clearly see Tarik's bloody knife at Field's throat. "Can't you see I'm busy?"

"No! Now! You must stop and come immediately!"

"Aghhhhh," Tarik said, shoving Field's head away. He pointed his knife at Decker and said, "I will not be gone long."

He growled something to his gunmen and, a moment later, he was gone. The gunmen remained and the door shut with a heavy clank of locking slide bolts.

"You see what I mean?" Fields said, massaging his neck. "He likes to leave an impression."

"Tell me about it," Decker said, motioning toward the decapitated sheep and then holding his arms out to display his own blood-soaked clothing.

Fields was shaken. "You don't stay clean very long around here. And apparently, he will be back soon. Otherwise, he wouldn't have left the guards."

Decker looked at Tarik's goons. They stood with guns trained awaiting the return of their commander.

"You all right?" Decker said.

"Yeah, I'm okay. A little hungry. Maybe they'll change their minds about all this planet domination crap for a minute and cook the sheep for us. Least they could do. A little mint jelly."

Decker allowed a brief smile at the private's attempt to lighten the air. "What's all that panic about with the guy in the lab coat?"

Fields shrugged. "I don't know."

"Who is he?"

"I don't know his name but I think he's the local mad scientist."

Decker nodded. "Looks like there's trouble in paradise."

One of the guards motioned with his gun and said in Farsi, "No more talk."

12

"What do you want?" Tarik called to Dulai, but his top scientist was running for the exit. Suddenly, Tarik heard an agonizing scream coming from the opposite direction. *The lab? What happened?* Tarik took a few steps toward the lab but stopped when he heard another scream. He then noticed something else that made no sense. Bugs. Flies. Dozens at first but then hundreds and the corridor to the lab was suddenly clouded with loudly buzzing insects. He heard coughing that turned to choking. A soldier appeared from the cloud with his hands around his neck and then fell to his knees, his eyes as wide as eggs. What was happening? Where was Hassani? He snapped his jaw toward the exit in time to see Dulai vanish. More agonizing screams. His eyes darted about. Cries, with blurred movements of arms flailing, followed the cloud that was almost upon him. Little wings scratched his forehead and then one found his nostril and another his lips. Tarik snorted and spit and bolted for the exit.

~

Decker looked at Fields. "Did you hear that?"

Fields frowned. "Sounds like people are getting skinned alive."

The guards looked at each other. One of them said something and the other knocked on the locked door behind them.

"Sounds bad out there," Decker said in Farsi to the disturbed guards. "I would have thought Tarik would be back by now. Hope nothing unpleasant happened to him. Could be the food," he said in mock concern and then turned to Fields and spoke in English. "Do you think it might be something they ate?"

"Maybe," Fields said, motioning toward the wooden bowl with the rat still nibbling next to it. "Maybe they should switch over to what they feed us. The rat seems to enjoy it."

"Shut up or you're both dead," shouted one of the guards.

Suddenly, the other guard dropped his gun and buckled over. "Aghhh," he cried, dropping to his knees and then screeching in agony. "My eyes, I can't see!" he screamed in Farsi, stretching himself prone on the dirt and then flipped onto his back. The screaming stopped as he gasped to breathe, then his eyes rolled back. Convulsive shakes followed.

The first guard frantically pounded on the door, shouting. His comrade's mouth opened wide and then his body became limp. The guard stopped banging on the door for a moment, frozen, as he watched the other guard's face and hands turned black. He gasped and screamed in Farsi, "Open the door, let me out." Suddenly, as if punched in the stomach, he jackknifed, dropped his gun and then plowed his face into the dirt, writhing in pain. "Aghhh!"

Decker turned to Fields and motioned toward the gun, mouthing the words, "Get the guns."

Fields, eyes wide as ping pong balls and unblinking, didn't move.

Decker looked back at the guard. His body was now fluttering, his mouth biting the dirt. Then just like the other guard, his body went limp and skin turned black. Both guards appeared not only dead, but burnt. As if they had been burned chemically from the inside out. But what kind of chemical would act so quickly... so independently?

"Fields!" Decker called in a harsh whisper.

Nothing.

"Private Fields," he shouted.

"Huh?"

"*Get the guns! Now! Before someone comes in!*" he shouted.

Fields pointed. "But what if..."

"Without the guns we're dead anyway, Private," Decker begged. "Just kick one over to me."

Fields crawled to his feet, held his breath and hurried over to the first guard. He grabbed at the gun like a hot rock from a fire.

"Gimme it," Decker said. He snatched it away from Fields and aimed it inches away from the shackle bolt. After three shots, he was free. He tossed the iron aside, scrambled to the other dead guard and retrieved the second gun. He gave one of the guns to Fields, who had retreated to the far back corner.

"Listen to me, Private, I don't know what's going on here but whatever happened to them hasn't happened to us... yet."

"What do you think happened to them?"

"Probably something that they intended to happen to someone else," Decker said as he moved over to one of the guards. He looked at Fields and then at the guards. "Stand watch at the door," he said and then took the head covering off one of the guards.

"What are you doing?"

"I think we'd be better off in their clothes than these orange jumpsuits."

"We?"

~

Tarik caught his scientist by the left arm a hundred feet from the cave opening and spun him around. Half of the artifact was in his right hand, the other half presumably still in the lab. Neither man had ever stood outside the cave in broad daylight due to the constant concern of being spotted on the mountainside by enemy drones flying thousands of feet above. Tarik reflexively glanced to the sky and pulled Dulai tight against the nearest boulder.

"Where do you think you're going? What happened?" Tarik demanded.

Dulai gasped for air. "It got out," he said, trembling, his face dripping with sweat.

"What got out?"

"*It!*"

"The germ?"

Dulai nodded. "I put a new monkey in. It was seized quickly. Before it died it lunged at my gloves and bit through the rubber. The lab— now the whole cave— is contaminated. We have to get away. Who knows how far it will spread? Fortunately, I was able to get this half of the pillar."

Tarik looked at the stone in Dulai's hand. The other half was in the cave. He looked back at the entrance and saw that the cloud of flies was now out, like a small tornado funneling from the cave opening.

Dulai brought his hand to his forehead, smearing sweat. "My god. The flies. They're gathering, reproducing. I knew there was something else mixing up in the translation. They started bubbling up on the monkey's hair and quickly seemed to be everywhere, coming from every direction."

"But what about the pillar? We can't leave without the other half!" Tarik demanded.

Dulai held up the other half of the artifact. "We're lucky I had this out of the case and was able to grab it on my way out. The elements from the pillar are crucial in production. What we need can come from this half. We don't need the other half anymore."

"But the writing from the other half?"

"Encrypted and saved in cyberspace. I can retrieve it anywhere at anytime. That and this is all I need."

"The pillar will fall into enemy hands."

"Only half. They'll never figure it out, and if they do, they would never dare use it. It's like a nuclear bomb. Only *you* would…"

Tarik quickly rose a finger in front of Dulai's face. "Watch your tongue, Doctor or these words will be your last."

Dulai quickly became silent.

Tarik took a step in the direction of the cave. "There must be a way to retrieve it."

Just then, a man staggered from the cave in a thick cloud of flies, holding his neck with both hands. He fell to the ground and sprawled face down, legs kicking. Soon the flies were so thick the body could not be seen. Then another man ran out with a gun. He sprayed bullets wildly causing Tarik and Dulai to crouch. Finally the man dropped his gun, grabbed his neck and fell into a plume of black flies.

Dulai leaned in to Tarik's ear and said, "You go ahead. I'll wait here for your return."

~

Decker stood next to the steel door in a braced stance, white knuckle grip on his newly acquired automatic weapon. The door would open any second. There was nothing to hide behind in the room so, as soon as the door was unbolted, he and Private Fields would bust out firing at anything that moved. He liked it better that way. Their odds of survival would be near zero if they tried to shoot it out in the prison room and a little bit better with their planned surprise attack. But the most important thing was that Tarik would be dead, that was first priority. Anything after that was a bonus as far as Decker was concerned.

"I can't get over how his skin felt." Fields said.

"Huh?"

"His skin. When we traded clothes. Freaked me out, man. Felt like wood. Can't believe I'm wearing the Haji's clothes. You're out of your mind, you know that?"

Decker nodded. His clothes actually fit fairly well. Fields was another story. He turned out to be much bigger than his Haji counterpart. Pants high and shirt tight. "We'll talk about it later. Be ready to pounce. Just remember, I spray to the left and you to the right."

Fields nodded and re-braced himself. "Tea merchant," he muttered skeptically.

Decker rested his ear on the door. There was still a lot of movement and shooting, though the agonizing screams had ceased. Decker deduced that there had been more deaths like the two guards but, like themselves, there seemed to be others who survived. Perplexing. And why the shooting? And why weren't there any voices anymore? Just movement and shooting.

"Come on... open the door," Decker whispered through gritted teeth.

A few moments later, the light bulb flickered, grew dim and then went out. The shooting stopped. Total darkness. Total silence.

13

Corporal Benjamin Bedell sat hyper-focused on his monitor, inside a trailer at Nellis Air Force Base just outside Las Vegas. The Army had changed his life, but not entirely. The uncountable hours logged playing computer games with his friends did have *some* value after all. Whatever the case, Bedell was considered the ground control station's most experienced operator. With the help of the high definition nose camera on the surveillance drone, he could spot terrorists on the other side of the globe in Afghanistan like a seasoned hunter could see a still deer in the woods. He moved the joystick slightly to the left and the view on the monitor shifted accordingly.

The Predator RQ-1drones were systems, not just aircraft, and Bedell controlled one of four drones working in unison and was one of eighty-two personnel engaged in continuous twenty-four hour operations. Flying drones ten thousand feet over Afghanistan's jagged mountainous landscape was easy, routine, almost boring, yet absolutely essential in the effort to find the enemy on his ground before he found you on yours.

Bedell's attention drifted to the aroma of an approaching cup of coffee. Captain Douglas Schultz seemed to always have a hot cup as he passed by monitors and looked over shoulders.

Schultz paused momentarily behind Bedell, bringing the corporal's full focus back to the monitor. "Still moving east, corporal?"

"Yes, Sir."

"Did we pass Zhawar Kili?"

"Five minutes ago, Captain."

"Hmmm. Let's make our swing. And bring it up to twenty thousand over the border. We don't want a repeat of last week," he said, referring to a downed drone that passed too low over the Pakistani border in the same area. Schultz continued on to the next operator.

Corporal Bedell was about to make the necessary adjustments when he saw something that gave him pause. A dark area on a distant mountainside. Not a shadow. He frowned. A year ago it would have meant nothing to him, but he'd come to know the landscape like a bank teller knows the feel of money. A counterfeit bill comes through their fingers and the counting stops. He centered and zoomed in. White dots in the dark area, but too far to identify. He needed to get closer.

"Captain?" Bedell said.

Schultz turned. "Yes, Corporal."

"Permission to break formation and deviate course to investigate an anomaly."

"Where?"

"Just northeast of Khost, Sir."

"Whose side of the border?" Schultz said, as he walked back.

"Ours, Sir. Just barely."

"What have you got, Corporal?" Schultz said, as he leaned over Bedell's shoulder.

"I don't know, Sir, but it doesn't belong. That area is usually smooth under the cliff. There should be no shadows there. When I zoomed in, the dark area turned black as coal. I've never seen ground that black before. And then those white spots appeared. They look like they could be sheep, but there's no grass up there and nothing's moving."

Shultz stared for a moment and then said, "Check it out. And push the throttle."

"Yes, Sir," Bedell said, maxing the predator's speed out to one hundred and thirty-five mph. As the drone drew closer, the white spots on the jet-black surface began to take shape.

"Jesus, Corporal," Schultz said. "Are you seeing what I'm seeing?"

Bedell nodded. "Bodies. Dead Hajis."

Schultz reached for a nearby phone, pressed numbers and waited. "Major? We have a sighting."

By the time Major Peter Joseph arrived, the drone had moved close enough to reveal guns randomly scattered among the motionless bodies. The major, sixtyish and clothed in the same desert fatigues everyone else wore, walked briskly to the small gathering and said, "What have we got, gentlemen?"

"Dead Hajis, Sir," Captain Shultz said. "We're thinking chemical. Possibly nerve gas. Assuming the black surface was flowing downhill, it appears to have originated at or behind a huge boulder. Possibly another cave."

"Gas?" Joseph said surprised. There had been zero evidence of chemical weaponry in Afghanistan from day one of the campaign.

"Look at the bodies, Major," Captain Shultz pointed out. "There's no evidence of blood. And they're out in the open, not hiding behind anything, as if they were fleeing something. Not one of them is holding a gun. Nerve gas would have caused them to drop whatever they were holding."

Major Joseph massaged his chin for a moment and said, "Or maybe they needed their hands for something else."

"Sir?"

"Why is the dirt so black?" Joseph said.

"We don't know, Major. Maybe from digging a cave out, but they wouldn't advertise themselves like that. Maybe an oil spill of some kind."

"Hmm. A lot of maybes, Doug. Let's get some men down there while we still have good light."

"Yes, Sir."

The major paused and cursed when he considered that they had been operating at MOPP zero, indicating the most vulnerable degree of chemical readiness, so chemical suits would be hard to find. "I want their masks on and make sure they bring an ICAM or whatever else they can find to monitor air quality. We don't need *our* boys looking like *that*, for God's sake," he said loudly, pointing at the viewing screen.

14

Sam watched a commercial for her upcoming interview with Larry King on one of several surrounding monitors at the CNN studio, moments before the show was to air. They were running footage cut from her last trip to Egypt, some of which she had never seen. She had no idea where they had gotten it, but there *were* many cameras running when she had finally climbed out of the well. They even had a shot of her with a cigar in her hand. She remembered an unusually liberal sheik wanting to pose with her and actually handed her the cigar. Since she was not a smoker, she handed it back, but apparently not fast enough to avoid the ever watchful lens.

A studio assistant clipped a wireless microphone under the collar of Sam's khaki shirt. CNN requested that she wear the safari-type shorts, tank top and boots she had on in Egypt. She was happy to comply, feeling most comfortable in the field attire anyway. She could remember a time not long ago when interviews of any kind made her nervous. Stage-fright would make her palms sweat. All that was in the past. Repetition had bred familiarity and now her palms were as dry as toast and she could talk to the likes of Larry King as she would her hairdresser.

"Tonight, Samantha Conway, famed archaeologist and ancient writing expert, known to many as a real life female version of Indiana Jones, will give her first interview since her ᵗent hidden treasure discovery near Egypt's famous Valley of the Kings. She also brought some of the treasure with her. Samantha Conway, next, on 'Larry King Live'."

Larry King took his seat as a makeup artist took a last second touch-up with him. King wore a solid blue shirt with his trademark suspenders, rolled up sleeves and gray rimmed eyeglasses. A massive array of lights in large black cans suspended above him were adjusted brighter. King surveyed his silver tabletop. A black coffee mug with who-knows-what inside, a pen and a small stack of light blue papers with notes. A studio tech counted down the seconds aloud and then silently pointed at King with the final finger. King leaned in on his elbows toward the giant potato-like microphone from decades past, probably his first in a half century career.

"Hello, everybody! We've got a great show for you tonight. A visit with Samantha Conway, the beautiful and adventurous treasure hunter who recently added to her fame and to the Metropolitan Museum's amazing collection of ancient riches. Later in the program, some of the artifacts of interest will be unveiled publicly for the first time ever, right here in the studio, but first... let's welcome our guest, Samantha Conway," King said, looking up and giving Sam a pleasant smile.

"Thanks Larry," Sam said, relaxed.

King looked briefly at his notes. "I understand your friends call you Sam. May I call you Sam, too?"

"I would be honored."

"The honor is mine. I'm a big fan. So, is that color from a tanning salon or did you bring it back with you from your last trip?"

Sam smiled, revealing perfect white teeth. "A gift from Egypt, Larry. Africa is the best place in the world to be in the sun. They still have a complete ozone there."

"And we have little holes in ours?"

"Big holes, and getting bigger every day. In Africa, practically right on the equator, I'll get less burned in ten hours than I would here in two. And that's a fact."

"Too bad you couldn't bring any ozone back with you."

"Yes, that would be a treasure beyond compare."

"Spoken like a true scientist. But I must ask, how do you do what you do? How does a woman as young and beautiful as you find what the rest of the scientists on the planet couldn't?"

"Just lucky I guess."

"It's said that hard work often accompanies good luck."

"The team puts in the hours but, when you love what you do and the reward is so great, it doesn't feel so much like work as it does passion. But from time to time we do get lucky, which is said to be better than being good."

"Well, apparently, you're both. Is it true you were able to find the treasure from your interpretation of the ancient hieroglyphics in a previously discovered tomb?"

"Yeah, well, sometimes the writing's on the wall, as they say."

King looked off the camera and said, "Can we get a view of the wall in question?"

Sam was a little surprised when a large screen LCD next to them came alive with the ancient writing she had deciphered from the tomb.

"Can you show us how you were able to find your clues in this?" King said.

Sam took a deep breath. This was turning into a commercial for the museum. She began by pointing out some basic character translation and continued to the more complex compound symbol combinations that led her to form the theories that finally brought her to the treasure.

"Just amazing," King said. "But I understand we almost lost you in the process."

"Things got a little riskier than I'd like to admit. But we can talk about that later just in case my boss is watching."

"Too late, Sam. We have footage from your own camera down in the well. You actually went scuba diving in a well in the middle of the desert?"

"The diving instructor was late and it was getting hot sitting around in a wet suit."

King smiled. "So you found the nearest well."

"Exactly."

"That must have attracted a little attention."

"A little."

"Well, we have video from that unique dive," King said, and the LCD filled with footage Sam had seen a dozen times since. "Maybe you can give us a bit of a guided tour. What are we seeing?"

Sam went on to explain, as requested. She found that her favorite part was pointing out where she had knocked the expensive camera and light set off the ledge. When she was done, it was time to go to a commercial.

"When we come back, Samantha Conway will show us some of the treasures. Don't go away."

15

Staff Sergeant Luke Kitt, squad leader, took the hand-held from the backpack on his radio-man and said, "Alpha Team Leader, how is it reading?"

Corporal Izzo, the point man at the head of the wedge, looked at the small screen on the ICAM, for any indication of air contamination. "Still good, Sarge. All levels normal, but the closer we get... that smell. Over."

"I know, it's bad. Let's keep it moving, Corporal. Slow. Over," Kitt said. The 'slow' command was often given to conserve air at their high altitude but, this time he wasn't just concerned about the men's endurance. The black ground less than fifty yards up the mountainside was unfamiliar. Nothing was more disconcerting than the unfamiliar. Ninety percent of the time Kitt and his men were rallied together, it was to chase ghosts. Deployment orders, like today's, were usually met with a shrug. On the infrequent occasion insurgents were engaged, bullets would fly, missiles would whoosh by and hidden caverns would explode with earth-quaking force. Helicopter gattling guns would disintegrate anything that moved. This was all comfortably familiar and the day's events might be remembered in dinner conversation after sports scores. Now, however, Kitt's attention was piqued.

Sergeant Kitt and his men were dressed, battle-ready and advancing cautiously in standard double wedge formation. Alpha Team, in front, was made of an eight-man wedge and Bravo Team, made up of another eight man wedge, followed Kitt and his radio man, who were in the middle. Apache helicopters had confirmed a cave opening behind the boulder, as suspected. They now hovered overhead to secure the surrounding area in order to shut down any potential escape routes and provide support in case of enemy reaction forces moving toward the complex. Neither was a concern to Kitt. Regardless of the surrounding technology, the fact remained that a trained "footslogger" remained the only effective way to explore a cave complex. Above the helicopters, the predator drone circled slowly for the viewing pleasure of those back at the ground station. Kitt was pretty sure a decent crowd was gathered around whatever viewing screen was linked to *this* drone.

A bottle of dead lightning bugs. The pungent stench grew thick and reminded Kitt of his childhood, when he and his brothers used to catch lightening bugs and jail them in a glass jar. The crowded jar would become a blinking lantern. The next day they would unscrew the jar lid and the smell would jerk their heads away. This was worse, far worse, and there was no escaping it.

Corporal Izzo stopped at the edge of the black soil and stared for a moment before slowly crouching down.

"What do you have there, Alpha Leader? Over," Kitt radioed.

Silence.

"Alpha Leader? Come in, Corporal," Kitt repeated.

"Flies, Sarge. Over."

Kitt paused. "Say again. You were broken up. Over."

"Dead flies. It's not dirt. Over"

"You said flies, as in, the bug? Over."

"Yes. Foxtrot, Lima, India, Echo, Sierra. F-L-I-E-S. Flies. A foot deep, at least. Nothing but dead flies. It's foul. Over."

Foul? Kitt had to consider for a moment *who* had just said 'foul' to him. Corporal Dominic Izzo's position as Alpha Leader did not come by random choice. He was the tip of the leading wedge, the point of first contact and response. He was there because he had proven himself to be fearless, intelligent, and undaunted. An expert in tunnel exploration where the unknown could be waiting around every corner. Excelled in everything he was taught. Foul? Not a word he would expect to hear from Izzo. "Any change in the ICAM, Corporal? Over."

"No. Over."

"Then let's keep it moving. Over."

"Okay. Over."

The soldiers continued forward until Corporal Izzo came to the first dead insurgent. "Sarge? I think you should come look at this. Over."

Kitt ordered Izzo to stay put and the rest of Alpha Team to continue toward the cave entrance. He then ordered Bravo Team to spread out and continue forward. When Kitt came to Izzo's side the corporal was using the barrel of his gun to stir dead flies in the man's open mouth. The insurgent's face and hands were covered in red spots, like measles.

"Mother of God," Kitt said, feeling strangely nauseated, his hand tightening on his M4 carbine.

"Little critters tried to eat him. Not too long ago... maybe less than a day."

"They're everywhere!" Kitt said

"Sarge?"

"*The flies! Jesus!* It looks like they all choked on them," Kitt said, shuddering at the thought of suffocating on flies. Seeing a man cut to nothing from a fifty caliber browning machine gun wouldn't move his pulse a point, but seeing the pained expression on the insurgent's face with the rancid dead flies overflowing his mouth and ears made him want to gag and run.

Corporal Izzo looked around and said, "Whatever happened here happened fast. Everything was alive and then everything was dead. Glad I wasn't here when everything was alive," he said and then shook out a shiver. "A can or two of 'Off' might have been a good idea."

"Yeah, right. Looks more like they were using 'On' than 'Off'," Kitt said, and then turned to see the rest of Alpha Team inspecting victims. One of the soldiers vomited. The sight of *that* coupled with the overpowering nasal assault was too much and a moment later he found his partially digested lunch form a sticky composite with some of the shin-deep insect bodies. He immediately heaved again.

The radio sounded. "Squad Leader, this is Captain Schultz. What is your status, Sergeant? Over."

Apparently, the drone had zoomed in. "The black dirt is dead flies, Sir. The Hajis are all dead. It looks like they choked to death on the flies. The ICAM is negative but the stench is pretty... foul, Captain. Over," he said.

There was a long pause, and then, "Proceed to the cave, Squad Leader. Over."

Sergeant Kitt had heard those exact orders dozens of times in the past. Standard procedure. Routine. Familiar. Never unexpected, until now. He looked at the small opening in the mountainside. It overflowed with death in the same way as the insurgent's mouths. "Yes, Sir," he said and turned to Corporal Izzo, who was staring at him in disbelief.

"I don't suppose they would consider blowing this one up first and searching it later?" Corporal Izzo jested.

Kitt smiled thinly. "And miss out on finding out what happened here?"

"God forbid," Izzo said, then proceeded back to his point position.

The closer Kitt got to the cave entrance the deeper the flies. The expression and body language of each insurgent he passed spoke of the horror that was. Golf ball eyes with red veins, hands around their necks and in their mouths, cloth wrapping faces, fetal positions, buried heads completely covered to the shoulders. And why were all the flies dead? Not a living fly anywhere. What killed *them*? More unknown. Just when he figured he'd seen enough to have nightmares for years, he saw something that stopped him dead in his tracks.

One of the insurgents, face down, had a bare arm that looked odd, even in this sea of oddness. He deviated a few yards for a closer inspection. The arm was darkest brown and very skinny. In fact, the skin seemed to drape the bones. Kitt wanted to leave but felt compelled to turn the man over. Using his foot and the butt of his rifle, not wanting to touch with his hands, he pushed and lifted against a mush of dead insects until the body flopped over. "Jesus!" Kitt gasped, paralyzed, and then turned away. He wouldn't look back. The man had somehow decomposed, as if he'd been in the field for months. He'd leave this for the forensic scientists who were bound to be here sooner or later.

Meanwhile the men were doing their best to surround the boulder— believed to hide a cave entrance, in their standard positions, as if anything about the mission was standard. Izzo hugged the mountain, his gun aimed at the cave entrance, finger on the trigger as he inched closer.

Kitt leaned against the mountainside and gave the nod. Private Roberto Mendez acknowledged and tossed a banana-size device on a thin wire into the cave entrance to trigger any potential booby traps. The device disappeared into the flies. Mendez pulled the wire slowly. The air was tense with anticipation of an explosion.

Nothing.

With half of Bravo Team's rifles aimed at the cave entrance, Alpha Team changed out their rifles for pistols with silencers, the weaponry of choice for cave exploration. Kitt's palms were sweaty. Before entering a cave, there was always the fear of ambush, but he and his men were well trained and equipped for anything American forces have ever encountered... until now. What good would their carefully planned procedures do against flies as congested as air molecules? He turned around and found Sergeant Kitt some fifty feet back, also against the cliff. Kitt motioned for him to continue. Izzo turned on the sealed beam flashlight on his helmet and stepped into the tunnel, leaving all natural light behind.

Walking through knee-deep flies was like trudging through snow after a blizzard. The tunnel was large compared to the small entrance. Kitt's men followed him in a diamond formation, the last man walking backward.

"Shultz to Squad leader. Do you read me? Over," cracked the voice over the radio.

"Load and clear, Captain. Over," Kitt said.

"What have we got inside, Sergeant? Over."

"More of the same, Sir. All dead, zero resistance. The flies are deeper and the stench is stronger. But there also seems to be another smell, like perfume. Over."

"Have you determined the source of the flies? Over."

"Negative, Captain. But at least the Hajis are covered better. We don't have to see their faces. Over," he said and continued his slow march. The caves man-made tunnel system was typical of many he'd explored. A main artery going straight down the middle with other tunnels and rooms off to the sides. The first room was off to the left. Fuel storage. Fifty-five gallon drums, stacked wooden crates and at least two dead insurgents.

And, sheep?

○

Maybe a dozen sheep all huddled together… all dead. Twenty feet further down on the right was another room, a little larger with tables and chairs, the flies up to the seats. At least one insurgent lay on a tabletop; if there were any on the floor they were completely covered.

There was something weird about the man on the table. Kitt moved closer and felt his stomach lurch. Another decomposition like the one outside. The man's face was sunken like a five thousand year old mummy, flies dripping from sunken eyes. He turned away and saw a steel doorway triple slide-bolted into stone. He pointed his gun-barrel at the door and waved his men over.

16

Decker's eyes popped open in the complete darkness when he heard one of the locking bolts slide on the door he was now leaning against. "Fields," he said, hushed.

"I heard it."

Decker stood up. His left leg was dead from sitting awkwardly. He checked his gun. "You ready?"

"Not really. Ask them if they can wait a minute so my knees can stop shaking."

"This is a shoot first, ask later deal," Decker whispered. He thought he heard movement.

"Hey tea merchant," Fields whispered weakly.

"Yeah."

"Same plan? Bust out shooting?"

"Yes. And tag Tarik first."

"Right, Tarik first," Fields repeated to himself.

Another bolt slid.

"At first glance, they'll think we're the guards. All we need is that one second of surprise."

Decker heard more movement, as if someone or something was brushing against the door. Then there was the unmistakable sound of the final bolt sliding.

"Right. But suppose it's..." Fields said, when the door was kicked open followed immediately by a wave of putrid odor.

Decker reflexively jerked back tight against the wall, surprised. Light beams danced about the opening and quickly found the dead guards in orange suits. Why would Tarik's men kick the door in? And what was that black stuff? And that smell.

"Fields, yell out your name, rank and number. *Loud*," Decker yelled.

Fields didn't hesitate, calling out from behind the hinge side of the door and ending in 'Sir' for effect.

After a moment of silence, the welcome sound of an English speaking voice with a southern accent said, "Sergeant Luke Kitt here, Private. Who's with you?"

"Uh, another prisoner, Sir. John Chase. A, uh, tea merchant."

Decker rolled his eyes.

"Okay then, let's confirm that, gentlemen. We're heavily armed and aimed. Show yourselves with your hands up and empty, real slow. We just need to verify and we don't want any mishaps."

Decker removed his head-covering and cautiously peeked around the corner. American soldiers, knee deep in some sort of thick black dust. What was it? It couldn't have been here before. He didn't remember seeing anything like it when Tarik's scientist stood in the doorway. Was there a cave in? He tried to imagine the insurgents yelling and the shooting in this, stuff. He wanted to reach out and touch it but he didn't want to do anything that might startle an anxious trigger finger. He dropped his gun and told Fields to do the same.

Decker stepped through the doorway, hands in the air, all guns and lights trained on his chest. Fields followed, wondering aloud about the soot. Both men trudged forward and the black peat moss like powder smelled worse than an open cesspool on a hot summer day. Two of the soldiers hurried around them to check out the room.

"There are two dead prisoners, a gutted sheep, and no flies," reported one of the soldiers.

"Flies?" Decker looked at the soot more closely.

"Yes," Kitt said, still holding a gun on them while another soldier frisked them. "You're lucky they didn't get to you. Seems like most of the dead choked on them."

Decker looked at Fields.

"They're clean, Sarge."

"You can put your hands down fellas. Good to see you, Fields. We've been looking for you for six weeks," he said and then turned to Decker. "But you're another story."

"The name's Decker. Captain. DIA. 079486613. And if you have some water? All we've had was raw lamb."

Kitt's brow raised. He handed Decker his canteen and called for the radio. "If you can confirm the DIA, Captain, ASAP, I'd appreciate it."

Decker nodded. "Put me through to your CO," he said as he handed off the canteen to Fields before drinking. "Sorry, Private, I would have told you but I had no way of knowing for sure who you were and what they could get out of you if they set their minds to it."

"No problem, Sir. At least I'll feel safe again when I buy tea," he said and then drank heartily.

Decker gave him a brief smile but then turned back to Kitt.

"Major Joseph," Kitt said, handing Decker the radio.

"Agent John Decker, Captain. Shadow Company, Ninth Special Operations Command, under Colonel Bain, Fort Bragg, 079486613," Decker listened as Major Joseph confirmed the information and sent his best regards. Decker gave Kitt the radio and the sergeant was brought up to speed.

Kitt put the radio away and looked at Decker. "I'm glad we found you alive, Sir. My new orders are to follow your instructions to the T and get some immediate attention to that gash over your right eye."

Decker nodded. "First, Private Fields needs medical attention ASAP. My eye will wait until we're out of here."

Kitt's brow rose. "If you say so."

"If I can be of help, Sir, I request to stay," Fields said.

"No. You have people in much greener pastures that can't wait to see you, Private. Everything is under control here. Have a safe trip home." Decker said, giving Fields a wink.

Fields held up his hands in mock surrender. "Yes, Sir."

Decker turned to Kitt. "Did you happen to notice a man in a white lab coat, or if one of the dead Hajis was Tarik?"

Kitt's eye's widened. "*The* Tarik?"

"None other. It was my mission to find him and, if he choked on flies, well, my vacation would start right about... now."

"Sorry, Sir. Haven't seen him yet, but there's more to search."

"Then let's get on with it," Decker said, taking the canteen. The water was cool and wonderful. He gulped and felt it run down his chin and into his beard.

"Are you sure you're up for it?"

Decker wiped his mouth with his dirty arm and passed the canteen back to Fields. "Better now than coming back later."

Kitt motioned to the prison room. "Who were the other prisoners?"

"They were our guards," Decker said. "We changed clothes with them after they died. We figured we'd have to fight our way out, but our gracious host never came back. We thought you were him," he said as he scooped up a handful of flies and pushed all off his palm except one. He examined it closely.

Kitt nodded and then pursed his lips quizzically. "Do you have any idea what happened here? How did your guards die?"

"Don't know," Decker said. They just sort of fell over screaming and then turned black. We thought it might be from some chemical weapon Tarik was working on. Whatever it was, it was very powerful."

Kitt was frowning. "If it was so powerful, why didn't it affect you?"

"No clue, but I'm not complaining," Decker said, and then held out his palm to Kitt. "I'm not a bugologist, but there's something different about this brand of fly. All together they make the ground look black, but the color's actually closer to purple, and they have orange eyes. Ever seen a fly with orange eyes before?" he said, dropping a single fly into Kitt's hand.

Kitt held his hand in the light beam. "Can't say that I have, Sir. The wings are weird, too. Definitely not of the Texas housefly variety."

Decker went back for the guards' guns and gave one to Fields. "Souvenir, Private. Now get your butt out of here," he said, and then rechecked his own chamber to make sure he was loaded.

17

Decker hastily smacked the turban off the facedown Haji, grabbed a fistful of black hair, pulled his head from the shallow grave of insects and shined the flashlight in his face. Eyes wide and bloodshot, mouth open and stuffed like an oven roaster. Not Tarik. He dropped the head and moved on to another a few yards away. Knocked off the turban, grabbed hair and pulled. Decker classified the dead into two distinct categories. Those that choked on flies and those who never had the chance to. He held the light beam on the insurgent's face longer this time. It was much more difficult to discern facial features when they were black and decomposed. Again, no Tarik. Next.

Kitt and his men were just ahead, plowing deeper and deeper into the cave with Decker checking the dead in their wake. They found two bunk rooms with a dozen beds each, all unoccupied. Further along was a large meeting room, and then a kitchen and food pantry.

A flashlight beam meant to catch Decker's attention caused him to look up. Kitt stood at an opened door and waved for him to see something. Decker dropped a face and trudged over.

"What have you got?" Decker said.

"You tell me," Kitt said, pointing his beam.

A black statue, about ten feet tall. The head of a dog on a human body. Shiny eyes. Dark long curtains on either side. And skulls in the walls. Decker's focus went to a large mound in front of the statue and moved to it. If the rumors were correct, this would be the sacrificial altar, he thought as he cleared the flies off. Stone top. He was sure forensics would find DNA matching the skulls on the wall. The bastard. *His turn will definitely come*, he thought.

"Let's keep moving," Decker said.

"Is this place what I think it is?" Kitt said.

"That and more," Decker said and motioned to continue.

The main artery veered left and upward and then opened into another large area. In the far right corner there appeared to be some recognizable mechanicals: tanks connected with copper tubing, white insulated wires, ventilation that disappeared through the rock ceiling room, some more fuel drums and what looked like the front end of a gray tractor or a generator. Sergeant Kitt and his men headed to the right toward a stainless steel door that was held half open with the bugs sloping out like grain from a silo. The soldiers, waist deep moved through the doorway, guns elevated, like they were crossing a swamp.

Decker shined his light back on the generator. It had shut off right after the shooting ended. It probably suffocated on flies along with the Hajis. He lumbered toward it, his light focused on the gray machine's service door. He turned a chrome lever and opened a hinged panel flap. Flies poured out, revealing a straight six cylinder engine. He followed yellow spark plug wires to electronic ignition, fuel injection and then spotted the air filter. He threw a couple of latches and pulled off the filter's black cover. Clogged solid with bugs. He emptied and shook clean both the cover and filter, blew away bug remnants, put it all back together and closed the panel. *Okay now, where's the… ah, there it is*. He turned the key. The engine cranked and sputtered. A plume of dried flies billowed out the sides as the engine started. Lights about the cave glowed and grew brighter as the generator engine evened out to a purr.

Kitt appeared at the steel doorway, gun ready.

"Relax, Sergeant," Decker said. "Just me turning the lights on."

"You turned on a hell of a lot more than that, Sir," he said, and then disappeared back inside the door.

Decker hurried by taking long high steps. Snowshoes would have been helpful, he thought. When he arrived at the doorway, he could see they had found a very brightly lit lab.

Considering they were in a remote cave in the mountain wilderness of Afghanistan, the lab was a remarkable collection of very sophisticated high tech equipment. Lights blinked on several humming supercomputer towers the size of refrigerators. A large glass box with long gloves. A counter full of microscopes and keyboards and monitors everywhere. There was also what looked like a distilling kitchen of sorts with glass flasks, burners, coiled glass tubing and a shelf-full of wood crates marked, *Angelica*. Fields was right, but this hardly looked like a tearoom. What the hell were they doing with Angelica?

Kitt said, "Never seen anything like *this* in a cave before." Kitt's gaze was on the same thing everything else in the room seemed to be on... the glass box, or more specifically, what was inside it.

Decker moved closer until he stood beside the box. It was surrounded by cameras, chrome stanchions and gauges that appeared to display temperature, humidity and pressure. He stood motionless for a moment and then carefully brushed off the pile of flies from the top of the box. Inside was a jagged piece of pottery or stone, yellow pages size, covered with writing. It looked like a small weathered tombstone fixed erect with thin stainless steel rods and mechanical dental-like tools on what looked like robotic arms, a sharp contrast of old and new. The letters were small, crowded and unfamiliar, like everything else on this mission.

"Squad Leader to Command. Come in, Command. Over," Kitt said over the radio.

"Command here. What have you got, Sergeant? Over."

"Cave is secure, Sir. We found a lab you wouldn't believe. Over."

After a pause. "Did you touch anything? Over."

Kitt looked at Decker who had just brushed off the flies. "No, Captain. It's all just the way we found it. Over."

Decker looked to his right and took in the ghoulish red speckled face of a tortured insurgent, viciously feasted on by the flies. "What the hell were they *doing* here?"

18

Tarik's attention was seized by the television. He pressed the intercom button on his large granite desk without blinking as he watched Samantha Conway give a mind-blowing ancient writing lesson on CNN.

"Dulai here."

"Come to my office."

"Uh yes. I will need a just few minutes to…"

"Now," he said calmly and disconnected, unable to take his eyes off her. The cameraman seemed to enjoy her also, keeping the camera on her face while she was pointing to the hieroglyphics.

Tarik's auxiliary headquarters was technologically more advanced and had much better access than the cave but, consequently, was that much harder to conceal. His plan had been to use the off-shore oil rig as a staging area in the final days of his attack, but now it would have to facilitate the experimental research and production phases as well. Tarik's office sat atop a four story building covering one third of the rig's platform. Four square skylights illuminated the room brightly, allowing tropical plants to flourish, and three-hundred and sixty degrees of glass revealed an expansive Red Sea view without a hint of land in sight anywhere. Just water and the occasional boat, usually tankers and war ships.

Tarik found it amusing that his hideout would be right under the noses of those who wanted him the most. In fact, his company, Spectrum Energy, comprised of seven such rigs, was mostly legitimate, in spite of its covert ownership. Rig-5 was only used within the company and was listed as "temporarily shut-in pending reentry evaluation", which gave no reason for inspections to take place. A ghost ship among rigs.

The elevator door opened and Dulai appeared in his white lab coat. "The precise combination of..."

"Look at this," Tarik said, still focused on the LCD.

Dulai sighed and walked across the white marble floor toward Tarik's desk looking across the way at a sixty inch screen. "A beautiful blond. Is this what..."

"Shhh, pay attention. The beautiful blond is Samantha Conway."

"*That's* Samantha Conway?" Dulai said, brows raised. "What's this? The History..."

"CNN. She just discovered one of the greatest Egyptian treasures of the century. Be silent. She found the treasure by correctly translating ancient writing that had been already available to the rest of the world for years," he said and picked up a pair of scissors from his desk top and waved them without taking his eyes off the screen. "And if you speak again the cook will be thickening his sauce tonight with your tongue."

Dulai looked at the scissor tip, swallowed, and then turned his attention back to the TV. After the writing lesson was over, the station went to some commercials and then brought out glistening ancient artifacts from the find. After the break, Conway gave a very impressive museum-like explanation of each item with its probable history and use. When it was over, Tarik picked up the remote and powered off.

Tarik swiveled his seat toward Dulai and sat back, his fingers folded on his belly. "So what do you think?"

"May I speak?"

"No.... Yes."

"Why would she help us? She's a scientist. You're trying to exterminate a nation."

"They are not a nation. They are thieves. Terrorists," Tarik said with eerie calm.

"Uh, true, but she will see them as a nation you are trying to kill with a plague."

"And therefore they will need a cure. She can find it for them."

Dulai paused.

Tarik sat back. "Besides, you're a scientist, and you're helping us."

"Do I have a choice?"

"You always have a choice."

"If I try to leave you'll kill me."

"And your family. Let's not forget them. But if you stay, you'll be very, very rich."

"You call that a choice?"

"Would you rather I remove the very rich part?"

Dulai was silent for a moment. "What if something were to happen to you? How will I get my money?"

"You won't. You and your family will die."

"You, you never told me *that*!" Dulai said.

"A precaution. It should be important to you that nothing unfortunate happens to me."

"You don't trust me."

"Don't be offended, Doctor. I don't trust, I control."

"And you think you will control Samantha Conway?" Dulai said incredulously.

"Absolutely."

19

Captain Harvey Ross had sunken comfortably into the passenger seat of a special issue Army vehicle. The Hummer had a stinger air defense weapon system mounted on its back. Ross had departed Fort Detrick, Maryland many hours ago on his way to Afghanistan and had been in his seat most of the way. With less than a year to go before retirement, he didn't mind the comfort of an actual seat now and then. The Hummer would use zero gas on the trip because it was one of six securely strapped to the floor of an Army C-5 Galaxy transport jet along with various other vehicles and supplies. A couple of team members were asleep atop a soft pile of camouflage tarps secured with netting. Flying in a C-5 was like flying in a huge barn.

Ross had been in and out of restless sleep most of the way. Every time he awoke his mind would remember their disturbing mission. The DIA's report and photos of what had happened in Afghanistan wasn't like anything he'd ever seen, and he'd seen a lot. As head of the Special Medical Augmentation Response Team-Aeromedical Isolation Team or SMART-AIT, he had become accustomed to rapid deployment to remote corners of the world. He thought of himself more as a fire chief than a medical researcher, racing to evacuate, extinguish and investigate burning cities. His firehouse was the U. S. Army Medical Research Institute for Infectious Diseases or USAMRIID, pronounced u-sam-rid, at Fort Detrick, Maryland. His fire engine was usually the C-5 and a Black Hawk. His fireman's hat was an airtight helmet with a glass bubble-shield and his uniform was more often than not a blue or orange bio-safety space suit. His firemen were a half dozen specially trained enlisted medics, a physician and a nurse. And the fire was usually made up of lethal contagious infections, including hemorrhagic fevers, plague, pox viruses and anything else requiring immediate seamless containment and analysis. His hope, as always, was a false alarm.

"Buckle your seatbelt and thank you for flying Air Pathogen," said a familiar voice.

Ross's eyelids were suddenly heavy. He didn't remember falling asleep and he didn't remember Captain Donald Drake, the team physician, getting into the Hummer's driver seat next to him. Drake tapped the photo envelope next to him and said, "We're going *here* and we should worry about *seatbelts?*"

The C-5 flying warehouse touched down lightly on the tarmac, taxied for a few minutes and stopped. The huge rear ramp door opened and Kabul's morning sun filled the transport cavity, followed quickly by the rural scented Afghani air and distant loudspeaker prayers... if that was what they were. The team climbed out of their various nooks and crannies, stretching squinting as they gathered by their equipment. As usual, they were to be last in, first out. To whatever degree the C-5 was loaded and whatever schedule it was thought to be on, all would cease and bow to the priority of getting the team loaded and to wherever it had to go. Subsequently, all their gear was at the door's edge for an easy grab and run.

Several soldiers in dessert camouflage hurried up the ramp to meet the team and off-load the equipment. Alongside the soldiers walked a plainclothes man with long hair and a full beard, who could easily pass for an Afghani local.

"Captain Ross?" the man called.

"I'm Captain Ross."

The man saluted and said, "Captain Decker, DIA, Sir. You

were my instructor a few years back during a training exercise at Fort Detrick."

Ross smiled, surprised. "Yes, I remember you. Advanced germ engagement training. Something only a handful of DIA were chosen for."

"They like keeping us well-rounded."

Ross snorted knowingly. "I didn't recognize you in your beard and long hair. And that's a nice little wound over your eye. I assume you're on assignment."

Decker felt his beard and said, "Yes, Sir. But I'll probably need to find some scissors. My cover has been recently compromised."

"Are you the agent we found in the cave?"

"Yes, Sir."

"Jesus! Don't you guys get a day off?"

"A what, Sir?"

Ross smiled. There was a commitment about Agent Decker that was special.

"The choppers are waiting. Hopefully, you can help shed a little light on our situation here."

"From what I've seen in the photo, you look a lot better than the others we found in there."

"Thank you. I try to avoid stress."

"Well, you've picked the perfect occupation for that. Seriously, though, what do you attribute your survival to?"

"The flies couldn't get to us."

Ross nodded. "It seems something else killed your guards... but not you. Do you have any idea what it was or why you were unaffected?"

"No."

Ross continued to stare at him. "Where is it?"

"About fifty miles from here," he said and then curiously watched the men carry out an isolator stretcher. One of several containment units of various shapes and sizes, the stretcher is a sort of airtight clear coffin on wheels or horizontal phone booth, able to bring back an entire body, dead or alive, to the USAMRIID "slammer" bio-contain for further examination.

The helicopters were quickly loaded. Ross was now wide awake. He took a seat next to Decker and put his earphones on as the engine revved high. He looked out the window and saw the Black Hawk's shadow smoothly move away from the craft and then squiggle in and out across the desert foothills as the team was once again on the move. A shepherd with a small flock shielded his eyes from the sun and watched them fly by.

Decker motioned to the envelope in Ross's hand. "Those the photos?"

"Yes."

"Any thoughts?"

"Yeah, scary ones. I've never seen anything like this. Very strange. My first inclination was chemical since there aren't any known germs that quickly kill both humans and insects," Ross said. Decker had no reaction, which was a little surprising. "And since the discovery, no one has had any adverse symptoms. Whatever hit them hit them fast and hard and then vanished."

Decker nodded casually and then produced another, smaller envelope and handed it to Ross. "Here's another photo. Something else we found in the cave that I didn't send over open airways."

Ross frowned as he took it. He opened the envelope and unfolded a photo.

"That's actual size," Decker said.

"What is it?"

Decker shook his head. "We don't know. It's made of stone and seemed to be the center of focus in the cave's lab."

"Looks like some sort of ancient writing."

Decker nodded. "Yeah, but what's its significance?"

Ross shrugged. "Maybe it's a part of their bible or something. Hang it on a wall for good luck."

Decker shook his head. "It wasn't hanging on a wall. They had cameras on it from every angle and some of the monitors had it magnified a hundred times."

"I wonder what it says."

Decker shrugged. "We also found a significant supply of Angelica."

"The herb?"

"Yes."

"Strange. You expect to find some kind of crude weapons manufacturing and we get antiques and medicinal herbs."

"We also got a lot of dead bodies. Whatever they cooked up, it packed more wallop than anything I've ever seen."

Ross frowned and held the photo of the stone artifact closer. "Huh."

"What?"

Ross shook his head. "Nothing."

"Nothing?"

"No. It's just that one of the characters looks like something I've seen under a microscope many times."

"A microscope?" Decker said.

Ross smiled thinly. "Yeah, this character looks like a thread virus."

"What's a thread virus?"

"A very small and simple virus. Very old with relatively no evolution. Sometimes, very deadly. Usually hemorrhagic. Nothing you'd want to bump into... but I don't think the fellow who wrote this had a microscope."

Decker nodded and seemed to disappear into his own thoughts while Ross took some more time looking at the photo. Soon the choppers slowed and hovered over a makeshift landing pad on a flattened area on the side of a craggy mountain. Decker pointed to an area about a hundred yards away and Ross saw a view somewhat familiar from the photos only the ground was not as black. Presumably the wind had taken away most of the flies from the mountainside, but the insurgents' dead bodies appeared to have been left the way they were found.

The area had now been secured, surrounded and landscaped by the army. Camouflage tents and other equipment had been snuggled into the rough terrain like a midway camp on an Everest expedition. Two F-15s roared by. Not much chance of a surprise attack.

The Black Hawk touched down, the doors opened and four soldiers were immediately there to meet them. Introductions were brief and routine with everyone anxious to get to work. Ross was handed a map of the cave complex and briefed on what to expect. The team wasted no time off-loading and getting into their space suits since the probability of contamination was impossible to estimate with so many dead and no one else dying.

Captain Ross and four members of the team moved clumsily forward while the rest stayed back awaiting instructions. The flies were now found in small drifts and between rocks, not thick and deep as in the report. Wind and time had removed much of the bizarre event's evidence. The dead bodies however were unmoved. Ross scanned until he saw the one he was looking for... one of a few from the photo that was different. He waved Drake, the team doctor, to follow him. The plastic space suit squeaked as his arms and legs moved but all he could hear was his own Darth Vader-like breathing echo within the helmet.

Ross stopped over the chosen body and looked in disbelief. Was this really a man who died less than a week ago? It didn't seem possible. His sunken black skin almost made him look like a burn victim, but his clothes were unscorched. "Put this one in containment," he said, then looked in the direction of the cave opening, where the dead flies were still deep, just as in the photo.

20

Sam sat with her brother, Jesse, at a large table in a plush conference room full of law books when the lawyer walked in. He took one look at Sam, stopped, snapped his fingers and said, "I almost forgot. I'll be back in a second," and then hurried out of the room.

She looked at her brother and shrugged. So far there had been no surprises. Her father had left everything for the both of them to divide equally.

"D-d-did you p-put any ice on that?" Jesse stuttered, getting a closer look at her black eye. Stuttering was just one of side effects from his car accident. He also needed a cane to walk, was blind in his left eye, had almost no use of his left arm and wore a large pronounced Frankenstein-stitch scar angling across his forehead from the ten-hour operation that saved his life. And then there was the coma. Sam had sworn at her parents' gravesite that she would always take care of him and she meant it with all her heart.

"No. But I gave him ice for his," Sam said with a wink, her hand settled on his. Sam's early morning martial arts training kept her and those around her used to an occasional lump or bruise. A good thing they couldn't see her feet. Kicking. That was where she really got her frustrations out. She enjoyed sparring with the big guys, knocking them around a little bit. She liked that she could kick higher than a guy's head and preferred using her feet to her hands because her hands were more fragile and she needed them for work. She could break five boards with a spinning back kick and knew confidently she could kill a man if she wanted to.

Sam's mother had died at the World Trade Center on nine-eleven. Her father, Jack, had been a top electronics engineer for Innovative Sound Technologies. He had spent the week that followed the terror attack digging and breathing hazardous soot, twenty-four seven, trying in vain to find his wife's body. Whether it was the loss of his wife or the pounds of hazardous soot he had breathed in, his health took a downturn and had never returned.

Sam played with a blond curl and thought of her mother. Mom said they were twins separated by twenty-two years. Same hair, same steel blue eyes, same wide smile, same second glance from lookers of either sex, but the physical was where the comparison ended. Lisa Conway never returned home with bloody knees, ripped jeans, mud in her hair or with a freshly caught bull frog like her daughter Sam had often done as a child. And Lisa was never the MVP on the town little league team. Nor did she ever even think about exploring the local storm drains. Sam drummed her fingers on the table and then looked at her watch. She needed to get back to the museum.

The lawyer, David Sterling, reappeared, his steps silent on the thick carpet, as he carried two packages. He handed a large envelope to Jesse and placed a taped shoe box on the table in front of Sam. Jesse hastily opened the envelope. Inside he found a framed photo and a DVD. The photo was of Jesse, age five, playing fetch with the family Saint Bernard, Clyde, short for Clydesdale. What made the photo unique was that Jesse was using a tennis ball shooter to launch the balls into a field next to their house. The photo was entitled, "Poor Clyde." The DVD was labeled, "home videos."

After smiling at the photo, Jesse held up the DVD and said, "We're g-g-going to have to wa-wa-watch this together."

Sam nodded but she wasn't ready for a home video. Not yet.

"O-open it?" Jesse said, and pointed to the box.

Sam frowned. She had no idea what could be inside the shoe box. No doubt, knowing her father, it would be something that would bring tears to her eyes and there was nothing she hated more than crying, especially in front of her baby brother and a perfect stranger. "I think I'll wait until..."

"Let's s-see what's in th-there."

She sighed. "Maybe now's not the right time."

"I opened m-mine," he said, motioning to the framed picture.

Sam rolled her eyes. Arguing with Jesse required too much energy. She picked up the box and shook it. Didn't weigh that much and nothing rattled. What could it be? "Ah, why not," she said and started opening it, both Jesse and Sterling watching intently. The tape came off, the lid opened and all she could see was bubble-rap. She peeled apart the corners like petals on a flower and then stared in disbelief.

Jesse peered into the box. "*O-oh... my... G-God!* I haven't seen that th-thing in years."

"Twelve," Sam said, unable to blink. "I was sixteen." She picked up an index card and read it aloud. "Please try to stay out of trouble with this thing. Love, Dad." Her eyes filled. She couldn't hold it back.

"What is it?" Sterling asked. "A camcorder?"

Jesse shook his head with a sentimental smile. "It's the s-sound sh-shooter."

"It's a what?"

"The WISP," Sam interjected, as she pulled it gently from the box. "Short for wireless infrared sound placer. I used to call it the sound shooter. It was my best friend, but Dad had to take it away from me. It became addicting."

"What does it do?"

Sam put it down on the table, wiped away a tear and proudly said, "Dad was brilliant. The smartest scientist they had at Sound Tech. He would always be making prototypes. Some went into production; some went back to the drawing board. Prototypes on their way to the drawing board would occasionally make detours instead of going to a shelf to collect dust. Dad would turn some of them into toys for Jesse and me. The WISP took one of those detours and was *by far* my favorite toy. Basically, it whispers into people's ears."

Sterling chuckled. "Really! How does it work?"

Sam looked at Jesse, who gave her a shrug. She picked up the WISP and walked over to a corner of the room where she was able to look through the doorway and down the hall to a young woman at a desk. She raised the unit to eye-level and explained. "When you pull the trigger an infrared laser beam is sent through the lens like one of those little laser pointers, only it's invisible to the naked eye. This little infrared scope on top allows the operator to see the beam so it can be aimed. You speak into the microphone and your voice travels through the beam. The beam stops at an ear and the voice empties."

"You've got to be kidding me?"

Sam pulled the trigger and watched the beam appear in the scope. She carefully aimed it directly into the young woman's ear and quietly said, "Mister Sterling needs you immediately."

The lady instantly turned her head and saw no one. She paused and then left her seat and hastened to the conference room. "Mister Sterling?"

Sterling looked at Sam, smiled and said, "Yes, Michele?"

She paused and then said, "Did you need something?"

"Why, yes. I was just going to call you. I need the files pulled on Freedman for my one o'clock. How did you know?"

"I, uh, just thought…" she smiled. "A little bird told me. I'll get those right away," she said, and then disappeared.

Sterling turned to Sam. "That's the most remarkable thing I've ever seen. Why did your father take it away from you?"

Sam looked mischievously up to the ceiling and said, "I don't know if I should say."

"Tell him, Sis," Jesse said with a broad smile.

Sam glared at Sterling. "You can't tell a soul."

Sterling held up his hands. "You can trust me. I have to know."

Sam shrugged. "Whatever. Nobody would believe you anyway. Besides, I'll deny everything."

"You wouldn't be the first."

"Well, the last time I used it was at Yankee Stadium, World Series. Yankees, Mets. I'm a huge Yankee fan and, according to my father, I let myself get a little too involved."

"J-just a l-little," Jesse said.

Sam smiled and continued. "I sat in the outfield and through the scope I was able to see the catcher signaling the pitcher. I was telling the Yankee batters what pitches to expect… and I lied to the Mets."

Sterling's face dropped. "You *are* joking?"

Jesse shook his head.

"But the batter's helmets…"

"H-have ear holes," Jesse said. "The Y-Yankees crushed."

Sam, deadpan. "Actually, we just made this up. Jesse and I do it all the time. But we had you going there for a minute, didn't we?"

Sterling smiled. "Regarding what?"

127

21

Sam smiled and gave a polite wave to a small group pointing at her on the corner of Park Ave and Forty-Seventh Street on her way uptown to the museum.

"U-unbelievable," Jesse said.

"Why do you think I was so quick to agree to you guys driving me? she said, referring to the museum's limo hire for her, Jesse and Miss Cox. "I used to like to take the subway."

"Y-yeah," her brother said. "P-people p-point at me, too."

Sam had to laugh. She had gotten used to Jesse's sense of humor finding laughs at his own expense. "I'm thinking they use a different finger."

"H-ha, ha," Jesse said. "S-so w-what are you g-going to do with the S-sound Shooter?"

"Absolutely nothing. That was from another time. Whatever trouble I could have gotten into then would be a hundred times worse now. The Sound Shooter will stay in the box and be taken out for fun at birthday parties only. Stuff like that."

"C-can I b-borrow it?"

She laughed again. He was on a roll. "Of course. That, my credit card and my shot gun. Anytime, Jess," Sam said and rolled her eyes. "Seriously, what would you do with it?"

"W-what, you d-don't think G-God can stutter?"

Sam laughed. "I suppose, if He wanted to. He's God. But most people might find your con questionable."

"B-but there's this g-girl."

"How did I guess?" she said, and then held her thumb to her lips like a microphone. "Isn't Jesse cute? When he asks you to go to dinner, say yes."

Jesse nodded enthusiastically.

"No. Remember Dad's note. Keep out of trouble."

"That note was for you."

"Right, and keeping the Sound Shooter out of your hands is honoring his request."

The limo pulled over in front of the museum. Sam gathered her stuff, leaned over and kissed Jesse on the cheek. "Cheer up, Jess. You don't need the Sound Shooter's magic. If you ask her, she'll say yes."

"Y-yeah," Jesse sulked. "Maybe you should use the Sound Shooter to get yourself a boyfriend."

Sam laughed. "I thought about doing that when I was a teen. Honestly, I wouldn't know who to shoot."

"H-how about one of the Y-yankees so we can get W-world Series t-tickets?"

Sam laughed. "That's a very bad idea. I like it."

"Y-you c-coming home tonight?"

"Of course," she said with a wink and then shut the door.

A cold wind cooled her ankles as she took The Metropolitan Museum's expansive front steps two at a time but then paused halfway up. A politician was using the museum as a backdrop for his campaign speech. She noticed his earplug and thought of the Sound Shooter in her hand. She thought about Jesse and smiled. Keeping out of trouble might be more difficult than she thought. She continued on her way up the steps and through the massive doors like she and most of the other museum employees did every day.

"Hi Sam," the security guard said, watching the monitor. "You looked great on CNN."

"Thanks, Willis," Sam said with a smile, then walked across the Great Hall and took the elevator to the restricted third floor. The door opened and Sam stepped onto the polished stone floor. Like the rest of the museum, the third floor was very old and impeccably clean. Two security guards down the hall quickly noted her presence with a nod. Her steps echoed through the tall hardwood walls and high ceilings as she turned two corners to her office.

Sam's brisk gate slowed. Her office door was opened and big Eddie Washington, the head of security, was standing outside it.

"Problem, Eddie?" she said.

"You have visitors, Doctor Conway" he said, his voice as deep and cavernous as the Great Hall.

Sam frowned. Visitors were *not* allowed on the third floor. None. Not since the nine-eleven World Trade Center attack. No media, no specialists, not even the police unless they were invited. She wasn't even sure if the Mayor would be allowed. Any visitors were to be met in lower floors, usually in the Great Hall, assuming they had an *appointment*. She stared at him for a moment looking for more of an answer, but all he did was motion with his eyes toward the open door.

Sam walked into her office and found two men of medium height looking out her window.

"May I help you?" she said.

The men turned. One man was wore a dark blue suit, black and handsome with a strong clean-shaven jawline, crew-cut and brown eyes. The other man was a rugged contrast. He wore faded jeans and a pullover sweater, a dangerously unshaven four-day beard, piercing blue eyes, recently cropped thick black hair and a white bandage over his right eyebrow. He dripped testosterone and held a black metal attaché.

"Hi, we're waiting for Doctor Conway," the suit said. The rugged one leaned over and whispered something into his ear which caused a raised brow.

"I'm Samantha Conway," Sam said.

"Great view of Central Park," the suit said nervously. "But I guess you hear that all the time."

"Not really," she said. "Not for the last eighty years, when we restricted the field trips and guided tours to the lower floors." She glanced at the attaché.

The man smiled. "Of course. It's a pleasure to meet you, uh, Doctor Conway," he said extending his right hand with a business card. "I'm Agent Walker— Bruce Walker. I'm with the Central Intelligence Agency. And this is Agent Decker," he said, motioning to the other man, who simply nodded. "Agent Decker is with the Defense Intelligence Agency. And no, you're not in any kind of trouble. Actually, we are. We need your help."

Sam was momentarily stunned. The CIA? What did they want? "The Defense Intelligence Agency?"

"DIA," Walker said. "They're more specialized than us and don't get as much press. They sort of like it that way," he said with a smile. Decker appeared disinterested in the explanation, his gaze moved to her shoe box.

"Well, I suppose that explains how you were able to get up here." She wondered what was in the attaché.

"Membership has its privileges. We get to see the world, although, not necessarily the way you might want to," he said with a wink in Decker's direction. Decker didn't respond with even the slightest smile and he still hadn't said a word.

Sam smiled politely. "I guess not."

"You have quite a reputation, Doctor Conway," Walker said. "We've been told you are the best in your field."

"I'm flattered, but what could I possibly have that the CIA wants?"

Walker cleared his throat, frowned and motioned to the four walls of her office, completely taken up with books. "All of what we know about ancient writing is in books. Ancient history has never been our specialty. As far as we were concerned, when it came to ancient history, there was nothing new, so to speak."

"Until now," Decker said, directly. "Would you please close your door?"

Sam frowned and didn't move.

"We need to show you something that is for your eyes only. I have to request that you shut and lock the door and then have a seat at your desk," Decker said, authoritatively.

Sam paused, but then stepped back to the door. "It's okay, Eddie," she said, then closed and locked the old hardware with a loud clack.

"We've come across something we'd like you to look at, Doctor Conway," Walker said.

"May I?" Decker said, and then set his attaché on her desk.

"Uh, go right ahead," she said, and then circled her desk and sat down as requested. She realized for the first time the attaché was handcuffed to his left wrist. *What was going on here?*

Decker unhandcuffed himself, played with the attaché combination lock and opened it. He carefully removed some gray foam egg crate protection, lifted out an olive green strongbox just smaller than the attaché and put it on the desk in front of her. "It's all yours, Doctor Conway. Open it."

Sam looked at him and then at the box. She unlatched two clips, one on either side, took the lid completely off and placed it on the desk. Surrounded by soft black felt was a stone tablet or at least a fragment of a tablet about the size of a thick loose-leaf binder, with writing on it. She smoothed her hand lightly over the etched lettering. She had never seen anything quite like this. And was it her imagination, or were her fingers tingling? A strange sensation that felt curiously comforting. She cleared her throat and refocused. The artifact wasn't flat; it had a distinct vertical curve. She zeroed in on the characters and frowned. After analyzing countless ancient cuneiform writings on clay tablets, this was beyond unique. The cuneiform system of writing was debatably the oldest and most primitive, where etched art told the story and numbers were represented by the repetitious use of strokes or circles. This appeared to have an Egyptian flavor, but was more complex than any hieroglyphics she had ever seen, each character crowded with detail. And it was stone, not clay. Without taking her eyes off the inscriptions she said, "Where did you get this?"

Decker was about to speak, but Walker held up his hand and said, "Before we tell you anything, we'd like to hear your thoughts, if that's all right."

Sam smiled. "My thoughts? I think someone's playing a joke on me."

"Excuse me?" Walker said.

"Normally, rare artifacts show up in straw stuffed wood crates, occasionally accompanied by the archaeologist who found it. Not secret agents with handcuffed attaché cases. So, where's the camera?"

"This is no joke, Doctor Conway. There is no camera. You are the archaeologist. We need the help of an archaeologist. If that's not you, then sorry for the inconvenience. We'll be on our way," Walker said in a serious tone that sounded genuine.

Sam shrugged. "Okay, I'll play along. I can't tell you how old it is, at least not yet. My gut tells me Egypt but there are indications here that are uncharacteristic with Egyptian writings."

"What does it say?" Decker said impatiently.

Sam opened a drawer and pulled out a magnifying glass for a closer look. "Well, that's the odd thing. It says a quite a bit."

"What do you mean?" Walker said

"Lots of data. Like this papyrus stalk," she said carefully pointing with the tip of a pen. "Normally it would appear as an elongated figure eight with an extended bottom and a bell top... this has complex and specific detail in leaves and flowers, indicating type and precise usage. More than I can interpret without further study. Is this all you have, or is there more?"

"That's it," Walker said.

"It's a shame. Taking random information out of context can taint the message... affect the translation."

The agents shared a glance.

"Honestly, I've never seen anything quite like it. Lots of instruction and trivia. Like a book of recipes and short sayings. Have you ever read the inside of a Snapple cap?"

"Yes," Walker said. "Real facts, I think they call them."

"I think you're right," Sam said. "Little snippets of truth, like the speed of a bee or the distance to the sun. This is sort of like that. But the info..." she said, and then paused as she continued to read silently.

"Yes?" Walker said.

"Is a bit ahead of its time."

"I thought you didn't know how old it was," Decker said.

"I know it's old but, some of this information isn't ancient, in fact, some of it might be considered... news," Sam said with a smile. "So, uh, really, where's the camera?"

"Does it say anything about flies?" Decker said. Walker gave him a look.

Sam thought the question strange but then took a moment to scan the writing. She couldn't get over how beautiful it was. Almost hypnotic, the way it drew her in. She ran her fingers over the stone as she tried to decipher the weathered markings. "Actually, yes, here and there, but again with added detail. Finding flies, by the way, is not unusual. Flies were holy to the Old Kingdom Egyptians and show up in many ancient writings."

"Holy?" Decker said, sardonically.

Walker gave him a corrective look, but Decker showed no sign of apology.

"Why do you ask?"

"How about herbs?" Decker added.

"Herbs?"

"Yes."

"Which herbs? There are actually quite a few here."

"Can you list them?"

Sam frowned but then looked back to the text. "Possibly some. I would have to know more about the origin of the artifact to be confident in my analysis."

"And this," Decker continued, pointing to one of the many tiny characters on the artifact. "What does this mean? It appears several times in the text."

Sam focused her magnifying glass on a character she had never seen before. "I don't know. Looks like a snake in a bumpy circle. Could be a snake nest, though it appears in repeated sequence with some kind of,.. staff."

"A germ?" Walker said.

Sam blinked and looked at him, wondering if he was serious. "The Egyptians were ahead of the times, but not quite that far. A *shepherd's* staff, like flies, snakes and sheep, were commonplace in ancient records."

"Sorry for interrupting. Please continue with your impression," Walker said.

Sam frowned and said, "Okay. Your tablet, if it's as old as it looks, is very peculiar. Writings that go back this far don't contain anywhere near this much information. They usually say, 'you owe me two camels and one wife' or 'two wives and one camel.' In fact," she said with a slight head shake, "It appears to be a modern piece of a hieroglyphics text book... written in stone. A bit conflicting to say the least."

"Does it matter how old it is?" Decker said. "We just need to know what it says."

"It matters in the translation," Sam said. "Some characters have different meanings in different eras."

"So maybe it's not old?" Walker said.

Sam shook her head. "I didn't say that. Some of the characters are consistent with early ancient writing and there is no visible evidence of recent tooling in the stone. My gut says it's old, which makes it rather fascinating."

"Hmm. How far back are we talking?" Walker said.

Sam shrugged. "We're not going to be able to cross-date it with anything I've seen in a predated site. The oldest writings found were from Egypt, Harappa and Mesopotamia. Clay tablets were uncovered in southern Egypt at a tomb of a king named Scorpion that carbon dated back fifty-five hundred years ago, but those were much more primitive than this. It's a shame we can't carbon date this."

"Why not?" Decker said.

"Because it's stone. In order to carbon date, you need organic matter."

"Organic?" Walker said.

"Yes, something that was once alive. Bone, shell, charcoal, even clay from organic sediments," she said, then turned the piece over and ran her fingers across the back. She then looked at the jagged side and leaned closer. "But with stone there are other ways that…" she said and then paused.

"What?" Walker said.

Sam didn't reply, staring intensely at the edge with her magnifying glass. She then turned it over and looked at the writing, closer, closer.

"Doctor Conway?"

"This,.. can't be possible."

"What can't be possible?" Walker said.

Sam put the glass down and the lid back on the box. She stood up and said, "Follow me." The container was lighter than she expected.

"Where?" Walker said nervously as Sam took box hastened away from him.

"To the lab."

22

Sam marched briskly down the wide hall with Walker, Decker and Eddie, the security guard, trying to keep pace with her. She turned the corner, slid a security card through a reader at the first door and went in, followed by Walker and Decker, but Eddie stayed out. The lab was a large room that would on first glance, look like a flea market devoid of customers. Giant tables with all sorts of priceless junk strewn about, or so it appeared. Their quick footsteps were loud on the stone floor as Sam made a quick left and entered another door. The room was white with stainless steel counters filled with electronic scales, scopes, computers and other scientific paraphernalia along with glass jars, paper towels and latex glove dispensers on the wall. Sam pushed a lab chair aside and stopped in front of the electron microscope.

"What are you doing?" Walker said, catching his breath. Decker breathed normally and watched in silence.

"Going in for a *much* closer look," she said, as she opened the box and placed the artifact on the scope platform. She turned it on. A stream of highly energized electrons poured over the fragment and an instant later a close-up, one thousand times its normal size, appeared on the viewing screen. Sam stared, unblinking. She couldn't believe her eyes. She slowly scanned across the artifact, stopping, staring, moving, and examining everything. Slower, closer. Her suspicion was correct. But how was it possible? Something must be wrong. There had to be a logical scientific explanation. There always was. She stared at the edges of the characters. This was not a recent work. The cells had been eroded beyond her belief.

"Helloooo."

"Huh," Sam said, tuning to Walker.

"I said, are you going to tell us what you see or not?"

Sam turned. "I'm back to wondering where the candid camera is?"

"Trust me. The CIA isn't big on practical jokes. What have we got here?" Walker said.

"I'm sorry, gentlemen. I've never seen anything like this. I don't think anyone has. At least not in the last several millennia, or more."

"What do you mean?" Decker said.

"I mean I need to know more. I *need* to know more. Where did this come from?" Sam was surprised at herself. It was natural for her to be curious and investigative, but why was she feeling desperate. *Get a grip*, she thought.

"I can tell you that the recent history of it is highly confidential," Walker said.

Sam gave him a look. "Right, and if you get any more specific than that you'd have to kill me."

Walker smiled. "We've encountered strange phenomena surrounding this artifact and we'd like to know what you think it is and what you think it says as quickly and quietly as possible."

Sam nodded. "Then we have to do some testing."

Decker gave Walker a grave stare. Walker gave a slight nod and said, "Testing might not be the best idea."

Sam rolled her eyes. "Testing is how we *find out* what it is."

"What kind of testing?"

"Carbon dating, for starters."

"But I thought you said stone can't be carbon dated."

"It can't. But *this* isn't stone."

"Then what is it?" Decker said.

"Wood. And I need to find out what kind."

"Wood!" Walker said, incredulously.

"Yes. A petrified wood of some kind. Wood that has turned to stone over time. Lots of time. It takes at least sixty million years."

"But the writing can't be *that* old," Walker said.

"Correct. But being that I've *never* heard of ancient writing on petrified wood before, because there was virtually none to write on in the Middle East, and because it's a lot easier to write on almost anything else, I have to repeat my first question to you."

"Which is?"

"Where, on this side of Hell, did you *get* this thing?"

Walker frowned thoughtfully. "Actually, it was on the other side."

"Come again."

Walker motioned to the lab chair and said, "Have a seat, Doctor Conway."

Sam wanted to stand, but she obliged him for the moment, not wanting to delay his answer.

"We don't know where it came from originally, but we found it in a cave in Afghanistan," Decker said.

"Cave? What kind of cave?"

After a pause, Walker said, "A recent hollowing in a mountainside near Kabul."

Sam shook her head. "More secrets. Whatever, there's no way it could have originated there. Afghanistan was a crossroad. Stuff came *in* before it went *out*. It's like telling me you found it on the first floor in the Egyptian exhibit. It had to get there from somewhere else. Bactrian, the oldest language in Afghanistan, came from Greece, compliments of Alexander. This thing *isn't* Greek."

Decker cleared his throat and ended his silence. "Before it happened, I was told by one source that local insurgents had found a 'Sutun'."

Sam turned to Decker and frowned. "A pillar?" She considered the slight curve to the surface. "Some ancient records were etched into pillars for public or group viewing. At city entrances laws would be carved into pillars, much like today's traffic signs, or in a temple you might find creeds or statements of faith etched into columns. I've never heard of a pillar made of petrified wood, though. I can't even imagine how it happened."

Decker nodded. "You speak Farsi?"

"If your business is ancient artifacts, you have to. You said, 'before it happened'," Sam said. "Before *what* happened?"

"I have some photos, but I must warn you they're a bit graphic." Walker said.

"Have you ever dissected a mummy?"

"Uh, not lately." Walker reached into his jacket pocket, produced a white envelope and handed it to Sam. "Agent Decker has been undercover human intelligence for DIA in Afghanistan since October two-thousand and one. In that time, he's blended into the landscape and has been our eyes and ears among the Kabul locals, some of whom are insurgents and relatives of insurgents."

While Walker continued, Sam opened the envelope and withdrew the photos. The first one was an aerial shot of a mountainside with bodies lying on black soil. The next was a close up of the black soil, dead insects or something, overflowing a dead man's mouth. Next were a couple of grotesque shots inside a cave and then one with the artifact in a glass case surrounded by scientific equipment.

"Whose lab was this? Doctor Frankenstein's?"

"Have you ever heard of Tarik?" Walker said.

Sam looked up. They had her attention. "I do occasionally pick up a newspaper. Is that who was behind this?"

"Not was... *is*," Walker said.

"Did he die in this mess?"

"No," Decker said.

"What happened?" Sam asked. The faces of her parents flashed in her mind. She could feel her pulse rise.

"We don't know," Walker said, and then pointed out small details on the photos. He also explained that the insects were all flies. "But, apparently, something went very wrong."

"Why are the flies all dead? What killed them?"

"We don't know," Walker said. "Whatever it was seems to have disappeared by the time we got there. Another mystery."

"So you think the secrets of this tragedy and whatever the insurgents were looking forward to is somehow locked up in the translation of the artifact," Sam said.

"We don't know," Walker said. "When can we expect your test results?"

Sam continued to handle the pictures. "What is this?" she said, showing the agents a picture of a dead insurgent that appeared to be decomposed. "The flies couldn't have done that, not without having weeks or months to work on him."

"Minutes," Decker said.

Sam shot Decker a look. "How do you know that?"

"Agent Decker witnessed two of the deaths personally," Walker said.

Sam looked at Decker. He said nothing, just stared at her with intense unblinking steel blue eyes. "You were there when this happened?"

Decker nodded matter-of-factly.

"I thought everyone died."

"There were two survivors," Walker said. "Agent Decker and another prisoner were locked away from the flies. Two guards who were locked inside their cell with them died of … well, actually, that's part of what we're trying to find out."

"We wouldn't be *here* if we had the answers," Decker said.

Sam nodded slowly and then looked back at the photo. The idea that the hellish scene was caused by the information written thousands of years ago on a piece of petrified wood sitting a few feet from her was chilling. Would her understanding and translation of the wood fragment result in more corpses somewhere? She would need help. She stood up and walked to the phone, then picked up the receiver and started to dial.

Walker's finger stabbed the phone's switch hook, disconnecting her call. "What are you doing?"

"Calling a friend. I want some help with this."

"I'm sorry, Doctor Conway, but this isn't for public consumption," Walker said. "We need to keep a tight lid."

"Tight lid," Sam said, incredulously. "Who are you afraid is going to find out? The terrorists? *You* got it from *them*, remember."

"Sam, we have our own scientists. Actually, they were the ones who pointed us in your direction. They don't want to make the same mistake the people in the cave made."

"They're scared," Decker said.

Sam handed him back the photos. "They should be. I assume you quarantined some of the corpses to a lab somewhere?"

"Of course."

"Where?"

"That's classified. When will your test results be back?" Walker asked again.

"Tomorrow morning."

23

Sam's mind raced on the way home. She scanned through a few channels and then turned her satellite radio off. Her busy mind kept revisiting the electron microscope's magnification of the ancient writing and disturbing photos. *Tarik*. She almost drove by Exit 39 on the Long Island Expressway but quickly downshifted her Mini Cooper S and cranked a right turn onto Glen Cove Road. She still had not gotten used to the fact that she lived there again but, with Jesse's needs and her father gone, Glenwood would be her home for the foreseeable future.

One place she was always able to relax and think clearly was her father's house. As a child, she was a classic tomboy and always in some kind of trouble but, those had been some of the best years in her life. She smiled reflecting on mischief she had been involved in as she turned into the old neighborhood. Her father's house backed up to an unfenced old ball field. She used to think the whole field was theirs and others were nice enough to mow the lawn for them.

Sam drove up to the house and was glad to see the lights on and Miss Cox's minivan in the driveway. Life on the home-front was normal and working. She got out of the Mini and for a moment imagined Deuce, her childhood Saint Bernard, running up to greet her with that deep barrel-chested bark. She walked into the back door. Open as usual with that weather stripping squeak. Her father never fixed it so he would always know when it opened, at least that what she thought. Miss Cox sat at the kitchen table reading her newspaper, her usual station. She looked up and smiled. The smile said all was well.

"You m-missed dinner," Jesse called from the family room. "Was g-good."

Miss Cox shrugged. "Hot dogs and beans," she said.

Sam smiled and went to Jesse. She dropped her coat over the back of a chair, plopped onto the couch next to him and gave him a peck on the cheek. "How's it going?"

"Today was h-hard," he said with a smile but couldn't keep his eyes from welling up. "I needed to w-watch one of D-dad's old m-movies. J-join me?"

"Sure," she said patting the top of her little brother's hand. "I just need a minute in Dad's office. Have to check on something before I forget it." Suddenly she felt better too. Being with Jesse, seeing the familiar pictures on the wall, hearing the radiator pipes bang and the scent of the cozy fire her brother liked to keep told her she was home.

Sam found a bottle of spring water in the fridge and then went into the basement to her father's office and turned on the computer. While it booted up, she took a second to look at the familiar wood paneling and drop ceiling panels. When she was a kid, this room had been off limits unless her father was present. She sighed deeply and started searching the museum's archives and the web for anything she could find on "Ancient Pillars". Sam placed a high-resolution glossy color photocopy of the CIA's artifact on the desktop next to the keyboard. She was barely able to keep her eyes off it, an exciting redundancy of unknown characters. Some patterns she recognized, sort of, like the reverse lineage at the top, but others she couldn't even guess at... yet. She had to wonder what really came first, Egyptian hieroglyphics or the pillar. Which was borrowing from which? The longer she looked at it, the more she thought the pillar was older. But how was that possible?

She reached into her hip pocket and felt for a small quarter-size piece of the artifact she had chipped off. She found it amongst some change and held it up before her eyes. She rubbed it between her thumb and index finger. "Where did you come from?"

Since this pillar had not been previously discovered, it would either be unknown or fall under the category of "legendary pillars." Any pillars from the legendary city of Sodom and Gomorrah would have been destroyed with the city, including the pillar of salt that had once been Lot's wife, according to legend, of course. Like any scientist trying to decipher between fact and fiction, she had to consider all legends with an open mind, as far fetched as they might be.

Sam was in an ocean looking for land. She scrolled and scrolled through text and illustrations of everything from historical legends to fairy tales. None had the connection she was looking for. She looked at the artifact photo. "What are you? Where did you come from? Who carved you?"

Jesse called down to her. *"Y-you coming?"*

Sam looked at her watch and cursed. "Sorry, Jess," she said and then pushed the mouse away, grabbed her water and went up to see her waiting brother.

"F-finally. Hey, I h-have a j-joke," he said.

"Okay, what?"

"S-silk, silk, silk… W-what do c-cows drink?"

Sam smiled and said, "At what time of day?"

Jesse pursed his lips. "In the morning."

"Café latte."

"Y-you were s-supposed to say m-milk."

"Milk doesn't do it for them in the morning."

"N-never mind," he said and hopped off the couch to the bookshelves where the DVDs and videos were. "W-what m-movie?"

"What's in the player?"

Jesse poked 'open' and the disc slid out. "The F-fugitive"?

"Maybe. What's in the VCR?"

Jesse pressed eject and waited. "P-planet of the Apes"?

Sam laughed. "Classic. 'Get your stinkin' hands off me you damn dirty ape.' Dad was always a softy for Charlton Heston."

"Y-you liked him too."

Sam frowned. "Me? How you figure?"

"J-just a second," Jesse said and scanned the shelves. He then plucked out a tape and held it up for her to see.

Sam leaned forward and read the title. "'The Ten Commandments'? It's probably worn out from all the times I watched it. Probably why I work at the museum."

"I l-like the s-special effects."

Sam nodded. "I remember thinking it was so cool when Moses' staff turned into a snake and ate the other snakes."

Jesse nodded. "P-poor Yul Brenner."

"What do you mean?"

"All the p-p-plagues and then h-his son was k-killed.

Sam smiled. "Yeah, the Ten Commandments and Jurassic Park. My favorites. Real chick flicks."

"Y-yeah, r-right. C-could Juras-sic Park h-happen?"

"No. The dinosaurs were a hundred million years ago. But how cool would that be?"

"V-very. D-did the Ten Commandments h-happen?"

Sam shrugged. "It's hard to say what's true. The Egyptians were famous for their records and they don't seem to have *any* on the Exodus story, which makes you wonder if Moses, whoever he was, was the real deal or just a good storyteller."

Jesse nodded and turned to another tape. "H-how about, 'The African Queen'?"

"The flies!" she blurted involuntarily.

Jesse frowned and then said, "We don't h-have that."

"No! Not that movie." Sam said, her mind suddenly somewhere else completely. "The *plague* of the flies."

"In the T-ten Commandments?" he asked.

"Not in the movie. In the Bible," Sam said, immediately up from the couch and over to a different bookshelf. She pulled out a Bible and flipped through chunks of pages until she found Exodus. She scanned subtitles: The Birth of Moses, The Burning Bush, God Promises Action and the section on, Water is Turned to Blood. At chapter eight she read quickly to 'swarms of insects'. When she finished, she stared into space, trying to gather a barrage of thoughts flying through her brain not unlike the plague she had just read about.

"H-how about 'Predator'?"

Sam waved her hand at him. "Start it, Jess. Something important just came to me and I'll need a minute to think."

Jesse gave her a look and shook his head. "I'll s-start it."

"Thanks," Sam said, off at a run to her father's basement office again. "I'll be back in a little bit."

"S-sure you will."

Sam couldn't help herself. There was no way she would be able to watch Predator or any other movie right now. She was shaking with anxious energy. She thought of the photos. The flies. The decomposed bodies. The final plague that killed the pharaoh's son. The death of the first born. *The fools*, she thought. *What were they thinking?* She hurried down the basement stairs and back into her father's chair. She hit the mouse and the screen woke up. She moved the cursor to her search site and typed: *Books of Moses- pillar.*

The computer was moving too slow for her. Her fingers drummed the mouse-pad. An index appeared:

Pillar of fire

Pillar of cloud

Covenants, Pillars and Theologies

Samson tied to pillars

Pillar of salt

Shalom's pillar

Jacob's pillar

She clicked onto each and found nothing she considered applicable. She looked again at the photo of the artifact. This was crazy. How could there be no record of this thing? There had to be. Somewhere. No Egyptian record. No Biblical record. What else? If some of Moses' divine help came in the form of information found on the pillar, the person who supplied it would be important to him and be recorded in his books somewhere. What if she cross referenced the names with extra-biblical sources? She punched up all the names in the Books of Moses chronologically. Adam, Eve, Lucifer, Cain, Abel, Seth, Enosh, Kenan, Mahalalel, Jared, Enoch, Methuselah, Lamech, Noah, Shem, Ham, Japheth and on and on. The list was enormous and, after thousands of years, so would the legends. She searched each name, starting from Adam, with any connection to a pillar. After about a dozen dead ends, she saw something that nearly stopped her heart.

Methuselah's Pillar.

As she read on she could hardly remain in her seat. According to legend, Methuselah's Pillar was a record of information Methuselah had received from his seven times great grandfather, Adam. *The Adam.* Sam sat back and began to tie legends together. According to legend, Adam, of course, lived with Eve in the Garden of Eden where they enjoyed the unfallen nature of man with God, with Adam presumably operating with, not one-tenth, but one hundred percent of his brain. According to legend, Adam lived for hundreds of years after the fall and would have been there to talk to Methuselah who, according to legend, became the oldest living human, ever. What kind of information did Adam pass on in the pillar? She looked again at the photo of the artifact and got shivers. Did Methuselah have any clue what he had received? She sat up and read on. After Methuselah finally died, the pillar was considered holy and moved to a place of sacrifice and worship where it remained until the time of Moses, when it was moved again to an unknown location.

Sam stared at the last sentence in disbelief. After a moment she pulled Agent Walker's business card out and calmly picked up the desk phone receiver and dialed his cell number.

"Hello!"

"Agent Walker? Sam Conway."

"Oh, hello, Doctor Conway. It's late. Are you okay?"

"Yes. Sorry. I lost track of the time."

"Find anything?"

"Yes. I need to see you and Agent Decker."

"Great. How about first thing in the morning?"

"How about now?"

24

"S-Sam!" Jesse called down the stairs. "Y-you have c-company."

Without taking her eyes off the screen, Sam yelled, "Send them down. And don't mess with them. They're secret agents."

Jesse laughed and left. She could hear his footsteps over her head and then other multiple footsteps coming back and then down the stairs behind her. She turned around. Jesse was no longer laughing. "Y-you were s-serious," he said.

"You two have a seat," she said, motioning to a couple of office swivel chairs. "And you go back to '*Predator*', Jesse."

"It's over."

"Watch it again."

"C-can't I…"

"No. We'll talk about it later."

"P-promise?"

"Yes. I love you. Now go. And shut the door." Jesse left and the door closed. She waited for his footsteps to reach the family room and then turned her attention to Decker and Walker. They were both silent, leaning forward, elbows on knees, hands clasped, all ears.

"Before I say anything, you guys have to promise not to put me in a straitjacket and call the men in the white coats."

"What have you got, Sam?" Walker said. "We're all on the same team here."

Sam curled her hair behind her ears and sipped some water. "Out of curiosity, did you guys happen to check out the flies?"

"I examined one pretty closely. It was purple with orange eyes. Different." Decker said.

"I assume, you brought some to a lab for testing?" Sam said.

"Yes," Walker said. "We wanted to find out what killed them."

"Did you find anything?"

"Not yet."

"Did you find out what kind of flies they were?"

"No. We're not sure yet."

"Well, do they match the existing flies in the area?"

"No," Decker said.

Sam felt a shiver run down the back of her neck. "Did they match any flies... anywhere?"

"We don't know what they've found," Walker said. "They're still testing. Why?"

"Because I got ten bucks that says you're *not* going to find them... anywhere."

"Ten bucks?" Decker said.

"Make it a thousand."

Decker frowned. "What makes you so sure?"

"Because, like all other living things, flies evolve. They change over time. Their size changers, wing length, eye color, speed, lifespan, growth rate."

"So?" Decker said.

"So, I think any fly you match these up against is going to be different, further evolved."

"Why?" Decker said.

"Because today's flies have had more time."

"Today's?" Walker said.

"You're saying what... that these flies are from another time?" Decker said, doubtfully. "They're time traveling flies?"

Walker snickered but Decker showed no hint of humor.

"Not exactly but, in a way, yes. I think we'll eventually find that these flies no longer exist."

"Extinct?" Decker said.

"Not as a species, of course, but as a type, yes."

Decker paused thoughtfully, and then said, "When do *you* think these flies are from?"

"From the time of the pillar. When it was first written, or possibly before."

The faces on both men froze.

"You mean like five thousand years ago?" Decker said, skeptically.

Sam didn't want to answer this question. "It depends. Maybe longer."

"It depends on what?" Walker said.

"On *who* the author of the pillar is."

Both Decker and Walker frowned and then Walker leaned closer and said, "It sounds like you have someone in mind."

"Who's the suspect?" Decker said. His expression was blank.

"I believe this pillar was a gift to Methuselah."

The agents looked at each other for a little help and then Walker shrugged and said, "The woman with the long dreadlocks who could turn you into stone if you looked into her eyes?"

Sam paused. "That's Medusa. Borrowed Greek mythology. Good try, though. If I didn't think you were serious, I'd laugh. While you were thinking of what you were going to do when Sunday school was over, your teacher told you Methuselah was a real person, the son of a guy named Enoch. Actually, a very distant ancestor of Jesus Christ."

After a long silence, Decker said, "You're joking, right?"

"I'm simply following a lead. Examining some details. Exploring a possibility," she said, handing them printed copies of her research. "Frankly, I never thought it really ever existed. As far as I was concerned, Methuselah's Pillar was total myth."

"Methuselah's Pillar?" Walker said. Decker was looking through the printouts.

"Yes. Nothing about this thing has made any sense to me until now."

"I've never heard of it," Walker said.

"It's not as well known as Noah's Ark or the Holy Grail or the Ark of the Covenant that used to be housed in The Temple. Methuselah's Pillar predates the Bible by thousands of years and, like those other aforementioned artifacts, it's a legend. We believe the Ark of the Covenant existed and may even still exist, because of the many records. We're not sold on Noah's Ark because the only record is in the form of a story. Methuselah's Pillar has always fallen somewhere in-between. Personally, I've never given its existence much credibility, until now."

"Well, what does the legend claim?" Walker said. "Who was the actual author of this thing?"

Sam took a breath and exhaled. "This is where it gets a little mind-boggling and impossible to actually prove. According to legend, Methuselah's Pillar is simply a record of information given to Methuselah from his seven times great grandfather, Adam."

Decker's eyes came off the papers. "*The* Adam?"

"As in Adam and Eve," Walker said.

"Yes."

Decker rolled his eyes and he looked at his watch. "Are you sure you're not confusing the word 'legend' with 'fairy-tale'?"

Walker's attention also seemed to relax. She may as well have just told them she thought the pillar was from the North Pole, written by Santa Claus.

Walker frowned and said, "I have a question."

She braced herself. She had summoned the CIA and DIA to Long Island late at night to hear her, an archaeological expert in ancient writings, give a fabled answer for a world threatening phenomenon. Now it was their turn to torture her with stupid questions disguised as realistic concerns.

"How was Methuselah able to have conversations with his great, great, great… Adam?" Walker said.

"Again, according to legend, Biblical legend in this case, Methuselah was the oldest person that had ever lived. Nine hundred and sixty-nine years, possibly as a result of this record from Adam, who, as according to legend, had unobstructed conversations in the Garden of Eden with God, at a time before a certain fall, that could have messed with human brain capacities and capabilities. Nine hundred and sixty-nine years. What do you think immortality would fetch on the open market these days?" She couldn't believe these words were coming out of her mouth any more than the two agents could.

"As a scientist, do you *believe* that?" Decker asked.

Sam folded her arms. "In a word, no. At least not verbatim. But as a scientist, especially an archaeologist, I have to be familiar with legends, whether they are true or not. They usually evolve around *something*. Scientists have to separate meat from bones, food from garbage."

"So do we," Decker said, pointedly.

"Look," Sam said. "There's a lot we don't understand here because it can get very complicated mixing legends and facts and faith when you can't determine where one starts and the other ends. Scientifically, immortality can't work. God supposedly created Adam and Eve to be immortal but, if that were true, mankind would already be extinct because we would have clearly overpopulated the earth by now and starved ourselves into extinction. And if we stopped breeding, we would die of eventual accidents, like trains and lightning. But faith would demand that

God already figured that out and would provide a way. So, no, I personally don't understand the possibility of a literal Adam and Eve but legends tend to come from somewhere."

After a moment of silence, Decker looked at Walker, dropped his papers on the floor and stood up. "She's got quite an imagination. Thanks for your help, Doc. It's been real... unreal."

Sam stood up and quickly met him face to face. "Does this mean you'll bet me the thousand bucks on the flies?"

Walker lightly pulled down on Decker's arm. "He's a little short on American currency at the moment." He looked at Decker. "We're here. She does have a history for finding things others didn't believe existed. Let's hear her out."

Decker seemed to resist, but then exhaled and sat down. "Please continue," he said.

"Thank you. I'll try to get right to the point. I admit I'm fascinated by the possibility of us having a piece Methuselah's Pillar. It would be the greatest archaeological find of all time. But my fear is that it could also be extremely deadly."

"More flies?" Walker said.

Sam shook her head. "The decomposed corpses. The flies were nothing. They were deadly to the insurgents because they were in a cave when the insects appeared faster than they could deal with. If they were outside at the time, the bugs would have been little more than a horrible nuisance."

"What killed the others?" Decker said.

Sam paused. "I hope I'm wrong. The flies give us direction. As time went on, it was given many names. The Book of Exodus said there would be a great cry in Egypt like never before, and there was."

Walker and Decker shared a moment of eye contact.

"Possibly, there was enough information on the pillar fragment to engage the final curse, or what scientifically could be found to be some sort of extremely strategic warfare."

"What *are* you talking about?" Decker said, impatiently.

"What kind of warfare?" Walker said.

"Possibly germ… chemical… but much more pinpoint. All so called miraculous phenomena has to involve science. I mean, God, according to legend, invented science. And where there's smoke there's usually…"

"Yes, yes, your point?" Decker said.

"The hand of the Lord, the plague of destruction, or what it was most commonly called; the Angel of Death."

After a silent pause Walker said, "What is the, Angel of Death?"

Sam took a sip from her water bottle and screwed the cap back on. "Okay. The legend also allows that Moses, many years later, had possession of, or at least access to, Methuselah's Pillar. This is the same Moses who eventually broke pharaoh's stronghold on the Israelites with plague upon plague," she said and then handed Walker a Bible opened up to Exodus chapter eight with the second half of the chapter highlighted. "Read this and take a look at the photos you showed me earlier today. I think that your terrorists inadvertently released the plague of the swarming insects upon themselves and possibly even the Angel of Death."

Decker rolled his eyes. "How can that be possible? The world's top scientists can't spontaneously create life at that rate, and a corpse can decompose quickly for any number of reasons. And that…" he said pointing at the Bible, "…is Moses account of what Moses did. The Pentagon is going to need more than *that* to go on."

"You're here because you can't explain how a blizzard of flies, thick as apple sauce, choked the air out of a small army intent on finding a weapon to put an end to the civilized world, starting with you. You needed an expert in a field you know nothing about and found me. My money says you brought me a piece of legend. If that's true, logic demands we start with the legend itself."

Walker looked troubled. He shared another eye exchange with Decker. "I want to hear more about the Angel of Death," he said.

"It was the last plague recorded in Exodus. The one that crippled the mighty Egypt overnight."

"Weren't the plagues supposed to be miracles?" Walker asked.

"Of course. But you're talking about an ancient people that explained all unusual phenomena as divine intervention. I suggest we don't let 'miracles' derail us from our research. Penicillin was a miracle."

"You're twisting definitions a bit, don't you think?" Decker said.

"You think so? I'll tell you a quick story. There was a poor Scottish farmer named Fleming, working his field when he heard cries for help. He ran to investigate and found a young boy stuck in a bog, struggling and sinking. He managed to get the boy out, saving his life. The next day he was again working the field when a nobleman's carriage pulled up. The nobleman offered the poor farmer money for saving his son's life. Fleming said he couldn't take pay for doing what anyone would have surely done under the circumstances. Just then the farmer's son, Alex, walked up. The nobleman then offered to give the farmer's son the same education his son could now enjoy. The farmer, who could not turn down a gift for his son, thanked the nobleman for his generosity. The farmer's son, Alexander Fleming, turned out to be the discoverer of penicillin and the nobleman was Randolph Churchill. His son, Winston, would later contract pneumonia and cheat death again with the help of the newly discovered antibiotic."

"Touching tale," Decker said. "But I still think your point is contrived to fit your imagination."

Sam rolled her eyes. "Who healed more people, Jesus or antibiotics? For my money, both are miracles from God."

After a moment of silence, Walker said, "How did the Angel of Death kill?"

Sam shrugged. "With extreme accuracy. It went after the firstborn. People, animals, dogs, sheep, cattle. This is, of course, what I see as the major concern. If it was a miracle and only a miracle, in other words something that could never be duplicated without divine intervention, then all is good. But, if the miracle combines scientific information, a recipe of sorts, then we're dealing with the most strategic weapon on the planet."

"What do you mean?" Walker said.

"Well, you guys would know this stuff better than me but, as far as I know, there are two strategic weapons; nuclear and germ. We don't use either, not because they don't work but, because they work *too* well. Especially germ. It's uncontrollable. When you shoot a bullet, you know what's going to happen and, if you miss, you can shoot again. Very controlled. Biological warfare is far less certain. You don't know where it's going to spread and who it's going to affect. It could come back and kill the ones pulling the trigger. The Angel of Death was very specific and, if you knew what kind of shield to use, in their case, lamb's blood… you could protect yourself. It worked with one hundred percent accuracy and efficiency. If it wasn't a miracle, it was germ warfare perfected."

"Lamb's blood?" Decker said, unblinking.

"Yes. Apparently lamb's blood kept the germ from approaching, like insect repellent. Insects don't stay away because they hate the smell. Insect repellent messes with their central nervous system at short distance, causing them to retreat. It's possible the lamb's blood has a repulsion of its own, specifically aimed at the attacking microbe.

"I'm a firstborn," Decker said, as if to himself.

Walker motioned to Decker. "Why isn't he dead?"

Sam paused. *He should be dead*, she thought.

"I had sheep's blood on me when our guards died," Decker said. "So did Private Fields, the other prisoner."

Walker's brow rose. "I wonder if he was a firstborn."

Decker shrugged.

"Why did you have the blood on you?"

"Tarik slit a sheep's throat in my face to show me what he was going to do to me if I didn't tell him what he wanted to know," Decker said and then his eyes widened. "And then he grabbed Fields hair with his bloody hand and put the dripping knife to his neck."

"Jesus!" Sam said.

"That wasn't in your report," Walker said to Decker.

Decker ignored him. "Did your Angel of Death go after birds, too?"

"I don't know, assuming your question is a serious one. Birds come from eggs. The rule may not have applied or it may have applied to all of them."

"How about bugs?" he said.

Sam took a second to digest. *"The flies?"*

Decker shrugged. "Assuming this legend of yours is true."

"What about the flies?" Walker said.

Sam got out of her seat and paced. "Maybe they were all firstborn," she said. "Maybe all insects are first born. Maybe *that's* why all the flies were dead. Gentlemen, we have to find out exactly what the Angel of Death does to the human body before it's too late. We also need to find the rest of the pillar."

"Are you sure there's more?" Walker said.

"A lot more. Part of the problem is that the information is incomplete, just enough to get everyone killed. And who knows what else we might find. Methuselah knew, and the people around him lived ten times longer than we do. Coincidence?"

"How do the herbs we found in the cave lab fit in?" Decker said.

"I don't know. There were some herbs Moses would have had available to him. Maybe an extract was a necessary ingredient for whatever cake they were trying to bake. You still want to know what herb was in the cave?"

"Tell us," Decker said.

Sam produced an enlarged copy of the writing and explained how she arrived at her analysis. She made references to the presumed culture, geography and shape of the leaves in sequence to other characters and positions. In the end, they both awaited her answer.

"So what is it?" Decker said.

"If I tell you correctly, you get me to a cadaver," she said.

"What cadaver?" Walker said.

"One of the decomposed from the cave."

Walker shook his head. "No. I can't get you that kind of clearance."

"It's in biocontainment?" Sam asked.

Walker's brow raised. "Uh, yes. And that's part of the reason. They don't let just anyone in."

"I'm not just anyone," she said boldly. "I'm your translator and I need more input."

Walker sighed. "Still. I can't promise you'll be allowed in."

"But you'll try?"

Decker leaned forward. "What's the herb?"

"Angelica."

The agents didn't blink. Finally Decker leaned forward and said, "What's the attraction?"

"I want in."

"You don't even know where 'in' is," Decker said.

"I don't care. I want in."

"Why?"

"That's classified," Sam said, without a smile. "You want answers. I'll get answers."

Walker looked at Decker and then said to Sam, "You'll need to clear your schedule for tomorrow."

"Maybe longer," Decker added.

Sam paused to study their faces. "To meet your scientists?"

"Yes," Walker said. "We'll meet with you in the morning to see what the lab tests have discovered as planned and then leave from there."

"To where?"

Again the two agents exchanged eye contact. "I guess you can call it *our* lab," Walker said. "There are other scientists there who need your input. We might have you back by the end of the day."

"End of the day?" Sam said in disbelief. "Where is your lab, underground in New Jersey?"

"Maryland," Decker said. "We call it '*The Institute*'. Maybe you've heard of it?"

"*USAMRIID?*" she said, pronouncing it you-sam-rid.

Walker gave Decker a look, annoyed. He then looked at her and said, "Yes.

Of course, Sam had heard of *The Institute*. USAMRIID, or the United States Army Medical Research Institute of Infectious Diseases, was one of a select few labs in the world that no scientist in their right mind was in a hurry to visit.

"BSL-4?" Sam said, referring to the strictest bio safety level at the institute, a place where the world's deadliest microbiotic monsters were jailed in extreme quarantine.

"Yes," Decker said. "You still *want in?*"

"Absolutely."

"There won't be any TV cameras following you on this one," Walker said.

"Good. They're never my idea to bring along in the first place."

25

Sam's career had posed many exciting challenges and her work had contributed to unlocking doors of mystery and tweaking the history of ancient times, but *never* with significant present day implications that stretched beyond the museum's bank account and her own fame and popularity. She sat in her office on the third floor of the Metropolitan Museum hunched over the lab results. The morning sun was still low and Central Park was still in the museum's shadow. But as surely as the sun would rise on the park and chase the frost off the grass, she would decipher the artifact's archaic data though, hopefully, with better results than the late insurgents of the Afghani cave.

Her normally clean and organized desktop was covered with printouts, photocopies in various magnifications, open reference books blooming with yellow post-it tabs , maps of the early middle east, a half empty cup of black coffee and, of course, the ancient artifact itself. She needed more time to study the writing. If only she could clear her mind of all the connective data and settle in with the characters and patterns, she was certain it would illuminate before her.

There was a knock at the door.

"It's open."

Eddie Washington stuck his head in. "They're here, Sam."

"Thanks, Eddie. Send them in."

Decker and Walker walked in, each with a Starbucks grande in hand. Either they were dressed in the same clothes as yesterday or so close to it Sam couldn't tell the difference. "Morning, Sam," Walker said. "How long have you been here?"

"I got here two coffees ago. I couldn't sleep very well. How 'bout you guys?"

"Couple hours, maybe," Walker said. "Couldn't get your stuff out of my head."

"Slept like a log," Decker said and then took a careful sip.

"Sweet dreams or nightmares?" Sam asked.

"Dreams," he said and sipped.

"Anything good?" Sam asked, with a smile..

"I dreamt I was sleeping."

Sam paused, and then returned her attention back to the report details. "Isn't that like a double negative or something?"

Decker shook his head. "Double positive. Turned five hours into ten. Did you get the artifact age test results back?"

"Yes. I was just looking them over."

Walker walked around the desk and looked over her shoulder. "Is your theory gaining support?"

Sam grunted. "Let's just say it's expanding."

Decker took another sip and deadpanned, "The artifact is a billion years old and was brought here from outer space by an alien who turns out to be a direct ancestor of Obama."

Sam looked up at him. "If only. Actually, the results present more questions than answers. The wood turns out to be one hundred and forty-five million years old. That's borderline between the Jurassic and Cretaceous periods. A landmark time, paleontologically speaking. The dinosaurs roamed the near-tropical Earth. No polar ice caps, no snow anywhere. Flowering plants had just evolved and were rapidly changing the face of the planet. Conifers dominated the landscape of continents that were close enough to pole-vault across to each other."

"Sounds like paradise," Walker said.

Decker nodded. "Yeah, for about an hour, then you'd be eaten."

Sam had to smile. "Dinosaurs didn't eat humans, gentlemen. On the evolutionary clock, humans didn't show up until, well, about now. Anyway, there was a minor mass extinction and most of the enormous sauropod dinosaurs, marine reptiles and clams died out."

"Clams?" Decker said. "Hard to imagine life without clams."

Sam looked up at Decker and had some brief eye contact. She smiled and shook her head. "Basically anything living in shallow waters. No one knows what caused this extinction but we have lots of petrified wood from this time. The only problem is that *our* wood doesn't match up with any of those or *any other* known tree species, living *or* extinct."

Decker shrugged. "So you missed one. What's the problem?"

"It's unnerving," Sam said. "Where there's one there *has* to be more, but there isn't."

"Can't it be a freak?" Decker said.

"We're talking about a tree, not a virus. There *are* no mutant trees."

Decker shrugged. "Again, so what? Why should we care what it's written on? Why would anyone care what the Declaration of Independence is written on? What matters is what it says... no?"

"Origin matters a lot. It helps us understand context. Obviously, the inscriptions had to be written when the wood was already petrified because man didn't exist when this tree was alive. But there *are* microscopic indications that some of the wood cells were divided before the wood had crystallized."

Decker rolled his eyes. " As if Adam had written on the pillar before it was petrified."

"But that's impossible," Walker said.

"I know!" Sam said loudly, tossing the report in his direction. *"You* tell *me* what it says. It would be nice if *something* would match *somewhere.* Cross-referencing is a logical and comfortable way to identify and translate ancient information. This artifact, across the board, has no equals."

Walker picked up the report and stared at it. After a few moments, he put it back on the desk and said, "I don't understand a thing I'm reading here."

"Well, don't feel so bad. I *do* and I don't understand it, either," Sam said.

Decker shook his head. "Look, it doesn't matter, we're going to have to pass on this for now and move on. There are more important things on the agenda and we have a schedule to keep."

"When do we have to leave?" Sam said.

"Right now if you're ready," Decker said. "There's a helicopter waiting ."

"Where is it, out front? I should warn you, the meter maids take their job seriously and we might go out to find it towed."

"I dropped a quarter. We have two more minutes."

"You didn't tell me I had to punch a clock."

Walker cleared his throat. "Speaking of punching a clock, I've been authorized to offer you a contract if it turns out we need your continued help."

Sam stared at him and then turned to Decker and said. "He's kidding... right?"

Decker shook his head. "Show her the fax," he said to Walker.

Walker paused. "Yes, there's something else. I don't mean to repeat myself, but I must stress that keeping this information confidential is of the..."

"Show her the fax," Decker repeated and then turned to Sam. "Food for thought on the ride down."

Walker reached into his blazer and pulled out a folded sheet of paper. He handed it to Sam and said, "Does this look familiar?"

Sam unfolded the paper and saw a dark circle that reached the borders of the page with a single pale image the size and bumpy texture of a golf ball, with occasional black dots and a squiggled line in the center. She didn't need to see it more than a few seconds before she recognized it. "Yeah, it's one of the characters from the artifact."

"The snake in the circle?" Walker said.

"Yes."

"It's also a photo magnified a hundred and fifty thousand times," Decker said.

"What!" Sam said.

"It's an electron microscope's photo of a single strand RNA virus. Our scientists found it in the body of *this* guy," Walker said, handing Sam a photo.

"He was infested with it."

Sam took the photo. "One of the decomposed insurgents." she said.

"That's right."

"So yesterday, when you asked if the character might be a germ, you weren't kidding."

"That's right."

"But that's impossible. It has to be a coincidence."

"That's what our scientists also said. But we thought you might find it interesting."

"Even Adam couldn't know what a virus looked like. There was no electricity, much less microscopes."

"You're the one with the active imagination here. You tell us," Decker said.

Sam stared blankly. She didn't have a theory for anything else the character could be.

Walker looked at his watch. "Can we talk some more in the helicopter?"

Sam nodded and motioned to a brown leather suitcase on the floor by the bookshelf.

"I *think* I'm all set. Though, I didn't pack any lamb's blood. Did I mention I'm a firstborn?"

26

Sam buckled-up in one of the rear seats behind Walker and next to Decker. They each put on headphones in order to hear each other talk over the noise of the engine and blade. Lift off was smooth and, in moments they were passing over the Statue of Liberty on their way to Fort Detrick, Maryland.

Sam glanced at Decker. Through all his glibness and attitude, she felt safe with him though she was sure there were many who wouldn't, especially if they were his enemy. He appeared relaxed in jeans, scraggly beard and a black leather jacket. As a DIA agent, she imagined he probably had learned to look comfortable in everything from a tuxedo to whatever they had him wearing to blend in with the Afghani insurgents. "I don't suppose they serve breakfast on this flight?" she said, trying to break the ice.

He turned and paused, taking a moment to see her. "Hungry?"

"A little. All I've had so far is coffee."

He frowned thoughtfully. "What you're going to see at the Institute will probably quiet your appetite."

"Don't bet on it. I like to eat."

His eyes briefly scanned her figure but said nothing. He reached into his jacket and said, "Have you ever eaten carob?"

"You mean, like in a protein bar?"

"No, like a carob pod," he said, producing what looked like a dark brown bean pod. "It grows on locust trees."

"What do you do with *that*?" Sam said doubtfully.

Decker bit off the end as if it were beef jerky and chewed. "They sell them in the Afghani markets. I kind of got used to them. They're not bad." He offered the pod to her.

"What else have you gotten used to?" Sam said accepting the pod. It was as hard as wood.

"You don't want to know. Don't bite the seeds unless you want to break a tooth."

She bit into the tip and tore off a piece. At first, it had all the taste and texture of dried leather but then a pleasant flavor, a little like chocolate, crept in. "Not terrible."

"Keep it, I have more," he said, then rested his head back.

"Thanks," she said. He nodded and disappeared back into his mental cave. *Whatever*, she continued to chew and looked out her window. At ten thousand feet, towns and cities came and went, each one with roads, or arteries, flowing to and from. She imagined the cars and trucks as cells traveling along the bloodstream, carrying passengers. Some friendly, some not. The cells traveled in and out of organs, possibly dropping off a passenger or picking up a new one. Her mind flashed back to the decomposed bodies in the photos. What could make them deteriorate so quickly? Even the deadliest thread viruses, at least the known ones, took more than the few minutes this needed. How could one of these cars damage a city so quickly, so utterly? A single man with a gun, a machine gun, unobstructed, could cause a lot of damage, but not enough to kill the whole city. And he *would* be obstructed. He'd be met as soon as the gun was fired... no... sooner. As soon as he got out of the car.

She looked back at Decker. He appeared to be sleeping. Maybe he hadn't gotten the good night's sleep he'd claimed.

Two hours later, the Blackhawk landed on a helipad in a field at Fort Detrick. The fort looked like a busy town surrounded by walls and high security fencing. They hurried from the helicopter to a white Suburban. The temperature was milder than the New York weather they had just left, and sunny. The SUV hurried them past what she was told was the gym and toward the iron fence of USAMRIID, as clearly indicated by a large brass sign on a green lawn.

"This place is like a fort within a fort," Sam said as they passed by another sign that said "Building 1425," and another that said "Crozier Building," at what looked like a main entrance.

"You haven't seen anything yet," Walker said.

They continued to a tall iron gate at the side of the building. With the nod of a soldier at a sentry booth, the gate opened and they drove in and stopped. The Suburban immediately emptied and she stood before a huge windowless yellow brick building. Several armed soldiers were watchful as Walker quickly led the way to what looked like a steel silo against the building and a door.

"It's hard to imagine anyone unwanted getting in," she said.

"Actually we're more concerned about something getting out," Decker said, following behind her as Walker slid a card in the card-reader and buzzed open the door.

"No finger print or retina scan needed?"

"Only card readers, no bio access," Walker said.

As she walked through, Sam felt a breeze follow her in. "Negative pressure?" she said.

Walker nodded. "Exactly. The building covers ten acres and nothing airborne gets out of the doors and there are virtually no windows. The tall smokestacks on the roof are HEPA exhaust filters that create a vacuum within the entire building and kill anything that passes through them, keeping the exiting air safe. Some of the stacks are specific to particular confinement areas."

"Like Level Four?" Sam said.

Walker turned and smiled thinly. "Especially, Level Four."

Inside were more soldiers in camouflage fatigues to greet them. Walker signed in and instructed Sam to do the same. "It doesn't matter who you are or what the occasion is, everyone must always sign in." Then they were all given color badges that would give them access to a place Walker called the "Slammer."

"What's the Slammer?" Sam asked.

"That's where we'll stay if anything goes wrong and then we'll stay in there for the rest of our brief lives," Decker said falling into step with Walker, alongside Sam.

"How comforting," Sam said as Walker gave him a look. They walked through a maze of corridors. Soldiers and civilians, probably scientists and technicians, wearing badges, were everywhere. Everyone seemed very busy, no one chatting or standing idle. They walked past a long windowed room that had a sign that said 'Biosafety Level Zero'. People inside were dressed normally behind mostly white and stainless steel equipment without any visible germ protection.

"So where do you guys make the bio bombs?" Sam asked.

"In Biosafety Level One," Decker said, to Sam's surprise.

Walker sighed, annoyed, keeping the fast pace. "You have to remember not to take what he says seriously. There *is* no Level One and there *is* no weapons development. We're strictly defense here. We research ways to protect soldiers against biological weaponry and infectious diseases. We specialize in drugs, vaccines and biocontainment."

"Come on," Sam said doubtfully. "It's hard to believe that the Army doesn't have some offensively minded bio program going on somewhere."

Walker shrugged. "A constant accusation we have to endure. During World War II, we did have germ warfare research going on here. The Army labs were experimenting with lethal bacteria strains and viruses that could be loaded and deployed in bombs. But in 1969, Nixon outlawed the development of biological weapons in the United States and USAMRIID was formed. The labs were converted to develop protective vaccines and discover ways to control lethal microorganisms. "

"Then ask him why there's no biosafety one," Decker said.

Sam looked at Walker to respond.

"I'm glad he finds time to joke at a time like this. I don't know. Why do women's sizes start at zero, skip one and go to two?"

"So you think a woman had something to do with the biosafety numbering?" Sam said.

Walker rolled his eyes. "Yes. That's my official answer," he said. "You can quote me on that." They passed by another window in the wall.

Around the edge, Sam could see that the glass in the window was much thicker than the others, like at an aquarium. She saw someone in a blue spacesuit amongst rows of caged monkeys. "And this is?" she asked.

"The Ebola Suite," Decker said.

Sam looked at him doubtfully. "More jokes?"

"Not this time," Walker said. "That's your Level Four containment right there. And that's Ernest. He's the caretaker. He feeds the monkeys, cleans their cages and checks on their physical condition. I would bet that no one on the planet has seen the effect Ebola has on a host more than Ernest."

Sam nodded in wonderment. "Must take a lot of getting used to. I'm a little freaked-out just being on the other side of the glass from the deadliest virus on earth."

"Used to be the deadliest," Walker said. "Until last week."

Sam looked at Walker. "That's assuming it's a virus."

27

Sam followed the two agents through another door that required Walker to swipe his card. More soldiers checking badges and nodded hello as they passed. She followed the agents, went up a flight of stairs and then past a conference room that had a map of the world on the wall. A meeting of some kind was in progress. Beyond the meeting room was a cluster of offices, one with the name "Captain Harvey Ross" inscribed on a half opened door.

Walker knocked lightly on the door.

A man sat behind a desk on a swivel seat; he spun halfway around to see who was there. The man was sixtyish with full pure white hair combed straight back. His face was full with a round nose and rosy cheeks. "Ah good, you're here," he said to the men and then picked up his phone and said, "Tell Captain Drake they've arrived." His face brightened. "I know who *you* are." He stood up, stocky and not tall. "Thank you for coming. I'm a big fan of yours, Doctor Conway."

"Call me Sam," she said, extending her hand across the desktop.

Ross met her hand. A firm but gentle grip. "There's no substitute for meeting someone in person," he said, then looked to Walker and said, "Is there, Bruce?"

Walker smiled. "Yeah, well sometimes a picture can be worth a thousand words, but we didn't have one on file."

Sam frowned. "I'm confused."

Ross piped up. "Agent Walker doesn't catch much news outside the agency. He didn't know you. He thought 'Doctor Sam Conway' was a man. Everyone assumed he knew so no one mentioned it to him. It doesn't matter. Have a seat," he said.

Sam smiled. "Why didn't you tell him?" she said to Decker.

"I did... in your office when he first met you. I whispered to him that you were 'Sam.' He recovered better than I hoped."

Sam nodded. "I remember that."

"Little things like that entertain him," Walker said.

"He's bad," she said.

"You have no idea," Walker said.

"Well, I'm glad to see we're all getting to know each other," Ross said and looked at Sam. "The men have filled us in on your theory, but there seem to be some pieces missing. Maybe you can take a minute to tell me in your own words."

"There are plenty of pieces missing, Captain. Literally. Regardless of the pillar's origin, we have only a small piece of a large record."

"So I hear. Do you think there's more somewhere?"

"I don't know. Obviously, there used to be, but without knowing where this came from, finding the rest of the pillar isn't likely."

"Maybe we'll find that out when we get Tarik," Walker said.

Decker shook his head. "Tarik wants it, too. If he had it, it would have been there. My guess is that he's barking up the same trees we are."

"But the advantage is his because he's probably planning something to do with it and we don't know what that is," Sam said.

Decker nodded. "That's for sure. And the test run will be attention grabbing."

Ross lifted a finger as he rose from his seat. "Ah, but he's already had a test run and the results are for both sides to see. Now here's where we get the chance to level the playing field a bit. He has a team and we have a team. His team has a jump on ours but he also lost a few members. We have a better translator in Sam and our lab is far more advanced than his."

Ross looked past Sam at the man who just entered the room. "Captain Drake. Sam, I'd like to introduce our team physician," he said. Drake stood tall, forty-something, with short thick black hair, craggy complexion, deep-set blue eyes and a substantial nose. He reminded Sam of Mister Spock with human ears.

Sam wasn't sure what team he was talking about or why it would need a physician but she smiled and shook his hand. "Hi, I'm Sam Conway."

"I know. Pleased to meet you. We're very grateful for your help."

"I haven't done anything."

"We're an optimistic bunch," Decker said dryly.

"Then let's get to work," Sam said and then looked at Walker. "I don't think we'll be getting me back to New York tonight."

"Is anybody hungry?" Ross asked. "Once we get into containment, we may be in there for a while."

"I had a carob pod, or whatever you call it, on the flight here. I think I can squeeze in a touch more," Sam said.

"Carob pod?" Ross said.

"Carob comes from the locust tree. Considering the direction our research is taking..." Decker said, straight faced.

"Actually I don't care what I eat as long as it's outside the containment areas," Sam said.

Ross swiped a sheet of paper from the fax machine as he passed. "Yes, well, Fort Detrick has its own dining facility," he said putting on his reading glasses for the fax. "Today's... Thursday. They're serving beef pot roast, Creole chicken, steamed rice, parsley buttered potatoes, lima beans and corn. They also have a decent salad bar and burgers are always available if you prefer."

"Let's go!" Sam said.

After a brisk walk to the café, Sam was ready to eat everything she saw. On the way over she had figured herself for the chicken but the pot roast looked too good to pass on. They carried their trays to a round table and quickly became comfortable with their meals. Curiously, Decker had passed on the menu and filled his tray with two cheeseburgers, a bowl of oatmeal and a bowl of fresh fruit from the salad bar. Sam was going to ask if he was in some sort of transition diet from Afghanistan but thought it better to mind her own business.

"The dining facility is fairly new and the food is good," Ross said. "It's open to both soldiers and civilians."

Sam nodded and looked around. A graphic of Martian Luther King hung from the ceiling. "Interesting décor," she said.

"They change it from time to time," Ross said. "It's in honor of Black History Month. Last month, it was Teddy Roosevelt."

Sam nodded as she squeezed a lemon and dropped it in to her water.

"Have you been able to make much headway with the translation?" Ross said and then filled his mouth with potato mopped beef.

"No. My focus has primarily been on the pillar itself. In a case like this origin greatly impacts the message. And considering the possible source and the aftermath of getting it wrong, a quick read isn't going to get us where we want to be. In fact, even though this is the oldest writing I've ever encountered, I need to consider that I may be reading post modern science. The process can't be rushed without great risk."

"It has to be rushed," Walker said.

"I agree," Drake said.

"We've witnessed the results of a partial translation, some of us more closely than others," Sam said with a glance in Decker's direction. He squeezed gobs of ketchup onto one burger and none on the other. Was he *trying* to be strange?

Drake pointed randomly with his fork while swallowing. "Their controlled environment didn't allow for much error. Our facility is the best in the world. Miscalculations and mistranslations will help *guide* our research in the proper containment."

Sam pursed her lips. "Maybe. But maybe not. Do we even know yet what we're trying to contain?"

Drake finished a noisy slurp of coffee as he nodded. "We're beginning to."

Sam was surprised. She looked at the others, who were all looking at her, except for Decker, who was clearly more interested in his oatmeal. "What do we know?" she said.

Walker was about to speak but Ross stilled him with the raise of a hand. "We know we're dealing with something we've never seen before and we know the artifact has something to do with it."

"You also seem to think there is some sort of super germ involved," Sam said. "Or why else would we be here?"

The men looked at each other, but none answered. The hamburgers eaten, Decker had now mixed his fresh fruit into his oatmeal and stirred in some Equal. Sam figured he was either a nutritional genius or retarded. In either case… cute for an assassin type.

"So, are we dealing with a chemical agent or a super germ?" Sam said, impatient for their answer.

"It's much more complicated than that," Drake said.

Decker spooned some oatmeal, swallowed and said, "Both."

Sam frowned. "Both?" she said, unsure if he was talking about his food or agents involved in the deaths.

Ross nodded. "I've heard about your theory and I must say it sounds rather... fantastic."

Sam chuckled. "I think the word you were looking for is 'impossible'."

Ross shook his head. "We are both scientists, Sam, and have a vitally important job to do. We believe half of what we see and experiment with possibilities until one seems to fit. Then we try to chop it down. If it stands, we invite others to swing the axe. We never get anything to a hundred percent. Our problem here is time. We have an extremely lethal entity in our midst and desperately need to get a handle on it before someone else figures out how to aim and fire it at us. Your credentials speak for themselves. What I believe doesn't matter. What seems to matter is what the artifact's message is. If your theory, right or wrong, helps you give us a better translation than our enemy, then maybe we win this round."

Sam nodded. "Speaking of the artifact, if you don't have any objections, I'd like to take it with us."

"Into BSL-4?" Ross said.

"Yes."

"Why?" Drake said.

"I'd like to keep it with me as a reference while we investigate."

After a moment of silence, with the exception of Decker chewing, Ross said, "I'd rather not bring the artifact itself into risk of bio-contamination. We can have an image downloaded for your viewing at any of several monitors in containment."

Sam nodded compliantly. "That's fine."

Drake finished, picked up his tray. "I need to make a few preparations for the viewing. See you on the other side."

28

Decker followed Sam and Ross downstairs and along a corridor to the Level-Four containment suite. He had been down this way only twice before. Both for training exercises. The first time was a visit that ended at BSL-3. For that, he'd received all the required vaccinations which included yellow fever, Q fever, Rift Valley fever, the VEE, EEE, and WEE complex, tularemia, anthrax and botulism. The study cadaver of that day was an anthrax victim, opened up like a Rand McNally road map highlighting all the pertinent points of interest the spore had ravaged. The second trip for Decker was more memorable. No vaccinations would have been required because a Level Four hot agent is lethal, without cure. There he watched the freshly dissected monkey's organs turn to jelly before his eyes. Anthrax had suddenly seemed safe and cozy. Ebola Zaire virus was the most feared hot agent at USAMRIID, causing the fastest and most devastating viral attack on living tissue ever seen by human eyes... until now.

There was only one locker room to change into the spacesuits essential for Level-Four entry. Ross tugged and opened the door against the suck of air. The usual hiss of negative air pressure designed to prevent deadly hot agents from drifting out, drafted around them. The room was small and had a few lockers along one wall, a few shelves and a mirror over a deep stainless steel sink.

"First we need to change into some surgical scrubs," Ross said to Sam. He reached to a shelf of green shirts and pants. "These should fit. You can't wear anything underneath. No underwear. No bra. Decker and I will wait outside for you to change."

Decker thought of a wise crack but resisted.

"Thank you," she said. "I'll just be a minute."

They stepped back outside and in what seemed like thirty seconds the door reopened.

"Your turn, gentlemen."

"What kept you," Decker said as he passed her and then sniffed the air. "Jasmine?"

"Yes... how'd you know?"

He smiled thinly. "I, uh, was once a tea merchant."

"You? Really?" she said.

He nodded. "Yeah." He couldn't remember ever seeing anyone look so good in scrubs before, but he kept his eyes straight. The last thing he needed now was a distraction and Sam Conway could be that and more.

Decker and Ross quickly dressed and let Sam back in. Ross handed her a cloth surgical cap. She put it on without hesitation, tucking curly blond locks under the elastic rim. She didn't appear nervous, but Decker figured she had to be. He'd heard of professionals freaking out, panic stricken, under the confinements of Level Four. They would be removed to the disinfecting shower area to calm down.

Ross led the way, barefoot, through the only other door, leading them into Level Two. Again the air hissed as they entered into a deep blue light... ultraviolet light. Viruses are destroyed by ultraviolet light, which sterilizes their ability to reproduce. The door sucked close behind them.

Sam looked back at Decker, her perfect teeth glowing bright white. "When do we get our UV sunglasses?" she said as they continued through a shower stall equipped with soap and more ultraviolet light.

"As long as you're not a virus, you should be fine."

The shower stall led into a bathroom. On the wall was a shelf that had clean white socks for their bare feet.

"Tube socks. One size fits all," Ross said tossing Sam and Decker each a pair.

Socks on, they pushed through another door into what was known as the staging area, Level Three. As in the previous room, there was a sink, but this room also had a desk with a phone.

"Nice chair," Sam said, referring to a cylindrical plastic hazardous box blazed with a warning symbol in the shape of a pointy red flower.

Ross smiled. "The government spares no expense. The hatbox might be a tad short for Decker but works perfect for my stumpy legs."

Decker shook his head. The old guy had a way of keeping you relaxed in an otherwise scary place.

"Hatbox?" Sam said.

"We call it the hatbox or ice cream container. Don't worry, it's empty."

"I won't ask what normally goes in it," Sam said.

"Just don't get too curious and open one on this side of Level Four," Decker said.

Ross smiled. "That's actually good advice. They'll put us all in the Slammer and that won't be fun, I can promise you that."

"What exactly happens in the Slammer?" she asked.

"A Level Four biocontainment hospital where all your doctors and nurses are in spacesuits to protect themselves from you," Decker said. It's usually a life sentence, which isn't very long."

Ross nodded. "Death is the quickest way out of the slammer." He dropped a box of latex gloves and adhesive tape onto the desk. "You die and go into the submarine, our morgue."

"Okay, no peeking into hatboxes, I get it. Now what?"

"Baby powder," Ross said and then underhand tossed a white plastic bottle to Decker. Ross began tearing off strips of sticky tape and hanging them in a row on the edge of the desk. Standard procedure.

Sam frowned. "Bab…"

"Keeps away diaper rash, and sticky gloves," Decker said, powdering his hands and then motioned for Sam to hold out hers. She did and he "salted" them liberally with powder before tossing the bottle back to Ross, who had finished with the tape. He then slipped his latex gloves on smoothly, took a strip of tape off the desk and began taping himself. First, he ran the tape around the cuff of his glove, attaching it securely to the sleeve of his surgical gown. Then he taped his socks to his pants. No drafts. One layer of protection completed. He looked over to see how he could further coach the rookie only to find that Sam had already finished, waiting for the next move.

"Sterile gloves that you would find in an operating room, for example, come with their own powder but, since we aren't concerned with infecting anyone or allergies to latex, we use the older cheaper version," Ross said.

"Very comforting to see the country's germ defense is so budget conscious," Sam said.

Ross had just put on the last strip of tape, his round face further reddened from bending over. He focused for a moment on the taping job of his two guests, and then seemed satisfied and motioned for them to follow to his right into an antechamber where bright blue 'Chemturian' spacesuits were hanging on racks. Ross pulled one off the rack with both hands and gave it to her.

"This is heavy," Sam said.

"That's okay," Decker said. "The thicker the better, as far as we're concerned."

"Absolutely," Ross agreed. "Lay it on the floor, open it and slide in feet first."

Decker chose a suit and stepped in. He pulled it up to his armpits and slid his arms through until his fingers filled the factory-attached brown gloves. He wiggled his fingers. A bit stiff. The gloves were made of even heavier plastic than the rest of the suit for the handling, or mishandling, of potentially dangerous needles, knives and sharp bones. The slightest puncture would mean time. Time in the Slammer to evaluate the probability of lethal contamination. Valuable time, needed to catch up with whatever Tarik was planning.

When Sam had suited up, Ross handed her the helmet and briefed her on procedures. This would be interesting, Decker thought, as he watched him lower it over her head and look into the clear faceplate to see her reaction. At USAMRIID, they say you can't predict when, if, or how bad a person will lose control of their mind inside a bio-spacesuit. Panic happens, mostly to the inexperienced, but sometimes even to the veterans. People have been known to rip off their suits and breathe in BSL-4 air in a moment of claustrophobic insanity. The first hint of trouble is usually given immediately after the helmet seals. Eyes begin to widen and flutter with fear. They sweat, turn blue, claw at the suit, try to rip it open for air, lose balance, fall down, moan, cry, scream.

"You okay?" Ross said loudly.

Decker heard a muffled, "Yes."

Ross nodded and closed the oiled zipper across the suit's chest. The zipper made a popping sound as it sealed shut. The instant the helmet sealed the faceplate fogged. So far, there wasn't any panic. Decker reached over to a wall and pulled down a coiled yellow air hose and plugged it into the spacesuit. He knew she would hear a roar of air flow in and pressurize the suit. The blue suit ballooned fat and hard and her faceplate cleared, revealing a broad smile.

"I feel a cool breeze blowing through my hair," she sang, muffled.

"As long as it's not from a tear carrying anthrax spores, I wouldn't worry about it," Ross said.

Decker shook his head and finished suiting up. *Definitely my kind of girl,* he thought.

Ross came over to Decker and peeked in his faceplate to check his face for fear.

"Is it okay if I don't sing?" Decker said.

"I'll guess we'll just have to live with the disappointment," Ross said, eying the suit closely.

Ross led the way through a stainless-steel door well decorated with a large biohazard symbol and warnings. CAUTION. BIOHAZARD. DO NOT ENTER WITHOUT WEARING VENTILATED SUIT. The door closed behind them with a loud clank. They stood silently for a moment in a small totally stainless-steel room. The Level Four airlock had been described by someone who understood its fortitude as a place where two worlds meet. A place where the hot zone of the planet's most lethal microbes touch the normal world. Some use this area to pray and cross themselves before proceeding through the next door. Though it is procedurally forbidden, some entering this area will wear religious amulets and charms under their suits.

Decker had no use for such superstitions. He was a subscriber of the "nothing to fear but fear itself" theory. He'd escaped death many times and, as far as he was concerned, he was playing with house money. If God wanted him dead, He could have left well enough alone years ago and had His wish. And if there was a God, which was a big *if,* considering the areas of creation he had the pleasure to visit, The Almighty didn't need little good luck charms to keep someone from the proverbial dragon's jaw. All dependence upon religious traditions was bred from fear and clouded rational judgment. Period. Maybe that was what he liked about Sam Conway. Yeah, she was crazy all right, but in a way he could like.

Decker looked at Sam. Ready to go. Wearing a bio-spacesuit and hungry for whatever was next. She was the real deal all right, not just some beautiful Hollywood impersonation designed for big ratings on the History or Discovery Channel. She was a modern day Lewis and Clark embodied in a raw scientist. And right now, she was blazing a trail in an uncharted wilderness. And maybe... just maybe... she could lead him across the path of a certain snake named Tarik. And maybe after that, he might allow himself some distraction time.

29

Tarik surveyed his three chosen operatives. At least that's what he told them they were. He glanced down to his desktop again. The names of the three men as they sat, from left to right, were sketched out on a piece of paper. His desk was shown as a rectangle and the men's names were in circles in front of the desk. Simple enough. If his new assistant, Ottah, had seated them or listed them in the wrong order, Dulai would have another volunteer for his experiments. With the turnover rate so high, it seemed that capable assistants were becoming increasingly difficult to find.

Tarik smiled proudly at the men. "I once sat where you men are now sitting. I was chosen for a great and glorious mission and now so have you. You were not simply chosen at random. Allah knows you completely and has decided that now is the time to pick you up as tools in his hands. Your record of service was of the highest, but you were not only chosen because you are the top of the top. In a vision I also saw each of you, decorated with crowns of honor," Tarik said, trying not to be distracted by the ticker tape on CNBC.

The big screen behind the 'chosen' was never off during trading hours and Isonics, a stock he'd acquired a week ago, was down again. His smile eroded and he suddenly wanted to kill someone. Maybe later. Take care of this business first. He exhaled and reminded himself that *that* stock, along with a few other security defense companies he'd been accumulating, would shortly be hitting new highs while the rest of the market would be crashing. All because of him. His focus returned. He read concern on the faces of the chosen.

"Your mission is completely confidential. Only I and your contacts know the next step you'll be taking. You will meet your personal contact in the airport of your destination. They will know you by your luggage. When you retrieve your bag at the distribution belt, you will be contacted by someone with a password. You will reply with your password and then you will be given your next instruction. Does everyone understand so far?"

All heads nodded.

"Are there any questions?"

The chosen took turns looking, shrugging and shaking their heads at each other and then at Tarik.

"Excellent. Another confirmation from above that I have selected the right men for this mission. Praise be to Allah."

Tarik pressed the intercom button on his desk phone labeled 'lab' and said, "Doctor?"

"Dulai here."

"Bring up the carry-ons," he said, and then looked back to his chosen with a comforting smile. "I have prepared everything for you to the finest detail to ensure the success of your missions."

They all smiled back, but none dared to speak.

Shortly, the elevator door opened and Dulai appeared with a box. He set the box on a short table in front of the chosen and took out three thin attaché cases, handing one to each of the men.

Tarik waved his hand and said, "You may open the cases. Doctor Dulai will instruct you."

Dulai waited as the three opened their respective attaches. "In the yellow envelope you will find all the documentation you need to get you to your initial destination. Tickets, passports, medical records, some miscellaneous brochures of local interest, a credit card and a date book with a history of activities you have been involved in over the last few months. Read them carefully."

"You are on a business trip, my brothers. God's business," Tarik said, and then motioned for Dulai to continue.

You will also find a small first aid kit with all the typical ingredients, less any fluids that would draw the closer attention of security. Band-Aids, some assorted pills and capsules should you get a headache or stomach pain. Airline food is different than what you're used to and can take a little getting used to. Combine that with the motion of the flight and you might find yourself nauseous. The yellow capsules should get rid of any discomfort... very quickly."

The chosen all looked through their papers and kits. One lifted out a zip-lock bag and looked at Dulai quizzically.

"Ah, Doctor, you didn't tell them about their snack," Tarik said.

"I was just about to get to that," Dulai said. "Our Sheik has instructed that I supply you each with jellybeans and a brownie to snack on during the flight."

"The jellybeans are from my own personal stock," Tarik said. "And the brownies... I had brought in from Italy."

Dulai slowly gave him a look.

"They are the best in the world. In fact, I would like each of your opinions on the brownies, as well as the jellybeans."

One of the chosen began opening the plastic bag.

"Not now!" Tarik yelled, causing the man to freeze in place. Tarik then exhaled and found his smile. "It's for the flight. I want you to have a relaxed flight before the real work starts."

All the chosen smiled with him, nodding, and neatly packed away their goody-bags.

"From this time forward, you will have no further contact with each other until the mission is over and we all celebrate your success together. When you land, your contact will find you at the luggage recovery. You will go with him and be briefed on the next part of your mission."

30

The door opened against the suction of air and Sam held her breath. She followed Ross into Level Four, Decker close behind. Her human eyes couldn't see the deadly germs that her spacesuit was protecting her from but, in her mind's eye, she saw microbes the size of tennis balls parting as they moved through a narrow cement block corridor, various rooms opened on either side. Yellow air hoses dangled from the walls for the traveler's convenience. She made a quick note of the thick goopy epoxy paint on everything. All electrical outlets and switches were sealed with more goop.

Decker gave her a thumbs-up and then held another one of those air hoses up for her view. "Remember this? It will be loud," he shouted with a muffled voice and plugged one of the air hoses into her suit. Suddenly, all she could hear was a roar of air filling her helmet. Again, the air was cool and felt good inflating the suit away from her body. Ross opened a cabinet and pulled out three pair of yellow boots. He read the sizes and handed them out. She followed his example and slid the soft feet of her spacesuit into the boots. Ross then unplugged his air hose again and waved them to follow him down the hallway. She followed his simple lead.

Sam paused at the doorway of the room filled with monkey cages. Some of the monkeys began to hoot and screech at her presence while others were motionless.

Decker tapped her on the shoulder and said, "Ebola."

Sam turned to look at him and then back to the monkeys. She had been to Africa many times and was aware of the horrors this virus had brought to unsuspecting villages. The monkeys that weren't wildly active, as they should be with visitors passing by, were not only motionless but also expressionless. One of the first areas attacked were the connective tissues in the face, leaving victims with the inability to frown, smile, wince or anything else that required facial muscles, leaving a mask-like appearance. All the monkeys here, active or comatose, were doomed.

"They're very close to a vaccine."

"Really?"

He shrugged. "So they say," he said and motioned for her to continue.

Sam hurried her pace to catch up to Ross and Decker as they traveled through a maze of hallways. Finally, Ross turned left into a room where a cadaver lay on a stainless steel table and Doctor Drake was off to the side viewing an electron microscope monitor. The cadaver was easily recognizable as one of the decomposed from the Afghanistan cave. The chest cavity was opened. Sam slowed to look as Ross went directly to Drake. Inside the cavity every organ had experienced the same decomposition as the skin. She suddenly felt she'd be more comfortable back at the Ebola Suite.

"Sam!" Ross called.

"Coming," she said.

The two men were hunched around Drake, who was pointing at the screen with what looked like a rubber chop stick. "This is what killed our friend over there on the table," Drake said, tapping on the screen. "Tiny but potent. Twenty NM of pure hell."

Sam leaned in for a closer look. Twenty nano-materials was small even in viral terms. Certainly smaller than anything she would be looking for in her field. A bumpy dotted sphere. A whitish ball with a structure resembling five petal, black flowers. Unbelievably similar to a character on the artifact that Sam had no other explanation for. "Can you split the screen with the pillar?"

"Sure thing," Drake said, typing unusually fat keys designed for glove use. A moment later, the screen was divided with the artifact occupying the left half. Drake pointed to the character in question. "Pretty good likeness, isn't it?"

"Yes, but it can't be more than a coincidence," Sam said.

"That's your Angel of Death, Sam," Ross said, pointing to the right side of the screen. "A Picomaviridae."

Sam frowned. "Pico-what?"

"Rhinovirus," Drake said.

Sam paused at the familiar name. *"The common cold!"* she said incredulously.

Drake nodded. "With one small caveat. It kills the host before it can give it a runny nose."

"Yes, a very minor difference," Ross said.

"I don't understand," Sam said. "Please explain."

Drake looked at Ross. "Should I or would you like to?"

"It's your discovery," Ross said.

Drake paused and then turned to Sam. "Unfortunately, you were correct when you said 'common cold'. Almost everyone has antibodies that instantly recognize Rhinovirus epitopes."

Sam frowned, trying to follow.

"All right, an epitope is part of a macromolecule that is recognized by the immune system, specifically by antibodies, B cells and T cells. Although epitopes are usually thought to be derived from nonself proteins, sequences derived from the host that can be recognized are also classified as epitopes. The part of the antibody that recognizes the epitope is called a paratope," he said and then pointed his chopstick at the surface of the sphere on the screen.

"Like most epitopes recognized by antibodies, T cells and B cells, these have three dimensional surface features that fit precisely to the correlating antibodies. And these particular epitopes seem to be cross reactive. This property is exploited by the efficient attacking immune system through regulation of anti-idiotypic antibodies. The antibody binds to the antigen's epitope and the paratope becomes the epitope for another antibody that then binds to it. The second antibody is of the IgM class and it's binding up-regulates the immune response. Of course, this is catastrophic to the Rhinovirus."

Sam rolled her eyes. "Of course."

Decker looked at Ross. "Your turn."

Ross appeared to shrug, but the spacesuit didn't give much away. "In other words, the propagation of the virus is immediately met with a supercharged immune response. However fast the virus spreads, the immune system matches it one for one and destroys."

Sam shook her head. "Okay, I think I'm following. The virus gets snuffed. So what's the bad news?"

"Ironically, *that is* the bad news," Drake said. "This, Angel of Death, as you call it, is well named. The antibodies find and recognize it quickly and easily and squash it like a grape. Easy prey. But it's an insidious decoy... a death trap. If the immune system knew what it was really attacking, it wouldn't go near it. It's a micro miniature land mine. It busts open and gushes out an extremely powerful toxin. The dead carnage is what kills. The immune system never gets a chance to clean up the cellular debris before this super toxin travels through the bloodstream to every part of the body and disintegrates the host from within... fast. *Real fast.*"

Sam looked at the cadaver. "So, it's both germ *and* chemical?"

"Yes," Drake said. "And not without possible redeeming qualities. Like snake venom, it has uses. For instance, we injected a cancerous tumor from a monkey with an infinitesimally small amount of the virus and the tumor disintegrated before our eyes with little to no damage to surrounding tissue."

"Are you serious?" Sam said.

"Quite," Drake said. We've been doing that with rattlesnake and cobra venom with some success, but this is much more potent."

"But why does it stop at the tumor? Why doesn't it run rampant like it did with that guy and the others?" Sam said.

"We don't know exactly. We know that the Angelica we found in the cave attracts and stimulates it," Drake said. "We introduced Angelica extract into the cellular environment and the virus came to life, so to speak. Immediately multiplying, but very controlled, not like wildfire."

But we don't know how to make it combust the way it did in the cave," Ross said. "We feel there must be something missing, maybe in the translation," he said, with raised brows.

Sam frowned thoughtfully, staring at the ancient writing. *Missing? What were they missing? Think, think, think. What did the terrorists have in the cave that they didn't have here? They had the Angelica. We have the Angelica too,* she thought. *What could make the virus suddenly multiply a million... a billion fold?* She considered their technology. Everything here was superior to what they found in the cave. "What did they have that we don't?"

"We don't have a clue, Sam," Ross said. "Throw something out to us. I promise we won't scoff."

"Don't worry," she said. "I'm used to scoff."

"You're also used to getting results," Ross said.

Sam wasn't listening, her focus burning a hole in the screen. "Can I get a zoom on the virus character, or whatever it is? Make it the same size as the real virus," she said motioning to the other half of the screen.

Drake tapped some keys and the character quadrupled in size.

She stared and stared, hoping something would click. If she was to try to etch a likeness of the virus on polished petrified wood, she wouldn't be able to do a better job. Amazing likeness. But comical that anyone, much less a scientist, would consider the character had anything to do with the virus. On the other hand, if it did, impossible as it was, what was the message?

She turned to the cadaver and stood over it. Black and shriveled to the bone. The hair, intact upon arrival, had since formed a halo around his shrunken head. *Unbelievable*, she thought. She'd seen three thousand year old mummies in better condition. Such complete devastation. The intense *agony* he must have suffered. She tried to imagine the super toxin from the pummeled virus riding the channels of the human circulatory system. Reaching everywhere. Every cell. Although the viruses that had survived the immune system assault no longer seemed to be contagious in its dormant state, she found comfort inside the spacesuit.

The others came along side and surrounded the cadaver.

"Your thoughts?" Ross said.

"I'm thinking, you're right. We're missing an ingredient, maybe more than one. I'm not aware of any disease that is capable of doing this to a body so quickly, so we are either looking at something totally new or something prehistoric. If it's prehistoric and somehow connected to the pillar, as we suppose, it very well could be the Angel of Death recorded in Exodus. And if it is, Moses may have been able to... conjure it up, so to speak, with only what he had on hand."

"No missiles, no electricity, no laboratories... maybe a primitive kitchen," Drake said.

"Right! Moses was able to bring about the Angel of Death without any modern conveniences. He certainly didn't have an electron microscope, even if he did have a symbol that looked a hell of a lot like a single-strand RNA virus. He had Angelica available. What else?" Sam said.

"Sand," Decker said. "Plenty of that."

Sam nodded. "Yes, but he had to have something we don't. Something the insurgents *did* have in the cave."

"He probably had the entire pillar," Ross said.

"Yes. According to legend he did."

"But what did the pillar tell him?" Drake said.

Sam turned to Drake. "Did you check the cadaver for trace elements?"

"Of course," Drake said. "He was loaded with dead virus and toxin, and some live virus, but all of it was dormant."

"Any Angelica?"

"No Angelica."

"Really. So the Angelica was used as a viral stimulant, but not as part of the transmission," Sam said.

"Correct," Drake said. "The herb seems to bring it out of dormancy, but whatever makes it multiply explosively is a mystery."

"It's not a mystery to Tarik," Decker said.

After a moment of silence, Sam said, "This is crazy. It must be right at our fingertips. What did Moses and Tarik have that we don't?"

Decker turned in the direction of the monitor and then turned back. "They had the pillar."

"So do we," said Drake.

"Not here we don't," Decker said and then pointed to the monitor. "We have the downloaded image."

"What's the difference?" Ross said.

Decker turned to Sam. "Did you ever find out what kind of tree the pillar was made from?"

Sam thought for a moment and then it hit her like a sledge hammer. "No!" she said enthusiastically. "It's completely alien to anything on record, past or present."

Drake and Ross exchanged eye contact and then Ross said, "Well, where is it?"

"I have a small piece in my pants pocket back in the locker," Sam said.

Decker smiled thinly and shook his head.

"We'll need some lab time to analyze the elements, separate the chemicals and prepare an extract," Drake said.

"Yeah, that's probably what Moses did," Decker said sarcastically.

"Decker's right," Sam said. "No lab, remember? Whatever he did, he did it with the raw material."

31

Sam hurried to the locker room with Decker on her heels to assist with decontamination procedures before reentering BSL-4. They kept their spacesuits on, spending extra time in the chemical shower and ultraviolet cleanse. At the locker, Sam grabbed clumsily with her plumped-up gloves for her pants. Unable to reach into her pocket, she shook them upside-down until the artifact chip fell to the floor. On her hands and knees, she pushed the chip with one finger along the floor until Decker got down and tried to push it from the other side.

"I hope no one's filming this," Sam said.

"It's being seen live on America's Funniest Home Videos as we speak," Decker said. "And Tarik's watching."

"Why do I think you're probably telling me the truth?" Sam said as the chip stood on end between her and Decker's finger tips. She pinched the chip and they started back to Ross and Drake. When they arrived, the two doctors were working over the cadaver's head. Ross held the skull while Drake worked a large set of pliers with both hands.

"Ah, you're back," Ross said. "Do you have the wood chip?"

Sam nodded and held up the match book sized fragment of the artifact.

"Good," Ross said when suddenly there was a pop and a crunch and the cadaver's skull cracked open like a walnut. He apparently noticed the pained expression on her face and said,

"We can't use saws or anything sharp in here that can puncture the spacesuits. Pliers are a bit primitive and sloppy, but they're not sharp and still do the trick."

"A bit on the brittle side," Drake said.

Sam exhaled at the sight of the split open head. If this didn't give her nightmares nothing would. "Why did you do that?" she said.

Drake put the pliers on a stainless steel tray with a few other surgical tools and found a pair of rounded safety scissors. "We need some live virus," he said reaching in and snipping off some brain tissue and placing it on a plastic dish. "The virus can hide from antibodies here, but it can't hide from me."

Ross took the chip from Sam and turned to the steel table. His fat fingers found what looked like a rounded file and he went to work scratching the edge of the chip over another plastic dish. Soon there was a white powder gathering like a small ant hill. Meanwhile, Drake untwisted an eyedropper cap from a small plastic bottle filled with an amber colored liquid.

"Angelica extract?" Sam said.

"Yes," Drake said. "The same we used to test the other live virus we found in a nostril scrape. We got lucky but now the tissue is destroyed."

The procedure moved to a stainless counter by the microscope. Sam watched the monitor with Decker by her side as the two scientists prepared their ingredients for combination. Sam and Decker shared a glance of mutual anticipation. On the outside, Decker appeared quiet and preoccupied, but Sam was getting to know him a little better. His power of observation was actually quite intense. He not only heard every word, but every sound. While he appeared to be catching up, he was in fact often ahead of them. His words, while few, showed he was thinking both in and out of the box. His extrapolation of the pillar itself, as being a possible missing ingredient, was simple, yet profoundly bright and resourceful. She was upstaged in her known arena, but without an ounce of envy. She was glad he was there.

"This will be crude, but we should get some idea of what we're working with," Ross said as he placed the prepared dish with brain matter under the electron scope. After some fine adjustments, the monitor projected a highly defined live microscopic image.

"Okay, just as we thought," Drake said, pointing at the screen. "Plenty of dormant virus. "Now watch what happens when we introduce the Angelica only."

Ross made his way back to the scope with the amber extract. Sam looked back to the monitor as the new solution washed into view like a rising tide. The sound of her own breathing was all she heard for the next few minutes as all watched silently. The beads of sweat on her forehead had merged and dripped down her nose and into her lips. Salty. There was nothing she could do about it.

"What are we supposed to see?" Sam finally said.

"Just watch the virus," Drake said. "We should see... there." The rubber pointer touched the screen. "They're coming out of dormancy. Looking to dock."

"Dock?" Sam said. The bumpy round microbes moved and turned, like slow-motion bumper-cars at an amusement park.

"Yes. They want to attach themselves to cells, eat and multiply. At this point, antibodies, if there were any, would be conned in to wage war," Drake said. "A lethal mistake."

"I suppose it's time for our next ingredient. We'll start with just a tiny drop," Ross said, starting back to the scope. "What should we call it?"

"Petrified sawdust juice," Drake said. "Since it comes from the artifact itself."

Sam smiled. "Dino juice is more like it," she said. "The only ingredient Moses would have had that hasn't been available to anyone else… until now."

"Forbidden fruit," Decker said.

Sam looked at him, curiously.

He shrugged. "Just playing with your legends."

Sam snorted. "You're joking… right?"

Decked shrugged again, staring at the monitor and said, "Of course. There was never a real tree."

"The Tree of the Knowledge of Good and Evil?" she laughed, incredulously.

"The day you eat of this tree you shall surely die," Decker said, quoting Genesis.

"Ha, ha. You can be pretty funny when you want to," she said and then considered that Eve, according to legend, had found the tree irresistible. She wondered for a moment if her *own* attraction was more than natural.

"Your theory, not mine," he said, still focused on the screen.

Sam looked at him for a moment, lost in his comment, and then turned back to the slow viral dance on the monitor. Another tide began to move through the picture as Drake introduced the next petrified tree dust and Angelica solution from the into the tissue.

The explosion was immediate. The virus erupted exponentially, multiplying so rapidly that the dish boiled and the screen blurred red.

"Jesus!" Ross yelled, quickly stepping back from the scope.

Drake dropped his pointer and started toward Ross and the dish.

Sam froze next to Decker. A ghostly crimson swirl was rising from the dish and vanishing into the air currents of BSL-4 like a steamy tornado, growing in size and speed. What next? Had they pulled the grenade pin of the Angel of Death? She felt fear rush on her like a strong gust of wind. Would their bio spacesuits protect them? She never had any doubt until now.

"I've never seen anything like this!" Drake said. "We should leave here until it calms down."

"Absolutely!" Ross said, backing further away.

"No problem here," Sam said.

Drake started shaking his right hand frantically, as if he had burned it. "What the hell?"

"What's the matter?" Ross said.

"I don't know," Drake replied. "My hand... ouch! Oh no! I must have punctured my... *Jesus!* Aghh!" he screamed and then buckled over, as if kicked in the gut. He dropped to his knees.

Sam took one step in his direction and was held back by Decker. "What are you doing?" she said to him.

"He's done," Decker said. "I've seen this before."

Sam looked at Decker's unblinking eyes and then back to Drake, was now stretched prone, face down, screaming and shaking. "There must be something we can..."

"He's done!" Decker said sternly.

How was this possible? She wanted both to run to him and away from him. The red tornado was still swirling. Ross was a statue. Drake stopped screaming and rolled over. He shook for a few more moments, and then stopped. Sam shook off Decker's hold and went to him. Whatever happened to him wasn't happening to anyone else. Inside his helmet, Drake no longer looked like himself and his skin was darkening before her eyes. She looked at his right hand and cursed. "His glove has a tear."

Ross came to her side and tugged on her shoulder. "Maybe a splinter from the cadaver's cracked skull," he said. "There's nothing we can do for him now. Let's get out of here before something else happens."

Decker opened the door and suddenly there was horrific loud screeching coming from the corridor. Decker looked back in. His eyes were wide. "The monkeys," he yelled, and then disappeared.

Sam hurried after him, down several narrow hallways, Ross at her heels. When she arrived at the Ebola Suite the screeching had ebbed. Decker kept his distance from the cages. A couple of the monkeys were still moving, but the rest lay still, face up, mouths open, eyes sunken. With a closer look, Sam could see that the monkey's pink palms and soles had turned black.

"It's going to kill all of them," Ross said.

"They couldn't *all* have been first born," Sam said.

"Drake wasn't," Decker said. "I guess that puts a hole in your theory."

"Are you sure?" Sam said.

"Youngest of four," Ross said.

After a blank moment Sam looked back at the monkeys. No more movement. All dead.

32

Shabaka Akil Mohammad pressed the black button and the screen went blank, again. He pressed the blue button and the smiling lady appeared on the screen and welcomed him, again. He stared at the remote and wondered what to do next. He tried the black button again. Blank screen. He pressed the blue button again.

"Oh... my... God! Excuse me. You uh, push *that* arrow twice," the pretty blond woman in the next seat said. All blond women were pretty. He had never seen one who wasn't.

Shabaka pushed the arrow twice on the remote and a movie list appeared on the mini flat screen sunken into the headrest in front of him. Embarrassed, he smiled thinly and nodded a quiet thank you. She smiled back, but just for a second, and then returned to reading her paperback. For the last hour he had been unable to get past the introductory Emirate Airline's commercial. Now if only he could get the sound to work. Fortunately, his headphones wouldn't let her know he couldn't hear anything.

After watching a silent version of The Sound of Music from the classic movie menu, Shabaka decided it was time to open his attaché and go through his papers. He had never had papers before. In fact, he had never been on a commercial airliner jet before. He opened his yellow medical papers and scanned through them, as if he actually knew how to read. Words with boxes next to them. Some of the boxes had checks. Some didn't. He didn't have any kind of medical examination or immunization, but this paper gave the authorities what Tarik wanted them to see. He folded the papers exactly the way he'd opened them and then examined his passport. He especially liked his passport. His picture was in it. He remembered having his picture taken months ago with twenty other men. The two other 'chosen' had been there, too.

He considered showing his passport to the pretty blond woman next to him, but he remembered rule number one. Strict orders not to talk to anyone unless spoken to and even then to say as little possible. He closed his passport and was about to shut the attaché when he noticed his goodie-bag. Jelly beans. He couldn't remember the last time he had a jelly bean. Must have been ten or more years ago. He thought it an odd snack, but who was he to judge what snack he should have on a jet airliner? The salted peanuts were very good and he hadn't had them in a while either. He opened the small zip-lock bag and took out a small plastic container with about five red jellybeans. Not many. But, come to think of it, there weren't too many peanuts either. He unscrewed the cap of the plastic pillbox and dumped the jelly beans into his palm. All the same color. He wished there were a couple of yellow ones. He thought to offer the blond woman one, but then remembered his instructions. So much to remember.

Shabaka picked one of the red candies from his palm and popped it in his mouth. Mmm, good. Very sweet, just as he remembered. He took another and then the rest. In a moment they were all gone. Just like the peanuts. He wanted more. What else is there? The brownie. Another zip-lock bag, but no inner container. Just the brownie. He opened the bag, took out the brownie and gave it a sniff. Smelled like chocolate, but there was another aroma also. He didn't like the other smell and was about to put it back in the bag, but then he remembered Tarik saying he wanted an opinion on the taste. His shoulders sagged.

He didn't like to offer opinions, especially to Tarik. A good opinion brought little more than, well, nothing. A contrary opinion could be bad. Very bad. No opinion, *that* would certainly be the worst choice. He turned to the woman next to him.

"Would you like to taste this brownie?" he asked, and then immediately remembered rule number one.

The pretty lady looked at him blankly, and then at the brownie between his fingers. "No, thank you. I'm full," she said, and then looked away.

How could she be full? On peanuts? He didn't see her eat anything else. Just a glass of Coke. Diet Coke, whatever that meant. Maybe she was just being shy, or polite. "Are you sure?"

"Yes. Positive," she said quickly, without looking at him.

Shabaka was about to say something else, but stopped himself. Her voice was beautiful. Deep and even. Smart too. There was no doubt in her voice. He liked that. He shrugged and took a bite of the brownie. Thick, sweet, grainy, chewy. Not terrible. He swallowed and took another bite and finished it. Gone. Actually, not gone. An aftertaste. Similar to that strange smell it had. Made his mouth dry and sticky. He needed something to drink.

"Coke," he called to the stewardess six rows up. She was wearing a uniform, a two-piece tan suit with big brass buttons on the blazer. She also had a flat head covering that looked like a red cloth plate with a long white veil out the back. She was very pretty, but not blond. "Diet Coke." The stewardess nodded and disappeared behind a curtain and then returned with a silver can and a glass with ice. She put the glass on his tray and poured.

"Would you like me to leave the can, sir?" the stewardess asked. Her black hair was pulled back under the red head covering. Her face was bright and friendly and dimples framed a very beautiful smile. She had a name tag that spelled M-s J-e-n-n-e-l O-r-t-i-z. He could not pronounce it. Not Arab. And judging by those diamond earrings, she had to be very wealthy. He knew wealth when he saw it.

Shabaka felt the warmth of power. "Yes," he said.

"Would there be anything else, sir?" she asked, as if he was the only person on the plane.

"Peanuts?"

She smiled and the dimples reappeared. "Yes, sir," she said and then left.

He had never felt so important in his entire life. *So this is what it means to be a 'chosen one,'* he thought, and then belched slightly. There was that brownie aftertaste again, only worse. There was also a bit of a sulfury rotten-egg taste. He drained the cold glass of diet Coke. Delicious. He poured himself another glass and drank it right down. The stewardess with the dimples returned with the peanuts.

"More," he said, holding up the empty can.

"Wow! Thirsty?" she said pleasantly.

"Yes. It is very good," he said and then turned to the blond lady next to him. She was already looking at him. *She thinks I'm interesting,* he thought. "Diet Coke is very good," he said to her, and then involuntarily belched in her face. She grimaced and turned away, coughing. His rotten breath was much stronger this time and made his nose scrunch.

Shabaka was very embarrassed, but his humiliation was short lived. His attention quickly shifted to his bloating abdomen. He loosened his belt, but that was not enough to relieve the pressure. He would need to open the top clasp of his pants. All he had was a small bag of peanuts, an even smaller portion of jelly beans, a small brownie and a diet Coke, but his gut was busting full, and heavy, like he'd swallowed a bucket of mud. His abdominal muscles tightened, cramping, as if he'd just done a hundred sit-ups. Another belch, and then another. Every eruption brought a newer stronger flood of rancid gas into his mouth and sinus cavity.

His eyes started to burn and tear, sweat beaded up on his face, the color of his face drained and nausea set in. He fought an urge to vomit. Suddenly, he remembered the headache and stomachache pills Doctor Dulai packed in the first aid kit. He wanted both, and now. Dulai had said the pills worked fast. He pushed papers back and forth, found the kit and opened it. Staring him in the face was the small bottle Dulai had called, "stomachache pills".

"Maybe you should try some ginger ale," suggested an old lady across the aisle looking over her narrow glasses. His eyes darted about. She wasn't the only one looking at him. He was not to do or say anything to draw attention to himself and now he seemed to be the center of attention. The stewardess was also looking at him, and talking to another stewardess.

Shabaka belched again as his fingers trembled and fumbled the cap off. The pill container label was completely blank, so even if he could read there was no way of knowing the dosage. He emptied four into his palm and shoved them into his mouth, chased it down with his Coke, and prayed to Allah for a rapid end to his pain. And was it his imagination or was his skin turning darker?

The prayer was quickly answered, though not as expected. Within seconds he vomited with force, propelling a bloody gush against the attaché lid.

"Jesus!" cried the blond.

The stewardess immediately turned and ran toward the station. "Call Med Link," she said.

Shabaka breathed heavily as fear bored into his chest. His stomach felt relieved for a few seconds but he could feel another build up gathering fast. Revelation flashed through his terror. The food Tarik had given him made him sick and the stomachache pills provided by Dulai made him even sicker. Why? He could not ponder more than an instant before a crimson mist swirled off the splattered spew like steam from hot soup. The abdominal cramps rushed across his entire body to every extremity. A red plume billowed from his mouth as he screamed in agony. Within minutes his torture was over, his eyes still open but no longer seeing, his ears no longer hearing but, the red mist was still pouring from his open mouth and nostrils.

33

"Call Med Link!" Stewardess Jennel Ortiz called out again as she hurried into the galley, threw open the lower cabinet door and yanked out the biohazard kit. Med Link was the industry standard help-line for medical emergencies in the air. She had seen air sickness many times, stomach viruses, a massive coronary that had forced a detoured landing, and once had a huge elderly woman pass out and fall on her in the aisle, trapping her until help pulled her free, but nothing even remotely close to this. She opened the kit and quickly rummaged through the contents, tossing aside two CPR masks, antiseptic wipes, a pair of shoe covers, and a set of instructions.

"What's wrong with him?" asked Sharon, another stewardess.

"I don't know," Jennel said. "Epilepsy, virus. You got Med Link yet?"

"We're connecting. Does it look contagious?"

Jennel looked at her for a second. "I'm sure as hell not going near him without some protection," she said, opening a paper gown from a tiny compressed bag. Jennel's coworker helped her on with the flimsy blue cloth and a face mask with a visor. If the man was having a heart attack she would have to perform CPR and, according to procedure, continue resuscitating until the aircraft landed and paramedics could come aboard and take over. No way was she going to do that without bio-protection.

Jennel took a deep breath. She looked like a cross between a surgeon and a janitor, a red biohazard garbage bag in the left hand and a container of absorbent vomit treatment powder in the other. This was not the way she wanted to walk down the aisle. Stewardesses were trained not to sweat... literally. Appear in control. Keep a smile. She remembered an old man had passed away on a flight once and they simply put a blanket on him as if he was asleep and then simply waited for all to depart the vessel before dealing with it.

When she got to the sick passenger, she suddenly stopped. She took a step back and unconsciously dropped the red bio bag from her hands as she watched the crimson mist swirl from the man's open mouth. CPR no longer seemed to be a question. He looked dead, in fact, he looked days... *weeks* dead. But how could that be possible? Just minutes ago he had asked her for another bag of peanuts and a second can of diet Coke. He'd been a little nervous maybe, looking around like it was his first flight, but otherwise young and healthy.

A child walked down the aisle toward her and an arm came out a few seats back to block the little boy's way. "Go back to your parents, son," a man said.

"What happened to him?" asked an elderly lady, tugging on her sleeve.

Jennel looked at the lady, curly white hair and concerned big eyes behind thick glasses. On her lap was a tiny white poodle... same hair and eyes, no glasses.

"He needs a doctor," came another voice to her right. "Is someone here a doctor?

"Did he eat the salad?" the lady asked. "I ate the salad. Where did the salad come from? Was it made fresh?"

"I told him to try some ginger ale," said another lady who was now getting out of her seat and limping away down the aisle. Another followed behind her, trying to push past.

213

"How do you get those air masks down from the ceiling?" said a man in a gray suit.

Regardless of the dead man's appearance, her concern now had to shift to the living. If he was indeed dead, of which there was little doubt, simply putting a blanket over his lap to feign sleep wasn't going to work. The passengers needed to be calmed. As bizarre and unique as this was, it had to be treated with a mechanical-like response to avoid panic. But what was the proper procedure for a dead man turning black with red smoke coming out of his mouth… and ears?

Sharon ran up behind her. "I have Med Link. What are his sym…" she said and then stared in silence.

The blond woman next to him in 6B was staring wide eyed without blinking when she suddenly let out a painfully high-pitched strident scream. The ear-slicing screech echoed through the fuselage, draining the color from every face. Just then the man on the other side of the screaming woman, buckled over in his seat with a loud sickening grunt, like he'd been stabbed in the gut with a bayonet. A moment later, he was crying out loudly in agony.

Jennel looked at her co-worker for advice, but the other stewardess was holding her own abdomen and breathing heavily before suddenly dropping to one knee.

"Sharon?" Jennel said.

"I don't feel very… aghhh!" she screamed in a high pitch, and then similarly to the man in the seat, buckled over into fetal position on the floor, shaking violently.

Jennel reached a hand toward Sharon to help still her when she heard another scream, and then another. Suddenly, the jet jolted and dropped before catching itself. Food and drinks had come off trays and people had come out and pounded back into their seats. Groans and screams came from every direction as others buckled in half and shook. Whatever the first man had was mind-blowingly contagious.

Why hadn't the captain reported anything about the air disturbance? Jennel struggled as quickly as she could through an isle littered with writhing passengers. She hurdled over someone and then ran into the flight deck. Her eyes widened. Captain Andrews thrashed about all the way back in his seat as his feet kicked the instrument panel. The copilot on the floor gasped and twitched like a live fish on a boat deck. She looked at the blue sky out the window when the plane took another plunge. Her feet came off the floor and suddenly she was on her back. She scrambled to her feet and went to the Captain. She grabbed his feet and looked at him in the face. His eyes bulged, his mouth hung open and he didn't appear to see her. His hands gripped the armrests tightly and then he stretched out and fell from the seat, joining the copilot on the floor. Jennel watched in shock but then darted for the door and stuck her head back into the passenger cabin.

"Dorothy," she yelled to the other stewardess, no longer so concerned about calming the panic as she was about flying and landing the aircraft.

Dorothy was right there in the galley. "Now what?" she said.

"I need your help, now."

Dorothy hurried to her and gasped. She started to reach for the pilots but Jennel held her back. "Don't touch them," she said.

Dorothy started breathing heavily. "But who's going to fly the…"

Jennel took hold of Dorothy's cheeks with both hands and forced her to look her in the eye. "I need your help. Are you with me?"

Dorothy nodded, tears dragging mascara lines down her cheeks.

"Okay, we need to get them out of here," she said, motioning to the pilots, who had stopped struggling. Their eyes were rolled back and their mouths opened.

A moment later, Dorothy helped her carry the pilots out of the flight deck and into passenger cabin.

"Are they dead?" a man asked.

"No," Jennel lied, dragging the captain from under his armpits. She propped him into a seat, his skin darkened.

Yelping. Jennel looked up to see the tiny white poodle yelping in pain, as if someone was sticking it through with a skewer.

"Sashi! Stop! What's wrong! Sashi!" The old lady cried.

Jennel turned to Dorothy. "Put a blanket on them," she said and the bolted to the flight deck. She slid into the captain's seat.

Dorothy came back.

"Shut the door, and lock it," Jennel said.

Dorothy shut the door and came to her side. "How are *you* feeling?" she said.

Jennel paused. "I feel, okay, I guess…. And you?"

"I don't know."

"Do you feel sick?"

"I don't know."

"What do you mean you don't know!" Jennel shouted, surprising herself.

Dorothy's eyes widened with shock. "I'm not dead or turning black, so I suppose I'm not sick… yet," she yelled back.

Jennel held up her hands in surrender. "Okay. Calm down. We have to calm down. I'm sorry for yelling," she said, and then moved past Dorothy to look out the cabin door. There was a lot of loud crying and sobbing, but the agonizing screaming had stopped. There were the dead and the living, but no one else appeared to be dying.

"How are we going to land?" Dorothy said.

"The first thing would be to find out if there are any other pilots on board."

"What are you going to do, make an announcement that we need a pilot? That should go over pretty well."

Jennel thought for a moment. "Ask the passengers individually what their occupations are. If you find anyone with any, I mean any, flying experience, bring them back here. Meanwhile I'll contact New York."

Dorothy nodded and disappeared. Jennel slid into the captain's seat, put on the headset and radioed the flight center at JFK airport.

"Center, center, this is the flight attendant from Emirates Flight 105."

"Go ahead Emirates 105."

"This is an in-flight emergency. Both pilots are, are, incapacitated. Searching for someone on board who knows how to fly the airplane. What do I do?"

"Say again, Emirates 105."

Jennel exhaled. "This is an in flight emergency. Both pilots are incapacitated."

"Did you say both pilots are incapacitated?"

"Affirmative."

After a pause. "Okay, first and foremost, do not panic. You're going to be just fine. The airplane will fly itself. If there is no pilot on board, then you'll auto-land. Do you understand?"

Jennel looked at the panel that the captain had smashed with his feet and felt fear swirl through her chest. Next to the auto-land label, several switches had been crushed and broken. She inhaled deeply and let it out. "Auto-land is also incapacitated."

"Please repeat."

Jennel closed her eyes. "I said, auto-land is incapacitated. No auto-land."

"Are you, I mean, how do you know?"

"Because the control panel has been destroyed."

"How?"

"The captain had some kind of seizure and smashed the panel before he died."

"Died?"

"Yes."

"And the copilot?"

"He died, too."

"Say that again, please."

"Both pilots are dead."

"I'm sorry. It sounds like you said that both pilots died."

"That is correct."

Pause. "How?"

Dorothy reappeared. "There are no pilots in the cabin."

Jennel closed her eyes tight, squeezing out a tear. "And it has just come to my attention there is no one on board who can fly."

No response.

"Hello, center?"

"Yes, I'm here, Emir... I'm sorry, what is your name?"

"Jennel Ortiz."

"Okay, Jennel. We're going to get through this together. I'm going to put you on with Captain Forsythe. He's very familiar with your aircraft and will instruct you with everything you will need to land."

"Me! You want me to fly this thing!"

"Stand by."

Jennel scanned what looked like thousands of switches and lights and gauges, some of them destroyed. "Jesus, you can't be serious."

"This is Captain Forsythe, Jennel. You're going to be just fine. I'm very familiar with your aircraft and I can just as easily land it with you on the radio as I could if I were there myself."

"But I've never flown anything, except a kite, and even that I crashed."

"That's okay. This will be easier than flying a kite. First, I want you to strap yourself into the captain's seat, okay?"

"Okay, I'm in."

"You are going to land in New York at JFK airport as scheduled. This is going to be very simple. The pilots already did the hard part for you. They already set the course for JFK runway one-nine. I want you to look at the switches just below the front windshield in the very center of the dashboard. Do you see a gray knob that says, AP?"

"Uh, yes, yes, there it is."

"I want you to turn it all the way to the right."

"Okay, I did it."

"Did a little orange light come on next to it?"

"Yes, it's on."

"Very good, Jennel. That's the autopilot. It's on and set. Now I want you to relax, you won't have to do anything until we land, and then you must do exactly what I say, so I want you to be calm, okay?"

"Right, calm."

"The controllers are working hard here to keep all other aircraft out of your vicinity and you'll have priority landing clearance in Kennedy. Meanwhile, Mr. Barry Morse from control center, says that he needs to talk to you. If you want to talk to me any time, I'm right here. Okay?"

"Okay," she repeated, but her head was spinning.

"Jennel, my name is Barry Morse, and I'm the head of security down here. I understand that both pilots are dead?"

"Yes, sir."

"What can you tell me about the death of the pilots?"

"Some sort of sickness spread through the plane and it killed about half the people on board, including the pilots and a stewardess."

No response.

"Mr. Morse?"

34

Sam had no sooner entered the staging area with Ross and Decker when the phone on the lone desk rang and Ross took the call.

Ross looked at Decker, brow raised. "Yes, Sir, he's here," he said and held the phone out. "It's for you."

Decker took the phone and listened silently without expression for a few moments and then looked at Ross and then at Sam. "Has there been any confirmation?" he said, and then listened more. "Yes, Sir. We'll be right there," he said and hung up.

"We'll be right there?" Sam said. "Right where?"

"Tarik's made an announcement and a strike. There's a video conference upstairs in five minutes."

"What's the announcement?" Ross said.

"What's the strike?" Sam said.

"Three jets. Two have crashed, one is still up but the pilots are dead along with half the passengers."

"Where is it going to land?" Sam asked.

"It was supposed to land at JFK, but that doesn't seem likely anymore."

"Why?" Sam said.

"They died of an unknown sickness. JFK security is not going to take the chance of letting an epidemic loose in New York. They also don't like that a stewardess is the one who's going to land."

"A stewardess?" Ross said doubtfully.

They raced through the decontamination and dressing stages like firemen and then hurried to the third floor for the video conference. When they entered Room 323, they were met by several other officers Sam had never met. After some fast introductions, everyone took a seat around a long wood-grain Formica table. At the end of the table the image of the Secretary of Defense, Tom Link, behind a clean desk, appeared on a large flat screen monitor.

"Good afternoon, gentlemen. It's time we updated each other with current intelligence and implement a plan of action. As you probably now know, our friend, Tarik, has moved us into sudden crisis. Three aircraft from Emirate Airlines were used in some sort of biological or chemical terrorist attack. Two have crashed with no survivors, but otherwise, with no catastrophic results. One crashed in the Swiss Alps and the other in the English Channel. As far as I know, there were no known damages other than to the affected aircrafts. You may, however, feel free to educate me differently. We also have a third plane still flying. From what I understand, half the passengers are already dead. What to do with it is the big question? We don't have the luxury of time with this. The other disturbing matter is a demand from Tarik. In the short time since we received it, our team has confirmed that it is authentic, and so far, non-traceable. I'll switch you over to the madman's brief video now."

The screen went blank and then Tarik appeared. In contrast to Tom Link, nothing but the terrorist's torso and head appeared in the screen. No desk. No plush office. Nothing to give a clue as to where he was. He wore a long white shirt with a white head covering. The wall behind him was also white. Sam glanced around the table. Decker sat unblinking, expressionless, as he stared at the face of his mission. Perfect poker face, but she felt the intensity.

"The time has come to illustrate the seriousness of our capabilities and intentions. Soon all of the atrocities committed against our people will be punished in the same manner they were inflicted. All authority and rule in the Middle East must be returned to the people who have known this land as home for thousands of years. A new kingdom shall emerge from the ruins. A list will be provided of imprisoned servants. These prisoners shall be released into freedom and safety. Another list will be provided of blocked financial accounts. All monies frozen on these accounts shall be released immediately. And finally, ten billion dollars will be funded to Asad al Adala and unrestricted in an account, the number of which you will be provided with at the conclusion of this message. Three airline demonstrations could very easily have been ten planes, or a hundred, or even a city. More and larger demonstrations will come unless our demands are met swiftly. Our desire is for a peaceful resolution. Three martyrs gave their lives for this purpose and will be rewarded accordingly for the rest of eternity."

The video ended abruptly and Secretary of Defense Tom Link reappeared.

"There you have it, gentlemen. Before I ask you about strategy, I would like to know what the hell killed the people aboard those planes."

Ross spoke up. "We've isolated a virus responsible for some of the deaths in the Afghani cave, Sir. We have strong reason to believe the same virus has been used with these aircraft."

"A virus?"

"Yes, Sir."

"A virus able to cause deaths within hours?"

"Yes, Sir. Actually, minutes."

Sam noticed the officers at the table were staring at Ross, in shock.

"But how is that possible? What virus can act like that? Some sort of super explosive Ebola or something?"

"Nothing like that, Sir. What makes this virus so swift and deadly is its deceptive innocence. It's completely asymptomatic in its infective state and multiplies explosively when in contact with a specific element or compound that we've only isolated in part. But when the immune system kills it without resistance, the carnage is as toxic as the most powerful snake venom and causes almost immediate decomposition of all cells in contact. The mortality rate is one hundred percent with those who become infected."

"One hundred percent?"

"Yes, Sir."

"But only half the passengers died from it."

"The others did not get infected."

"How? I mean, why not?"

"We don't know, Sir."

"Well, we had better find out."

"Yes, Sir. Right now, we're getting conflicting results as to why some get infected and others don't. I would like to study the passengers on the jet still in flight."

"Very well. I understand that flight isn't going to be allowed to land in New York."

"If it lands here, Sir, we could bring the victims directly into USAMRIID for investigation and put the survivors through a few tests that could help us form a defense," Decker said.

Ross nodded concurrently.

One of the officers opposite to Sam, with short white hair and a long chiseled but craggy face, spoke up. "Yes, but the plane has no pilot. It's being flown by autopilot."

"There's a stewardess flying. She's being instructed by a retired pilot very familiar with the Airbus A-340. Auto-land is disabled. It's going to be very difficult, extremely risky, for her to land, much less navigate to a different airport off AP."

Ross looked at Tom Link. "If the plane crashes we lose a valuable opportunity to research the virus."

Sam understood and followed the practical logic of saving the jet to study the virus further but, she was surprised there was no mention of the human lives that could also be lost.

Link nodded. "What are her chances of successfully pulling it off?"

"Not good," said another unknown officer.

"She'll crash it," Decker said.

Sam was a bit surprised Decker joined in.

"Captain Decker?" Link said. "Do you have a suggestion?"

Captain? Sam thought. And the Secretary of Defense knew him by name?

"The plane needs a pilot."

"This is, of course, correct. But there isn't any on board. Not even a hint of one."

Sam noticed everyone at the table had Decker's undivided attention.

"Then we need to get one on board."

"And how do you suggest we do that, Captain?"

"With the V22 Osprey."

"Osprey? How?"

"Cabling to the EE hatch under the flight deck."

"EE hatch?" Link said.

Decker nodded. "It's just behind the nose landing gear. Mechanics use it to access the electronics bay. From there, a person can climb through a hatch in the floor of the cockpit in most of these aircraft."

"At what, five hundred miles per hour?" one of the officers said doubtfully.

"The jet would have to be slowed to approach or landing speed by lowering the slats and flaps. It would lose altitude, so the time window for access would be small."

"How fast are we talking?" asked Link.

"About one hundred forty-five knots, or one hundred and sixty miles per hour."

"One-sixty? Is that doable?" Link asked.

"With rock climbing equipment and suction cups, maybe. The climb would be hard, but the Osprey is stable enough to hold a steady cable and can fly twice that speed to get into position."

Link shook his head in disbelief and exhaled. "How do you know all this?"

Decker took a brief glance around the table. "I'm a pilot."

"What *kind* of pilot?"

"The kind of pilot you need, Sir."

Link's brow rose. "And what kind is that?"

"One that can get on board."

Link smiled thinly. "Captain, your reputation precedes you.

After a pause, Link said, "But can you really float one of these birds?"

"Yes."

35

Sam caught up to Decker as they walked briskly down the hallway. "You can fly one of those things?"

"Probably."

"Probably? You told the Secretary of Defense and all…"

"I'll figure it out," Decker said quietly.

"You'll figure it out!"

"Shhhh. They're easy to fly. It's called an Airbus. Air-bus. Do the math. Like driving a bus."

"And you can *probably* drive a bus."

"Probably."

Sam rolled her eyes.

"Look, it's not an F-16."

"Can you fly an F-16?"

"Hmm, I don't know, probably not."

"What have you flown?"

"Helicopters, mostly. Before DIA, I flew rescue and evac."

"Helicopter? she said, incredulously.

"Relax, Sam. I'm dual rated."

"What does that mean?"

"Means I'm certified to fly fixed wing also. Most of us had to get our fixed wing certification first. Now you can get just helicopter, but most of us had to start in a fixed wing."

"Are you serious?"

"What?"

"And you're going to fly a jumbo jet, *with passengers?*"

"Half empty."

"Half full."

"Do you have a better idea?"

"Let the stewardess fly it. She's getting competent instructions from an experienced pilot."

"This isn't a movie, Sam."

"I think someone should tell *you* that."

"Look who's talking. I don't go scuba diving two-hundred feet into ancient wells."

"No, you just climb aboard jets in flight. She'll probably crash it trying to get you inside," Sam said as they turned a hall corner.

"It's not as crazy as it sounds. Hey, you're not afraid for me, are you?"

Sam paused. "I just don't want us to lose our best chance of getting Tarik."

"Which is what?"

"Which is you."

"He's my mission."

"Mine, too. When do we get the Osprey?"

"It will be here in five minutes, but you're not going."

"Are we going to go through this again?"

"No. Too risky and we need you alive. If you feel the need to be there, then you go with Ross to the airport. I'll meet you there when I land."

Sam grabbed Decker by the arm and spun him to look at her face to face. "I'm a member of this team and I go where the virus goes. Besides, you need me."

"I need you to translate the artifact, not crash in a jumbo-jet."

"I thought you could *probably* fly it? Make up your mind."

"Too risky."

"I need to get clues everywhere the virus goes. Which reminds me, don't forget your protection."

Decker's brow rose. "What protection?"

"Lamb's blood."

"Half the people on the flight survived. The virus is probably now gone," he said then continued to walk with Sam right next to him stride for stride.

"We don't know that. Someone should check to see if the victims are first born."

"Drake wasn't, and he died."

"We can't explain that yet, Decker. We still have many tests to take. Lambs blood might have protected Drake."

"Better than space suits?"

"Possibly. Remember your cave experience."

Decker nodded.

Sam followed Decker out the door and into a white Suburban that shuttled them a short distance across the main street in Fort Detrick to the helipad on which they had arrived. A couple of jets roared by and behind them another plane followed, unlike anything Sam had ever seen. Decker spoke to a small assembly of soldiers and then turned to Sam. He followed her gaze to the sky.

"Good, its here," he said.

"Is that the Osprey?" Sam asked.

"Yes, let's give it a little room," he said, leading Sam backward by the arm.

The battleship grey V-22 Osprey had a wide transport fuselage, like a pregnant bus with huge propellers at the end of each fixed wing. The craft approached swiftly but slowed as the massive engines tilted upward, in essence changing the transport plane into a transport helicopter. "Marines" had decorated the rear fuselage, allowing no mistake as to which branch owned this bird. Its agility on approach reminded Sam of a bumble bee, forward, slow, hover, and settle down on the pad. The props slowed but never stopped. A side door ahead of the wing opened and two soldiers in large green jumpsuits and white helmets exited. Decker engaged one of them and shouted into his ear but Sam couldn't hear what was being said over the noise of the engines. The soldier nodded and pointed back to the Osprey. Decker slapped the man's back and motioned to Sam to get into the Osprey.

"Aren't you forgetting something?" Sam said.

Decker motioned with his hand for her to wait as another white Suburban drove up, the door opened and Ross hurried out of the passenger door with a brown bag in his hand. Decker looked at Sam and said, "Fort Detrick has its own butcher shop."

Sam was shocked. "You asked for blood? Then what was all that…"

Ross, winded and sweating, handed off the bag to Decker, and said, "I could only get a pint. I hope that's enough," he said, looking at Sam.

Sam shrugged. "We're untested."

"There are a few jump suits inside. You have thirty seconds to find one and get into it before we're gone."

Sam scrambled inside and found the suits in one of many open compartments that surrounded the interior. Three suits. She unzipped the smallest one, a medium, slipped her pants off, slid in and zipped up as the soldiers rushed in.

"Put a helmet on." Decker said as he snagged one of the other suits. "The helmets have radios built in so we can talk and all hear each other over the noise."

36

Sam found the Osprey's interior surprisingly spacious but cluttered, its walls and ceiling were covered with exposed wire harnesses, conduits of various diameters, brackets, aluminum compartments, hoses, electrical junction boxes, grids and six wall mounted seats with harnesses. The soldiers found their seats and buckled in. Decker did the same and yelled to the pilot to "Go!" and looked at Sam who took the seat next to him and then put on a helmet. It was big, like the suit, but she could immediately hear everyone's conversations over the noise. The engine sound increased and the Osprey began to rise, quickly, smoothly, and then forward. Faster, faster, faster. With no time for introductions, Sam read the name "Kelly" on one soldier's name tag and "Baker" on the other.

"When do we intercept them?" Sam asked.

"*If* we intercept them, it will be in about thirty minutes," Decker said.

"If?"

"JFK is trying to explain to the stewardess how to slow the jet down to a workable speed. If she doesn't slow it down, we'll never catch them."

~

Jennel Ortiz could not believe her ears. "Please repeat that," she said to Captain Forsythe, her ground instructor.

"We want you to slow the jet down to landing speed and lower the landing gear," Forsythe said.

"But, you do know we're over the water?" she said, skeptically.

"You're not going to land, Jennel. We are going to bring a pilot on board and your present speed and altitude would make that impossible."

"I wasn't aware you could bring a pilot on board in mid flight, *at any speed*," Jennel said.

"Behind the nose landing gear is the EE hatch. He'll be coming in through there."

Jennel laughed nervously. "Oh," she said. "Is he waiting on a cloud somewhere?" She could not help herself. Fear saturated her. Their solution sounded too desperate to work.

"A special unit has been dispatched, Jennel. They are extremely experienced and qualified."

"Has this ever been done before?" she asked.

"Apparently, they have someone with experience. They are on their way and are very specific in their instructions. We need you to do your part."

Jennel exhaled. "I'm listening, Captain."

"Good. The first thing you have to do is turn the AP switch to the left."

~

"There she is, Captain," the pilot yelled back to Decker.

Decker unclipped and went up front. Sam followed. Through the Osprey's windshield, the Airbus appeared stable enough. Giant wings and landing gear down. Their approach was rapid. The Osprey was like a sparrow maneuvering around an eagle. As they passed, the stewardess was at the windshield waving.

"Get directly in front and match its speed," Decker said and then retreated to the rear of the Osprey.

"How can I help?" Sam said.

"Just stay back and watch," Decker replied.

Sam nodded. Baker and Kelly followed Decker to the rear and pulled equipment from compartments and cubbies. Decker climbed into a cable harness and tightened the straps. Kelly pulled down the end of a cable from the ceiling and clipped it to Decker's harness. Baker handed Decker small hand tools not unlike mountain climbing gear and Decker quickly attached them strategically to his harness.

"We're in front, Captain," the pilot yelled.

"What's our airspeed?"

"One hundred and fifty knots."

"Altitude?"

"Eleven thousand feet and falling."

"Open the hatch. Let's go," Decker yelled.

"The blood!" Sam yelled.

Decker stopped and then motioned for Sam to bring it to him. She carefully opened the container to avoid spillage.

"Take off your helmet," she said.

"Just…"

"Take it off, let's go."

Decker sighed, ripped off his helmet and allowed Sam to paint his head liberally.

"Ok, that's enough," he said. Baker and Kelly were clearly puzzled. "Don't ask," he told them. They didn't.

"How do you feel?" Sam asked.

"Wet and smelly."

"Besides that."

"Like eating a bacon cheeseburger, but since I'm all geared up and hooked to this hoist up here at ten thousand feet, I may as well try to get into that jumbo jet out there."

"They'll have food on board," Sam said and then grabbed his vest and pulled his bloodied face close to hers. "When we're done, the burger's on me."

"That's very generous of you."

"I want to give you some extra incentive to come back."

"Then I'll hold you to that. Go tell the pilot to open the transport hatch and then buckle up," Decker said, then secured his helmet and lowered his visor.

Sam told the pilot and found her seat. The rear hatch opened, filling the cabin with thunderous noise from the engines of both the Osprey and the airliner, which was amazing to see just a few hundred feet away. Sam's heart pounded, which surprised her. She couldn't decide whether Decker was brave or insane, but she immediately prayed for him.

37

Decker did a final check of his harness, tools and cable in about 10 seconds. "All good. Let's do it," he said.

Sam watched the Airbus through the open ramp, moving up and down. She was in awe of Decker's bravery, inspired.

The airmen looked at each other. "You sure, Sir?" Kelly said.

Decker stepped off the ramp, descended briefly but was picked up by the high air velocity, floating horizontally, as the cable unwound him further and further away. His target: the landing gear behind the nose.

"Clouds," the Pilot said. Sam turned and saw clouds nearing. She wasn't sure what that meant but knew it couldn't be good. She looked back to Decker. He had made it sound easy back at the fort but this was insanity. The two craft were anything but stable. One moment he was on target and the next he was by the windshield. She could only imagine what it looked like to the stewardess at the helm.

Into the cloud and freezing rain, Decker became a blur.

"How are you doing, Sir?" Kelly said.

"Thanks for the cloud," he said.

"They come with the sky," Sam interjected.

"Now you tell me. How much more line?"

"Almost maxed," Kelly said.

"Then you have to get closer," Decker said.

"We're dangerously close now," the Pilot said.

"This isn't a safety first mission, Major. "I need another fifty feet," Decker said loudly.

The cloud was breaking up and the view was getting clearer. The cable reached its max and Decker wasn't there.

"Let's go, Major," Decker said sternly.

"This is crazy, Captain," the pilot said.

"Not as crazy as what's happening inside the jet. A little more— and that's an order."

The Osprey inched closer and Decker touched the nose of the Airbus but needed more to get to the landing gear.

"More!" Decker yelled.

"More dammit!" Sam yelled. She wanted to do something… anything. The Airbus was so close she felt like she could touch it, but they needed to get closer.

The pilot cursed and backed up. Decker slid down the nose.

"You're almost there!" Sam yelled.

"If I go back any further, we'll hit," the pilot yelled. "They're in our draft. The slightest pocket will….

"Another inch!" Sam yelled.

"Got it!" Decker said. "Hold it steady."

Sam held her breath. The entire hatch was filled with Airbus nose. No other view was possible. The stewardess in the Airbus had eyes as big as Frisbees. Decker immediately strapped himself to the upright holding the wheels and unsnapped the hoist cable.

"He's on! We're free!" Kelly yelled.

"Altitude?" Decker said as the Osprey gave some distance.

"Seven thousand and falling," the pilot said.

"Tell her to depressurize," Decker said.

"Flight Six hundred. Have you been instructed on depressurization?" the pilot said and listened for the answer. "Then do it now. We're coming in."

Decker struggled with his tools, each one attached to a line. He had tied himself to the upright and worked both hands. "Altitude?"

"Sixty-three hundred and falling. We need to increase speed."

"You can't," Sam yelled. "You'll tear him apart."

"Come on, you mother!" Decker snarled.

"What's happening, Decker?" Sam said.

"It's not opening."

"Why?"

"I don't know. It's stuck"

"What do you mean, 'it's stuck'," Sam said.

After a few grunts, Decker calmly said, "I mean, it won't open."

"It has to open," Sam said.

"Right, you want to give it a try?"

Sam looked at Kelly and Baker, her eyes drilled into theirs. "He has to get in. How

do we get him back?"

They both looked at each other and shrugged. "We could try sending the cable back out but, without someone on it, it will whip in the current." Kelly said.

"Altitude," Decker said.

"48 hundred," the pilot said.

"Increase speed," Decker said.

"No," Sam said.

"That's an order," Decker said.

"We're sending out the cable," Sam said.

"How's that going to help?" Decker said.

"You can grab it and get back in here."

Decker laughed. "I think I'd rather chance the high speed and landing than getting whipped to death with that cable."

"Then I'm coming to get you."

"No, send Kelly."

Kelly's face turned pale.

"I'm lighter," Sam said "and I should be on board if you get it opened."

"It's not opening and you're not expendable. We're losing altitude. Kelly, hook up and get out of here."

"Yes, sir," Kelly said.

"Clouds," the pilot said.

Sam turned and saw more clouds coming fast. She also saw something else.

38

Sam reached into the open cabinet behind the pilot and pulled two pistols from the holster. Familiar with the 9mm, she checked the clip and loaded the chambers. "You're crazier than he is," she said under her breath, then tucked the two guns into her vest pockets. "Let's get her back into position," she said to the pilot.

The pilot nodded and started aligning the Osprey back to the Airbus. Sam took a last look at the clouds ahead and then turned her attention to the rear. The pilot displayed his newly learned experience as the Airbus nose came smoothly into alignment.

The end of the cable lay on the ramp floor. She picked up the end while Kelly prepared to go. Unnoticed she released the tension on the cable and then picked the end up to give it to Kelly.

"Ready for this?" she said.

Kelly gave her a look. "No, but when you gotta go…"

"Well, I am," Sam said before he could finish his sentence, snapped the hook quickly and securely to her vest and then ran and jumped off the ramp. The hoist spun freely as the wind caught her and lifted her up. The cable reached its end and snapped her in tow.

"Kelly, what kind of crazy stunt was…" Decker yelled.

"This isn't Kelly, Deck."

"Sam? I thought I told you…. Where's Kelly?"

Sam didn't answer. A few yards from the front of the Airbus, she pulled out both guns and waved the wide-eyed stewardess to get away. The woman didn't respond. Sam waved again, then pointed the guns directly at her. The stewardess vanished into the passenger cabin. Sam knew she had just seconds before she would be cranked back to the Osprey by its shocked crew. She pointed both barrels at the far left windshield and opened fire. Like fat snowflakes, white circles appeared on the glass. She kept firing away. Web-like cracks appeared around the white spots. The cracks spread through the entire shield but then, click…click…..click….click. No more bullets. She dropped the guns and they disappeared over the Airbus's wings.

"Bring me closer."

"We're bringing you back ma'am."

"We don't have time! Bring me closer!"

"Captain?" Kelly said.

Decker didn't respond.

"Kelly, I'm right here, dammit," Sam yelled. "Give me ten feet and thirty seconds."

"Captain?" Kelly repeated.

"Bring her closer. Ten feet for thirty seconds, no more. Then yank her the hell out of here."

Sam held the cable with both hands as the Osprey closed the gap. The cloud was upon her and both aircrafts bounced in the turbulence. Her feet touched the middle windshield. She stepped left until she stood directly on the pelted glass. She stomped her heels. The crack stretched but the windshield stayed intact. She stomped with both feet and felt flex. Rain pounded the glass, making it slippery.

"Times up," Decker said.

"I'm almost there," Sam yelled.

"Three thousand feet gentlemen," the pilot said.

"Pull her in," Decker said.

Suddenly, the Airbus dropped and she was yanked off but, just as quickly there was slack in the line and the Airbus bounced back. Sam slammed into the cracked windshield hard, knocking it through; she swung into the flight deck and bounced off the controls and hit the floor. She was inside, but then the cable pulled and slammed her against the windshield. It loosened again and she fell back to the floor. She grabbed at the hook latch with both hands, fumbling with the release then, just as it cleared, the cable whipped out the windshield, denting the frame on exit. Dazed, Sam stared at the open window for a moment as air and rain stormed in at one hundred and sixty mph.

"You all right, Sam?" Kelly asked.

"Yes. Where's the EE hatch?" she yelled and then saw the stewardess peeking around the corner.

"Are you all right?" she asked Sam.

"Where's the EE hatch?"

She looked down and then up. "You're laying on it."

"We need to open it right now," Sam said and rolled off.

The stewardess nodded, dropped to her knees and reached for a D-ring latch.

"Turn this, and pull," she said as she opened the door.

Sam looked down a ladder with wires and circuits everywhere. The area was lit, probably from opening the hatch, she thought. At the bottom of the ladder she saw another hatch in the floor.

"You're bleeding," the stewardess said.

Sam hopped onto the ladder and hurried down the rings and then jumped off the final six feet. She found a similar latch to the one on the flight deck. She grabbed the ring handle and tried to turn it. Nothing. Frozen? She looked around, her eyes darting. She looked up to tell the stewardess the problem but she was gone, but only for a moment. She reappeared with a short metal rod in hand.

"Try this," she said, stretching it down to Sam's reach.

Sam grabbed it. Solid, about two feet. "What is it?"

"The Captain's closet rod."

Sam stabbed it through the ring and turned. It started to bend, but suddenly the ring moved. She pushed with all her strength. It unlocked. Sam ripped open the hatch and ear-crushing wind blasted into the compartment. Decker was right there. The amazement of his expression lasted only a second on his face but she would never forget it.

"Give me your strap," she yelled.

Decker released his tie from the landing gear and handed it to Sam. She tied it through the ladder rung and then reached for his arm. He stood on the wheel and grabbed the edges of the hatch but the wind held him, his legs and feet flailed in the powerful wind.

"Pull," Decker yelled.

Sam pulled with everything she had but she couldn't overcome the hundred and sixty mile per hour force pulling him from her.

Another pair of hands grabbed his vest. The stewardess. They both struggled and pulled and, finally, Decker was in. Sam closed the hatch and silenced the roar of air.

"One thousand feet."

Sam looked at Decker eye to eye.

"I'm not used to being rescued," he said.

"I know how you feel," she said.

"You're pretty crazy, aren't you?" he said and then grabbed the ladder ring and climbed.

"I guess you inspired me," she replied and climbed right behind him.

"I owe you one," Decker said and then climbed through the hatch into the windy flight deck.

"That's what they all say," Sam said, but only Jennel heard her.

39

The roar of wind in the flight deck was deafening. Sam took the copilots seat next to Decker, who stared at the control panel a frighteningly long time.

"Five hundred feet. You can't land on water," said the pilot's voice over the helmet's radio.

Decker took off his helmet. "Where's the stewardess?" he said.

Sam looked at the stewardess and then back to Decker. She didn't believe her ears. "I thought you said you could fly..."

"Just get the stewardess," he said.

"I'm right here," said the stewardess.

Sam turned, her name tag said "Jennel". "Point to the controls as they instructed you."

"Ok."

"Landing gear."

"Here," Jennel said pointing.

Decker pulled a lever and Sam felt mechanical movement under her feet.

"Flaps," Decker said.

"Here," she pointed again.

Decker pushed a lever and then another and then another. The engines increased in pitch and the wind coming through the windshield grew louder and louder. Decker's hands kept moving and there was a bump.

"What was that?" Sam yelled to Decker.

"Nothing," he said and smiled as the water outside the window got further away.

"What do you mean nothing?" Sam said and Jennel also looked interested in an answer.

Decker turned toward them, apparently satisfied in the speed and direction for the moment. "The tail hit."

Jennel's eyes grew much wider.

"Hit the water?" Sam said. "As in zero altitude?"

Decker nodded. "Yeah," he said and looked at Jennel. "Thanks for the jump start. I think I can figure it from here on out. But, uh, don't wander too far."

"No problem, you have blood all over your face," Jennel said. "Are you hurt?"

"No, it's not my blood," he said and then looked at Sam. "Where's yours?"

"I... forgot," she said. Her knees suddenly felt weak.

"Relax," Decker said. "You're safe."

"How do you know?" Sam said, unable to think as visions of decomposed bodies flashed through her mind.

"You'd already be dead. Just like in the cave. It came and left fast."

Sam exhaled. "Please let me hear you say it again."

"Well, how do you feel?" asked Jennel.

Sam took a moment to ask herself the same question. The adrenaline rush was calming. She had several cuts and her left shoulder and left thigh ached, but no severe stomach cramping, paralysis, or decomposition as far as she could tell. "I guess I feel normal."

Decker smiled thinly, "Normal for someone who shot their way through the front window of a jet in flight. How'd you come up with that one?"

Sam shrugged. "It was there."

"*It was there?* That's some answer. Anyway, thank you."

"No problem, just treat me like I'm on the team."

Decker nodded. "Ok. Check out the cabin while I radio in and set our new course."

Sam gave a quick nod and motioned for Jennel to give her the tour and followed her into first class. She gasped. As much as she had prepared for what she expected to see, she was completely unprepared for this. The Afghanistan photos and cadavers were one thing. Watching Drake die had been awful, but the scientific clinical aspect took some of the edge off since it had happened within the confines of a BSL. But these were civilians in business suits and street clothes. Mothers, children, businesswomen, families on vacation, the pilots.

Sam turned to Jennel. "Who was the first to get sick?"

"Shabaka Akil Mohammad. A strange character from the onset."

"Take me to him."

Sam followed her through first class into the main cabin. The smell of death was nauseating. Apparently no one wanted to touch the dead, leaving them dispersed throughout where they had died. Every eye was on her. Many of the living passengers were huddled in one area, some standing.

"What's happening?" called one lady.

"What were those shots?" said another.

The questions came rapid fire and Sam held up her hands. "There is no present danger. Everyone stay calm and we'll get through this, ok?"

"What happened?"

"It's all under investigation," Decker said from behind.

Sam turned on a dime and gave him a look.

"It's cool," he said. "Auto pilot at ten thousand feet. Where are we at here?"

Jennel pointed to a man who looked like many of the other dead men. "Here he is. Victim number one."

"Our suicide bomber?" Sam said softly.

Decker shook his head. "Tarik doesn't generally ask for volunteers. He gives 'special' assignments. I'm sure this guy thought he was going to New York."

"So how did it happen?" Sam said.

Decker turned to Jennel. "Did you notice anything strange about him prior?"

Jennel nodded. "He acted like a five-year old boy on his first flight. Kept asking for peanuts and coke and then eating from his own food. We were all keeping an eye on him."

"His own food?"

"Yeah, he had his own goodie bag."

"Goodie bag?" Decker said then reached and took the man's attaché and opened it on the empty seat next to him. Assorted papers, passport, the usual and a small leather zipper bag. He opened it carefully and pulled out the items and placed it next to the bag.

"One empty bag," Decker said. "Did you see what was in here?"

Jennel shook her head.

"We'll give it to Ross to play with. He'll find out what was in it,"

Decker said, then pulled more out. Another plastic bag with crumbs.

"A brownie?" Sam pointed to the bag. "How much do you want to bet we have our ingredients in these bags?"

Decker pulled out a pill box that read "stomachache pills.' "Ah-there's one left. Guaranteed whatever he ate in these first two gave him a wicked stomachache."

"Then the pill would be the pillar," Sam said.

"Pillar?" Jennel said.

"A theory we're entertaining," Decker said.

Sam raised a brow. "Entertaining?" she said and then turned to Jennel. "We need to know if anyone who is still alive is the oldest of their siblings."

Jennel frowned. "Excuse me?"

"Firstborns," Decker said. "We need to know if there are any firstborns alive."

Jennel's frown increased. "Why would….."

"Are you a firstborn?" Sam interrupted .

"Uh, no. I have an older brother."

"Well maybe that's why you're still alive." Sam said.

"Part of the theory," Decker said.

"You are joking," Jennel said and then her face went pale.

"What?" Sam said.

"The other stewardess. She was the oldest," Jennel said. "And Dorothy is the third."

Sam saw a little dog on a seat. "Who owns the dog?"

"Her," Jennel motioned to an older lady.

"See if she knows about the dog, too, and no, I'm not joking."

40

The sun was setting and the Osprey and two fighter jets led the way to the municipal airport next to Fort Detrick. Decker, in constant radio communication with an experienced airbus pilot, appeared in good control as the runway came into view.

"I don't think this neighborhood is used to jets this size scraping their rooftops," Sam said from the copilot seat.

"Relax, Sam. The real problem is the runway length."

Sam looked at him.

"Don't look at me."

"You never mentioned the runway length was a problem."

"It became a problem."

"When?"

"When we didn't crash."

"Oh. Now I understand where you get your confidence. You see the glass all full when it's only half."

"Well, I didn't want to be stick in the mud and sound discouraging."

"Thanks for that. Should I worry now?"

Decker pursed his lips. "Well, I guess."

"Are you worried?"

"About what?"

"Ugh, you're an idiot."

A few minutes later Decker pushed and pulled levers, threw switches, and pressed buttons. To take advantage of as much runway as possible the Airbus touched down at the earliest possible moment and Decker frantically worked the air brakes to slow it. The end of the runway came and went. The jet plowed through fences, barricades, and lawn before coming to a bumpy halt.

Sam and Decker looked at each other.

"Don't quit your day job, Captain Decker," Sam said.

"A bird couldn't have landed better."

Sam laughed. "Right! If the bird was a rotisserie chicken!"

"You're jealous."

"You're delusional."

"Perhaps, but the plane's on the ground."

"Where all planes eventually end up."

"Mission accomplished."

"Through organized chaos."

The door opened and troops took control. The aircraft was quickly evacuated and readied for Ross and the SMART-AIT.

Kelly and Baker stood at the bottom of the steps as Sam and Decker stepped off.

"Doctor Conway, you surprised me," Kelly said.

"Sorry, Sergeant. I kind of got caught up in the moment."

"Under the circumstances, apology accepted."

Decker shook his head. "Not so easy on her, Kelly. She's in a lot of trouble and will remain in my custody, indefinitely."

Just then, a white Suburban pulled up and Ross and his team stepped out. Decker turned to him and said, "We have to stop meeting like this." He handed Ross the insurgent's goodie bag. "The ingredients to the bomb that went off in there were carried in this. I don't think you'll find any surprises." Ross nodded. "Another scene like Afghanistan?"

"Yes. Only this was no accident and the survivors weren't firstborn."

Ross sighed. "How does the virus know who's who? Why did it kill Drake and not the others on the flight?"

Sam wanted to engage in the conversation but she needed a break from the action. Her jump suit and harness had glass, blood, and who knew what else on it. She felt supremely disgusting after being in the same cabin as all the decomposed victims.

"Hey, Deck?"

Decker turned. He looked as bad as she felt. "What's up, Sam?" His voice had a tone that had been missing prior to this. A tone of acceptance.

"Where does one get a shower and a nap around here?"

"Remember, you're under custody," he said.

"Shouldn't a prisoner be entitled to a shower?"

"Hmm, I guess you haven't spent too much time as a prisoner."

"Not lately."

"Grab our clothes from the Osprey and I'll get us a ride."

"Deal."

"And, Sam."

"What?"

"Don't try to escape."

Sam smiled and left. The clothes were where they left them. She didn't dare put them on. A white suburban drove up and the passenger door opened. Sam climbed in with a spare jump suit stuffed with their clothes.

"What's that?" Decker said, looking at the stuffed jump suit.

"Our luggage. I'm afraid of anything touching us. Sorry, but your job is officially grosser than mine, dissecting mummies included."

"Funny, I was going to tell you the same thing," Decker said, driving away from the busy scene.

Sam lowered the visor to look in the mirror. "Yikes! My hairdresser couldn't do this if he tried. I'll need a shower and a head transplant."

"The fort has some rather impressive accommodations set up for you."

Sam looked at him. "At your recommendation?"

"Nah, CIA figured you might be spending the night."

Sam smiled. "You're lying, Decker. Thanks."

The drive to the fort was a very short trip from the airport and Decker carried the overstuffed jumpsuit to Sam's room.

Decker looked at his watch. "It's seven o'clock. How about we take those showers and get some food before a nap. I'm pretty hungry and, if you shower and nap, you'll probably be done for the night."

"Dinner on the CIA?"

"Whatever you want. You earned it."

"See you in an hour?" Sam said.

"Perfect," Decker said, and then showed her in, separated his clothes from hers without remark and left.

41

Sam glanced around. Very nice but she craved an immediate hot shower. She went directly into the bathroom and painfully eased out of the jump suit and kicked it into the far corner, never to be touched again. The water took five seconds to get hot.

Sam looked at the mirror. A cut on her left cheekbone and a scrape on her chin. Her leg and shoulder hurt and a couple of colorful bruises were visible proof. She stepped under the hot water and sighed. What a day. The water pressure and heat felt good on the back of her neck. She soaked it in for a few minutes and then lathered up her hair. She rinsed and shampooed again, and then washed her body thoroughly. She felt an unusual need to be clean. Sterile.

After she dressed, Sam noticed several missed calls on her cell phone. The museum. She didn't recognize the next two. Jesse? The last time she saw him was two days ago, or was it three? So much had happened, she had to think. She looked at the night table clock. Decker would be here any minute. She pressed in Jesse's number. It went directly to voice mail. She listened to her messages. Delete, save, delete; weird. Jesse didn't leave a message. Actually, he started to, but didn't say anything. She immediately called him back and left a brief, "Call me, Jess," and then called Miss Cox.

"Hello, you've reached the cell phone of Judith Cox," was all Sam heard before pressing pound to jump to the beep.

She left another brief message to call her back, and then stared at herself in the mirror and said, "Where the hell are they?"

A knock at the door startled her focus. She slowly and painfully opened the door but, what she saw was not at all what she expected. Decker was barely recognizable and she was pleasantly drawn to his stunning appearance.

"You've shaved," Sam said, unblinking.

"Yeah," Decker said massaging his clean chin. "Second time this year."

"I'm flattered."

Decker smiled thinly and hidden dimples appeared. Who was this man? "To be honest, I almost shaved my head, too," he said.

Sam was staring at him and forced herself to look away. "I know. You need to feel clean. Me, too. I almost scrubbed my skin off."

"Well, you look ... great."

Sam laughed. "I feel like something the cat dragged in. But thanks. You look pretty great yourself."

"So what do you feel like eating?" Decker said.

"Anything, I'm starving," Sam said.

"Steak?"

"Perfect. You read my mind."

"If we had time, I'd take us down to the Waterfront in Baltimore, but we need to stay close right now. I know a great little steak house about a mile away that..."

"Sold, Deck. I can already taste it."

Parking was easy at the Santa Fe Grill. The interior décor was a hodgepodge of everything from old civil war pictures, to license plates, to lobster traps. The hostess showed them to a small round table with a red and white checkered table cloth. The menu was all about steak. A waitress quickly appeared.

"Can I start you off with a drink?"

Decker looked at Sam.

"Normally, I would go for a Merlot." Sam said.

"Merlot for the lady and I'll have a Grey Goose on the rocks."

Sam's brow rose. "Make that two. Maybe the inside needs a little sterilization too."

Decker smiled. "My thoughts exactly."

The waitress returned with the whiskeys and said to Sam, "Has anyone ever told you that you look like Samantha Conway?"

"Who?" Decker said.

"The archaeologist treasure hunter lady," the waitress said.

Sam smiled. "From time to time, her name pops up."

The Vodka warmed the atmosphere, and the steaks were thick and juicy. Just the way Sam liked them. They ate with silent fervency, cutting and stabbing and sopping until the plates were virtually shelf clean.

"So what's next?" Sam asked.

"You have room for dessert?"

"I mean what's next with our mission," Sam said.

"For me, find Tarik – for you – translate the artifact."

"How are you going to find him?"

"I have a few ideas, all involving research. We may find some clues from the crashes and from the jet that didn't crash. Saving it was big for our side. I also want to go back to the videotape. There was something I'd like to examine a little closer."

"What?" Sam said.

"I'm going to look at it later. You can review it with me if you like."

"Sure. I'm in custody, remember?"

"And don't you forget it."

"Dessert?" The waitress asked.

Decker looked to Sam for the answer.

Sam stared blankly, lost in thought. "He didn't leave a message."

Decker frowned. "Excuse me?"

"Jesse, my brother. He called me and didn't leave a message."

"Maybe he didn't want to bother you while you were shooting out the window of the Airbus at a hundred and sixty miles per hour and will try you later."

Sam shook her head. "You would think," Sam deadpanned. "But he always wants to bother me and loves leaving me messages."

"Call him now."

Sam nodded and found her phone. She dialed and it went right to his voice mail again. She looked at Decker and said, "I'm worried."

Decker waved the dessert off and asked for a check. "Do you want me to send someone to the house?"

"Unless you have a key to the Osprey."

"Always out of the box, aren't you? I'll get someone to make a call. No problem."

"Thank you," Sam said and then reached over and squeezed his hand. "I appreciate it. Jesse's well-being means everything to me."

Sam and Decker sat in front of a huge screen, playing back the Tarik's announcement.

"Stop it there!" Decker said and stood up.

Sam hit pause on the remote control.

"Tell me what you see?"

"Hmm. At first glance, a lot of absence. He could be anywhere. He's standing in front of a white wall. I don't see anything about his clothes that stand out. His words seem to be his own."

"Forget his words. Nothing he says is what he means."

"Then what does he want?" Sam asked.

"Immortality and power," Decker said.

"Murdering innocent victims doesn't seem like a prudent way to get to heaven."

"He doesn't care about heaven or hell or seventy-two virgins. He believes in the ancient Egyptian Gods."

"Like Hitler?" Sam said.

"Hitler believed in Egyptian gods?"

Sam nodded. "Yes. In fact, the golden eagle symbol the Egyptians worshiped was common Nazi imagery, appearing everywhere from belt buckles to flagpole caps. Maybe he wants to be like Hitler."

Decker shook his head. "Hitler's a bad guy historically. Tarik wants to be like Attila was to the Huns or like Genghis Khan was to the Mongolians."

"Someone who will inflict punishment to one to get glory from another."

"Exactly. A hero to the distant masses."

"Even if some of his people need to be sacrificed for the cause."

Decker nodded. "No problem. He just sacrificed three of his own men and possibly hundreds of his own people."

"To give an example of his power?"

"That, but I suspect also as an experiment. I think this was a test of his own ability. He's not just flexing for us; he's flexing for himself."

"For what?"

"We don't know."

"Probably something to catch everyone's attention."

"I think that's a given."

"Something bigger than three jets," Sam said.

"One would think."

"Something with unmistakable credit to him."

"Do I smell a theory coming?"

"Just a thought."

"I'm all ears, Sam. Let's hear it."

"Would you consider Tarik to be a romantic?"

"I suppose, in a twisted sort of way."

"Dramatic?"

"Absolutely."

"Do you think he might be interested in revenge."

"On who?"

"Well, what do you think Pharaoh would do if he had the recipe for the Angel of Death?"

"Who?"

"Ramses. The Pharaoh that Moses set the plagues against."

Decker nodded thoughtfully. "I suppose he would return fire with fire."

"Exactly. Direct payback for what Moses did, what, three-thousand years ago? Moses was God's tool to wipe out the Egyptians' firstborn and deliver the Jews to the Promised Land."

"So, Tarik is obviously Pharaoh, and Moses represents who? Israel?"

"I can think of a few possibilities.

"Do you have a calendar?"

"I'm sure I can get one. Why?"

"When is Passover? If he wants to make a dramatic statement, what better time?"

Decker stared at her blankly and then, without saying another word, he got up and left the room. In a few minutes, he was back with a calendar with animal pictures on it, turning pages. He dropped the calendar in front of Sam and turned the pages. He stopped at April, scanned with his index finger and then jabbed it on a square. "Passover!"

"April second," Sam said.

"What's today? March Sixteenth?"

Sam thought. "I'm lucky if I know what day of the week it is." She flipped the page back. "The seventeenth."

"That gives us, two weeks!"

"More or less."

"Which city?" Decker said.

"My immediate thought would be Jerusalem. By far the most poetic justice of a vengeful mind."

"How about New York? There is a larger Jewish population in New York than in all of Israel," Decker pointed out.

"Maybe in the mind, but not in the heart. New York is a nice place to visit, but Israel is home and Jerusalem is where God wanted the Ark of the Covenant to dwell: in the city of David."

Decker nodded. "Or both."

"Maybe. But it's not unlimited. New York is a big city. The virus does have its limitations. We need to know more about it, find its weakness.

"Or stop Tarik before he sets it loose."

Sam nodded. "What did you want to show me on screen?"

"Oh, look above his head on the wall behind him. What do you see?"

Sam looked. "Nothing."

Decker motioned for the remote. "Let me have that a second." Sam gave it to him and he magnified the area above his head.

Sam nodded. "A smudge —no, a few smudges."

"Okay, that's two-hundred percent."

"Bumps?"

"We might be looking at three rivets," Decker said. "If those are rivets, the white wall behind him is metal."

"Okay, does that help us?"

"Hey, you're the treasure hunter here. To me, metal and rivets mean industry, and what industry uses rivets to hold its walls together?"

Sam shrugged. "Marine?"

"Or something that either keeps in or keeps out liquid. Bridges, shipping, oil tanks, water tanks, navy, tankers."

"Well that narrows it down to the whole world."

"He's in the Middle East. He can't chance traveling too far. He's right now the most wanted man on the planet. Especially now."

"Still a big area."

"If he didn't put the rivets there to send us off track."

Decker's cell phone rang. He answered, said "uh-huh" a few times, then hung up.

"Jesse's not home," he said.

"What!"

"There's no answer and the door's locked."

"That's impossible."

"Why?"

"Because Jesse doesn't go anywhere at this time of night and Ms Cox would be asleep. She's an early riser."

"There's no car in the driveway."

"It's in the garage," Sam said and then immediately called Jesse again. No answer, right to voice mail. She left another message pleading for Jesse to call her. *"He doesn't answer and he's not home,"* she stressed.

"Could be anything, Sam. Does he have a girlfriend?"

"No."

"He might just be out of signal range."

"He called me and didn't leave a message."

"That *does* happen."

"Not with Jesse. He either couldn't leave one or someone else made the call."

Decker paused. "You're not going to be worth anything until you know, right?"

"Right," Sam said emphatically.

"Ok, I'll make you a deal. Get to bed now and I'll get us a lift at the crack of dawn."

"How about now?"

Decker gave her a look. "It's been a long day, Sam, and we're going to have nothing but long days for the foreseeable future. I need you at full strength. You're not going to be much good translating with your eyes closed. And not for nothing. I'm wiped. Okay?"

Sam nodded, looked him square in the eye and said, "I'll see you in the morning."

"Good," Decker said and got up to walk her to her room. However, when they left the viewing room, Sam turned left instead of right.

"Hey, it's this way," Decker said.

Sam kept walking and said, "Not for me. I'm going to Long Island."

42

Sam followed Decker into the Osprey and, a minute later, they were headed for Long Island. Decker gave the pilot some instructions and then went into the rear with Sam, who sat buckled into a seat.

"What are you looking for?" Sam said.

"This," Decker said, pulling what looked like a folded yellow tent from a cubby. He pulled a thin rope and the yellow sack instantly inflated.

"A life raft?" Sam said. "Getting a little paranoid?"

Decker grabbed an arm full of jumpsuits and then tossed them inside the raft. "I don't see a life raft. I see a bed," he said and got in. He leaned up against a side, closed his eyes and patted a spot next to him with his hand. "Queen-size."

"You think I'm that easy?"

Decker smiled. "You think I am?"

"Probably," Sam said, as she unbuckled and stepped in. She adjusted the jumpsuits a bit and got comfortable. "Thank you," she said.

"No problem," Decker said sleepily. "Any time you need an Osprey, just let me know."

Sam smiled. "You're a good guy, Deck," she whispered and snuggled closer to him. Decker appeared to be completely asleep.

Two hours flew by like two minutes.

"Captain?" the pilot called.

Sam opened one eye. She was more tired now than when she had first laid down. She watched Decker climb out and sit up front with the pilot. She realized she had asked a lot to fly up to Long Island and Decker was more than a good sport. She rolled over, crawled out of the raft and tried to keep her balance as she moved toward the lights of the flight deck. She rubbed her sleepy eyes and recognized the area, even in the moonlight.

"That's the field," She said, pointing to the local sports field she had always known as her back yard. Her father's house bordered it and her father always referred to it as, "Our yard, but the county mows it for us."

"Your neighbors are going to think they're being invaded," Decker said.

Sam shook her head. "No, they'll just think I'm back from work. You have no idea what we used to do here when I was a kid. What time is it?"

Decker looked at his watch. "A little after two."

"The police will be around if not the neighbors."

"They've been notified," Decker said. "The basement lights are on. Maybe he's home."

"If he was home, he would have shut them off and gone to bed," Sam said. "And there's no way Ms Cox would miss that. Her bedroom is right next to the basement door and she's incredibly detailed," she said as the Osprey settled in the grass field. The door opened and they jogged to the rear of the house. Sam grabbed the door knob.

"It's locked," she said, shocked.

"It's very late," Decker pointed out.

"This door hasn't been locked in thirty years," Sam said and knocked hard. "Ms Cox, Jesse," she called.

"Don't you have the key?" Decker asked.

"There is no key. Why would there be a key to a door that's never been locked?"

Decker looked like he was going to say something, but didn't.

Sam clenched her hand and took aim at the glass. She threw the punch but Decker quickly caught her fist in front of the glass.

"Do we really want to add a late run to the ER to the itinerary? Didn't I see a keypad on the garage door?"

"Yes," Sam said and ran around to the garage door. She flipped open the keypad, punched the number one four times and hit enter. The door started rising.

"High security," Decker said.

Sam didn't respond. Ms Cox's car was there as it should be. Then why was the door locked and why didn't anyone answer the knock? She ran past the car to the house door and found it was also locked. "Locked! What the…" was all she got out when the sole of Decker's shoe hit the door and it busted open.

Sam ran through the door and down a short hall that led into the kitchen and switched on the light. A dirty frying pan sat on the stove. Ms Cox sat at the table, face down in a red puddle.

"No!" Sam gasped.

"Stay back," Decker said and picked up a butcher's knife from the counter top.

"Jesse!" Sam called, ignoring Decker's order, and then ran to the family room and turned on a light switch. The floor was littered with books and DVD cases. A table lamp was on its side. "Jesse!" she called and ran up a half flight of stairs to his bedroom. She swatted the light switch on. Neat as a pin. No Jesse.

"Where the hell is he?" she cried. She stormed past Decker, through the family room and saw the basement door cracked open with light coming through. She ran for it, raced down the steps and gasped. The place was a wreck. The computer was on with a note typed to the screen and it didn't look like Jesse's handwriting. The note read, "Press enter, click send, and you will hear from Jesse!"

Sam ripped the note off the monitor, clapped it into Decker's hand and hit enter. The screen saver vanished and Jesse's email appeared with a letter already written, waiting to be sent. The draft simply said, 'Samantha Conway'.

"What do you make of this?" Sam said.

Decker frowned and read it. "A letter from Jesse to Jesse. Non-traceable yet viewed by anyone who has his address and password. Someone has his password and will communicate with you through email and now that they know you have been here, will contact you on your cell phone – probably with Jesse's".

"Jesse's been kidnapped?" she shouted.

Decker paused. He looked around the room. There was debris all over the floor. "Signs of struggle down here and upstairs. No signs of blood, except from your housekeeper, who was probably shot on entry."

Sam couldn't believe her ears. She grabbed his jawbone and turned his eyes to hers. "*Her name* is Judith Cox." Sam had a rush of anger as she thought of how Ms Cox, though reserved in personality, had faithfully cared for her brother. "She's dead and my brother's been kidnapped."

Decker removed her tight grip from his chin. "We'll get him back, Sam."

"Alive?"

"Yes."

"He's been through so much."

"I know. I'll bring him home."

Tears ran freely down Sam's cheeks. "Do you promise?" she said holding his hands – holding his gaze.

"Yes," he said confidently, without a blink. "I'll bet my life on it."

Sam was unable to think. "What do we do first?"

"Click send. No one knows you were in Maryland except the people connected with our team. Whoever did this is probably expecting a quick response. The note promises we'll hear from Jesse. It doesn't say when, but let's click and hope for the best."

Sam clicked "send" and paced. "Why would anyone kidnap Jesse?

"To get to you." Decker said. "Your name was on the letter."

"Why would they kill Ms Cox? She's harmless," Sam cried.

"Guaranteed harmless when dead, and it sends the message they mean business."

"*Mean business?* So call me, for God's sake. Knock on my door. That's what *you* did," she said and started picking things off the floor."

"Don't," Decker said. "This is a crime scene. Don't touch. Let's go upstairs."

Sam nodded. Her head was spinning. "What do we do about Ms. Cox? Shouldn't we call the police?"

"No. Leave that to me, Sam." Decker took her hand and led her up the stairs and into the family room.

"Tell me, Deck. Why take Jesse when I would be more than happy to help someone? Do they think I'm rich? On the museum salary?"

"No one wants your money Sam."

"Then what?"

"Same as us, Sam. They want your expertise."

"Who?"

"The competition. Try to remember you're world famous."

Sam tried to think but her thoughts weren't connecting. "I'm sorry Deck. Help me understand."

"Do you know anyone else with ancient writings that might need translation? Someone you would deny in a heartbeat?"

Sam suddenly realized what Decker was trying to make obvious. "*No.* You're a liar!" She said.

"You read my mind?"

"They're nowhere near here."

"You're probably right," Decker said.

"Shut up!" Sam said and fled to the front door.

Decker allowed a minute to make a phone call, and then followed her carefully.

Sam sobbed and then turned to Decker. "You want it to be Tarik, don't you? This will give you a connection."

Decker got closer but Sam moved away. "Sam, that's not true."

"But you'll take it."

"I don't want it but it is what it is. They came here looking for you and found Jesse. They couldn't leave him to warn you but they won't hurt him and risk the chance of you not helping. They need you both healthy, at least at first. Jesse is a bonus to them. He ensures your cooperation."

"I can't believe I'm hearing this. You could be wrong."

"Maybe – maybe not. The timing is too coincidental, wouldn't you say?"

Sam couldn't respond. To admit it would make it real. Just then her cell phone rang. It was Jesse's number. Sam looked at Decker.

"Answer it," he said.

Sam's hands shook as she flipped open her phone. "Hello?" she said.

"Put it on speaker," Decker mouthed. She did.

"Doctor Samantha Conway?" The voice had an Egyptian accent.

"Yes. Who is this?"

"We are a client of yours."

"I don't have any clients. Who are you and what do you want? Where is my brother?"

"Your brother is presently in most excellent condition. With your cooperation, he will stay in perfect good health."

"If you harm a hair on his head, I swear, I will kill you."

Decker motioned with his palm down to tone it down. Sam gritted her teeth and gave a nod with her eyelids.

"Doctor Conway, you misunderstand our position. Your brother became an unexpected passenger. We seek only your assistance. If you help us you will be rewarded beyond anything you can acquire in lifetime. You and your brother will be very, very rich. He has special needs that will receive care for rest of life."

Bull, Sam thought. "And if I refuse?"

"You are intelligent person, Doctor Conway. Refusal not intelligent."

Decker mouthed for her to agree to help.

She exhaled and nodded. "What do you want me to do?"

"You will perform work that you are expert in. Detail come later."

"You want to speak to Jesse," Decker mouthed.

"I want to talk to Jesse. I need to know he's all right before I agree to anything."

"Jesse will be waiting for you when you arrive."

Sam looked at Decker. He shook his head.

"No good. This works both ways."

After a pause, the caller said, "As show of perfect mutual very good faith, we connect you with him. This will take minute."

"A minute?" Sam said to Decker, with her hand over the microphone.

Decker nodded. "It won't be a direct connection. Jesse will be on another line and we'll communicate speaker to speaker. The only number we'll ever see will be Jesse's and the only written communication we'll get is Jesse's email."

"As long as I hear his voice telling me that..."

"H-hello?" Jesse's voice sounded distant.

"Jesse?"

"H-hi."

"Are you alright?"

"Y-yes."

"Did they hurt you?"

"N-no. W-what's h-hap-pening?"

"Doctor Conway." The Egyptian was back.

"Where's Jesse?" Sam said. Her heart needed more.

"You spoke to your brother and he was in perfect condition. We have acted in good faith but to keep him in excellent health, you must respect the agreement. Yes?"

Sam wanted to tear his head off. She looked at Decker who mouthed, "What do you want me to do?"

The cell phone shook in her hand. "Yes. What do I do?" she said.

"We could not help but notice you arrive in military aircraft. We also know there is man with you. In next sixty seconds, we need him enter aircraft and leave and you drive in your car. I will direct you as you drive car. Key already in ignition. No deviation from instruction will be tolerated," the man said.

Decker shook his head. "You need more time," he mouthed.

"I need more time. I need to get Jesse's pills and some other…"

"No more time. Fifty seconds."

Decker shook his head.

"But…" was all Sam said.

"Forty-six seconds," the man said and then disconnected.

"No," Decker said. "We need to set up control and security. You can't just drive away unprotected. I won't let you."

Sam put her phone in her pocket and left. "You can't stop me. They'll kill him. And you have to leave in the Osprey. They're watching."

"This is crazy, Sam," Decker said, chasing her.

"Thirty seconds, Decker. Get your ass out of here."

"Take my phone," Decker said. "It has a homing device. I'll call you immediately after you start off in the car. We'll triangulate your position."

Sam took his phone and stopped as they passed the kitchen and stared at Ms Cox. "What about…"

"I'll take care of Ms Cox," he said.

Sam nodded and then bolted to the car in the garage and saw the key in the ignition as told. Decker made a quick check of the back seat.

"I'll follow from the Osprey," Decker said. Don't forget. You're in my custody. I'll be one step away."

"Promise?" Sam said.

Decker gave her a quick, strong kiss. "I promise," he said, then sprinted to the Osprey. Sam opened the driver's door but, before she could get in, she felt something stick her in the back.

"Step way from the car, Doctor Conway," said a man's voice with an Egyptian accent.

Sam backed away from the car and another man entered, started the car and drove away. She watched it turn onto the street and race away. The Osprey lifted off and followed.

"We will walk to your neighbor's house. Any resistance will mean your instant death and the disposal of your brother. Do you understand?"

"Yes," she said. Decker's cell phone vibrated.

"I'll take that," the man said. Sam reached into her pocket and handed it to him, the barrel of the gun pressed hard in her back.

"Thank you," he said, and then opened it and placed it on the ground. He then pressed her to walk toward her neighbors.

The Osprey had disappeared. They went through a gate and into her neighbor's driveway.

Your neighbor was kind enough to give us the keys to her car."

"Debbie Reuben?" she said. "Did you hurt her?"

"Of course not," he replied. "She felt nothing."

"Like Ms Cox?" Sam snarled.

"We take no pleasure in this task, but our instructions are very specific and cannot be adjusted by the individual. I'm sure you understand."

"I understand that you won't get away with this," Sam said.

"For your brother's sake, I hope you are wrong." The man led Sam to her neighbor's Honda SUV. Sam was told to climb into the passenger seat from the driver's side and the man slid in right next to her. He then produced a hypodermic needle.

"This will only make you sleep. When you awake, you will be rested and with your brother, both safe and unharmed. The alternative will be very unpleasant for both of you so please do not resist. Roll up your sleeve."

Sam looked into the barrel of the gun, unafraid. She considered knocking the gun away and stabbing him with his own needle. But then what of Jesse if they didn't show up? She rolled up her sleeve and was promptly injected.

"Thank you, Doctor Conway, and good night."

43

Jafari Amen drove his own car into the massive multilevel parking complex at Roosevelt Field shopping mall. He had switched cars twice, once under a bridge and again in another multilevel parking complex a few miles east. Other cars had been set up for him if he needed, but the military helicopter and the other helicopter that joined the chase were long gone. He couldn't help but smile. He had not only done well as a decoy, but he had managed to completely escape. He had told them he would, that he was meant for the job. His family would be proud.

He parked and grabbed his gym bag from the trunk and walked to XSport, the 24/7 gym he belonged to. At 5:00 AM, he would be virtually alone and have the gym to himself. He took the escalator to the basement passing dozens of large screen televisions, with beautiful models dancing and singing ridiculous American songs. He passed his key chain code bar over the scanner and heard the beep that authorized his entry. A pretty girl in black spandex pants smiled and welcomed him with a "Good morning, sir." He smiled back.

"Good morning," he said. If only she knew who he was. She would be even more impressed.

As he figured, the place was empty. He usually wouldn't check his emails, but the internet café was also empty. He glanced around and then took a seat, one of ten, and checked his email. Nothing new, but he decided to send a little note to his supervisor.

He typed in English, "All good," and clicked "send". Next stop was free weights. He did a little bench press and then used a few machines. His routine was haphazard, having never exercised as an adolescent or trained by one of the many pros at the facility. His favorite time to go to the gym was after work when it was busy and lots of women occupied the machines and exercise classes. He had come to learn that in this country things were much different.

A half hour into his casual routine, it was time for a rare sit in the whirlpool before work. Upstairs in the mall, he worked at a cell phone kiosk but, he wasn't due there for another hour. He went into the locker room, changed into some bathing trunks, and entered the pool area. He liked it better during prime time when more women in bathing suits walked around, but after being chased all over Nassau County by the government, a peaceful sit in some steamy water felt well deserved.

The water was hot as he eased in. The pool was about five yards in diameter with a large rock in the middle and a waterfall in the corner. He sat under the waterfall and closed his eyes as the healing water massaged his shoulders.

Jafari reflected upon his life: how his family was being taken care of by Tarik and how everything was falling into place. He didn't know what, but something very big was going to happen soon. The recent airline crashes were just the beginning of a master plan to bring his people the respect and authority they had fought for. He didn't know when they would call on him next, but he expected it to be in the near future.

"That waterfall is great, isn't it?" A voice said.

Jafari opened his eyes and saw a man sitting across from him. He wasn't aware anyone had entered. The man looked very strong and defined. He was probably a regular at this time in the morning. "Yes," he said, and then closed his eyes again.

"You don't usually come here this time of day do you?"

Jafari opened his eyes again. *Why did this man think that he wanted to converse?* "No, I usually come at night."

"So what brings you here so early this morning?"

Was he writing a book? Jafari sighed. "I had business that I needed to be awake for and, afterward thought I would come here before work."

"Ahh, where do you work?"

"In the mall upstairs."

"Really, where?"

Jafari paused. He wanted to ignore the man but he didn't want the attention that could come with rudeness. "The cell phone kiosk in front of J C Penny's."

"Yes. I know the one. Well my name is John Decker. Yours?"

Another pause. "Jafari Amen."

"Where are you from, what country?"

"Egypt."

"Cool. Do you like America?"

"Yes."

"You plan on staying here?"

"I think so."

"Good, good. So uh, what kind of business got you out of bed so early?"

Jafari had enough of these questions. "It is getting late for me and I've been in the heat too long. If you want good deal on cell phone come see me…"

"Decker, you can call me Decker."

Jafari got up. "I will see you again, Decker." He said and, then grabbed his towel and left.

"You can bet on it, Jafari," Decker said and then followed Jafari out of the water.

Jafari turned to see that Decker was in his underwear not bathing trunks. *What was wrong with this man?*

"Do you come here often, Decker?" Jafari said as he walked to the locker room.

"No. This is my first time."

Jafari was surprised. He entered the locker room with the Decker man close behind. Strangely there was no one else there. Other people should have arrived by now. Jafari walked down the hall to the showers.

"Oh, uh, Jafari?" Decker said, still behind him.

Jafari turned, "Yes?"

Decker had a roll of duct tape in his hand.

"I found this in the parking lot. Is it yours by any chance?"

Jafari felt his eyes widen. "Why would it be mine?"

"Because I found it in the trunk of your car," Decker said in perfect Egyptian.

44

Jafari didn't blink. He suddenly dashed to get by Decker. Decker saw it coming a mile away. He hit Jafari in the throat with the roll of duct tape, knocking him splat on his back.

Decker smiled. That felt good. He had the gym completely to himself, his friends from the CIA and FBI had evacuated the facility while Jafari was in the whirlpool. He had asked for twenty minutes alone. If he wanted more time, he would ask and get it. No witnesses on this one.

Jafari held his throat, choking and gasping. "We're going to get to know each other real well, Jafari. I'm really looking forward to it. How about you?" he said and then grabbed him by his thick black hair and dragged him into the sauna. He brought his face within a sniff of the electric heating elements, just long enough to get a good scream and then threw him onto the bench.

"Now that we've been properly introduced, there are a few questions I'd like to ask you. Are you good with that or do I have to explain your rights again?" Decker asked.

Jafari was gagging, spitting and sweating. He appeared confused and scared. "What do you want to know?"

"For starters, I want to know where Samantha Conway and her brother are?"

Jafari snickered between deep breaths. "Do you think they would tell me that?"

"For your sake, I would hope so."

"I have no knowledge of where. You— whoever you are— should already know that."

"What is your supervisor's name?"

"If I tell you that, I will be killed."

"If you don't, you'll wish you were dead," Decker said calmly.

"It is very hot in here," Jafari said.

"What is your supervisor's name?"

"I cannot tell you. Kill me if you must."

Decker shrugged. "Okay."

Jafari's eyes widened as Decker came at him. Jafari tried to get away but promptly got hit in the throat again, a quick jab with Decker's crossed index and middle finger. Jafari fell back grabbing his throat again, spitting blood.

"Out of curiosity," Decker said. "Which was more effective, the duct tape or the finger? I only ask because you just had both and it's unusual that the same person can make such an educated comparison with such objectivity." He rolled him on his face and duct taped his hands behind his back and then his feet together.

"I wouldn't imagine, since you have this tape, that Jesse got similar treatment. Am I right on that Jafari?" Decker said, as he dragged the terrorist by his armpit out of the sauna and into the shower. Jafari curled into fetal position on the shower floor while Decker left him momentarily to get a towel.

"You are not police. I want police."

"Did I mention that whining annoys the hell out of me?"

"You are not permitted to treat me like this," Jafari said.

"Give me Tarik's address and I'll send him a personal apology, with a couple of your favorite body parts. My choice, of course," Decker said. He turned the shower on and adjusted the spray to a single solid stream. He ripped the towel and kept a piece the size of a face rag and soaked it on the floor. He then turned

Jafari onto his back so that the water was hitting hard next to his face and then straddled his chest and sat on his abdomen.

"Now are we comfy?" Decker said. "Before we begin our next exercise, I want to give you the chance to answer the questions I already asked you. In case you forgot. Number one. Where did your friends take Samantha Conway?"

"I told you, I don't know."

Decker shook his head. "Wrong answer. Number two, who is your supervisor?"

"I can't tell you," he said, his eyes looking at the water.

Decker pursed his lips. "You know, I was kind of hoping it would go this way. I'm sure you're familiar with or have at least heard of water boarding?"

Jafari's eyes grew very wide.

"It's kind of a poor man's lie detector. Most people last from five to ten seconds. A couple of your group have lasted an outstanding one to two minutes. Anyway, I won't tell you how long I've lasted because I find it embarrassing. The gag reflex it triggers makes your brain and body actually believe you're drowning. It's quite uncomfortable even though you don't actually get hurt. Unless, of course, you break your own bones trying to escape. I've seen that."

"Please," Jafari said.

"Please?" Decker said. "Do you want me to say please?"

"Don't do this. Please."

"Okay, even though you didn't give that chance to Jesse or Sam, I'll ask you once more."

Jafari exhaled. "I can't tell you."

Decker sighed. He then touched Jafari in the throat just below the Adam's apple, where he had already been hit twice. Jafari screamed, and in that instant, Decker shoved the soaked towel in his open mouth. He then grabbed the hair above his ears and dragged his head so that the water was hitting the rag.

Jafari instantly gagged and buckled and writhed in agony. Decker was hardly able to hold on. After about fifteen seconds, Decker slid his head away from the water and pulled the rag out. Jafari screamed a few times and then coughed and choked, his body limp with exhaustion.

"So, Jafari. I trust you've reconsidered the answers to my questions. Or do you want to have another go at it?"

Decker walked out of the locker room and into the cardio area where dozens of CIA and FBI agents waited. He spotted Walker and said, "He's all yours... in the shower."

"You just left him there?" Walker said, incredulously.

Decker grabbed a dry towel and started using it. "He'll be happy to see you," Decker said. "Anyone see my pants?"

Walker motioned to a few men to go into the locker room. "I have to tell you Deck, it sounded pretty scary from out here."

"Do they make smoothies here?"

"Are we going to need an ambulance?"

"Nah, he's fine," Decker said pulling his pants on.

"You know, it's not your fault Sam was kidnapped," Walker said. "Tarik wanted her and with or without us he was going to get her."

"We should have anticipated that," Decker said. "I should have."

"And what, put an eye on every writing expert?"

"I feel responsible."

"Well, you're not."

"Look, don't worry about me."

Three agents carried Jafari past them. The man was completely limp, his eyes bloodshot. When he saw Decker, he screamed and struggled. Walker watched him exit surrounded by agents.

"You seem to have made an impression on him."

"I was hoping he'd last a little longer."

"Did you get what you wanted?"

Decker wavered. "I got what he knew. His supervisor's name is Masud Zahur."

"Excellent," Walker said. "We'll check it out against the email."

"What email?"

"When he came in, he went to the internet café and sent an email. We pulled it and are running it down."

"How did you know?"

"The receptionist saw him go in there and the camera showed us which terminal he used."

"What did the email say?"

"It just said, 'All good' ".

Decker nodded. "Don't take Zahur."

"Excuse me?"

"Don't take him. Locate him. Keep him under surveillance. He can't know we're onto him. I have an idea."

"What?"

"Later."

"What did he say about Sam?" Walker said.

"They took her to an airport. He didn't know which one."

"To go where?"

"He didn't know."

"Are you sure?"

Decker gave him a look.

"Ok, you're sure. We'll check them all for private flights departing."

Decker nodded. "Listen, call me when you get Zahur located," he said and gave Walker his current number.

"Where are you going?"

"Back to Sam's. Can I use your wheels?"

"Sure, I'll hitch."

"Later on I need to get back to USARMRIID. Can you get there?"

"Are you going to let me in on what you're doing?"

Decker nodded. "You're part of the program but, I can't tell you about it yet."

"Figures. They told me I would get used to you but they didn't say how long it would take."

"Wow, they're still telling people that?"

"Ha ha. By the way, you look tired," Walker said.

"I'm fine," Decker said. "Remember to call me when you locate Zahur. And…"

"I know, don't take him," Walker said and tossed him his keys.

Decker left the gym and went directly to Sam's. A twenty-minute drive. On his way to the rear door, he saw his cell phone open on the ground. He picked it up and continued. Inside he rummaged around until he found what he was looking for in the basement office. On the desktop next to the monitor was the box Sam had when he first met her. He opened the box and stared at it for a moment, wondering the best way to pick it up. Finally, he carefully cradled it like a baby and held it up in the light. It looked a little like an old style camcorder with a scope on the top. He looked through the scope. It had adjustable magnifications like most rifle scopes. He pulled the trigger. Nothing seemed to happen. He looked through the scope and pulled the trigger again. A laser beam appeared. He smiled. He took his eye out of the scope again and pulled the trigger and heard a quiet hum. He saw nothing, but in the scope he saw the beam clearly. "Infrared" he said.

"Testing, testing," he said into the microphone. He pulled the trigger and spoke again. According to what Sam had told him, his voice was being channeled through the beam. He put it back in the box and went upstairs. In the living room, he was momentarily captured by some family photos. There was one of Sam in a little league uniform. Another picture had her and a boy at about twelve years old and she was holding the same sound instrument that was in the box.

Written on the bottom of the photo it said, 'Sam and Tyler with Sound Shooter'. "Sound Shooter," Decker said and smiled. *Very cool kid,* he thought. He touched another photo of her in khakis in a desert somewhere with a few others in front of a jeep. He touched the photo and said. "Hang in there, Babe… I got you into this and I'll get you out."

Decker left the house and drove into a strip mall's parking lot. There was a supermarket, a bagel deli, a pizzeria and a card store. He parked, rolled down the window and took the sound shooter out of the box. "Okay, let's see what Sam was talking about." He watched a lady pushing a cart about a hundred feet away. He pulled the trigger, heard the hum and looked through the infrared scope and saw the green beam. He focused the magnification until he was easily able to place the beam in her ear. "*Stop*," he said into the microphone. The lady instantly stopped, as if he had spoken to her from a couple of feet away. She turned around a few times and, seeing no one there, she continued.

Decker looked at the Sound Shooter and feathered his fingers over it. "Where were you when I was a kid?" he said when suddenly, his cell phone vibrated. It was Walker.

"Yeah?"

"We found Zahur."

Decker drifted in and out of sleep in the driver's seat of Walker's car, waiting for Masud Zahur to appear. Walker watched from the passenger seat, allowing Decker a much needed cat nap. They had stationed themselves in a parking lot across the street from Empire Electronics.

Zahur turned out to be the co-owner of a successful electronics distribution company. Ten years earlier, his brother had opened a small electronics store and chose to specialize in cell phones. Together, they had since expanded the business to forty-five stores nationwide. In the years that followed, phone companies generated their own stores so Zahur moved into accessories. Changing within the major company constraints and guessing right with public demand for new technology, had kept them ahead of the competition. His origin and connection with Tarik was unknown… until today's email. And, as far as Zahur knew, his identity was still secret and everything was, "All good."

"Deck," Walker said, smacking him in the leg with the back of his hand. "Deck," he repeated.

Decker awoke with a start. A man was getting into Zahur's car alone.

"Looks like we have a lunch date," Walker said.

Decker started the car and followed the black Mercedes at a safe distance.

"Don't lose him," Walker said.

"Don't worry. It will be worse if he spots us. We know where he'll come back to. We can get him later if we need to. We need the right situation and I'm going to stick with him till we get it."

"Situation to do what?" Walker said.

"Trust me," Decker said. "If I tell you first, you'll leave."

Walker rolled his eyes. "Maybe I should leave now."

"Then you'll miss the fun."

Zahur pulled into a parking place and went into a delicatessen.

"Is this good?" Walker said.

Decker shook his head. "No, this doesn't work. I need a clear shot at his head."

Walker looked at him. "I think we need to talk."

"Just pay attention, here he comes."

Zahur came out of the deli with a brown bag and then got into his car and drove away.

"I guess we follow him back?"

"Yup," Decker said.

Zahur surprised them by making a turn that wasn't directly on the way back to Empire Electronics. About a mile later, he pulled into a gas station.

"This could be good," Decker said.

"A gas station?" Walker said incredulously. Zahur pulled up to the pump, got out and set the nozzle. He then got back in the car and closed the door.

"Shit!" Decker said

"What?" Walker said.

"He's in the car."

"So?"

"He has to be outside. It won't work though glass."

"What won't work through glass?"

They waited until Zahur got out, hung up the nozzle and then got back in the car and drove away. Decker followed. They were heading back to Empire.

"He's got his right directional on. Isn't Empire to the left?" Walker said.

"Yes."

"What now? A car wash?"

"A car wash would work if he waits outside. It's nice and sunny out. Not cold."

"When are you going to tell me what we're doing?"

"We're going to tell him to bring us to Tarik."

Walker sighed. "Sorry I asked. Maybe one of these days, I'll get a straight answer."

Decker smiled. "You won't even know when it happens."

Zahur continued to drive for another mile and then made another unexpected turn.

"Eisenhower Park?" Decker said.

"This park cuts through to Hempstead Turnpike. Maybe he's going to Hooters."

"With deli food?" Decker said. "Don't think so." Zahur drove down the main avenue and then turned into a parking lot and parked. Decker passed the lot and pulled into the next one. They watched him get out with the deli bag and walk down a path.

"Let's go!" Decker said.

"I'm following you."

Decker got out, opened the back door and picked the box up off the floor.

"What's that?" Walker said.

"A gun," Decker said closing the door. "A very special gun."

"I knew we needed to talk. I think it's time I told you that killing Zahur like this would be against my companies normal policy."

"We aren't going to kill him. At least not yet. This is Sam's gun and it doesn't shoot bullets. It shoots sound. She named it the Sound Shooter when she was, like, twelve."

"The what?"

"Don't you remember Sam telling us about the Sound Shooter?" He said and started jogging.

"Uh, no," Walker said, trying to keep up.

"The toy her father, the scientist, made for her to play with?"

"Uh, vaguely. What's it do?"

"You'll see, I hope," Decker said, running to catch up to Zahur.

Decker reached the pond where Zahur disappeared and slowed to a cautious walk. A little further a large duck pond appeared with park benches scattered around it. Zahur was approaching a bench on the opposite side. A woman was sitting on it.

"Whoa!" Walker said. "A rendezvous?"

"Maybe," Decker said, and then pointed to a large rock with foliage around it. "Right there," he said.

Walker followed him around the top of the hill surrounding the pond, then they descended behind the boulder. Decker took the Sound Shooter out of the box.

"That's a toy?" Walker said.

"Yup."

"Wish my father gave me toys that looked like that."

"You and me both, pal… Shhh."

"Is that a girlfriend or a contact?"

"I don't know," Decker said, "It doesn't matter. He's going to be saying good-bye to her soon."

"How do you know?"

"Because I'm going to tell him to."

"How?"

"With this toy."

"Right," Walker said doubtfully. "Who are you going to say you are?"

"I don't know. I'm hoping he'll think I'm his god or something."

"You're out of your mind, you know that?"

Decker set the Sound Shooter on top of the boulder and looked into the scope. He pulled the trigger and the beam instantly appeared. He let Walker have a look.

"Infrared?"

"Yeah. And when I speak into the microphone the beam will channel my voice into his ear. Meanwhile, she won't hear a thing."

Walker paused and then said, "You're either insane or genius."

Decker snorted and said, "This is Sam's device, not mine. I'm just grabbing for straws."

"And she's used this?" Walker said, incredulously.

"So she says. When she was a kid."

Walker shook his head. "Go for it, man," he said and backed away.

Zahur was about two hundred feet away. He reached into his deli bag and pulled out what looked like two sandwiches and two bottles of some kind of beverage. The two seemed engaged in casual conversation.

Decker pulled the trigger, heard the hum and saw the beam. He focused the scope until Zahur's ear was an easy target for the beam. He cleared his throat and put his mouth to the microphone as the beam sat in Zahur's ear.

"Masud Zahur," Decker said.

45

Zahur's head quickly turned toward them. Decker didn't move a muscle. Zahur then turned around and looked up the hill and then said something to the woman. In the scope, Decker could clearly see the woman shrug her shoulder.

Decker took aim again and pulled the trigger. *"Masud Zahur, she cannot hear me. I am speaking to you only, my son,"* he said in perfect Egyptian.

Zahur stood up quickly and looked around. He spoke to the woman again. She turned her palms up and shook her head. Decker took his finger off the trigger and looked at Walker. "Can you believe this thing?" he said and then translated what he had told him.

"This can't be happening," Walker said.

Zahur sat back down, still talking. He then faced the pond and Decker pulled the trigger. *"Quiet your mind and listen, my son."*

Zahur looked at her. She shook her head. He looked forward again and Decker immediately took advantage.

"Tell her to leave."

Zahur didn't move. He glanced in her direction but didn't say anything. He then got up and walked to the edge of the pond.

"Tell her to leave, my son. I have a great mission for you."

Zahur turned quickly, looking in every direction. He appeared confused.

"Whatever you're saying, he's not buying it, Deck," Walker said.

Decker frowned. What else could he safely tell him? God wouldn't make a mistake and if one happens, the game is over. He looked at Walker. "Get on the phone. I need to know if he's married, his wife's name and get into his email and phone and find out who the hell this woman is." As Decker was speaking, Walker was already connecting.

Decker exhaled and pulled the trigger again. *"I have chosen you as a messenger and a tool, my son. You shall deliver my word. If you obey you will be rewarded beyond your dreams, if you ignore my instruction, you will not receive this or any other blessing already stored up for you in my kingdom,"* he said and let go of the trigger. Zahur turned toward them and Decker didn't move, hoping Zahur didn't have excellent vision. Zahur turned back to the pond and put his head in his hands. The woman was talking to him. Decker would give anything to know what she was saying. He looked at Walker, who held up a finger, listening to something. Had he had the time to plan this better, he could easily have set up a listening device that would work in tandem with the Sound Shooter. *Sam must have ruled her little world with this thing as a kid*, he thought.

Walker hung up the phone. "No emails to anyone about any meetings. He has a wife, but that might be her."

"How long have they been married?" Decker asked.

"I don't know," William said.

Decker looked back into the scope and tried to get a close up of the woman. Black hair, sort of Arabic looking. Why would he meet his wife in a park for lunch? Maybe she insisted. Maybe tradition? Decker knew virtually nothing about Zahur yet. What would God say to him? He had to word this just right, so it could be taken more than one way but, Zahur would take it the only way it made sense.

Decker pulled the trigger. *"If you don't tell her to leave right now I will smite your wife with... leprosy,"* he said and then told Walker.

"Leprosy?" Walker whispered, doubtfully.

Decker shrugged. "What should I say, measles?"

Zahur turned to the woman, whoever she was, and said something. Decker would have loved to have known what. The woman just stared at him, speechless. After a moment he spoke again, this time with a little hand language. The woman said something back. They seemed to be arguing and then she suddenly stood up, threw her sandwich at him and stormed away.

"Leprosy," Walker said. "I'll have to remember that one."

"Shut up," Decker said.

Zahur stood up and brushed the sandwich leavings off his clothing. He then looked to the sky and spoke, but Decker couldn't hear him.

"I can't miss this opportunity," Decker said to Walker. He pulled the trigger. *"You have pleased me, my son. Listen carefully and record my words."*

Zahur pulled out a pen and picked up the lunch bag. Decker almost laughed.

"There is a humble hut outside Kabul," Decker said and then gave him specific directions. *"My word awaits you there on an ancient tablet. Tell no one. Your hands only shall touch it and your eyes only shall see it. You are to bring my word to my servant Ramses al Tarik. My will be done,"* Decker said and then translated for Walker as a gust of wind blew across the pond swirling some leaves near Zahur into a miniature tornado. The terrorist dropped to his hands and knees and put his forehead to the ground.

Decker glanced at Walker and said, "Sometimes it's better to be lucky than good."

Walker nodded. "This is spooky."

Decker shrugged and changed the subject. "Okay, I need the tablet drilled and filled with a tracer. Make it good. He's going to check it thoroughly. And I need to get it to get to Kabul ASAP, so get your men on it now."

Walker smiled and started dialing. "I'm impressed, Deck. By the time Tarik realizes he has his own property back, we'll have him."

Decker looked him in the eye. "Not we. You have to promise me you won't tell a soul of this plan. Give orders, put pieces together, but don't explain the plan. I don't want any leaks."

Walker nodded. "I agree. But after we find him..."

"He's mine," Decker said, emphatically. "Wherever he is, I don't want an invasion. I sink the hook, I reel him in. Remember Sam. I want first shot."

Walker frowned. "You can't let your emotions dictate the safety of a country."

"I'm not. Run ahead of me and we'll have a disaster. I got us this far. Follow my lead and I'll deliver Tarik. You owe me that."

Walker nodded. "You can stay a step ahead, but if you trip, we'll be coming through."

"I won't trip."

46

Consciousness came slowly. Sam heard the familiar sound of a helicopter blade. She couldn't see anything but the inside of the white sack over her head. *How long had she been asleep? How far had she traveled?* There was a hole cut out of the cloth that covered her head for her mouth, but she found her hands tied, her feet also. She tested her limitations and discovered she couldn't move but a couple feet before being held. Her eyes quickly became heavy. Whatever she was lying on was comfortable. So sleepy. What had they drugged her with? Where was she going? Where was Jesse, Decker? Dreamy. She saw her dad. She rolled over, her hands pulled.

A change in movement. Was she in a helicopter? Did she know that already? Vaguely remembered waking once before. Descending, like in an elevator. Slowing, slowing. Touchdown. The engines slowed. The door opened. The smell of saltwater in the air, and… oil. Maybe Decker was right. But maybe this was just another stop to transfer to another craft. She wondered how many times that had happened while she was out. *How long had she been out?* It was light out. She had left in the dark, but was that earlier today or yesterday?

Someone was getting inside with her. Her heart began to race. She almost jumped when her ankles were grabbed and then her arms. Did they think she was still asleep? She remained limp but her brow rose when they picked her up and made a comment about her athletic body in Egyptian. Was she in Africa?

The warmth of the sun felt good. The helicopter blade slowed and went silent. Waves could now be heard… and seagulls. Others were speaking Egyptian, in fact, it was the only language she heard. Only one place she knew of would account for that. A door hinge squeaked and the warmth of the sun vanished. The door clanged closed and she began to descend at an angle, the echo of footsteps on metal, level, angle, level, angle, level. A real high class place, she thought. No gurney. No elevator. More metallic footsteps level for a while and then she stopped and another door opened. Moving again.

Sam was placed on something soft and the handcuffs were removed. Someone squeezed one of her breasts a couple of times and laughed. She continued to feign unconsciousness. No one else laughed and someone called someone an idiot. A moment later, she heard a door close and lock with a slide and a clack. Footsteps leaving. Gone. Silence. Eerie silence. Her hands felt good to be free. She lay there for a few moments and then pulled the sack off her head.

Sam was a little surprised. She was expecting a jail cell and found herself in a bedroom. The walls and ceiling were appliance white. The floor was high gloss natural cement but most of it was covered with a large Persian rug. The bed she was on was plush with sheets and blankets and several fresh pillows. There was another room with an open door. Probably a bathroom. There were three small porthole like windows and, as she figured, a camera in the corner of the ceiling. She waved hello at it and then decided to check out the porthole view. She stood up and then almost fell down. Whoa. The drugs were still very much with her. She wanted to sit back down but, consciously placing one foot in front of the other, she worked her way to the little round window and looked out.

Bright and sunny and nothing else but endless water as far as the eye could see. She was apparently on an offshore oil rig, probably near Egypt. She tapped the glass. Thick, solid, too small to fit through.

Sam knew she was being watched through the camera and then wondered if there was one in the bathroom. She felt a little better after being upright for a little bit and baby-stepped her way to the open door. The light switch was on the right and went on with a loud click. Toilet, shower, sink, towel on a bar, medicine cabinet. Basic, small and clean. All the walls were metal with the same rivet heads Decker pointed out in the video. She opened the cabinet. Toothpaste, toothbrush, Q-tips, stick deodorant and a pack of single edge disposable razors. All new. Soap and shampoo were in the shower on a metal shelf. And yes, there it was in the corner of the ceiling; a camera. Probably being viewed right now.

A door opened.

Sam left the bathroom to find three men in her room. One was armed with some kind of machine gun and the other two were in white lab coats.

"Good morning, Doctor Conway. I am Doctor Mandihr Dulai and this is my assistant Doctor Harshit Patel," said the thinner man in decent English but with an Indian accent. The assistant was heavy with maybe three or four hairs on his head and just nodded his hello. He also carried a small briefcase.

"Doctor Dulai and Doctor Horseshit," Sam repeated.

"Harshit," the fat man corrected.

"Right, must have been a very popular name that year," Sam said. "Where's Jesse?"

"Your brother is well and will be brought to you when we leave."

"Then leave," Sam said.

Dulai smiled. "We have our instructions, Doctor Conway. We are told, not asked, what we do… as you will surely observe during your stay with us."

"You have your rules, I have mine. I want to see my brother now."

Dulai sighed. "I had hoped it would not come to this, but I was advised it might. Tarik has just prepared a demonstration for your, let's say, education." Dulai motioned to Harshit, who promptly opened his briefcase and produced a small laptop computer. Dulai took it and opened it. He hit a few keys and then turned it for Sam to view.

Sam saw a man lying on a floor, his arms fully extended out to his sides, tied at the wrist by white cloth. His ankles were also tied and stretched in the same manner. Behind him a man sat calmly in a chair. Dulai nodded to Harshit who brought a hand radio to his mouth and said, "She's watching," in Egyptian.

A moment later, the man in the chair stood up, a shiny knife in his hand.

"What's he going to do?" Sam said, anxiously.

"The man who is tied fondled your breast while you were asleep," Dulai said.

Sam frowned. "Yeah, and?"

"It was inappropriate."

"So you're going to kill him?" Sam said in disbelief.

"No," Dulai said as the man with the knife grabbed the tied man's right hand and with a few quick strokes, cut the hand off and dropped it to the floor. The man tensed, writhed and screamed, but the computer emitted no sound.

Sam gasped. "Jesus! You cut off his hand!"

"There had to be a consequence for the action. An example."

"Couldn't you just garnish his paycheck?"

"We are expected to operate with zero tolerance, Doctor Conway. Your resistance to cooperate will be looked upon as a one time exception to that rule because you were an uninformed guest. Now you are informed. If you continue to speak of 'your rules,' Tarik will have your brother cut the man's head off. If your brother refuses, the man on the ground will be instructed to cut off your brother's head with his less coordinated left hand. Do you understand the situation, Samantha Conway, or do we need to continue your education?"

Sam just stared Dulai in the eye. She hated him. How dare he kidnap Jesse and bring him and her into this madness?

Dulai turned to Harshit and said, "Have Doctor Conway's brother brought to the discipline room and have him cut off..."

"Okay, okay. You win," Sam said. "Why am I here?"

47

Decker awoke as the helicopter touched down at Fort Detrick. Another cat nap. He figured he would have time for some real sleep on his way to Kabul. A soldier standing outside a white Suburban waved him over. The late afternoon sun felt good on his face. If all went as planned, he would only see it again briefly before sunrise, in Kabul. Moments later, he was escorted to the lab to meet Ross. The lab seemed unusually busy and Ross, who had just looked up from a microscope, saw him and waved him over.

"Is it ready?" Decker said.

"Is what ready?"

"The artifact. Is the tracer in yet?"

Ross looked over his glasses. "I think so, but what makes you think anyone will bring it to Tarik?"

"Let's just say Moses wasn't the only one with divine help."

Ross frowned. "I'm not even going to ask. But take a look at this," Ross said motioning toward the scope. "We've made an interesting discovery."

Decker looked in the scope and said, "I'm listening."

"Can you spot the virus?"

"Yes."

"You're looking inside a fly. The flies host the dormant virus."

"Flies?"

Ross shook his head. "You must be tired. Not flies. *The* flies. The flies that were in the cave were flies that don't exist in our world, or at least in our time period. The flies from the cave were unique and common to another millennium."

"So Sam was right?"

Ross nodded. "Somewhat. This explains how the Angel of Death was able to spread so quickly and disappear. In the airplane, the human host created unknowingly by the terrorist had limitations. The virus was able to spread within the confines of the aircraft, but not for long and not outside."

"The flies were everywhere in the cave and preceded the Angel of Death," Decker said, thinking out loud.

"Yes. And Moses plagued Egypt with flies prior to the death of the firstborn. Ancient flies. These flies."

"Setting the table for the Angel of Death," Decker said.

Ross nodded. "Wherever the flies go and die, the virus explodes into life when triggered by the trace element from the pillar. Like a spark igniting a brushfire."

"Where does the Angelica come into play?"

"We think the flies are attracted by it and ingest it, taking the virus out of dormancy and then killing the fly. It would pretty much end there if not for the pillar."

"Have you isolated the pillar's element?"

Ross shook his head. "No. There are several elements that are completely unique. There are elements from this tree that exist nowhere else on earth as far as we know."

"As if this tree was from another planet?"

Ross frowned. "As far as we know, there aren't trees anywhere else in the universe. But we don't know very much, do we?"

"Less every day, Doc," Decker said and then paused. "Do you think it's possible that Sam's..."

"The legends?" Ross said with a smirk.

Decker nodded.

Ross raised a finger, liked he was checking wind direction. "She's had me thinking. But, no."

"Really?" Decker said, surprised at Ross's quick dismissal.

"Most legends start with or at least run parallel to truth. How and where they deviate through passages of time and imagination we can't know. The Tree of the Knowledge of Good and Evil is an extreme example. Could it possibly have existed? Before seeing what Sam describes as the oldest writing she's ever seen and it being on a petrified tree having properties never seen by modern science. I would have said, no."

"And now?"

"I'd still say no, just now with a little hesitation. In reality, the history can help some, but where it comes from won't help us as much as what it says. Without Sam helping us translate, we can only concentrate on what we know."

"Which is?" Decker said.

"That Tarik will try to use the Angel of Death as a biological weapon intent on massive casualties."

"That's for certain. What's your cure?"

"You mean like a vaccine?"

"Yes."

Ross snorted. "There is none and there is no way we could have one anytime soon. What we need is a disinfectant."

"Any leads?"

"Yeah. The lamb's blood. We simply slaughter thousands of sheep and spray their blood over whatever city he infects."

Decker frowned. "Hmmm."

"Exactly. We're experimenting with what makes lambs blood unique. What makes it different from, let's say, a cow's."

"And?"

Ross shrugged. "We're early in the game, Decker. The scientific process doesn't always move as fast as we'd like it to.

As far as we can see, there is no significant, eye-opening difference."

"Then you'd better start gathering a very large flock," Decker said as Walker walked up with an attaché.

"Your ride just got here," Walker said and then handed off the briefcase with both hands. "But first, check this out."

Decker put the heavy attaché on the counter and opened it. As before, the artifact was inside a second container. He opened that as well and examined the tablet for any trace of the tracking device hidden inside. Impressed, he said, "It's installed, right?"

Walker smiled proudly. "We don't kid around here, Deck." Walker pointed to an edge. "Right there. It transmits a single ping every five minutes so it allows us to stay in virtually constant contact but the chance of electronic discovery is very small."

Decker looked closely and ran his finger across the spot and then nodded approvingly. "Excellent." He put everything back in the case and tucked it under his arm. He turned to Ross and said, "Neither of us can fail, you know."

"Just worry about yourself, Captain," Ross said. "Both our plates are quite full."

Decker gave him a nod and then turned to Walker. "You said my ride was here?"

"Sitting right outside."

"What is it? Remember, I have to get to Kabul before Zahur."

Walker smiled. "I remembered. You won't be disappointed."

"I've heard *that* before," Decker said and then tapped a few numbers on his cell phone. "It's Decker. I'm leaving now. Meet me on the runway."

"Who was that?" Walker said.

"My laundry."

"Laundry?"

"I'll need a change of clothes at some point."

Walker looked at him doubtfully as they left USAMRIID and got into a waiting Suburban. They drove through the iron gates and a minute later turned into the airfield, the runway in clear view.

"Your ride," Walker said, motioning to the lone waiting aircraft.

Decker frowned when he saw an F-15 Eagle sitting on the runway. "You're not giving me a Raptor?" he said.

"The Raptor's a one-seater. We want to make sure you get there. Time to suit up."

Decker hurried out of the Suburban and a van door opened with a couple of airman coming out with his flight-suit and helmet. Just then another white suburban pulled up and a tall lanky soldier with a black duffel-bag got out and hurried to Decker. "Here you go, Sir. Good luck with it."

"Thank you, Corporal, just put it down there," Decker said, as he stepped into his suit.

"Your laundry?" Walker said.

"Yeah."

"You don't pack very light do you?" Walker said. He opened the bag's zipper and peeked in.

Decker watched the agent's brows rise.

"You're out of you mind, you know that?" Walker said, and then zippered the bag back up.

A few minutes later, the vehicles had cleared the runway and Decker sat comfortably under the F-15's rear seat canopy with his black duffel bag and attaché. The powerful thrusters thundered them down the asphalt and into the sky. Soon they were flying Mach 2.5 at forty-five thousand feet, pointed toward Afghanistan. He wasn't going to get as much sleep as he thought.

48

Sam was escorted by multiple gunpoint down a poorly lighted corridor through a steel door and into another all white room. In the middle of the room was a large steel table on which sat a steel box with a large monitor on it. Two of three guards waited outside and the door was closed with a loud clack and locked. The remaining guard took his position at the door and stood silently, machine gun shoulder-strapped and ready. Sam drifted observantly through the room. Identical to her bed-quarters, but no bed. Same porthole window. Same view. Same bathroom. Same camera watching her every move.

The door opened and Dulai walked in with his assistant, Harshit.

"Please have a seat," he said firmly, motioning to the lone seat at the table.

"When do I see Jesse?"

"We will not engage in this same conversation at this time. Your visit with us has a schedule that must be kept. This is your workroom. It has been specifically designed for you and our purpose. Our purpose will be your priority. After you have become familiar with your job, your brother will be brought to you for a short visit."

"May we share our meals together?" Sam asked as humbly as she could stomach.

Dulai paused in silence, staring at her.

"Please. If you want my undivided attention to your work, then allow me to stay more focused. Sharing meals with my brother under armed guard should not be too scary for you, should it?"

After another pause, Dulai said, "I will consider your request. But now we must turn our attention to our task. Please open the metal case on the table."

Sam exhaled and looked to the metal case. She flipped up two latches and opened the lid. She tried to remain ambivalent as her heart rate jumped. In one second flat, she realized she was looking at another piece of the artifact. In fact, it was a previously connected piece that had apparently broken off.

"Have you ever seen anything like this before, Samantha Conway?"

Sam didn't know what Dulai knew of her. With no reason to believe the man had any knowledge of her involvement with the CIA, Sam wanted to give away as little as possible. "Of course. Some sort of ancient writing on polished stone. An artifact fragment. Origin and language unknown."

Dulai massaged his chin. "Hmm. Is there nothing else that strikes you?"

"Well, it appears to be very old. The characters seem to be ancestral to ancient Egyptian, but showing more information than I would expect from anything that far back," she said and then looked up at him. "It is an interesting anomaly to most others I've seen. Where did you get it?"

Dulai took his usual frightening pause and then said, "So you've never seen anything else quite like this?"

Sam shrugged. "Not really. If you'd like, I'll try to translate some of it for you."

Dulai turned to Harshit. "Please bring Samantha Conway's brother to the execution room and have him behead our prisoner.

If he resists, remove one of his eyes and lead him back to his quarters."

Harshit nodded and then said, "Which eye?"

Dulai waved his hand casually, as if being asked if he wanted cheese on his pasta. "Just pick one. It doesn't matter."

"Yes, Sir," Harshit said, and then turned to leave.

"Jesus!" Sam screamed. "Stop! Don't!"

Dulai frowned and stopped Harshit. "Excuse me. Is there something else you'd like to add to your observation?"

Sam caught her breath and exhaled deeply. "Yes."

"Ah, good. But before you do, I think you should look at this photograph," Dulai said, and dropped an eight by twelve on the table.

Sam picked it up and her eyes widened.

"I do believe the man you are walking down the museum steps with is DIA agent John Decker. Tarik had thought he was dead before this snapshot of the two of you came to his attention. Clearly, the DIA has need for your talents for the same reason we do. So, Samantha Conway, we know you are familiar with the ancient artifact before you. Please don't insult our intelligence any further or your brother will see a side of our business that will cripple his mind for the rest of his abbreviated life. One more lie, or even perceived lie, will be treated swiftly and mercilessly, without further redemption. Do I make myself clear?"

"Yes," Sam said quietly. "Very."

"Good. Now you may finish your answer, very carefully."

Sam nodded. "I will but, first I must tell you, that if you perceive something I tell you as a lie and it isn't and you hurt my brother in any way, there is nowhere on earth you will ever be able to hide from me."

Dulai smiled. "I suppose it is important for you to say that for us to proceed efficiently. Now, please continue with your observation and turn on the monitor. "

Sam reached over and turned the monitor on. Within seconds she had a picture of the sister artifact piece back at USAMRIID.

"We know you have this and have been studying it," Dulai said.

Sam returned her attention to the artifact. The correlation between the two pieces was immediately evident. If only they would have had the two pieces all along she would have been able to take Decker and Ross further, avoiding much of the trial and error.

"Is there anything in particular that you want clarification on?" Sam said.

"Our previous translator died in the Afghani cave. To be honest, he had his limitations. Our hope is that you can help refine his observations and add to them with your own."

"May I see his notes?" Sam said.

"Yes, of course," Dulai said. "They are filed in Word documents and you can access them from where you sit. The computer has been sectioned off for the convenience of your usage."

"You seem to have thought of everything," Sam said.

"One learns very quickly with Tarik to limit one's oversights to zero."

"Did someone mention my name?" said a deep voice from the doorway.

Sam looked up. Was it her imagination or did the presence of death fill the room? She recognized the man from the many newspaper covers he'd polluted with his face alongside horrific headlines of murder and destruction.

Dulai turned curiously pale at the sound of Tarik's voice. "Tarik, Samantha Conway understands what we expect of her and she is willing to diligently help us translate the pillar and keep to our schedule."

Tarik had not taken his eyes off her. Intense eyes. Deep, dark and piercing surrounded by thick black brows. "I hope our dear doctor has extended my sincere appreciation for you joining our team."

Sam wished she had a machine gun to properly demonstrate her sincere appreciation in return. But her most effective weapon at the moment wasn't force. "To be honest, I think what you've done here is amazing, but it's hard for me to appreciate it fully and concentrate on my work knowing my brother's safety is in jeopardy. And do I have to spend all my waking hours inside these walls? A girl can use a little sun once in a while to keep her mind from imploding."

Tarik's expression softened almost imperceptibly, but Sam saw it, if just for an instant. A crack in the door. Or was it the lusty anticipation of another murder through the eyes of a psychopath?

"What is it that you want?"

"I'm hungry. I would like to eat something... with my brother."

Tarik turned his palms upward. "This is not unreasonable," he said.

Dulai looked at him in shock.

"Doctor, please have Samantha Conway's brother brought here immediately and have food served," Tarik said, all the while keeping his eyes on her. "Is there anything special you would like us to include in your meal?"

Sam thought for a second. "Yes. My brother likes peanut butter and jelly."

Tarik's head tilted slightly. "This I believe we have."

"And avocado," Sam said. "Unpeeled. I want it whole."

"Avocado?" Dulai said.

"Yes, it's my favorite food," Sam lied.

Dulai looked at Tarik.

"Get it for her," Tarik said.

"But, I don't know if…"

"I said get it for her," Tarik said and then smiled at Sam. "Is there anything else?"

"Yes, information. I would like to know what your intentions are with us."

Just then another man without a gun came into the room and went straight to Tarik's ear, whispering. Tarik listened and frowned earnestly and then turned back to Sam. "I understand your need. You and I will talk soon, privately."

49

Decker woke with a start. The constant roar of engine thrust suddenly stammered, sputtered, jerked and coughed as the F-15 dropped to sub-sound speed. "What's happening, Colonel?" Lieutenant Colonel Gary Martin had been chosen specifically by Walker. The man was said to be the best pilot he knew and had no fear. That was all Decker had to hear.

"We, uh, seemed to have lost one of our engines."

"How?"

"I don't know."

"Can you fire it back up?"

"I'm trying, but there's no response."

Decker had lost power in props before but never in a fighter jet. "Fuel?"

"We have fuel, but maybe it's not getting through," the Martin said, pushing levers and throwing switches.

After a moment of impatience, Decker said, "Our time is of the essence, Colonel. What are our options?"

"First, we need to find a place to land."

Decker looked left and right and saw nothing but ocean. "Where?

"I'm not sure. And there's nothing friendly coming up soon."

Decker looked at the attaché next to his left leg and cursed. "Call home and report and then have me patched in to Walker."

"Roger that."

Decker thought about continuing on one engine. Sub sound would be too slow. And what if the second engine was to fire down? There was no third engine. The mission would be lost along with the artifact. He listened to the pilot informing the base of their situation and considered how Zahur might be slowed down. But then it occurred to him that slowing Zahur down meant allowing Tarik more time to send another plague and more time that Sam was at the madman's mercy.

"Walker," said the familiar voice.

"The plane you gave us sucks," Decker said.

"It's an F-15."

"A lemon F-15. I asked for a Raptor."

"Let's not go there. We have to talk about Plan B."

"Does Plan B include getting to Kabul on time?" Decker said urgently.

"That is the goal but, you still have to land."

"We know. But we're over the Atlantic Ocean and this plane you stuck us with probably doesn't have pontoons."

"It's an F-15."

"*Now* you tell me."

"Ok, let's calm down and reason this out. Our best bet is Ramstein."

"*Germany?*" Decker said, incredulously.

"Yes. But we'll have our best chance of getting you right back in the air."

"Another F-15?"

"I don't know. If we're lucky we have options there or something close enough to move there."

"You feeling lucky?"

"At the moment, not very."

"Well, Ramstein takes us way off our flight path."

"I'll have Zahur slowed down."

"I don't want that. Where is he now?"

"We don't know."

"What!"

"We, uh, lost him."

"You what!"

"Lost him."

"How!"

"He pulled a little bait and switch."

"He spotted you following him?"

"No, but apparently they have some travel procedures we didn't account for. He's not on the jet we thought he was. He must have taken another."

"Wonderful. We're going to stand him up for our own date."

"We might not know where he is, but we do know where he's going. We'll slow him down when he gets close."

"No! Stay away from him. If everything isn't perfect, he'll never bring us to Tarik," Decker said, angrily. "Besides, I don't want this slowed down."

"Then he'll be there before us."

"No," Decker shouted. "We have to beat him. We will beat him. Get me something that's fast. I don't care if you strap me to a cruise missile. We *have* to beat him there. Do you understand? We cannot fail with this. There'll be no second chance."

Walker paused. "I'll have to check our options. I'm not sure, but I might be able to get you that cruise missile you speak of."

Decker blinked. "Whatever you've got in mind, bring it on. I like when you reach out of the box."

"With you, I have to. You're never *in* the box."

"Excuse me, gentlemen," Martin said. "We have to refuel and our scheduled rendezvous isn't on our new route to Ramstein."

"Hear that?" Decker said.

"Yeah, yeah. I'll take care of that too. You get all the glory, but we do all the work."

"Sounds like you want my duffel bag."

Walker snorted. "We'll keep our roles just the way they are," he said.

The jet suddenly bucked as the remaining engine sputtered.

"Jesus!" Martin said.

"What's happened, Colonel?" Walker said.

"Momentary loss of power," Martin said.

The engine suddenly went silent and then reignited.

"Wonderful!" Decker said to Walker. "When was the last time you changed the spark plugs in this thing? Are there any aircraft carriers nearby?"

"Give me one minute," Walker said.

"Better make that thirty seconds," Decker said.

"No. Nothing close enough."

"Great. What's plan C?" Decker said.

Walker was silent.

"Where's our gas station, Colonel?"

"We were scheduled for a fifteen hundred rendezvous with a KC-135, but we changed course."

"Bruce, get us a refueler," Decker ordered. "If we can stay up long enough for it to get here and connect, it can tow us attached to the fuel line to Ramstein, since we don't even know if our problem is the fuel."

"Tow us with the fuel line?" Martin said, incredulously.

"I've never heard of that being done before," Walker said.

50

Sam couldn't focus on what she considered the most important archeological discovery of all time. Possibly the two most important finds if her job was to translate the legendary Tree of the Knowledge of Good and Evil. She considered that Methuselah's Pillar could also be the most infamous tree of all time from the mythological Garden of Eden, where man walked with God in perfect innocence with one hundred percent of his brain, and all she could think about was her kidnapped brother. Dulai had been sent to retrieve Jesse and every second he was gone hurt with anticipation.

The guard at the door was creepy. In fact, everyone she'd seen so far was creepy. Machine gun in hand, the guard kept staring at her up and down. Made her feel like taking a shower. She checked her top shirt buttons to make sure none of them had inadvertently opened. She thought hard about how to subdue the guard without getting herself shot or alerting the others outside the door. Were there others outside? There always seemed to be. Whatever the case, she needed to be very careful. Nothing too crazy. Her death would certainly mean the death of her brother. Why would they keep him alive if they no longer had her? They wouldn't. Dulai would probably use him in an experiment. The bastard. She exhaled and tried to shake off the thought of Jesse contracting the Angel of Death.

The door bolt slid and clacked. The door opened and Dulai stepped in.

Sam sprang to her feet. "Where is he?" she demanded.

Dulai stepped away from the doorway and waved. Jesse appeared head drooping, dragging his feet and pummeled countenance behind him. He looked up and his saddened eyes jumped to life. *"S-sam!"*

Sam bolted to him and he embraced her, but with half his usual strength. "Are you okay?" she asked, running her fingers through his thick rusty curls.

"B-better now," he said, a detectable slur in his words. "Y-y-you have m-messed up friends."

"They're not my friends," Sam said glaring at Dulai. "They're terrorists."

Jesse paused and then said, "You th-think?"

"Sorry, Jess. They have an ancient artifact that, before now, was only legend and they want me to translate what it says so they can release deadly viral plagues on innocent people," she said still looking at Dulai.

"Only y-you."

Sam held his face back and examined him closely for damage. His right cheek bone was flushed and a little swollen. She touched it and he winced slightly. His eyes looked tired. She took his hands and examined each one closely. The knuckles were scraped and swollen on his right hand. She felt tears forming and bit her lip. "Anything else bumps and bruise-wise?"

"I'm al-r-right. P-pills and n-needles m-make me t-tired."

Sam glared at Dulai. "Whatever he's on I want him off," she snarled through gritted teeth.

"You brother is on a mild…"

"I don't care what he's on, I want him off now."

"I'm sorry Samantha Conway, but you are not in any position to order me to…"

"My brother's well-being is number one. Tarik didn't go through the trouble and expense and risk of bringing me here to have me refuse to cooperate because you're sedating my brother while under heavy guard. I'm unhappy. I can't work if I'm unhappy. I want to talk to Tarik now."

Dulai paused, unblinking. "We had already determined that your brother had received his last dose of…"

"I don't care," Sam interrupted. "I still want to talk to Tarik now. There are things I need."

"You are to tell me your needs and I will evaluate…"

"I 'evaluate'. Get Tarik, now."

Dulai paused and shared a long glance with Harshit and then turned back to Sam's glare. "Tell Tarik that Doctor Conway requests his presence."

Harshit gave a nod and left.

"Are you hungry, Jess?" Sam said sweetly.

"S-sort of."

"What have they been feeding you?"

Jesse shrugged. "I d-don't know. S-stuff."

Sam looked at Dulai, wanted to choke him. "Where is the food?"

"It will be here momentarily."

"What have you been feeding him?"

"He eats what the others eat."

"What you eat?" she said pointedly.

Dulai paused. "My meals are not of your concern."

"Maybe not, but his are and…"

Just then, Tarik entered the room. Behind him entered several men, arms full with chairs, a table and other accessories.

"I'll be joining you for your first meal," he announced.

They quickly set up a dining arrangement by the porthole and were followed by three other men with covered trays. In moments, the help were gone and the table was bountifully set with a colorful feast.

"Please be seated," Tarik said with an extended hand as he took his own seat. The man was different than she had envisioned. She had only seen stills of him in magazines and news inserts that gave mug shot appeal but, in real life, his appearance was captivating and his presence filled the room. She felt as though she had just met Satan in the flesh.

Sam led Jesse, shuffling his dragging feet, to a seat furthest away from the terrorist. The food smelled and looked delicious. A large bowl of salad greens, bowls of rice, corn, hummus, beans, yogurt sauce, meats that looked like chicken and lamb. Two glass pitchers dripping with condensation, one clear and the other with a purplish tint. And, as requested, whole avocados.

Tarik made a waving gesture over the table. "Please eat freely and enjoy. I am honored to have your company. I have become a big admirer of yours, Samantha Conway. May I call you Samantha?"

"Yes," Sam said.

"Good. I want you to feel comfortable."

"Thank you. Everything looks delicious," she said and meant it, in spite of the present company. Sam began by dishing Jesse some rice.

Tarik cut a lamb chop away from a rack and de-boned it in one bite. "I had the avocados immediately flown in," he said, smacking his lips.

Sam looked at him. "Really?" she said, shocked.

"Of course. This was not a big problem. I can give you anything you can want," he said and then pulled off a moist drumstick.

"I want my brother off medication and free to see me when he chooses."

Tarik chewed and nodded. "It shall be done."

"I would also like to be in the sunlight from time to time. And a change of clothes."

Again, Tarik nodded seemingly without thought. "Provide Dulai with a list of items," he said and then cut a chop from the rack and served her and Jesse.

The chop was amazing. Soon she was spooning seconds of sweet corn and yogurt sauce and wiping her plate with warm bread.

"Samantha, you will find that great pleasure is only a request away. But you will also find that great pain comes just as quickly for those who oppose my will."

"I'll try to keep that in mind," she said, and then divided and pitted an avocado, one of four. She discarded the huge pit onto her empty bread plate.

"Good. Because I desire for you to have a prominent role in my kingdom."

Sam almost choked. "Really?" Sam said, and then drank some water. "Do you mean like Dulai?"

Tarik laughed. "No," he said, appearing genuinely amused. "I envision a time when Dulai will do as you tell him."

"And why would he do that?"

"Do you believe in destiny, Samantha?"

"As in a predetermined destination or existence through some sort of higher power?"

Tarik looked upward to the left, as if the answer to her question was somehow written on the ceiling. "Yes. As in being born for a great purpose."

"A specific purpose?"

"Yes. A predetermined plan."

"Predetermined by whom?"

"The gods."

"The gods."

"Ancient Egyptian gods?"

"They answer."

"Interesting theory."

"Not theory."

"Really. I stand corrected."

"Then you believe in destiny."

"I believe in freedom and hard work. Does your kingdom leave any room for that?" She took another sip of water and glanced at Jesse, glad to see him eating.

"Of course. But what I have in mind for you is a more... royal position."

Sam almost choked on her water. "Really," she said casually and reached for another avocado. "Jesse, have some avocado."

Jesse looked up from his plate. "N-no, thanks."

"Yes. It's good for you," she said, then cut and pitted it and gave him half, putting the second pit with the other on her bread plate. "It's very good with salt and olive oil."

Jesse scrunched his nose. "B-but I d-don't like..."

She kicked his foot under the table and with widened eyes said, "Eat it, sweetie."

"Eat your avocado, Jesse," Tarik said authoritatively. "Your sister is right. It is good for you."

Sam looked at Tarik. "Is everything just a means to an end with you?"

"Explain," Tarik said.

"You show concern for Jesse's health, but your plan is to murder thousands of innocent people."

Tarik surgically removed an avocado pit with frightening dexterity, scooped out a spoonful and filled his mouth. "And that bothers you?"

"Of course."

"Good. That is what I hoped for."

"It is?"

"Yes. You are the perfect person for the job."

"And what job is that?"

"The job of finding the antidote."

"The antidote?" Sam said.

"Yes, this will be your job here," he said and then bit into another perfect lamb chop. "I don't expect that you will help me create a biological weapon anymore than a vegetarian would guide a hunting safari. But you would be motivated to save lives and, if you happen to see something dangerous in what we are already doing, you will report it to us for the safety of Jesse here," he said, chewing.

"Sounds like you have the whole situation figured out," Sam said.

Tarik nodded. "Yes," he said with his mouth full. He then swallowed, dropped the cleaned bone on his plate and took another.

Sam imagined Tarik ordering his guard to shoot them on the spot if she didn't agree but, in truth, he was correct.

"You do not have to answer. But you must understand that your job is not to assist in the execution, but in the salvation. Your efforts can save thousands of lives."

"And you want this?"

"We already know how to destroy. We desire more understanding so we can control our weapon better and hopefully, you will help us with that as well. But the real work you will be doing is finding the cure."

"What if I can't find it in time?"

"Then I will proceed without it, but as Moses had a cure in place for his people, I desire to show the same benevolence for mine, if I can."

"If you can? But you'll proceed with your plan *without* a cure?"

Tarik shrugged. "Of course. But not without giving it my best effort. You."

51

Decker and the F-15 fell into the shadow of the massive KC-130J Hercules aerial refueler. They had continued to have intermittent flameouts but managed to stay in flight while waiting for the Hercules to arrive. The two aircrafts pointed toward Ramstein air base so there would be as little maneuvering as possible once in tow. Decker watched the telescoping fuel line and cable reach across the top of his canopy and connect behind him to the extended fuel arm. No fuel was exchanged to keep the F-15 as light as possible as they limped across open sea.

"How's your status, Deck?" Walker said.

"Slow. Too slow."

"But it's working?"

"Seems to be," Decker said, reluctant to admit to any good news.

"Good. Landing might get tricky."

"Worried about your plane?"

Walker sighed. "No."

"Good, because we might want to crash it."

"Why?"

"Spite."

"Oh. I never know if you're serious."

"I'm as serious as a heart attack. Just make sure that cruise missile's gassed up and ready to go."

"I may have found the next best thing, Deck. Less windy than the missile. It's going through preflight as we speak."

"Is it fast?"

"You might say that."

"What is it?"

"Let's wait till after the preflight, Deck. I don't want to piss you off anymore than you already are.

"No surprises," Decker said. "I can't be further delayed."

"Don't worry. If it works out, you won't need refueling. That will save some time."

"Won't need refueling? Sounds big and slow."

"Calm down."

"Can it do Mach two?"

Walker laughed. "It can do Mach *three* point two."

Decker frowned. "Does it explode on impact?"

"Actually, we stopped using them because they tend to explode without impact. But that shouldn't bother you."

Decker rolled his eyes. "Stopped using them? Explode? Have you ever considered a career in sales?"

Three miles from the airbase, the F-15 was still sputtering, but the pilot felt more confident landing solo, without the unpredictable assistance of the tow. The fuel line was released and the jet landed uneventfully, though substantially later than Decker wanted. Now for the fire drill, Decker thought. Several vehicles followed the braking jet. The second the jet came to a stop, the two canopies opened and Decker hit the tarmac running toward two airmen in gray jumper suits that waved him and the pilot to go with them. One took Decker's duffel bag and the other tried to take the attaché.

"This stays with me," he said and then hopped into a jeep. After a short race down the runway, Decker's eyes widened and he turned to Martin. "Do you see what I see?"

"That's us?" Martin said, shocked.

"Yes Sir," said the airman.

Decker smiled. "Son of a bitch. Now that's what I'm talking about. Where did he find it?"

"Probably at a garage sale. The SR-71 Blackbird has been out of service for over a decade."

"Who cares? It's the fastest jet ever built."

"Which is why so many of them disintegrated midair."

Decker looked at him sharply. "We put the pedal to the metal and keep it there."

Martin exhaled and nodded slowly. "My orders are to help you in any way I can, Captain. Now I know why."

Before the jeep came to a full stop, Decker was out the door. The Blackbird, named for its stealthy black exterior, had both canopies open and was already aligned for takeoff, engines purring. Decker hurried up the steps with the attaché in hand and slipped into his seat. His duffel bag was handed over to him as Martin stepped into the front seat. The Blackbird was slightly roomier than the F-15 for his bulky luggage. He took a moment to take in his impressive surrounding. Walker had done well this time.

Martin gave the ground crew the thumbs up and the canopies lowered. The runway was quickly cleared. "Let's see what this baby's got," Martin said. "All set back there?"

"Punch it, Colonel," Decker said, the anticipation of raw power through record setting thrusters was not lost on the urgency of the mission.

Lieutenant Colonel Gary Martin had never flown a SR-71 but no one watching takeoff would ever know it. Lift off was more level than the F-15 but the acceleration never stopped coming as they roared through clouds and quickly reached sixty-thousand feet, still climbing.

"Happy?" said the familiar voice of Walker.

"It'll do," Decker replied. "But I asked for a cruise missile."

Walker snorted. "Some people are never satisfied."

"Maybe when Sam is safe and Tarik is dead."

"We're doing our best, Deck."

"Have you found Zahur yet?"

After a pause, Walker said, "No."

52

Sam was finally able to concentrate on the artifact. A pair of magnification glasses Dulai had given her were excellent, bringing to life details she was unable to pick up with unassisted vision. She zoned into a world she was renowned in. A world of ancient characters and symbols that told stories of all but forgotten origins. She hyper-focused on mankind's most privileged record. Writings that could unlock thousands of years of scriptural mysteries and recipes for history's most infamous plagues.

Antidotes and cures for the plagues were harder to find. No wonder they kidnapped her. The wrong remedy could be disastrous. That was probably what happened in their cave calamity. Regardless, she was still translating from partial information. A simple error in character interpretation could have catastrophic results.

She craved the missing pieces of Methuselah's Pillar. She was utterly convinced now of its identity as she scribbled theories and notions about the artifact's tiniest details into a notebook. All of her notes were written with a sliding substitution code she had created. She also spent time evaluating the prior translator's notes. If what she believed was true, everything, every jot, every scratch, had a specific scientific meaning. Every mark had a purpose. Every stroke was part of the whole.

Sam suddenly became aware of Dulai's presence at her side. She threw off her glasses and turned to him. "What?"

"How is your work progressing?" he said, eying her notes.

"It *was* going fine. You distracted me."

Dulai's face brightened. "Really! Is there any way I can assist you?"

"How about a better lab? Put me back where you found me where I can attack this with a team."

"That would not be according to Tarik's wishes."

"So you admit he's crazy."

Dulai sighed. "Is there anything I can assist you with?"

"Yes." She grabbed a piece of paper off her desk and slapped it in his hand. "I'll want everything on this list as soon as possible," she said.

Dulai took the paper suspiciously and read, his brow rose and then fell into a frown. He looked up. "Two bikini bathing suits?" he said doubtfully.

"ASAP."

He shook his head. "How is this to help find a…"

"And make sure they're halter tops," Sam interrupted. "I'm very picky so don't get that wrong."

"We don't have anything like this here."

"You have a helicopter. I'm a sun worshiper, and I don't mean Ra. And don't forget the tanning lotion. Nothing over SPF-15. I like it deep and dark and since you guys still have somewhat of an ozone here, I intend on taking advantage of my time off. And speaking of here… where exactly are we?"

"Ra?" Jesse said, at the table playing solitaire.

"The ancient Egyptian sun god," Sam explained.

"Oh."

"This is not time off, Samantha Conway. I'm afraid you are missing the purpose of why you are here," Dulai said.

"If you want me focused, I need what's on the list."

"I don't understand how… size seven and a half running shoes are of any use on an oil rig."

"We're on an oil rig? I wasn't sure about that."

Dulai closed his eyes and sighed. "Our mission does not allow for leisure."

"Maybe you need to open your eyes a bit more, Doc. There's more happening here than deciphering ancient text."

"What are you referring to?"

"Like translating Tarik's ultimate intentions with me."

"You are treading in very dangerous waters, Doctor Conway. Try to remember why you are here and who brought you here."

"Tarik brought me here. And you want to fill me in on where *here* is?"

"Our location, for obvious reasons, cannot be revealed to you."

"But I'm already here. What's the harm in letting me know where that is?"

"You will not find me underestimating you, Samantha Conway," Dulai said and left. The armed guard at the door stepped aside and allowed him to exit. When the door closed, the guard stepped back in front of it, his attention back on Sam and Jesse. Sam smiled and gave the guard a little wave. He didn't respond at all. *Perfect*, Sam thought and returned her focus back to the artifact.

Sam understood the connections needed to produce the Angel of Death. Moses released the plague of the flies on Egypt prior to the Angel of Death. No coincidence. With the added information, she believed the flies to be the necessary precursor to spread the virus as widely and rapidly as possible. Like the distance across a city or region.

Sam had no illusions of what her real purpose was here. She was an excuse. A conscience soother. In order for Tarik to go ahead with his horrific plan, he had to tell himself he'd made the best effort, employing the best ancient writing translator on earth. It didn't matter if her task was insurmountable. In fact, he probably didn't want her to succeed and make his plan any more complicated than it already was.

Where was Decker? she thought.

53

The SR-71 came to rest on the tarmac of the solitary runway of Kabul International Airport. The canopy opened and Decker was quickly out and onto the ground with the attaché in one hand and duffel bag in the other. A tan Hummer pulled up next to him and a man Decker recognized as Captain Shultz got out and saluted. Decker tossed him the duffel, eyes scanning for Zahur. "Did he get here yet?" he said, bracing for the worst.

"Yes," Shultz said.

"He came? Where is he?"

"On the road to Baghlan."

"How long ago?"

"About thirty minutes."

"Not good!" Decker said. He looked at the duffel bag and wondered if he should dip into it yet. "How's the traffic?"

Shultz shrugged. "The usual for this time of the morning. No delays. Do you want us to create one?"

"No," Decker snapped. "Who knows about this besides you?"

"No one. Walker called me direct. He basically told me if I told anyone, you'd kill me."

"Basically," Decker said and almost smiled. "He's come this far without our help. If he smartens up the game is over."

"Game, Sir?"

"Sorry Shultz. The less you know the better. How fast can I get a chopper?"

"Five minutes."

"Do it in two."

"Yes, Sir," Shultz said and was immediately on the radio.

Decker surveyed the landscape while Shultz threatened a pilot with a transfer to Iraq if he wasn't there by the time he hung up. The barren, jagged mountains rose steeply to the north. The road to Baghlan, where Zahur had been instructed to go, cut through sharp ravines. The final destination was an unremarkable farmhouse used by a sleeper CIA agent who worked closely with Decker to gather information on Tarik's whereabouts. The sleeper agent's current instructions were only to stay in the house until further contact by Decker himself. Decker didn't want to chance more than that in the open airways.

Decker turned at the sound of the chopper coming in low and fast across the tarmac. Shultz waved his hand in the air, as if the chopper could miss the only Blackbird on the only runway. It had barely touched the ground before Shultz opened the door. Decker threw the duffel bag in, jumped into his seat and they were off.

Decker put on his headphones and pointed. "Head for that ridge as fast as it'll go," he said and then buckled in.

"Yes, Sir. What's our destination?"

"Baghlan. But don't follow the ravine. Stay on the other side of the ridge and then come in from the North."

The pilot nodded. "What's our mission?"

"Your mission is to get to Baghlan ASAP, land behind an old barn, shut down and stay absolutely silent while I take care of some business."

"Yes, Sir," the pilot said and accelerated toward the ridge.

Decker looked back and watched the Blackbird become smaller and smaller. He considered the jet to be a huge visual risk. Something very different that might catch Zahur's eye and instill undue nervousness en route to Tarik. He called Shultz.

"Yes, Sir," Shultz said.

"Hide the blackbird."

"Hide it?" Shultz repeated incredulously.

"Yes," Decker said. "I want the airport to appear as normal as possible and there's nothing normal about the SR-71. Fly it to another airport if you have to. Just get it out of there. Now."

"Yes, Sir. Consider it gone."

Decker signed off and looked at the airspeed. Two-hundred and seventy-five KPH. About a hundred and eighty miles per hour. "Can you squeeze any more speed out of this thing?"

The pilot shook his head. "The wind's at our back."

Decker closed his eyes. At first, he saw images of Tarik's face. Smelled Tarik's rancid breath. He made a fist and felt his fingers tighten around Tarik's throat. *Not good*, he thought. Deep breath. Clear the table. Zero in on the now. Deal with Zahur. The bait was in place. The trap was set. The prey was being successfully lured. Execute the plan. Step back.

"Where to now, Sir?" the pilot said.

Decker's eyes sprung open. After taking a moment to gain perspective and refresh his memory, he pointed. "You're going to follow that river around that slope. Get low. Very low. I don't want to chance anyone from the pass seeing us. And don't slow until you have to."

The pilot nodded and dove steeply, not letting up at all on the throttle. He followed the river just yards above the water. He came around the bend of the jagged slope and Decker pointed again.

"That old utility barn, across the field. Set down behind it.

The pilot veered right across a desolate rocky field, missing occasional shrub and boulder tops. When they reached the barn the pilot inched close to the deteriorating clay walls and set down.

Decker swiped his fingers across his throat and said, "Kill it."

The Huey went still and the stiff wind swept the dust quickly away. Decker grabbed his gear and opened the door.

"Want some help with that?" the pilot said.

"No. Stay exactly where you are. I require complete silence. No radio. No nothing. Breathe only if you have to. Piss in your pants. I would have you leave now but I don't want to chance anyone spotting you go."

The pilot gave a silent acknowledging salute and Decker was off running. He stopped at the barn corner and peeked around. No cars in sight. Good. He opened the barn door and tossed in the duffel bag and then sprinted with the attaché to the clay house a hundred feet away. The rear door opened and the sleeper agent waved him in.

"Decker, it's good to see you," the man said. Haco was a short, fifty-something, Turkish man who had been a sleeper for the CIA for many years. Decker didn't know how long, but Haco had been his first contact when he had arrived several years ago.

Decker said nothing, hurrying to the front of the tiny house and looking out the window. "He should be here very soon, so we don't have much time, Haco. Good to see you as well."

"Who will be here? What's happening?" Haco said. "Walker only told me you'd be arriving and to do exactly what you say."

Decker put a pen in Haco's shirt pocket. "This is a wireless microphone so I can hear your conversation from the barn with this ear plug," he said, putting a tiny device in his right ear.

Haco looked down at the pen in his pocket, his long graying beard flattening on his chest. "Conversation with who?"

"You're not to know. I don't want you to slip and call him anything. You're not supposed to know who he is or even that he's coming." Decker opened the attaché. He took the inner box containing the artifact out and opened it as well.

The old man's eyes widened when he saw what was inside. "I've never seen anything like that."

Decker looked Haco in the eye and said, "Pay close attention, we don't have much time."

"Maybe less than you think," Haco said and then motioned for Decker to turn around.

A white car crept to a halt on the roadside. Decker could clearly see the solitary man in the driver's seat. Zahur. The man stared at the house, but didn't get out of his car.

Decker turned and looked intensely at Haco. "Put this at the bottom of a chest or wherever you consider your most secret place. When he comes to the door, he'll ask you for it somehow. Play hard to get, but then ask him for the holy word."

"Holy word?"

"Yes. You need a good reason to reveal this to a perfect stranger."

Haco thought for a moment and said, "Okay, what is it?"

"I'm thinking of one."

Haco rolled his eyes. You don't have one yet?" he said disbelievingly.

Decker gave him a look. "Look, it's been a rough few days. If you want to be useful, suggest something."

"Life... death... fruit... vine?"

"No.... The sword."

"The sword?"

"Yes. The sword. The words can be used as a weapon or as a tool... like a sword."

"Okay, fine. But if we just made it up how will he know it?"

"Don't worry about that. Just act surprised when he says it."

"It won't be an act," Haco said with a thin smile.

"When he tells you 'the sword', bring him to it."

"Where did I get it?"

"If he asks, tell him this has been passed down to you from your father or something."

"Or something? Shouldn't we rehearse this?"

"There isn't time."

Haco sighed. "Decker," he said, as if *that* said it all.

"Just keep it simple," Decker said. "And open the windows in the back and try to get him in my view if you need help," he said and then grabbed up the attaché and hurried out the back door toward the barn, careful to stay behind the shield of the house.

"Testing, one, two, three," Haco said through Decker's earpiece.

Decker turned and gave Haco a thumbs-up before disappearing into the barn. Haco nodded and opened the rear windows.

54

Tarik's forehead cooled against the sanctuary's sandstone tile floor as he paid homage to Anubis. Above him, eight small sanitary travel kits rested on the stone altar. Four black and four brown. Each was designated either north, south, east or west. Behind the altar, the black wooden statue kept a constant watch with emerald eyes. Suddenly, a blinking red light overpowered the golden glow of the scattered oil lamps. A signal that his presence was required. Was it already time? He had told them two hours. It felt like five minutes. He stood up and straightened his black robe.

"Come in," he said.

The steel door opened and eight hand-picked soldiers came in with Dulai and his assistant, Harshit. None of the soldiers had been in this room before and all gazed about. Anubis and the sacrificial altar seemed to gain most of the attention.

"Can we proceed?" Dulai asked.

"Yes," Tarik said. "Which do you want first?"

"The brown."

Tarik picked up the four brown travel kits, lifted them to Anubis and then handed them to Dulai.

The doctor in turn handed them to four of the eight men. "You four will immediately be escorted to Jerusalem. At dawn on the day before Passover, you will each be shown to one of four gates in the Old City. North, south, east or west, as indicated on the bag. There you will open your travel kit and find two small plastic aspirin bottles. Pour the contents of one bottle into the other and then fill the bottle almost to the top with water. Put the cap back on, shake and then pour it out on the ground where you stand. Then leave," Dulai said and then turned to Tarik for the black travel kits.

Tarik lifted them to Anubis and then handed them off to Dulai who, in turn, gave one each to the remaining four, all of whom were firstborn.

"A day and a half after these men accomplish their job, it will be your turn. At midnight, on the day *of* Passover, you will each be escorted to respective gates of the Old City. In each of the black cases are two bottles of pills and a bottle of water. You are to take three pills from each bottle and swallow them. All of them. Make sure you wash them down with all the water provided."

"This will protect you from the flies," Tarik interrupted.

Dulai glared at him.

"Please continue," Tarik said with a wave.

Dulai cleared his throat. "Yes, as Tarik has indicated, there should be many flies there. More than you can imagine. And, yes, after you take these pills, the presence of the flies will become unimportant to you," Dulai said, giving Tarik a sidelong look."

"Are there any questions?" Tarik said, drumming his fingers on the altar.

After a moment of silence, Dulai said, "Then that is all. Very simple. Please follow Harshit out. He will lead you to your escorts and the helicopter will leave shortly after."

A moment later Tarik and Dulai were alone.

"I thought you were going to completely explain to them what this mission was about and what would happen to them," Dulai said.

"It's a secret mission. I will not chance unnecessary exposure."

"Unnecessary exposure? The four with the black kits are going to die."

"I asked if anyone had questions. Besides, they had sworn their lives to me when they joined."

"They were afraid to ask, especially with you leaning on that altar and lifting each kit to your statue."

"It is appropriate procedure and nothing that I should have to explain to you, unless of course if you want a detailed explanation."

"Dulai paused and then looked to the ground and shook his head."

"Good. So, they are firstborn, correct?"

"Yes, but…"

"That's what is most important."

"Passover is just days away and we don't have a practical antidote."

"This is your fault, not mine."

Dulai sighed heavily. "As you wish but, without an antidote, your people will die along with the enemy."

Tarik glared at him. "And your point?"

"Postpone it. Wait until we have the antidote."

"I cannot. This is your problem, not mine. The schedule is what it is. If any of my people die, it will be on your conscience. I am clear. We each have our jobs."

"With all due respect, you seem to almost not want an antidote to be found."

Tarik paused. "And why would you say that?"

"The plague gives you power that would be considerably lessened when a cure is discovered."

"You should be smart and watch your words more carefully, Doctor. If I didn't want a cure I would have told you. Do your job and speak less."

"But I can't possibly..."

"Enough, I grow tired of this conversation. Check on Samantha Conway and report back to me immediately on her progress. The items she requested have also arrived. Make sure she gets them."

55

Sam looked up from her work when the door opened. Dulai walked in with a cardboard box and placed it on her desk.

"Your items," He said. "Do you need any assistance?"

Sam lifted her glasses onto her hair. "Are you supposed to ask me that whenever you see me?"

"Yes. But the request is genuine, nonetheless."

"Do you really want to assist?"

"Yes. I take no pleasure in seeing this virus at work."

"And you would like to see a cure?"

"Yes," Dulai said and she believed him. "Time is running out. Do you have anything to report?"

"Actually, I do. But if you really want to help, get me out of here. I can do my best work in a real lab with real scientists who aren't guarded at gunpoint."

"I am a real scientist, Doctor Conway," Dulai said.

"A real scientist who has sold his soul to the devil."

Dulai broke eye contact. "I am not at liberty to engage in this conversation. You said you had something to report."

Sam paused. Did she hit a nerve? Was Dulai developing a conscience? A weak trait when working with Tarik. "Strap on some glasses," Sam said and lowered her own back over her eyes.

Dulai promptly found his magnifying glasses in his lab coat pocket, put them on and leaned over. Sam used a pen tip as a pointer, which appeared too fat under the magnification.

"These symbols over here represent sheep, some larger than others."

"Sheep and lambs," Dulai said.

"Correct. Above them on a diagonal, we have two wavy but parallel lines. And between them are tiny verticals."

Dulai nodded.

"I believe this is the key. We know that Moses was told the antidote was to put lamb's blood on the door posts to ward off the Angel of Death. We know it worked. We don't know through what medium he received this information, but I think we see clues right here. I think the parallel diagonals represent a river, and the river, in Moses' case, would have been the Nile. I think the small verticals between the sheep and the river represent food. Lambs absorb nutrients better than the older sheep and, therefore, will receive higher concentrations of minerals and other elements in their blood. I would also bet that the Nile, which flows north and ends in Egypt, has concentrations in the silt that make any food by the shoreline unusually rich in some minerals. In other words, I don't think it was the lamb's blood, per se, that shielded against the Angel of Death, but something the lamb's blood carried."

Dulai nodded. "But wouldn't the Egyptians eating grains from the Nile's shoreline also receive the same minerals?"

"Yes but maybe not in necessary concentrations. The sheep herd's primary food was grass and they ate high quantities of it. Humans can't eat grass."

"Did the sheep in the cave die?"

Sam shrugged. "Yes but, they likely suffocated on the flies. In fact, Decker reported that he and the other prisoner had been drenched in sheep's blood from Tarik and they both lived when the guards in the room died."

"This is true. I saw him covered in blood," Dulai said, nodding.

"Decker didn't specify how old the sheep was but, it's possible that any sheep's blood would have worked in such high concentrations if the necessary minerals were present from their food source."

Dulai pulled off his glasses and looked Sam in the eyes, speechless.

"Of course, we'll never be able to figure out what that missing element is in time if you don't get me the hell out of here. I have to get some grass from the shore of the Nile in Egypt and analyze the mineral concentrations."

Dulai continued to stare, unblinking, and then snapped out of his trance. "I believe what you say is a brilliant deduction. But to allow you to leave will mean our deaths."

"What about the death of millions of innocent people?"

Dulai was silent.

"What is the target?" Sam said.

"The target?" Dulai shook his head as if amused by the question. "The target is what it has always been."

"Jerusalem?" Sam said quietly.

Dulai stared again for a moment, and then stood up. "I will pass on your findings to Tarik and ask that further avenues be opened for research and practical testing."

"He's holding the lives of your family over your head?" Sam whispered.

Dulai paused.

Sam pulled over a writing pad and was about to write, but then stopped and tore off a single sheet and wrote on the table so as to not leave any indented trace on the pad. She quickly wrote Walker's email address, her theory and sketched the important characters and then handed it to Dulai. "This will get us the antidote."

Dulai took it and stared at it for a moment and then walked into the bathroom. Sam hurried after him and saw him crumble the paper and flush it down the toilet. "That would get us killed within the hour. Next time, I will report you to Tarik." Dulai turned and left the room.

The guard watched the door close and then returned his attention to Sam. Sam forced herself to make eye contact with him for an uncomfortable five seconds, smiled a little too brightly and then looked at the box Dulai had left on the table.

Sam wasted no time in opening the box. She quickly found her two bikinis and held them up for the guard to see. "Yes!" she said with mock excitement. Identical type but one black and the other yellow, just as she'd asked. "I'm going to try these on right now!"

Jesse looked up from his computer, shook his head and then went back to his game.

Sam took the bathing suits and went to the bathroom. She shut the door and immediately took off all of her clothes and wrapped them in both bath towels, forming what looked like a pillow. She put the cushion in a corner and then began to examine her bathing suits. Halter top bikinis, as ordered. She put on the yellow suit and gave it a quick look in the small mirror. Perfect. *Maybe better than perfect,* she thought, checking her top. She then picked up the black top and examined the size of the cup. This should work well, she thought, and then opened the lid off the toilet tank and reached inside until the water was all the way to her elbow. Found it. She pulled out her hand and then dried off both her arm and the wet avocado pit with the black bikini bottom.

Sam took the pit, placed it in the bikini cup and held the top of the halter strap. She curled her wrist a few times, testing the weight of the large pit. Felt like a rock in a sock. She then twirled the top over her head, careful to keep the pit in the cup. No problem. She exhaled and pitched her arm at the cushion on the floor. The pit flew out of the top, but missed the towel by a good foot, making a loud bang against the metal wall.

"Ugh!" she said and immediately put everything down and walked out he door. Jesse and the guard were both looking at her.

"W-what was that s-sound?" Jesse said.

"The toilet seat fell. How do I look?" she said with a huge smile, turning around.

"You l-look like you've l-lost your mind," Jesse said.

Sam kept the smile on and then turned to the guard. "I'm going to try on the other now and then shower," she said and then went back into the room and then shut the door and lost the fake smile. A moment later, she twirled the black bikini top and let the pit fly again. This time, she hit the pillow with a hard thud. She successfully repeated the exercise a few more times, then turned on the shower and practiced more, aiming for the center, throwing harder and harder with the sound of the shower in the background.

56

Decker stood behind an old dirty table which was hidden in the darkness of Haco's barn. Sam's Sound Shooter sat on a small tripod on the table by an open window. The scope was aimed at Zahur, who was still in his little white car. Zahur's cautiousness bought Decker precious time to set up but, waiting for the man's next move to the house was maddening. Finally, Decker decided to give Zahur a nudge. He looked into the infrared scope and squeezed the trigger. The green laser instantly appeared. Decker figured the distance to be about two hundred feet. Not a problem. He focused the scope and brought the laser into the cavity of Zahur's ear.

"You have done well, my son," Decker said into the microphone and then took his finger off the trigger.

Zahur had zero response. Nothing. Not even the raise of an eyebrow. He apparently didn't hear the voice. Decker tried again.

"You will be rewarded greatly for your obedience," Decker said, a different message, if by chance Zahur actually did hear him the first time.

Nothing. In fact, Zahur looked at his watch.

"Son of a bitch!" Decker whispered. "What's wrong with this thing?" Without the Sound Shooter, the odds of failure were dramatically increased. And Haco would be waiting for a password that Zahur wouldn't know. "Shit!"

The car door opened and Zahur climbed out slowly. He stood there for a moment and then looked casually in every direction.

"The glass!" Decker remembered. The laser was light and could penetrate the glass, but the solid wall of the car window would stop the sound dead in its tracks, separating it from the light beam. He quickly re-aimed the Sound Shooter, looked into the scope and pulled the trigger.

"You will be rewarded greatly for your obedience," Decker said into the microphone.

Zahur snapped his head. Froze. Through the scope, Decker could see he wasn't even blinking. Amazing, he thought. For a moment, he felt close to Sam. Imagined her doing something similar. Wished she was with him... safe. He pulled the trigger again and quickly adjusted the laser to Zahur's ear.

"My gift is safe inside this home."

Zahur looked to Haco's home. He said something, but Decker had no way of knowing what. He figured the safest thing would be to respond as if nothing was said.

"Ask for the sword."

Zahur looked into the sky, threw his hands in the air and yelled angrily. Decker still couldn't make out what he was saying, but there was no mistaking the temper.

"Be at peace. Your reward will be great."

Zahur's shoulders slumped. He waved and then turned to get back into the car.

Decker was stunned. He quickly aimed and fired as Zahur was bending. *"Life or death."*

Zahur stopped.

"Choose life."

Zahur remained painfully motionless. Decker felt a drop of sweat drip off his nose. He wanted to speak again, but resisted.

Let it stew, he thought. *Let it stew*.... Finally, Zahur shut the door and walked toward the house.

"Here he comes," he heard Haco say into the microphone pen.

"I know," Decker said to himself and then adjusted his earpiece for comfort and listened. He heard a knock at the door.

"Show time," Haco whispered. "I'll let him wait a bit."

"Don't lose him, you old bastard," Decker said, but in truth, believed Haco was the perfect man for the job. There were a dozen sleeper agents in Afghanistan, but Decker would trust this assignment with no one else.

Another knock. Louder this time.

More waiting.

"He's leaving the door," Haco said.

Decker rolled his eyes. "Answer the damn door before he finds me and the helicopter, will you please?"

Decker heard the door latch and the creaking of the opening door. "May I help you?" Haco said in Farsi.

After a pause, Decker heard, "Do you live alone?"

"Why... do you ask?"

"Because I am unsure to whom I am to speak."

"I see. Then it must be me. I live alone."

"Hmm, are you expecting a visitor?"

"No. I wasn't expecting you, either. Who are you?"

"That is not important."

"Then what do you want?"

"I was told to come here... and ask someone for something."

"Your words are strange, Sir."

"I know. This is *all* very strange. I was told to ask for the sword."

There was silence. Decker could imagine Haco's surprise. "How... I mean, who told you to ask for the sword?"

"You know of the sword?"

"Yes."

"This is unbelievable. I was sure I had lost my mind. Or that…"

"Come inside."

Decker heard more movement, the door shut and then footsteps sounded.

"Please sit," Haco said.

Decker could hear more steps, louder and then quieter. *Zahur's footsteps*, Decker thought. He wasn't sitting.

"Sir, where are you going?" Haco said and then whispered into the pen. "Decker… he's looking nervous."

The footsteps got louder again.

"Please sit," Haco repeated.

"*You sit*," Zahur said sternly. Then there was the unmistakable metallic click of a pistol readied close to the microphone.

"What are you doing? Please put the *gun* away," Haco said, trying to emphasize the word 'gun' into the microphone.

Decker ran to the barn door, but then stopped short. To rescue Haco would be as good as killing Sam.

"The sword," Haco said, desperately. "You need the sword."

"Who are you?" Zahur said. "Tell me what this is all about or I'll kill you now."

"I don't know what you are talking about."

"Who are you with?"

"I live alone."

"Tell me who you're with," Zahur shouted. "CIA?"

"I don't understand."

After a long moment of silence, Zahur shouted, "Why don't you speak to me now!"

"What do you want me to say?" Haco said.

"Not you!"

"Not… then who are you talking to?"

Zahur sighed. "I don't know. A voice that knows *everything*."

"A voice? A voice told you about the sword?"

"Yes."

"A voice from… the air?" Haco said, in mock doubt.

"Yes!" Zahur insisted. "I'm not crazy."

"Did the voice describe it?"

"Not really."

"Hmm. The voice told you about the sword, but didn't tell you what it was or what it looked like?" Haco said.

"Yes," Zahur said angrily. "It is not for you to believe or not."

"When does the voice speak to you?"

"Different times. There is no pattern. I ask and it doesn't answer, and it speaks when I do not ask, only when it has something to say."

A pause. "Do you want to see the sword?"

"Yes. Now."

57

Sam took a deep breath, exhaled, tried not to think about the insanity and desperation of her plan, and then exited the bathroom in her new yellow bikini.

Jesse looked up from the computer and his brows arched. "I d-don't think y-you should w-walk around here l-like that. "

"How's the game going?" Sam said, ignoring his comment as she walked over and looked over his shoulder at his monitor. Some bizarre game with hundreds of characters, everything moving and exploding. She had her back to the guard, giving him her best posterior pose.

Jesse looked at her hands. "Are th-those a-avocado pits?"

"Uh huh," she said pleasantly. And then under her breath, she calmly said, "I want you to go into the bathroom and not come out until I come and get you."

Jesse's chin snapped in Sam's direction, his eyes large.

"Have I ever asked you to do anything unsafe?" she said and then started juggling the three avocado pits in a classic pretzel pattern.

"As a m-matter of f-fact...."

"Just do it," she whispered, motioning to the bathroom and then, pivoted toward the guard, still juggling. As a child, Sam had practiced juggling with tennis balls and various fruits to amuse her friends. Now she figured to give the guard all his eyes could manage. She went over toward her desk, walking as seductively as she could. She had his undivided attention.

"I was going to throw them out, but I needed something to practice with. They're a perfect size, don't you think?" Sam said in Egyptian.

The guard said nothing.

"You like?" she said, smiling innocently.

The guard stared, saying nothing.

Sam began to wonder if he could speak. She was about to ask him if his tongue had been cut out, but then it occurred to her that maybe it actually had been. "Sometimes I like to do it like this," she said, changing the juggling pattern to an alternating two-one-two-one.

The guard showed no expression, his eyes looking straight at her, not moving with the pits. *Perfect,* she thought.

"And if you like variety," she said, and then changed the pattern again, tossing the pits in a circular pattern. The camera was over the guard's head. She wondered if anyone else was watching. There was probably a crowd forming at the viewing monitor, wherever that was. She had to assume she was being watched and would soon turn their entertainment into a crisis.

"Would you like to see my favorite way?" Sam said in Egyptian.

The guard remained silent, but made no attempt to stop her. His eyes surveyed more than the avocado pits as she slowly swirled her hips.

Here goes, Sam thought. "I'll only need one," she said in Egyptian, and then placed the next two she caught on the desk. She juggled the final pit alone in her left hand as she untied the back of her bikini. She then pulled her top over her head with her right hand, exposing her breasts.

The guard, who had been a perfect statue up to that point, straightened up. The white of his eyes became much whiter and the sides of his mouth began to curl into a thin smile as Sam dropped the pit into one of the cups of her top. She then took all the straps firmly in her right hand and swung the bikini top around over her head in rhythm with her hips swinging hard from side to side.

"In my country, this is called slight of hand," she said in English. "While you can't seem to take your eyes off one thing, you're not watching what is really happening," she said and then took a long step toward him and whipped her arm, releasing two of the straps in rapid sequence, like a pitcher hurling a fastball. The hard avocado pit zipped and hit the huge guard directly in the forehead with a loud crack.

The guard dropped to his knees, the machine gun falling from his loose hands. Sam quickly grabbed the gun and ran to the bathroom door and kicked it open.

"Jesse, let's go! Now!"

Jesse stepped out and gasped at the sight of his topless sister with a machine gun and then gasped again at the guard on his hands and knees. "Oh, m-my God! Not g-good."

Sam quickly ran back and hit the guard hard on the back of the head, crumbling him limp to the floor. She then tossed Jesse the gun and put her yellow top on in an instant. "I don't want to die with these guys ogling my naked body."

"W-we're going to d-die." Jesse said.

Sam grabbed the gun back from him and racked the ammo to fire. "Follow me and do exactly as I say."

"I w-will go b-back in the b-bathroom till you're d-done?"

"We're not coming back," Sam said and opened the door. She looked both ways and saw nothing, but heard running steps echoing from somewhere above.

"W-what's the plan?" Jesse said.

"The plan part is done. From here on, I shoot from the hip. Let's go!" she said and ran down the right corridor to the metal stairs. Just as she was about to run up the stairs, several soldiers rushed through a doorway down the other end of the corridor.

Sam immediately opened fire over their heads. They turned and dove back into the doorway. Sam ran up the stairs. Gunfire exploded behind her and bullets ricocheted off the steps and walls behind them.

Sam remembered coming down the stairs but didn't remember how many flights. She turned the corner on the first flight, ran down a short corridor and then fired the gun at the top of the other stairs before running up the next flight. Jesse was right on her but so were the soldiers running up the stairs a flight behind them. There was a door at the top of the next flight. Sam only remembered one door. Before opening it, she fired a burst down the stairs and then opened it slowly. She was on the roof and a helicopter was some fifty feet away. The blades were moving slowly and someone was in the pilot's seat. As soon as Jesse got through the door, she slammed it shut and fired a few rounds into the handle mechanism, hoping to jam it, then ran for the chopper.

They're going to have to shoot us down, she thought.

Sam jumped into an open cargo area behind the pilot and Jesse jumped in right behind her. She pressed the gun barrel into the back of the pilot's head and said "Fly or die," in Egyptian.

"Hey!" Jesse yelled.

Sam turned to see Tarik in the back of the cargo area behind Jesse, his arm tightly around her brother's neck. He pointed a pistol at Jesse's head.

"Samantha Conway. This is very disappointing. Where do you think you are going?" Tarik said.

"If people are going to be saved, I have to get to an unrestricted lab with real scientists."

"I had so many plans for us. You broke our agreement."

"I'll never be able to finish my work here and you know it. I've found the means for an antidote, but I'll never be able to research it through in time, much less implement it."

"Your job was to try."

"My job was to fail."

Tarik pursed his lips. "I understand that you always strive for the highest standards and will excuse your little break from concentration. But there must be consequences or you'll try this again."

"Let us go now or I'll shoot your pilot!" Sam shouted, pressing the gun harder.

"Like this?" Tarik said and then, cat-quick, pointed his gun, fired a round into the back of the pilot's head and returned aim to Jesse's jaw. The pilot fell forward, dead, blood and brain splattered across the windshield. An instant later, soldiers had the chopper surrounded, all their guns pointed at Sam.

58

Decker looked at his watch. One minute had ticked off since the last time he looked. He didn't know where Haco had hidden the artifact, but there was very little conversation and a lot of shuffling sounds. The scam was in high gear.

"Excuse me," Haco said and then more shuffling.

"Where is it?" Zahur said.

"In here. The gun makes me nervous," Haco said.

Decker shook his head. He knew Haco would need all of ten seconds to disarm and incapacitate Zahur. Less to kill him.

"The gun stays. I can't take any chances," Zahur said.

"Here. It's in this blanket."

"It doesn't look like a sword."

"The sword is not a real sword as you know it."

"Then what is it?"

"Unwrap the blanket," Haco said.

"*You* unwrap it! On the table," Zahur ordered. "Slowly."

More footsteps. "Is here all right?" Haco said. Decker could see him at an open window. "The sunlight will make it easier to see," Haco said.

"Yes, yes, just show it to me."

"The sword has been in my family for many years. Passed down through generations. Now, only I am left."

Good line, Decker thought, and then saw Zahur stand next to him, a gun in his hand. Haco delicately peeled back the folds of a red blanket.

Zahur stared for a moment and then whispered, "My God." He then touched it, feathering his finger across the ancient writing.

"Careful," Haco said. "It's very old."

Zahur pointed the gun at Haco's head. "Stand aside. Over there where I can see you."

Haco humbly obeyed.

Zahur appeared mesmerized, "What does it say?"

"I'm not sure," Haco said. "It supposedly holds secrets of great power, wealth, healing as well as destruction.... That is why it is called the sword."

Perfect, Decker thought.

"It's broken," Zahur said.

"Yes."

"There's writing missing."

"Yes."

"Where is the rest of it?"

"I don't know."

"Have you tried to get it translated?"

Uh, oh, Decker thought. *Dangerous question.*

"No... I was afraid it would be stolen. I didn't want it to fall into the wrong hands."

That's exactly where I want it, Decker thought.

"My instructions are to take it," Zahur said.

"Instructions from the voice?"

"Yes," Zahur said, and then clicked the hammer back on the pistol. "The problem is, I have to go and I can't leave you to report me stealing it from you."

"Why would I do that?"

"Let's just say that I can't afford any undue attention with the government," he said and then leveled the gun at Haco's head.

"Jesus!" Decker said, and then pointed the Sound Shooter into Zahur's ear. Suddenly he saw a red light blink on the battery. Low battery.

"Allah decides my fate… not you. It is his voice you hear. Ask him," Haco said.

Decker squeezed the trigger. *"No… do not kill him. He is my faithful servant."*

"There!" Zahur said. "Did you hear that?"

"No."

"You're lying."

"I don't really believe in voices."

"I told you, I don't care."

"What did you hear?"

Zahur lowered the gun. "Not to kill you."

Haco sighed. "The voice is wise."

Decker squeezed again. *"You are my messenger. Complete your task. Bring the sword to my servant, Tarik. My time of fulfillment is near."*

"I suppose you didn't hear that either?"

"It spoke again?"

Zahur nodded.

"What did it say?"

"It is not for you to know. Be thankful you live," Zahur said and then carefully re-wrapped the artifact and left the table.

Decker heard footsteps and a door close.

Haco's face appeared at the window. He tapped the pen and said, "I don't know how, but you've driven the poor bastard crazy."

Decker squeezed and aimed the beam into Haco's ear. *"Sometimes hearing is believing, faithful servant."*

Haco's eyes widened. "Oh, my God," he said.

"Exactly."

Decker watched Zahur hurry into his white car and drive away.

59

Ali Shakib stood under the tall Roman arch at the Lions' Gate in awe of his surroundings and wondering why he had been selected for such an important mission. He didn't know what the mission was but he did know it was extremely important. So why him? He had never been in the Old City of Jerusalem before. For that matter, he had never been in Israel. He had seen many pictures of the famous Dome of the Rock taken from the Mount of Olives but until this moment, he had never seen the actual mount. Rising from the Kidron Valley just a few feet away, it was so close he felt he could just reach out and touch it. And so many people. Dulai had told him Passover would be a very active time, but not that it would be *so* busy that he would have to perform his secret task in a mob.

Ali stepped out from under the ancient arch and stopped breathing. Soldiers. Israeli soldiers. Two of them, one sitting and one standing. They didn't seem to pay him any attention. *But why should they*, he thought as he tried to breath normally. He wasn't doing anything illegal, at least as far as they could tell. He wove through the crowd and found a couple of steps to sit on. The stone was hard but warm from the midday sun. He unshouldered his leather satchel and found Dulai's sanitary kit and a small bottle of water. He drank half the water and then emptied the powder from the two pill bottles into what remained. The water turned a cloudy white. He screwed the cap back on the water bottle and shook it.

He reminded himself that his job was not to understand but just to follow the instructions, as he stared at the milky contents of the bottle. He unscrewed the cap and spilled the entire solution onto the ground and watched it disappear in the cracks between the cobblestones. That was it. That was his secret mission. That was what he was flown to Israel to do. That was why he was specially picked. Now he was to return. Mission accomplished. People passed and paid him no attention. The soldiers were still where they had been, still chatting. He shrugged, screwed the cap on the empty bottle and put everything back in the satchel.

Ali stood up and stretched. The sun felt good. He looked at the Lions' Gate and thought about going into the Old City. His instructions were to leave after spilling the liquid, but if he only had one glass of cold carob tea on the way out it would be the same as leaving and he would get to see the famous mosque. Maybe stop for a few minutes and say a prayer. A prayer of thanks for a mission accomplished and another prayer for future success. And maybe a Turkish coffee. He looked to where he had spilled the solution and the ground was already dry. Between the hot sun and the hot stone there was no longer any trace of liquid. He was about to walk away when he noticed an insect climb from between the cobblestone and then another and another. Soon the entire stone was covered with crawling insects.

He wanted to crouch for a better look at the bugs but then remembered his instructions to leave. Insects continued to come from the cracks and spread like a growing puddle of thick black oil.

"Look!" said a woman's voice.

Ali looked up to see that a few people had stopped. He stepped back from the object of the their attention, afraid he may become part of it. To his surprise, a few insects flew away. He didn't even know they had wings. One flew past him close enough for him to think it was a fly. A fly? When did flies ever crawl out of the ground? The thick puddle continued to spread and more people took notice and pointed. He wanted to stay and he wanted to run but his instructions were for him to do neither. He faded back as more people stopped and stared. More flies took flight until steady streams were leaving like bees from a busy hive.

He glanced at the soldiers. They had stopped chatting and the one that was in the chair stood up. The growing crowd had their attention. One started to walk over and the other talked on his radio. To who? What was there to report? A few people stopping to look at something? Or was he receiving a call? It was then that Ali remembered he was not alone in this mission. Three other Tarik agents were also at city gates. What was happening there?

The gathering crowd suddenly gasped and rippled backward as the swarm erupted into flight. A dark swirling cloud funneled into the air like a small tornado and dispersed into the sky. Over the city walls, he could see another swarm thicker and larger to the south in the direction of the Dung Gate. The two soldiers yelled at the crowd to back away and other soldiers were running toward them from the gate.

Ali tried to stay calm while his heart pounded. Tarik had done this. He had created chaos, fear and confusion in Jerusalem with the mere spilling of water on the ground. Tarik was great and he was Tarik's chosen agent. God's chosen agent. Ali walked proudly through the Lions' Gate. He would definitely stop at the great mosque and pray and then, if anyone was left in the Old City, he would have a Turkish coffee.

60

Sam and Jesse had their hands tied behind their backs and were held fast by four guards, one on each arm, in a large room that reminded Sam of an Egyptian tomb. The light from a dozen bronze oil lamps in carved niches splashed an amber glow on limestone walls. Ancient etchings and prayers were inscribed on walls, floors and ceiling. Wooden shelves showcased artifacts of various sizes. Tarik had clearly lost his mind. In the front of the room, a purple curtain hung from ceiling to floor. The large guard that had the unsuccessful task of guarding Sam and Jesse in their room had Sam's right arm in a vise grip. He also had a bump on his forehead the size of the pit that hit him. The steel door behind them opened and a familiar voice was speaking quick and angry.

"I did nothing! Nothing! This is wrong! Wrong!" Dulai pleaded as he was dragged by the armpits toward the curtain, the black soles of his shoes leaving a scuff trail on the concrete floor.

The curtain was drawn, revealing a tall statue Sam immediately recognized as Anubis, the Egyptian god of death and a stone altar at its feet. Dulai was quickly laid down on the altar and strapped securely by the neck and knees.

"What are they going to do to him?" Jesse asked Sam.

Sam wasn't a hundred percent sure, but she had heard rumors through Decker and Walker and, historically, there was only one use for the ancient altar. "I don't know, Jess. They're probably trying to scare us."

"They're doing a good job."

Sam looked around the room as best she could. There must be something she could do.

Another door opened behind the altar and Tarik walked in wearing a black robe that touched the floor. He nodded to Sam and Jesse. "I think it is good that you join me here for this unfortunate but special event because you caused it to happen. Doctor Dulai will bear the consequence of your decision," Tarik said and then immediately turned to Dulai.

"My decision, Tarik," Sam called. "Not Jesse's. Your own justice demands you not to include him in this."

"In what?" Jesse said.

"Anubis demands true justice from you," Sam said, hopefully.

Tarik paused. He looked up to Anubis for a moment and then turned and studied Jesse. He motioned to the guards and they immediately took Jesse away.

"What about me?" Dulai cried. "What have I done wrong?" He struggled against the straps, violently testing their strength. "You cannot do this to me. I've done nothing wrong."

Tarik held up a small sheet of paper. "Do you see this?" Tarik said, bringing the paper close enough for Sam to read. "This was found in the helicopter pilot's pocket."

Sam read it and was shocked. It was Walker's email address and the sketch of the characters and explanation that Sam had given to Dulai about the antidote. Dulai had tried to warn Walker.

"If you hadn't attempted your daring escape, the helicopter would have made its normal run and this would have undoubtedly found itself quickly into the hands of the CIA. But this is what happens when the gods are with you," Tarik said and turned to Dulai. "Are you going to try to deny that this is your handwriting?"

Dulai's eyes were wide in his silence.

Sam spoke up. "Please don't hurt him. We need each other to continue. Hurting him hurts you."

Tarik paused.

"Allow us to produce the antidote. You will only miss your target date by a few days. What would it matter?" she said.

"No. He has betrayed me," Tarik said and then felt through Dulai's lab coat for the top of his leg.

"What are you doing?" Dulai cried, jerking his hip.

Tarik did not reply but continued to search with his hand.

"Think of what you're doing," Sam pleaded.

"You're mad!" Dulai said and struggled.

"Stop moving," Tarik said calmly and put the point of the knife at the top of Dulai's thigh so any upward movement would be painfully punished.

"Aghh!" Dulai cried. "Think of all the innocent lives you're going to kill."

"There are no innocent lives. Least of all yours," Tarik said and then pushed on the knife.

"Aghh! Dulai screamed and then breathed deeply and screamed more.

"Jesus!" Sam said.

Tarik pulled the knife out, waited a second and then frowned. "This is embarrassing," he said to Dulai who was breathing in short puffs. "There is a woman here, Doctor. I was hoping to work through your clothes." Tarik shrugged and then parted Dulai's clothes. "I'll try again."

Sam exhaled at the sight of Dulai's puncture wound as Tarik felt around.

"Ah, here it is," Tarik said. "And we seem to be lucky. I should be able to sever your artery through the same entry. Correct me if I'm wrong, Doctor," he said matter-of-factly, "but should I proceed from here at this angle?" he said, and paused for Dulai's approval.

"Please, Tarik. You need me."

"We'll let Anubis decide that," Tarik said and then slowly pushed the knife in at an angle. Dulai screamed in agony. After burying half the length of the blade and twisting the handle, Tarik pulled out the knife. Blood instantly gushed out three feet into the air.

Sam closed her eyes.

"It appears that Anubis is making his decision clear," Tarik said. He put down the knife and picked up a goblet. He caught some of the squirting flow and held it high to the statue. He recited a prayer of recognition and then drank from the cup as Dulai watched. He turned to the guards who sipped and then offered the cup to Sam, blood dripping from his mouth.

"I'll pass," Sam said.

"Then I will require your brother to drink in your place."

Sam looked at Dulai, who was shaking. She took the goblet and sipped and then Tarik reached over and lifted it at a steeper angle. Warm liquid poured through her teeth and filled her mouth. She reflexively spit it out as it flowed off her jaws and around her bikini top.

Tarik smiled. "Clean up and dress for dinner," he said and then turned to Dulai. "I don't suppose you'll be joining us this time. A pity you won't be able to witness the fruit of your labor. CNN should soon have some breaking news very soon."

61

"Say that again?" Decker said and adjusted the volume on his headphones as the chopper quickly rose and banked away from Haco's home. He had waited thirty minutes and verified Zahur's location and progress with Walker before leaving. Although Walker was almost halfway around the globe at CIA headquarters at Langley, he was watching Zahur's car on a satellite fed big screen. Also, the white car on the screen produced a blinking red light indicating the artifact was indeed with Zahur.

"I said he's making great time," Walker said, too loud now that the volume was turned up. "I hope he doesn't get a speeding ticket."

"Make damn sure he doesn't," Decker said.

"How am I supposed to do that from here? If we alert the authorities, we'll have a leak for sure."

"Then bomb something for God's sake. I want him given a wide path."

"No problem. We'll call up an F-15 to take out a police car," Walker said sardonically. "That should get their attention."

"Take out the whole damn department if you have to. Just make sure he's given a clear road," Decker said.

"Well, unfortunately *that* won't be necessary. He's driving into the airport as we speak."

"Good. Make sure there's no air traffic either. Clear skies."

"Already done. We can figure out a few things in your absence, Deck."

"And don't lose him this time."

"The tracer will make that difficult."

"Belts and suspenders. No one is better at hiding than Tarik. If he disappears..."

"Relax. We've got him."

"Sam's life depends on it."

"Uh, not to mention a city," Walker said.

Decker frowned. Did Sam's well-being mean more to him than what Tarik was planning to do to a city? Whatever. At the moment, there were no conflicts. And no time to analyze priorities that ran parallel.

"You there?" Walker said.

"Yeah."

"You'll be visible soon. Do you want that?"

"No. We'll slow down and hug the hillside," Decker said and then looked at the pilot, who gave an acknowledging nod and banked into a ravine.

"He's out of the car and headed for the jet."

"Excellent."

"He's climbing the stairs. He's on board. Door's shut. We've got him Deck."

"Easy, partner. It's Tarik we want. We have nothing until we have him."

"Something is wrong."

"What?"

"Shit!"

"What!"

"We lost signal. The jet is readying for takeoff but no blinking red light. The fuselage is blocking the signal."

"How?"

"I don't know."

"Could they have found the tracer?"

"No. It happened too quickly. Maybe some sort of auto-jammer to protect the jet's electronics from outside radio waves."

"Thank you, Professor Einstein. Can you keep view of the jet?"

Silence.

"I said, can you…"

"I don't know. We couldn't last time. Clouds, range, night. Without the tracer, it's a crap-shoot. "

Decker closed his eyes, but then something occurred to him. "I'm coming in," he said and then looked at the pilot. "Fast."

The pilot nodded and opened the throttle.

"What are you going to do?" Walker said.

"Tail him."

"They'll see you."

"Not in the Blackbird. We'll follow him at eighty-five thousand feet."

"It's probably not ready. It has to be fueled."

"Start pumping. Is Martin still around?"

"I don't know."

"Find him. He got me here and, the fewer people involved, the better."

"We're already looking."

Decker looked at his duffel bag. He didn't know if he'd get another chance to change. In the Blackbird there was simply no room. The chopper swooped into Kabul international air space in time to see the jet leave the runway. The Blackbird was being fueled. The chopper landed next to it and Decker jumped out, emptied the contents of his black duffel bag onto the tarmac.

"I was going to ask you what was in the duffel bag," the pilot said. "But now that I see it, I still don't know."

"I'll send you a postcard when it's over, Colonel," Decker said and then saw a white car coming straight at them, fast. Light reflected off the windshield. Decker felt for his gun. The head lights blinked and the car skidded to a halt. The door opened and Decker's gun leveled at whoever was getting out.

"Can't a guy finish a beer around here?" Martin said and slammed the car door behind him.

Decker holstered his gun. "How many have you had?"

"Maybe five, ten. I would have had more if I knew I had to fly you again… Captain," Martin said and then climbed the Blackbird like a cat. *Maybe one beer*, Decker thought.

Decker motioned for the fuel truck to leave and quickly dressed into the contents of the bag. He climbed into the jet, dropped into his seat and snapped in. A few moments later, the Blackbird was in the air, climbing to eighty-five thousand feet at three times the speed of sound, west by southwest, the direction the jet was last seen on radar.

"It seems like we're making this plan up as we go, Captain," Martin said.

"Plan?" Decker said. "If I told you the *plan* you'd eject, Gary."

"Understood, Sir."

"Anything yet?" Decker said impatiently.

"No, Sir."

"They couldn't have turned the tracer off," Decker said, thinking aloud.

"Tracer?"

"Nothing. Just talking to myself. Been doing that a lot lately."

"If I were you, Captain, I'd listen. What you have to say is usually important."

"Always important, Colonel," Decker said.

"Uh, yeah. That's what I meant to say."

"But not always correct."

"Corporate jet, Captain, of unknown type."

"Is it them?"

"I don't know. I'll go in a closer look."

"Negative. Not an inch. If they even think they're being spied it's over. Take photos and send them back to Walker."

"Another Kodak moment," Martin said and zoomed the recon cameras in on the jet. Moments later the report came back from Walker.

"No good, Deck. Wrong jet," Walker said.

"How can it be the wrong jet?" Decker said, in disbelief.

"It is."

"Are you positive?"

"One hundred percent," Walker said. "Wrong tail number."

"Maybe they changed it."

"They can't change numbers mid flight."

"Why not?"

"How?"

"I don't know. We changed *pilots* mid-flight. Is there anything else on radar?"

After a pause, Martin said, "Actually, no."

"That's impossible," Walker said. "They have to be on radar by now, unless they crashed."

"It's them," Decker said, emphatically.

"But the tail number doesn't…"

"I don't care. Stay on them, Gary," Decker said.

"You got it."

Decker watched the sun setting in the horizon. Darkness would help them stay out of sight but make further photos much more difficult.

"We're coming up on Iranian airspace," Martin said.

"Will we be picked up?" Decker said.

"Probably not," Walker said. "But the corporate already has."

"That doesn't appear to concern them too much," Decker said. "They know exactly where they are."

"Why am I not surprised?" Walker said. "The back door opens, the back door closes. No one sees, everyone is innocent."

"What's more important is that they don't see us," Decker said. "If they do, they'll let Zahur know somehow and it's over."

"Hold on, Deck," Walker said. After a long pause, he was back. "Deck."

"Yeah?"

"You better sit down for this one."

"What?"

"Jerusalem suddenly has a major fly problem."

"Did you say Jerusalem?"

"Yup. People can't leave their houses."

Decker paused. "When does Passover start?"

"I, uh, believe tomorrow."

62

Sam and Jesse picked at their food, neither of them very interested in the new menu. The table was no longer decorated with a colorful array of scrumptious delectables. No rack of lamb. No greens. No fresh squeezed fruit juice. Instead, some sort of chickpea and rice mush and cold, dry meat from another era.

"Th-they aren't g-giving us any m-more avocados," Jesse said.

"No, I guess they weren't happy with the way I disposed of the pits," Sam said.

"N-no. I know I w-will never look at them the s-same way again."

Suddenly, the door opened and two armed guards entered, one of them was the mammoth guard with the large avocado bump still proud on his forehead. He motioned with his gun barrel for Sam to stand up. He didn't look like he was going to ask again so nicely.

"What's h-happening?" Jesse said.

"I'll be fine, Jess. Don't worry," she said and rose from her chair.

The other guard produced a white cloth strap and quickly tied it around her wrists. In an instant, she thought about grabbing his dangling gun but the big guard's muzzle in the small of her back reminded her not to try anything heroic. Tied snuggly, she was motioned to the door.

"W-where are they b-bringing you?"

"Hopefully to the kitchen."

Sam was escorted down two steel hallways with one guard in front, the other behind her. They stopped at a door that turned out to be an industrial elevator. There were no numbers in the car but it seemed to travel more than one floor before it stopped. The door opened and she was pushed into a large, plush room with a white marble floor, wall to wall. The elevator door closed and only the large guard remained with her. The room was surrounded on three sides by windows. Her eyes were immediately grabbed by the tail end of a beautiful sunset. She noted her global directions and saw Tarik behind a large granite-top desk staring at her, his eyes bright. He stood up and rapidly waved her over, unable to hide a wide grin. Had she ever seen him grin before? Sam felt the nudge of a gun barrel in her back.

"Hemsi, hemsi," Tarik said in Egyptian, telling her to sit. "My faithful obedience to Anubis has brought me the desires of my heart."

Sam was pushed into a black leather swivel chair and spun around to face a large LCD screen. CNN was on. From what looked like the interior of a van, a female field reporter pointed through a windshield to a dark blizzard of flies. She had to yell to be heard over the loud buzz that sounded like chainsaws. The screen flashed to earlier scenes. Film clips were blurred by unbelievably thick swarms. Close-ups of deserted cattle lying dead on hillsides. More close-ups of abandoned cars with doors left hastily open and loose camels running insanely in circles and into stone walls. Screams of people running to and from an unguarded Wailing Wall. A clip from the Mount of Olives showed the once panoramic postcard view of the Old City with such a thick black cloud around it that the golden dome of the mosque was completely invisible.

Tarik came around the desk, stood in front of Sam and pointed proudly at the breaking news. "*This* is just the beginning," he said. "Three thousand years ago today, *they* did this to *us*!"

Sam frowned. "Today?"

"Yes," he said, his jaw tight. "They did this to Egypt and now I am doing this to them."

"*They* had a reason," Sam said to herself. Or at least she thought she did.

"What!" Tarik said. "What did you say?"

"I said they had a reason. They were a trodden down abused nation of slaves asking for their human right to freedom. They were denied. They took action and asked again. What's your excuse?" Sam said.

The veins in Tarik's neck and forehead swelled. Sam thought he would grab a guard's gun and cut her down right there, but he rebounded quickly, his grin returned and he shrugged. "Times have changed," he said and then looked back to the screen, chin high. "And they will change more. Today, begins a new era. Today the power has shifted. Today, Anubis has taken vengeance and validated my decisions."

Sam wasn't sure which section of an insane asylum Tarik would be kept if the world was so fortunate to have him in one, but she was sure that, execution aside, he should be in one with the key destroyed. The man was basking in his success. "Shifted from where to where?"

"What?" he said, apparently too busy with the applause in his own brain to hear her.

"Power for who? Egypt?" Sam said doubtfully. "Is there a government who will share this power?"

"No government. Not Egypt. Not anyone. As long as I have ingredients from the pillar, I will decide who kneels and who stands."

"Fear? That's what you want? There are so many more worthwhile objectives that could come from the pillar. If we can find the rest of it, we might even be able to unlock the aging process. Methuselah supposedly lived to Nine hundred and sixty-nine years."

"Then you will be happy to hear that the fly plague is only the first part of today's good news. Another reward has confirmed that the spirit of Anubis has heard my prayers and answered them because of my faithfulness."

"Tarik, there aren't too many out there who would consider a fly plague to be good news. Doesn't that tell you anything?"

Tarik smirked and pointed to the TV screen. "Three thousand years ago, they thought it was good news."

Sam sighed. "I guess I walked into that one. Okay, what it the other 'good' news?"

"Another piece of the pillar is on its way and will be here very soon."

Sam stopped breathing. She must have heard him wrong. "Did you say you found another piece of the pillar?

"Not found. Given to me from Anubis. Given on the same day the flies appear in Jerusalem. Given as confirmation Anubis is pleased with the Angel of Death."

Sam wanted to blow apart his Anubis theory but didn't think it was the smartest thing to do at the moment. "From where?"

"Afghanistan. Perhaps this other piece will help you with the cure."

"Do you care?"

"Of course."

"Well, you might be right, maybe it will. Hold off your attack until we have it."

"No. The timing is perfect."

"Millions of lives can be saved. Doesn't that matter to you?"

"No. It didn't matter to Moses or his God when the firstborn of Egypt died. Why should it matter to me if the ones who first infected us die of their own plague? Besides, it is too late," he said, motioning to the LCD. "It has already begun."

"You've released the Angel of Death?" Sam said, her voice higher and breaking to get the words out.

"Yes, I've given the orders and they're irretrievable."

"You have to stop it! There is no antidote yet!" Sam pleaded.

"What will happen is meant to be."

Sam closed her eyes humbly and prayed, as her parents had taught her when she was a child. She had failed and now thousands, maybe millions of lives would perish, consumed by the most horrifying of deaths.

"Are you saying something?" Tarik said.

Sam didn't realize she was speaking. "I was praying for the innocent lives you are going to murder," she said and then looked at her guards. "He has no regard for you or your families. He will kill us all. Stop him now while you can."

The guards looked at each other and then smiled.

"You are a very unusual person, Samantha Conway. You sit there tied with gun barrels leveled at your head and you challenge me. No one would dare such foolishness, except maybe Dulai. Such a shame. I wish he could see this," Tarik said.

"You didn't have to kill him."

"Yes, I did. You both betrayed me. Anubis required a life."

"Why his?"

"You are a prisoner. Your betrayal was expected. His was treason."

Sam felt helpless. This conversation was going nowhere. She had to somehow reach the outside world. According to the news coverage, the only problem so far was the flies. Soon, the Angel of Death would be released and millions would die. And where? New York? Japan? Washington? What was Ross doing? And where was Decker?

63

Decker vividly remembered the flies in the cave. If he hadn't waded through them himself, he wouldn't believe any of this new plague news. Walker said people couldn't leave their homes. Sam's nightmare theory had become a reality, or at least part of it. With Tarik able to inflict plagues, the CIA would launch a full scale assault when his location was confirmed. To delay the confirmation could jeopardize the mission but might be Sam's only chance of survival. He looked up from the cockpit. The stars looked like they could be touched. The only other illumination was an orange glow from the instrument panel. Everything else was black. Black jet, black interior and he was wearing a black jumpsuit. Below were some clouds and then water. Zahur's ride had brought them over the Persian Gulf, Saudi Arabia and now, the Red Sea, with Egypt dead ahead.

"They're descending, Captain," Martin said.

"About time," Decker said.

"It looks like he's landing at Marsa Alam International," Walker said.

"Keep back at maximum radius, Gary."

"That would put us over Saudi Arabia," Martin said.

"Anything new with the flies?" Decker asked.

"A buzzing cloud around the whole city and nowhere else. Thick as rain," Walker said.

"And they're alive?"

"Of course."

"In the cave, they died. All of them. Sam said it was because the Angel of Death was also released and the flies were all firstborn."

"And you scoffed at her."

"I did, but that was centuries ago."

"Uh, maybe a couple of weeks."

"I'm open-minded now."

"You are many things, Deck. Open-minded is not one of them."

"You don't know what you're talking about. I'm very open-minded. And one more word and I'll open your mind."

Walker snorted. "Whatever you say. So far, no reported deaths, fly or human."

"That will change," Decker said.

"He's landing," Martin said.

"Let's hope it's the right jet we've been following," Walker said.

"It is," Decker said.

The corporate jet touched down and was quickly met by a little white car. A single passenger exited the jet and got into the car. A moment later, the car was racing across the airport and then came to a stop next to a helicopter.

"The tracer's giving off a signal, Deck. It looks like we're back in business."

Decker exhaled. "Good. Stay at maximum distance, Colonel. We want both pair of eyes on them."

"In sight. And the chopper's off the ground heading south east."

"Back the way they came. Over the Red Sea," Decker said.

"Correct," Martin said. "And hanging low. He can't be more than ten feet off the water."

The Blackbird kept at an invisibly far distance while Walker kept up a constant monitor of the tracer. Twenty-three minutes later, the helicopter came to a stop.

"In the water?" Decker said.

"Yes, about three miles off shore," Walker said.

"That's correct," Martin confirmed. "Wait, they're on the move again. Back the way they came."

"No, they're not," Walker said. The tracer is still motionless."

"What's going on Colonel?" Decker said.

"A boat. They've boarded a boat. And there it goes."

"What kind of boat?" Decker said.

"A fast one," Walker said. "The tracer's moving at eighty miles per hour and climbing."

The boat continued for thirty-two minutes before coming to halt.

"They've stopped," Martin said.

"They've stopped," Walker said.

"I hear an echo," Decker said. "Where are they, Gary?"

"Nowhere. They just stopped in the middle of the Red Sea. All alone."

"Barely drifting," Walker said.

Forty-four minutes passed like hours. "What's the latest with the flies?" Decker asked.

"It's horrible," Walker said. "Jerusalem is paralyzed. CNN called it a black blizzard. It's on every news channel."

"If Tarik succeeds with his plan, it will be on every channel, period," Decker said.

"We have company," Martin said.

"What is it, Colonel?" Decker said.

"Another chopper, coming from the south."

"A different chopper?" Walker said.

"It would have to be," Decker said. "The only instruction the first bird had was to meet the boat. The boat only knows where to pick up and where to meet the second chopper. I can guarantee you that Zahur has no clue where he is or where he's going."

"And if anyone asks the wrong question, it's their last," Walker said.

"We have a rendezvous," Martin said.

A few moments later, both vehicles departed in opposite directions, the helicopter returning back the way it came.

"This could go on all night," Walker said.

"I don't think so," Decker said. "Are any tactical measures being taken with the flies?"

"Yeah, stay inside. Hide. The Israelis are considering insecticide," Walker said. "Basically, crop dusting Old Jerusalem."

"What does Ross think about that?"

"I don't know except that he says he's in contact with them. Other than that he's being very secretive. He's buried himself in the lab working on something but I don't know what," Walker said.

"A couple of blips on the radar coming from the north," Martin said. "Jets."

"Whose?" Decker said.

"I don't know," Martin said. "Could be Saudi, maybe Israeli."

Decker paused. "Or maybe ours. Walker? Are they ours?"

"Don't worry. We're keeping our distance."

"You're on our screen, dammit!" Decker shouted. "Back off!"

"I can't, Deck. Jesus! Tarik has implemented a bio attack on Jerusalem. The order is to find and destroy."

"Chopper has stopped," Martin said.

"Another boat?" Decker said.

"No. It landed."

"Where?"

"On a platform of some kind."

Decker wanted to stand up. In his mind, he saw the rivet on the wall behind Tarik in the video. "Move in, Colonel. Drop us to sixty-thousand feet but keep us just sub-sound."

"You got it," Martin said, and immediately banked out of their circular pattern.

Decker felt weightless as the SR-71 rolled and dove. He felt for his straps and clips and knife. Everything was secure for the moment, but he wanted no mistake or delay during his separation.

"Are you sure they're at their destination?" Walker said.

"No," Decker lied. "Now get the hell away. You're crowding the kitchen and someone's going to get burned."

"I can't Deck."

"Let me get Sam out for Christ's sake. Without us you'd be nowhere."

"The tracer is moving," Walker said. "Is the chopper moving?"

"No," Martin said.

"Then he must be on foot," Walker said.

"How far are we from them, Gary?" Decker said.

"About sixteen miles and closing fast."

"When you get to six, drop us to thirty-thousand and slow us to two- hundred miles per hour," Decker said.

"Did you say two-hundred miles per hour?" Martin said, doubtfully.

"Affirmative," Decker said.

"That's close to stall, Sir."

"You'll just be there for a moment, Colonel. Just long enough for me to get out."

"Get out? *Eject?*" Martin said, shocked.

"Yes," Decker said, matter-of-factly.

"Nice of you to mention it."

"Sorry, Colonel, but we have to operate with zero outgoing information."

Walker snorted. "Not much incoming, either."

"Closing in on six miles at thirty-thousand feet, slowing to—two hundred—for a moment. Sir, you'll land in the water."

"That would be a problem. And Bruce," Decker said to Walker.

"Yeah, Deck?"

"Stay out of the kitchen till I'm out, or I'll come after you with a cleaver."

"You have ten minutes."

"Fifteen," Decker said. "It will take me five to get there."

"Fifteen, Deck. Starting now," Walker said. "At fifteen minutes and one second Tarik's hideout is a vapor."

Decker looked at his watch. "Time to go to work."

"Good luck, Captain," Martin said.

Walker sighed. "Get in and get out fast, my friend. The clock is ticking."

The glass canopy above Decker's head exploded off a millisecond before his seat blasted into the frigid darkness. The seat's ballistic chute auto-deployed and slowed him to a virtual halt at thirty-thousand feet. He calmly but quickly found his knife and cut the chute lines and accelerated in a free-fall to earth while the abandoned white chute drifted away above him. At one hundred and twenty-five miles per hour, blood rushed from his legs to his head. He replaced his knife and felt for the harness buckle and released it. The seat immediately separated from him. The black wingsuit from his duffel kept him invisible in the night sky. Decker spread his arms and legs until the wingsuit's web tightened, giving him the appearance of a human flying squirrel. His pin-drop descent swooped into a diagonal and his speed slowed to a hundred miles per hour. The new Mylar ribs in the arm wings kept the fabric from flapping and made his flight silent. With the acrobatic maneuverability gained from years of base-jumping in a similar suit, he aimed himself in the direction of the platform where the chopper had landed and looked at his watch. He was at thirty thousand feet and one minute had passed.

64

Sam watched CNN report on what appeared to be an extraordinary Israeli effort to deal with the flies. The screen repeatedly flashed to a concentrated effort of aircraft unloading large sacks of insecticide and of crop dusting planes taking off from remote agricultural runways. Tarik appeared amused by the scramble.

"Kill the flies," Tarik said to the screen. "Who cares if they die? They merely set the table."

Sam worked her wrists but the strap was very tight. She kept a longing eye on Tarik's laptop. If she had it for thirty seconds, even with her wrists tied, she could warn her team of what was really happening. It was already too late to stop the Angel of Death, but the city needed to be evacuated.

"Does the gun have to be pointed at me all the time? What if he sneezes and accidentally pulls the trigger?" Sam said.

Tarik looked at her calmly and smiled. "Then he would be disciplined and told to clean up the mess. Accidents are not tolerated."

"You don't trust me," Sam mumbled.

"Oh, but you are wrong," Tarik said, his eyes not leaving the screen. "I do trust you. I trust you to do whatever you can to stop me. I trust everyone."

Just then, two quick beeps sounded on his intercom and Tarik pressed a button. The large screen switched from CNN to an in-house view of two guards and a man in casual attire carrying a suitcase. "Yes, yes, come right in," Tarik said enthusiastically.

A moment later, the elevator door opened and the three men entered the room.

"Masud," Tarik said warmly to Zahur, he stood up and gestured to his desk top. "Put it here. It has been a long time, my brother."

The man Tarik called "Masud" bowed and smiled broadly as he carried a suitcase to the desktop. He briefly looked at Sam but then placed the suitcase down and the two men embraced.

"Of course, you know Doctor Samantha Conway?" Tarik said proudly. "I wanted her to be here to witness the unveiling of your treasure. Samantha Conway, this is Masud Zahur."

Zahur turned to Sam, the gun still leveled at her head. "Uh, yes. How are you Doctor Conway?"

"Wonderful, thanks for asking."

Tarik smiled. "Masud was very instrumental in bringing you to us and now he has brought us another piece of the pillar for our collection."

"Really?" Sam said with mock enthusiasm. "So resourceful."

Zahur frowned and then turned his attention back to Tarik. "It has been too long my sheik," said.

"Yes, yes. Please, show me what you have brought me," Tarik said, like a child.

Zahur nodded and unzipped the suitcase and flipped open the lid. Inside was an old red blanket. Sam craned her neck as Zahur unfolded the crimson cloth. Both men stared at the content as if looking at life from Mars. Tarik's face was bright with enthusiasm as Zahur patted him on the back.

"This is a gift from heaven," Zahur said with a proud smile.

Tarik nodded in agreement but his nod slowed and smile faded until his stare was like stone. His eyes widened and did not blink. Only his lips moved when he said, "Where exactly did you get this?"

Zahur frowned at the tone of the question. "North of Kabul."

"From who... exactly?" Tarik said, evenly.

Zahur paused, his eyes searched the air. "I... don't know his name. Why do you ask my Sheik? Is something wrong?"

Tarik reached for his computer mouse and clicked and then stared at his monitor and then at what his guest had brought him and then back again. He finally looked at Sam. "Come over and look at this, Samantha Conway."

Trouble in paradise? Sam thought, hopefully. She stood from her seat and walked to the desk, the barrel of the gun followed her closely. Zahur and Tarik separated enough to give her adequate room to step in and examine the artifact. She looked down over the artifact. In three seconds she realized it was the same piece Walker had first laid on her desk in New York and indeed the same characters she had been studying ever since. She also realized Tarik's sudden concern. She restrained her immediate reaction to laugh as a cautious but euphoric hope grew in her heart that Decker was near.

"Am I correct to say that this piece is the same as the one on the screen?" Tarik growled.

Sam knew that Tarik knew but wasn't sure how to respond. There didn't seem to be a way for her to convince him they were somehow different when they were obviously one and the same. To try would probably explode the rising pressure in her direction. To agree seemed to safer path.

Sam nodded. "Zahur? Is that your name?"

"Yes."

"If you don't mind me asking, how did you find this piece?"

Zahur paused and looked at Tarik.

"Answer her, Masud," Tarik ordered.

Zahur paused. "The truth is, I was led to it by God," he said, sheepishly.

"I see," Sam said. "And how exactly did God lead you to this?"

Again, Zahur looked to Tarik who waved impatiently for him to continue.

"He spoke to me," Zahur said. "I could not believe it at first, but then I could not deny it."

"Uh huh, and this was a voice in your head or audible."

"I am not crazy. I do not hear voices in my head. Obviously, the artifact is proof enough that the voice was true."

"I'm sure it was. So you heard the voice audibly?"

"Yes," Zahur said, annoyed.

Sam nodded, smiling and amazed at what had happened in her absence. *Decker,* she thought warmly. But then it also dawned on her that the entire rig might be in the cross hairs of a bomber. "Then let me ask you, Zahur. I have heard about this but there is something I always wanted to know," Sam said.

"And what is that?" Tarik said.

"Does God speak into both ears or only one?"

Tarik frowned but Zahur's eyes opened wide with surprise. He stared at her, frozen, and said, "One…. How did you know that? This is not possible."

Tarik's shoved Sam aside, picked up the artifact and examined it closely. He turned it over and over and finally threw it with force to the hard marble floor where it shattered in every direction. One piece hit Sam in the foot and she immediately stepped on it. Sam winced at the sight of priceless ancient characters in pieces but then she saw it. Tarik picked it up in his hand and displayed a small triple-A battery sized cylinder. He tossed it to Zahur who caught it.

"This is the priceless treasure you have brought me, Masud. You have brought me the CIA," Tarik said.

Zahur looked at the tracer in disbelief. "This is not possible."

"They will be here very soon," Tarik said.

"Game's over, Tarik," Sam said. "Time to give it up and, help put a stop to the virus. Maybe they'll consider your cooperation at your sentencing," she said, *when they decide on the method of your execution,* she thought.

Tarik's face flushed as he marched over and grabbed the gun from the extra large guard.

"My Sheik, she lies," Zahur said an instant before Tarik spun the gun and opened fire. Zahur's body danced to the impact of bullets and fell motionless to the floor, pooling blood.

Tarik turned to Sam, the gun clenched knuckle white tight in his fist, pointing straight at her head.

65

Yusuf Mustafa stood alone in the night under the tall Roman arch of the Lion's Gate, his head and face wrapped so only his eyes could peer through a narrow slit. The temperature was much too hot for the amount of clothing needed to shield the flies away. He had been to the Old City of Jerusalem twice, the last time five years ago. Back then, it was the enchanted history and spiritual presence that seized his attention. Now it was the unbelievable blizzard of flies and cloud of frosty white powder settling to earth from those crop dusting planes and helicopters flying overhead. In fact, the flies more than had his attention, they were unnerving him to the bone. Tarik had created chaos and, from what he understood, this was just the beginning and he and his three brothers were here to initiate the next wave of destruction. More than that he did not know, but he was honored to be a part of the new history that would again reshape the rich ancient ground where he stood.

Mustafa unshouldered his satchel and crouched. Dead flies and fine white powder blanked the ground like dirty snow. He opened the satchel and pulled out the black sanitary travel bag given to him by Dulai. He unzipped the black bag and quickly found the two pill bottles and bottle of water. He opened the bottles and found three pills in each. He didn't understand anything about what was to happen except that, after taking the pills, the flies wouldn't bother him anymore and that he would be ready for the next stage of Tarik's plan which would soon arrive.

Whatever the case, Mustafa wasn't going to ponder Dulai's simple instructions with flies buzzing so loud he couldn't hear himself think. He opened one of the bottles and pulled his turban scarf low enough to expose his mouth. He tossed the pills in his mouth and opened the water bottle. He felt movement in his mouth. A fly. He felt like spitting but that would end his mission in failure and make him vulnerable for whatever was next. He quickly drained half the water and then repeated the process with the other three pills. Again he swallowed a fly, maybe more than one. Ugh, definitely more than one. And what was with the water? It was clear but had a very strange aftertaste. *Or was that from the flies?*

Mustafa wrapped his face up tightly and stood up. *Now what? Just stand here?* That was his instruction but when were the flies supposed to stop bothering him? Tarik had clearly said that after he took the pills and water, the flies would no longer bother him. He swung his arms at the soupy air. And what kind of insecticide was being sprayed? It wasn't working. It was everywhere, on the ground, in the cracks of the stones, in the air. The flies seemed to be immune to it. Yes, there were thousands of dead flies on the ground but the air was thick with healthy flies unaffected by the white powder mist. He felt flies under his clothes and under his head-wrap. He wanted to run and scream. This was insane, he could no longer wait for the pills to keep the flies away. He had to get away, far away, from Jerusalem.

Maybe he had done something wrong. He hated the thought of facing Tarik after failing to follow simple instructions. Were his brethren at the other gates having the same problems with the flies? Amir was at Herod's Gate, which was very close. Just around the northeast corner. Unable to stand still, he found himself at a dead sprint for the Herod's Gate. Halfway there, he felt a sharp cramp in his abdomen. Probably swallowed the water too fast. He belched and the foul taste of rotten eggs filled his scarf. He cursed and wanted to open his face wrap but the flies were so thick he feared he would suffocate.

Mustafa turned the outside northeast corner of the great walled city and knew that Herod's Gate was very close, but his cramp stopped him. He leaned on the towering stone wall and then walked. The hillside to his right seemed to move. Actually everything seemed to move. Did the temperature rise? His clothes were suddenly drenched in his sweat. He stumbled and fell to his knees. What was happening? He struggled to his feet and continued to the Old City's northernmost gate. The abdominal cramps were so intense now he wanted to scream. He looked up and, in the dizzying movement of landscape, he saw Herod's Gate but no one was there. Where did Amir go? The question lingered in his mind only a moment. As he dragged himself closer, he discovered the answer.

Amir was on the ground, face up, and a strange crimson mist was flowing steadily from his mouth. Another belch and stabbing abdominal pain caused Mustafa to cry out and drop to his knees. Tarik was correct, the flies, though just as intense, commanded less and less of his attention. He did, however, notice that Amir's uncovered hands were very dark, almost black. He looked at his own hands and to his shock they had also turned darker. He cried in agony and fell over, his trembling body cushioned by dead flies and white powder. His belches were longer now and each one not only stank of sulfur but was red in color.

Mustafa lay next to Amir, the flies crawling over his face and into his nose and open mouth, but they no longer were of any concern to him.

66

Sam figured she had one entire second left to live. As a scientist, she had learned to measure time in both eons and picoseconds. A lot can happen in a trillionth of a second. A zillion atoms can split into a nuclear explosion. A universe can be born.

"Anubis!" Sam blurted.

Tarik paused. "What?"

"Today is your big day. Anubis requires your homage. If you shoot me who will you have to sacrifice?"

Tarik's wild eyes narrowed. "You want to be sacrificed?"

"There are lots of worse ways to go," she said. "Well, maybe a couple."

"Silence…. I don't know how but, you are somehow responsible for this," he said, and motioned with his chin at the broken artifact on the floor. "Simply sacrificing you is not enough." He glanced at the two guards that had come in with Zahur and said, "Kill her brother."

"No!" Sam screamed. "Please!" she begged.

The two guards immediately started for the exit.

"He has done nothing to you!"

"But *you* have. I brought you here to help and even offered to have you share in my kingdom but, you have caused me nothing but trouble."

Sam dropped to her knees, quickly covered the broken artifact fragment with her hand, and said, "I'm sorry. I will do anything you ask."

"Anything?.... Wait," Tarik said to the two guards just before the door shut behind them.

The guards stopped. "Would you sacrifice Butrus to Anubis?" Tarik said to Sam, motioning to the guard she had hit with the avocado pit. The big guard looked at Tarik, unable to blink.

Sam paused. There was only one answer she could give. Anything that would buy time. "If that's what you order. Yes."

Tarik laughed, but the guard was as still as a statue. "Do you really think I would put a knife in your hand? After you sacrifice him you would find a way to kill me too," he said and then looked back to the halted guards. "Bring her brother to the sanctuary," he said calmly and then looked at Sam. "Jesse Conway will witness his sister's sacrifice on the altar but, as she dies, *her* last sight will be her brother's execution."

The guards gave a quick nod and disappeared.

Sam prayed. She silently screamed to God inside her head and then said, "You don't have time for this. Shouldn't you try to leave?"

"Thank you for your concern for my well-being, but I will be fine. After today, I will control everything in spite of your efforts." Tarik gave Butrus his gun back and told him to take her to the sanctuary. Sam's eyes grew wide when she saw that the little tracer was now on the floor next to her. She grabbed it as Butrus pulled her up by her hair and pushed her forward. Tarik then picked up a few pieces of the broken artifact off the floor and followed them into the elevator.

"What good will that be to you without a translator?" Sam said, motioning to the broken pieces in Tarik's hands.

"It's the missing ingredient from a world long gone," Tarik said. " I can always find another translator but this cannot be replaced."

"You don't even know what you have," she said as she cut against her straps with the edge of the fragment.

"The promise of power."

"Actually, the only promise I know of concerning it is the promise of death."

"Yes, death to those who oppose."

"As I said, you don't know what you have there."

"I know that, at this very moment, the firstborn in Jerusalem are dying and, by this time tomorrow, the world will be ready to surrender to my demands. And you will be dead."

The elevator door opened and Sam was propelled out with the barrel of the gun. She bumped into Tarik and dropped the tracer into the side pocket of his long shirt but managed to keep hold of the other fragment. Tarik led the way to the sanctuary. Sam's heart pounded through her chest. She was not afraid to die but was quite certain that Jesse being executed while he watched his sister bleed-out could not have been what her father imagined when he told her to take care of her little brother. She wanted to run. She would be shot instantly but that would spare Jesse from witnessing her death. Where was the CIA? Where was Decker? Her wrist strap suddenly loosened.

Another poke in the back pushed her into the doorway. She stopped, and anticipated that another jab of the barrel to punish her defiance was a millisecond away. She spun to the right and caught the barrel with a forearm block and kicked upward as hard as she could, catching the big guard in the groin with her shin. His eyes instantly bulged as he groaned and dropped to his knees. She shook off the wrist strap, spun again, grabbed the door, slammed it shut, slid the bolt to a secure clack and turned to meet Tarik. His eyes darted to the sacrificial knife on the altar and then back to her. Sam bolted for the knife at the same time he did. She grabbed the ancient knife with her right hand and Tarik grabbed her wrist tightly and tried to peel her fingers free with his other hand. She bit into a piece of his sleeve and the top of his hand with all her might, cutting through his flesh and ripping the sleeve. He screamed, let go of her fingers and pulled on her hair. She clamped on as tight as a pit bull until he let go of her wrist. She spun, slicing his shirt across his chest. He jumped back in shock, but then looked as though he might try to rush her.

Sam spit his blood and a piece of white cloth on the floor and said, "I've never killed anyone but, if you take a step closer, I'll run you through in a second."

Tarik paused and straightened himself. "What are you going to do, swim away?"

"Yes. I'll rather take my chances in the water than on this floating bull's-eye with you." God, what she wouldn't give to be treading water with Jesse right now. Somehow, she needed to find him, subdue the guards and jump, hopefully with something that floated. She kept her glare on Tarik. She held the knife out and edged her way toward the rear door she had seen him enter when he murdered Dulai. Tarik held his bloody hand and smiled. She hated his smile more than any frown. He slowly backed up to the door, unlocked and opened it. She thought she would see Butrus with a gun pointed at her but no one was there. With Anubis' glowing emerald eyes behind her and Tarik's creepy smile in front, she dashed for the rear door, opened it and gasped.

Butrus stood in the frame of the door and, before she could slam it on him, his hand was at her throat. She swung the knife at his massive arm but Tarik was quickly there; he grabbed her wrist and pried away the knife.

"Put her on the altar," Tarik said.

67

Decker streaked through the midnight sky at a hundred miles per hour, like a hungry eagle eager to strike. The blinking red light in the distance was his visual target. His plan was to pull his black chute at five hundred feet, about hundred yards away from the landing pad and float into a shadow somewhere. Then he would have just minutes to find Sam and Jesse before Walker made them expendable.

Again, he had to chase away the flies. Not the actual real living insects but the memories cluttering his thoughts. If Jerusalem looked anything like Tarik's cave, then Tarik had proven he was capable of infecting entire cities at will. And, if the Angel of Death followed the flies as in the cave and killed all of the firstborn on Passover, then he could name his price and the world would pay.

Decker did a quick check of his wrist for an update of altitude and time. Shocked, he looked at it again. "Shit!" he said. "Shit!" he repeated. He was low. He wanted to check his watch again but didn't dare. He needed to keep his arms stretched out from his side to maximize his glide ratio. Normally, he had a four to one ratio. Four feet in distance for every one foot in descent. He had miscalculated. His angle of attack had been too steep. Maybe three to one. He hadn't attributed enough height to compensate for the lack of lift from the Red Sea below. If he fell short of the target, he would end up in the sea and lose any hope of reaching Sam before Walker's blitz. He thought about leaving his straight line to fly over land, but the deviation would mean extra time and, late at night, the natural lift from dry land might not compensate for the extra distance. "Shit!"

He considered the glide ratio of his chute. Three to one at best. Desperate, he thought again about how far away the land was. He looked left for a shoreline and saw something else. A helicopter at eight o'clock. A little behind and lower and moved about the same speed, in the same direction. *No, that would never work*, he thought. The slightest miscalculated and he would get cut up in the blades or drown. And he didn't come this far to drown. He stayed his course.

In the final moments of flight, the target became very large in a hurry. An old oil rig. An erector set complex of platforms, containers, stanchions, cables, cranes and a helipad with a helicopter. Tarik was hiding in the open, which meant he'd be doing his best not to attract attention with anything out of the ordinary for a rig. That would mean a minimum of soldiers, at least on the exterior, and a maximum of cameras. He saw two armed guards patrolling the perimeter. They were facing him. If he had more altitude, he would be able to silently land in the shadows and figure it out from there. But he didn't have that luxury. He would be lucky if he could open the chute and slide onto the platform like he was stealing second base.

Decker couldn't see the guards' faces yet, but they seemed to be cupping and lighting cigarettes. They exhaled, turned toward him, leaned on the railing and looked into the night. He figured he would be difficult or impossible to discern at his hundred mile per hour approach. They might see a growing black image in the black sky or nothing at all until it was too late.

Decker unzipped the length of his sleeves to free his arms from the wing's webbing. He was almost level with the platform when he pulled his black chute, just high enough to clear the railing. The chute had barely opened before he made his first contact: his boot soles with their faces. He slid to a stop and turned cat quick, knife in hand. The guards were on their backs, motionless. In ten seconds he was out of the wingsuit and then scrambled low to examine the guards. Eyes open, they appeared dead, but he didn't want to take the chance of them being seen on a camera so he quickly pushed them under the railing and off the platform. Their bodies splashed about sixty feet below but, other than that, all was quiet. He dashed into the shadows in search of a door. Six minutes had passed. Nine minutes to vaporization.

The first door he came upon was a storage room with hoses, jumpsuits and helmets. Probably a worthwhile disguise but not enough time. He kept moving and hurried up a few metal grid stairs. Another door flanked by well-lit windows. He peered in and saw two soldiers in an animated discussion, machine guns over their shoulders and lots of hand movement. Decker calmly walked straight in. Both men ceased their conversation and turned.

"Excuse me, I'm looking for Samantha Conway. Do you guys have her imprisoned here?"

The stunned guards looked at each other and then reached for their guns. In one motion, Decker pushed down a rising gun barrel with his left hand, slit the man's throat with his right, kicked the other gun away with his left heel, spun, pulled down on the other soldier's left sleeve, pushed on his right shoulder, tripped him onto his back and brought a quick bloodied knife under his chin.

"Where's Samantha Conway?" he said, while the other soldier gurgled on the floor with his hands on his blood-soaked neck.

The soldier froze.

Decker pushed on the knife hard enough to arch the guard's back and cause new blood to drip down the blade. "I am in a hurry so I'll only count to one before you see the tip of this knife coming out the top of your nose."

"She's in the sanctuary," he said.

"And where's that?"

The guard motioned with his eyes.

"Show me," Decker said and then pulled him up and forced him forward with the knife tip in his back. "And remember, I'm in a hurry. If I get there fast without trouble, you live. If not, you die. I live a simple life."

The guard led Decker down two hallways and up a flight of metal stairs before he heard other footsteps. Decker cupped the guard's mouth and put the tip of the knife in the back of his neck as he stopped to listen.

"*This* way, fool," he heard a man's voice say in Egyptian.

"I d-don't know w-what you're s-saying. W-where are you t-taking m-me?"

Decker pulled the guard backward around a corner and whispered directly into his ear. "Are they going toward the sanctuary?"

The guard nodded.

"Whisper your name to me? And if I think you're lying, I'll kill you."

"Dabir Abdul," he whispered.

"Ok, Dabir Abdul, I'm a man of my word tonight. You helped me and I'm going to let you live. In ten minutes, U. S. Forces will be here from every direction. If I were you, I would jump off and swim as fast and as far as I could."

The guard continued to nod, his eyes were wide open, sweat dripping down his forehead.

"This is a once in a lifetime opportunity. Leave fast. Leave quiet. If I ever see you again for any reason, I will kill you instantly. Understand?"

The guard closed his eyes and silently mouthed his thanks.

He released the guard and the man vanished. Decker listened. Jesse's words and footsteps were further away. He sprinted softly through the hall, knife in hand. When he caught up, he cleared his throat to get their attention. When the last guard turned to see who was behind him, the knife Decker had thrown on the run, sunk deep into the side of his neck. When the other guard started to raise his gun, Jesse grabbed the barrel and Decker, flying horizontal, hit him as high and hard as a linebacker, taking him off his feet and onto his back. A quick solid elbow to the Adam's apple and the guard was out.

Jesse bounced with excitement. "W-where did y-you c-come from... h-heaven?"

Decker looked in both directions and sprang to his feet. "Hell. Do you know where the sanctuary is?"

68

Sam struggled against Butrus' massive arms and powerful grip. He hog-tied her wrists while Tarik strapped her legs tight to the altar.

"Keep away from her teeth," Tarik warned and picked up the sacrificial knife. "She bites," he said showing off his wounded hand and torn white sleeve.

Butrus smiled and his eyes widened as Tarik pulled down on her scrub pants and felt for the femoral artery at the top of her leg. While he searched, he took liberty to explore further. Sam tried to twist and squirm but, with all her strength, she managed little, except to excite Butrus further.

"You could have been my queen," Tarik said.

Sam continued to strain and wanted to scream but was determined not to give them that satisfaction. "No, thanks. I'd rather be your enemy."

"You prefer death?"

"Absolutely," she said, gasping for air.

"Then you shall have it," Tarik said and put the tip of the knife on the artery.

"S-Sam!" Jesse yelled.

Sam quickly turned her head. Jesse stood at the door, but there were no guards. He then stepped to the side.

"Ah, just in time," Tarik said, his intense focus on the careful placement of the knife. "Bring him closer so he can have a better view," he said with a smile.

Sam watched Decker's black knife cut though the air. The sudden impact was almost silent but had an immediate affect on Butrus. His viselike grip loosened, the knife, handle-deep, in the giant guard's right ear.

Sam hit Tarik in the arm as hard as she could as he plunged the ancient knife into the top of her leg. "Aghh, Jesus!" she screamed and grabbed at Tarik's hand.

Tarik turned in shock as Butrus melted to the floor, Decker's knife proudly staking its claim. He glared at Sam, yanked the sacrificial knife out of her leg and dashed out the rear door.

Sam pressed hard on her wound. The pain was intense, her leg drenched red. Decker appeared next to her. Without saying a word, he quickly pulled the knife from Butrus' head, cut the straps that tied Sam's legs to the altar and started to retie them around her leg as a tourniquet.

"Go! Go after Tarik," Sam said. Jesse put his hand on her shoulder.

"We have to leave." Decker said, then tightened and knotted the straps.

Sam gasped in pain. "Go. Get that bastard."

Decker looked her in the eye. "In four minutes, this place will be leveled. He'll be gone."

"Yes, but not dead. He'll have escaped."

Decker's eyes widened. "How?"

"I don't know, but go. We'll be right behind you. Get Tarik!"

Decker bolted through the door. Sam looked at the straps tied around her leg. Bloody but not soaked. If her artery had been severed she would have been half drained out by now and getting cold. He must have missed. She slid off the altar, her right arm around Jesse's shoulder.

"We have to hurry, Jess," she said.

"Y-you're the s-slow one," he said as they made their way through the rear door and into a room with a large column in the middle. There was one other exit. Sam and Jesse hobbled quickly toward it. Suddenly the door burst open and Decker appeared.

"Did you get him?" Sam asked.

"No," he said angrily. "That door leads into a mechanical area but there's no way out and he's not in there."

"Are you sure?" Sam asked.

"Yes, I'm sure," he snapped. "It doesn't matter. If he's hiding, he's history in three minutes and so are we if we don't get off this rig."

Sam could feel the blood dripping down her leg. She looked at the floor and saw her pant leg was soaked. She felt light-headed but then saw something else on the floor that made her frown. At the bottom of the column was a piece of cloth that looked like the same material she had torn from Tarik's sleeve with her teeth.

"What's that?" she said, motioning to the cloth.

"What?" Decker said.

"That cloth. It's the same as Tarik shirt."

"Are you sure?" Decker asked.

"Positive. I had it in my teeth."

"Your teeth?"

"Just check it out," she said, still using Jesse as a crutch.

Decker crouched and tried to pick it up but it was stuck. "It seems to be caught under this column."

"What *is* this column?" Sam said.

"I think it's an oil shaft housing that goes through the water and into the ground," Decker said.

"How do you know that?" Sam said.

"I don't," Decker said.

"Then why is Tarik's shirt under it if it's a solid shaft?"

Decker frowned and pulled harder on the cloth but it wouldn't budge. He looked up to the ceiling and Sam followed

W.G.Griffiths

his gaze. There was a narrow gap where the ceiling surrounded the column. Sam looked back to the cloth.

"Scratch the floor next to the column with your knife," Sam said. "Then hit it and see if it moves from the scratch."

Decker understood. He scratched the floor and then hit the column low and hard with his shoulder. It moved fractionally away from the scratch. "It doesn't go through the floor," Decker said. He looked back at the ceiling. "It must rise into the ceiling."

"He's in there," Sam said.

"But how does it raise? Where is the mechanism?" Decker said, as he put his arms around the column and tried to lift. After a long grunt and no results, Sam looked around the room.

"There has to be a switch somewhere," Sam said.

"We don't have time to find it. In two minutes from now, this place will be a fireball."

Sam nodded with regret as Decker supported her other arm and helped her hurry back toward the sanctuary. "It's probably hiding in the open like the column," Sam said.

"Forget it, Sam. If Walker's on time, we might not make it as it is."

"F-fireball," Jesse said.

"What?" Sam said.

Jesse reached for a red fire alarm lever on the wall and pulled it. There was no alarm but there *was* a mechanical sound behind them. They all turned. The column was rising.

69

Sam ignored the deep pain in her leg in light of the imminent air attack less than ninety seconds away. She started toward the rising column.

"No," Decker said, and pulled back on her shoulder. "Hold her, Jess," he said as he pulled out his knife and hurried to the column.

"Come on, Jess," Sam said ignoring Decker. The column wasn't a column at all, but a hatchway.

Decker picked up the torn piece of cloth and handed it to Sam as he peered into a hole in the floor that had a ladder. "Is that from Tarik's shirt?" After a quick scan, Decker sheathed his knife and slid down the ladder.

"Yes," Sam said. "A piece from the sleeve I tore."

"He must have snagged it when the column closed. Whatever, he's not here, but I think I know where he went. Sam, you and Jesse come down here. In less than a minute from now, all hell is going to break loose."

Sam grabbed the rails and hopped down the rungs on one leg. Jesse followed. The ladder entered a narrow circular room below. At the bottom of the room was another hole, a shallow shaft with water in it.

"This was the escape route he alluded to," Sam said.

"It's the only way out," Decker agreed. "He probably had a mini-sub or something docked to this shaft."

"A s-sub?" Jesse said.

Decker shrugged. "Probably, I don't see any trace of scuba equipment and I doubt he just jumped in and swam away. In any case, he's clean gone... again, and by the way he spoke to you, he probably has everything he needs to continue with the Angel of Death."

"He's gone, but maybe not so clean," Sam said.

"What do you mean?" Decker asked.

"You know that tracer you put in the artifact?"

Decker's eyes brightened. "Yes."

"I slipped it into his shirt pocket. We tossed around a lot but, if it's not here and I haven't seen it, it's probably still with him."

Decker allowed a rare smile. "You're amazing. We have to get out of here and let Walker in on this."

"How much time do we have?" Sam asked.

Decker looked at his wrist. Suddenly, the room shook and his face went blank. "None," he shouted. "Go now!" he said looking straight into her eyes. "I'll follow. When you clear the shaft, *swim to the right* and stay under as long as you can."

Sam's apprehension of suddenly jumping into a dark hole filled with water, without first having tested and confirmed its length and where it actually went, vanished with the deafening explosion from above. With the blast came a jolting quake that took all three to the round sidewall for support. Sam pushed off the wall, jumped up on one foot and pin dropped into the hole. After a few feet, the shaft ended and she was in open water.

Sam immediately swam to the right. Deep sonic concussions and rumbles reverberated heavily as she reached far and fast with each stroke, ignoring the deep pain in her thigh. Bright lightening-like flashes illuminated the crystal clear waters and revealed the outer stanchions that supported the rig above her. The stanchions were just ahead but rocked ominously. Like a snow globe, debris big and small sank past her. Adrenalin surged through her veins. She saw Jesse right behind her. But where was Decker? *Where was Decker?* She paused, but then continued forward to lead Jesse.

A bright blast sent sonic reverberations through her body like a jack hammer. Large debris crashed and speared through to the surface. Currents pushed her one way and then the other. She wanted to swim deeper to get away from the thrash but her lungs were ready to explode. *Air.* She desperately *needed air.* She had to get past the buckling stanchions. Jesse was still there, but still no Decker.

Unable to hold her breath any longer, she burst through the surface, gasped for air and swam arm over arm. Another bright explosion, much louder above the surface, sent her back under. She could feel Jesse's stroke next to her. Another blast took out whatever support held the rig behind them and in the flash she could see the closest stanchion fall toward them. The whole rig was coming down. But the legs were so tall that, as it fell, it moved past them overhead and finally plunged through the surface. The ensuing wave was tremendous and pushed them away as if they were bodysurfing at the beach.

Darkness. Quiet. A burnt stench in the air reminded Sam of an iron welding shop.

"Jesse?" Sam cried.

"R-right here."

Sam spun around and saw Jesse maybe ten feet away. She raced to him and hugged and kissed him until they sank.

"O-ok, ok," Jesse said. "W-we didn't g-get away s-so you can kill me. W-where's D-Decker?"

"I don't know. Last time I saw him was before I jumped into the hole. Didn't he follow you?"

"I d-don't know."

Sam turned her head and called Decker's name as loud as she could and listened for a reply. She heard nothing but her own

heart beat and heavy breathing. She called and called but was interrupted by the sight of searchlights scanning the water's surface. She wondered for a moment if she was going to be rescued or recaptured? Then she considered how far away Tarik probably was and how unlikely the terrorists would be anywhere near the bombing. As they drew nearer, she could hear the *thwap, thwap, thwap* of helicopter blades. She didn't have the strength to wave *and* tread water. How much blood had she lost? They would find her soon enough, she told herself. But would they find Decker? Without him, Jesse would be dead, now. She would be dead too. In fact, they wouldn't have even been around for the bombing. She felt sick. *Where's our hero, she thought?*

The helicopters were very close and there were more of them than she had first thought. One of the searchlights passed over them and then quickly came back and stayed. The chopper lowered and water sprayed in her eyes. Suddenly, two men were in the water next to them.

"Doctor Conway?" one of them said.

"Yes. Take him up first," she said.

Within seconds, Jesse was snapped into a harness and hoisted up.

"Did you find Decker?" Sam asked.

"I don't know," said one of the divers. "If he's out here, we'll find him."

The cable came back down and they quickly surrounded her with the harness and buckled it. A bucket seat pressed against her bottom. As she rose into the air, she looked around for Decker. It was too dark to see anything but the searchlights scouring the calm sea. A moment later, she was next to Jesse. He had apparently filled them in about her leg. Lieutenant Elizabeth Bercow, in a helmet and jumpsuit, told her to relax and lie back. Sam resisted.

"Did you find Captain Decker?" Sam asked.

"Not yet," Bercow said.

"Where are we going?"

"To the USS Nimitz," Bercow said. "Ten minutes away."

"But what about Captain Decker?" Sam demanded.

"The search is ongoing," Bercow said. "Our orders are to get you to the Nimitz, ASAP."

"The air craft carrier Nimitz?" Sam said.

Bercow smiled. "Yes, that Nimitz."

"What's the news from Jerusalem?" Sam said.

"Jerusalem?" Bercow said with surprise.

"Yes. What is happening there?"

"You mean about the flies?"

Sam frowned. Had the virus kicked in yet?

"They found him, Lieutenant," came a voice from the front.

Sam felt suddenly awake. "They found Decker?" she asked.

"Affirmative," said the voice.

"Is he all right?" Sam called.

"He's alive. But he wasn't alone."

Sam frowned. "Not alone? Who was with him?"

70

Sam opened her eyes one at a time. She felt drugged, and when she saw the IV tube traveling from her arm to a hanging plastic bag, she figured she probably was.

"Looks like someone's waking up," said a familiar voice. It was Walker, the CIA agent. He stepped up to the foot of her bed and smiled. *Where the hell was she?*

"Where the hell am I?" she said.

"Yup, she's awake," Walker said over his shoulder. "You're on the USS Nimitz… recovering."

"How's Jesse?" she said.

Decker limped up to her bedside. "Better than you," he said.

"Deck!" she gushed, and felt her eyes well up. She reached for him but then a stabbing pain in her leg sent her back.

"Easy Tiger," Decker said. He had a white bandage around his head along with a black eye and swollen cheekbone.

"What happened to you? The last thing I remember was you telling me to swim right."

Decker smiled thinly and shrugged. "I don't remember. I guess I didn't swim right. After you and Jesse jumped into the hole, things came apart pretty quickly. The next thing I remember, I was being strapped into a rescue harness and loaded into the chopper."

"He was rescued by one of Tarik's men," Walker said.

Sam looked at Decker for acknowledgment. He shrugged. "That's what I'm told," he said.

"Really? Who, I mean why?"

"His name is Dabir Abdul," Walker said. "According to him, Decker spared his life and warned him of the coming attack."

"Why?" Sam said.

"I was in a hurry," Decker said with a glance to Walker. "I told him if he got me to you fast, I would let him go."

Walker laughed. "It gets better. He also told him he would kill him instantly if he ever saw him again."

Sam looked at Decker. "And?"

Decker almost smiled. "I haven't seen him yet."

"That's a lie," Walker said. "Decker thanked him and told him they were even but, if he didn't cooperate with us, he would kill him anyway. Dabir Abdul is currently... cooperating earnestly."

Sam nodded. Decker seemed typically phlegmatic but, she was confused by Walker's light mood. "What's happening in Jerusalem?"

"A major clean up," Walker said.

Sam's heart sunk. "How many dead?"

"All of them," Walker said. "Flies, that is. They're cleaning up dead flies and potassium."

Sam shook her head. "I'm sorry, but I didn't have my coffee yet. Potassium? What about the firstborn?"

Walker smiled proudly. "Your idea for the antidote worked."

Sam stared at his face in search of a clue as to what he just said. "Antidote?"

"Yes. In short, the Metropolitan Museum received an email from a Doctor Dulai carrying a theory from a Doctor Samantha Conway. The Met passed it on to us and we gave it to Captain Ross. Ross went to work and found out that the grass by the Nile where the Israelite's sheep would have grazed was extremely rich in potassium from the Nile silt. While everyone thought crop dusting aircraft were spreading insecticide to kill the flies, they were in reality dusting with potassium to kill the virus. It worked."

Sam sighed. "The Angel of Death passed over on Passover," Sam said. She felt muscles relax that she didn't even know were tight. But then she thought about Dulai. He must have known about the email when Tarik showed him the information for the antidote.

Walker nodded. "Thanks to you, Sam. Your antidote worked."

"Without Dulai, you wouldn't have gotten it."

Walker's smile vanished. "He was killed in the bombing?"

Sam shook her head. "Tarik caught him. Killed him."

Walker nodded. Decker looked obviously disturbed but Sam didn't think it was because of Dulai's death.

"And Tarik?" she asked.

Walker pursed his lips and then said. "We found the tracer."

"He got away," Decker said.

"Explain," Sam said.

"The tracer brought us to an abandoned mini-sub. In the sub, was a shirt with the tracer in the pocket," Walker said.

"There was a note with it," Decker said.

"A note?" Sam said.

The tracer was wrapped in a note," Decker said.

"Wrapped? What did it say?"

"We don't know," Walker said. "He wrote it in a way that would require a translator. I suppose he figured we would ask you."

"Show it to her," Decker said.

Walker nodded and reached into his pocket. "Sorry to put you to work so soon, Sam. But if you can make it out," he said and then opened it and handed it to her.

Sam held it up in the light. She saw two lines of simple characters. On the first line was a semi circle stone and a vulture next to it. On the second line from left to right was a foot, a vulture, a jar stand, a reed, a squiggly water sign, and then a repeat of the reed, water and jar stand. Sam handed it back to Walker.

"What does it say?" Walker asked.

"It's ancient Egyptian. Hieroglyphics. A lot of symbols but the English translation is quite brief and to the point," Sam said, looking into Decker's intense eyes.

Walker looked at Decker and then back to Sam. "Well? What does it say?"

Without breaking eye contact with Decker Sam said, "The beginning."

Epilogue

Sam's knife met Decker's in the butter dish. Afghanistan's only bar was known as much for its bread as for its beer and they were beyond ready for both. The day had been long, hot and dry.

Sam looked at Decker with mock intensity. "Ok, you first," she said.

"No, you," he replied.

"Ok," she said, dug into the butter and spread a healthy amount on a fresh tear of warm bread. She bit in, washed it down with a swig of cold Heather Ale and closed her eyes in ecstasy.

The Irish Club was located on a secluded side street in central Kabul and concealed by a nondescript outer concrete wall with no sign out front and not even a number on the door. In Taliban times, a fully stocked Irish pub serving cold beer in the heart of Afghanistan's ultra-Islamic capital would have been unimaginable. In the post-Taliban era, it was still unthinkable, at least for Afghans. The bar was officially licensed by the state to sell alcohol, but only to foreigners. Just inside the bar's entrance, a couple of capable bouncers kept Afghans out, which made it the perfect place for Sam and Decker to relax, dine, and review their search.

The steak for two was thick and delicious. They attacked it and spoke only in moans until the bone was clean.

"What makes you so certain he'll be back here so soon?" Decker said.

"Oh, he will," Sam said emphatically.

"Well, I'm not so sure. I've been chasing him for a long time and I don't find him that predictable."

"That's because you haven't been chasing him with me," Sam said with a smile. "Remember, first and foremost, I'm a treasure hunter."

"I wouldn't exactly call Tarik a treasure."

"No, but Methuselah's Pillar definitely is. And we are probably in the area he found it. Our paths will cross. Then you can do your thing."

"Sounds too logical."

"Totally. But that pillar is like love."

Decker raised a brow. "Like love?"

"Yup. Once you've tasted of it, you want more and, if you lose it, you'll spend the rest of your life trying to find it again. Besides, if the pillar is actually made from the Tree of the Knowledge of Good and Evil, the draw would be irresistible... and deadly. Hey, maybe that's really why I'm here and I don't know it."

Decker pursed his lips and grunted.

"Ever been in love, Deck?"

Decker took a long gaze into her eyes and smiled. "That's classified information."

Sam laughed and looked up to see the owner, Sean McQuade, walk toward them across the decorative tile floor.

"Excuse me, Doctor Conway. There is a man outside that says you want to see him," McQuade said with a thick Irish accent.

"*I* want to see *him*?" Sam said, incredulously.

"That's what he says. He's Afghan, so he only comes in if Samantha Conway invites him in. But he can't drink."

Decker shrugged and played with his steak knife. "Why not? Let's talk to him."

"He's unarmed. We already checked," McQuade said.

Sam smiled and rolled her eyes. "Send him in," she said.

A moment later, McQuade returned with a young man in worn clothes, sandals that had walked more soil than cement, and shouldering a handmade lambskin satchel of some kind. He had a prominent scar that ran from his cheekbone across to his left ear. McQuade pulled a seat for him and the young man sat.

"Doctor Conway?" he said in a quiet voice.

"Yes," she said.

The man looked at Decker and then back to Sam.

"It's all right," she said.

The man looked about and then reached into his satchel. Decker moved his hand against the steak knife but Sam gave him a discouraging look. The man pulled out his hand, a closed fist, and then opened it before her. A flat stone the size of a match book. Inscribed on its face were a few small ancient characters Sam had become extremely familiar with.

Sam's eyes grew wide. She reached and said, "May I?"

He nodded. "Only you."

Sam could feel her heart beat as she felt it between her fingers. "Where did you get this?"

The man smiled warmly. "The rest is buried."

"There's more!"

"All the rest."

"A pillar?"

"Yes."

"Where?"

"Buried."

"Can you bring us there?"

"Yes. Two day's walk."

Sam anxiously agreed. "We're ready when you are."

"I will wait outside," the man said and started to leave.

"Wait, who are you?" Sam said.

The man turned and said, "My name is Hakeem Salim."

Acknowledgments

While doing some research for Driven I came across a long out of print illustrated timeline of human history that, once opened, stretched eighteen feet. Within the first few inches I found the illustrated legend of an ancient artifact that claimed to be given to Methuselah from his seven times great grandfather, Adam, and later possessed by Moses. As I considered the implications and possibilities I reported my thoughts to Michelle Rapkin, my editor at Doubleday. After a quiet pause, she told me to immediately cease with any other projects and write Methuselah's Pillar. So a lot of the blame goes to her, but there are others. U S Army Captain Chris Devine, for his extremely detailed personal tour of Fort Detrick and USAMRIID. Ace Air Force and commercial airline pilot Gary Martin for helping me figure out the most practical and realistic ways to board a jumbo jet in flight. And then there's those readers and all their constructive and encouraging feedback that pushed the publication date right off the calendar. For this, the fault lies with William S. Griffiths, Dorothy Griffiths, Susan Walsh, Kate Hill Cantrill, Joyce Lopez, Anthony Mauceri, Billy Martin, Craig Feagins, Bill McCarty, Dawn Cartolano, Deborah Marchini, Doug Kelly, Chris Sorenson, Norm Sorenson, Meg Davis, Jessica Faller, Kathy Airey, David Breitkopf, Kevin Campbell and Andrew Syrotick. And the final finger pointing goes to my sons Luke and Stephen, for their artistic skills in developing the cover and to my publisher, Headline Books and the tireless and daring Cathy Teets, who is renowned for being simply the best.

About the Author

W. G. Griffiths lives on Long Island, New York, and is the multi-award winning author of both fiction and non-fiction books including: *Malchus*, *Driven*, *Takedown*, *Stingers*, and *Talons*. Griffiths believes the reader should live the story so research from the internet alone just won't do. First hand experience is essential for proper description. If his character has to sky dive then so does the writer. If his character has to travel through the neighborhood sewers then so does the writer. Research has brought him to the deserts of the Middle East, the bush of Africa, the tundra of the Arctic and even the U. S. military confines of germ warfare at USAMRIID in Fort Detrick. Griffiths has also appeared on television many times including The Oprah Winfrey Show and speaks on writing stories at both grade schools and universities. For more information and news visit www.HeadlineBooks.com and www.WGGriffiths.com.

Books by W.G. Griffiths

Malchus

Driven

Takedown

Stingers

Talons